COMPLETE

ACCESS

David Bannat

Chapter 1

Why me? Jay thought to himself. When will he grow up? The rain was getting heavier now and the wipers were not keeping up. After all, Jay thought, he's an adult now and should be able to take care of himself.

Earlier Jay got a phone call from his mother, "Could you please check on your brother Brian while we are on vacation?" I guess I will never outgrow a request from mom, Jay thought as he smiled to himself.

The pouring rain, and the sound of the wipers going back and forth, back and forth, caused Jay to start daydreaming. He remembered back in college when he played football. Southern Ohio Tech did not have a big team, and was really in a smaller regional district, but the games were taken seriously by the local crowd. Jay could remember how his brother yelled and screamed at him for throwing a pass to his tight end instead of the wide receiver. "But my wide receiver was not open," I said.

"Yes, but I told you if you throw the ball on the right side of the defensive wing he won't be able to block it. He strained his right shoulder and won't be able to block the pass" was Brian's answer.

Jay stopped asking long ago where his brother got his information. He seemed to get all of the medical records, or any other records he wanted, on every member of the other team. Somehow he could tap into people's records through his computer. If anybody from the other team so much as bought an aspirin with a credit card, or saw a doctor, Brian knew about it. Jay really did not understand it, something about writing a program to decipher password codes, but since his brother was a little impatient at explaining things he never really asked for details.

"Finally," Jay said out loud as he pulled into the driveway. The house Jay grew up in was a typical bi-level from the 1970's. He can remember riding his bicycle all over the neighborhood. It was a nice place to grow up, Jay thought to himself. The rain was still coming down, but at least the thunder and lightning stopped.

Jay ran to the front door fumbling for his key. He opened the door and stepped inside. Jay yelled "Helloooo," but he already knew that nobody was home. Brian's car was not in the driveway. He probably went to the store or something during the storm. It was typical of Brian to shut down his computer during an electrical storm. Since he did most of his work on line, he could work any time of the day and download his latest computer project to his company. Brian had a gift for programming like no one else Jay ever met. What exactly Brian did Jay didn't know. He didn't have any money problems, and although Brian still lived with his parents, it seemed like Brian was taking care of them. Nothing was ever discussed, but Dad's retirement and the trips they took didn't match. Jay was grateful that Brian took good care of them.

Jay decided to watch a little television and wait for his brother. He hung up his coat, and plopped himself on the couch with the remote. Five minutes of the evening news was enough to put Jay to sleep.

Jay woke up to the sound of someone in the kitchen. Brian was fixing dinner. "I hope steaks are okay," Brian said. "Did you have a good snooze?"

"Hey Brian, I'm sorry to drop in unannounced, but you know how mom worries."

"To tell you the truth," Brian said, "Mom called. Why do you think I ran out for all this food? Now how about lighting the grill? It looks like the rain is finished."

Jay just gave a nod followed by a yawn, scratched his head and walked toward the back door.

During dinner Brian turned on the TV and switched to one of the cable news channels. They were interviewing Bob Stone, the incumbent Senator who was up for re-election this year. The Stone

2

platform was mostly conservative, although like all career politicians the latest pole occasionally influenced his voting. This weakened his support from his own party base. When combined with the standard attacks from the other side his re-election would be close at best.

As casually as he could Jay asked Brian why he wanted to see this interview. Jay knew that Brian disliked Senator Stone but did not wish to get into any heated political discussion. Such debates were easy to start since each brother's political beliefs were very different. Brian, fighting a smile, said, "Just wait, you'll see in a couple of minutes."

Jay rolled his eyes but didn't say anything else. They continued to watch the interview, in which Stone was getting his usual grilling from Alfred Sumner, who really didn't care for him. Stone was doing pretty well so far, but Brian's excitement made Jay suspicious. Jay knew that Brian was up to something, but he wondered if it was possible for Brian to get an advanced copy of the questions. He couldn't have seen this interview earlier since it was live.

Sumner's next question was about allegations made by his opponent a half-hour before this interview. Senator Stone looked puzzled. He said, "I am not aware of any new allegations, but with all the things my opponent has accused me of it's hard to keep track of all he has said."

Sumner then held up a document showing the Senator and Bill Tyburg, a CEO from Jamerson Pharmaceuticals registered in neighboring hotels during the same weekend in Puerto Rico. The Senator shrugged his shoulders and said that he didn't see any big deal in the coincidence. "You mean to say that this was not a planned trip to discuss the new cholesterol lowering drug that Jamerson is trying to get through the FDA?" asked Sumner.

"No way," Stone quickly insisted. "I was not aware that he would be there."

Sumner then held up another document and said, "Although it appears that you used your own credit card to make your reservations, it was a Jamerson secretary that made the actual call." Sumner then held up the phone records from Jamerson showing the time of the call, and how the timing matched up perfectly with the exact time that Stone's credit card was charged for the room. Stone mumbled something about illegally obtaining private documents, but it would not matter what he said. This would cost him a lot in the polls.

Jay, who was quite shocked about what had happened, had forgotten all about his brother until now. Brian was quickly pacing back and forth unable to sit still due to the adrenaline rush he felt during the kill. Jay was a little nervous for his brother. What was he getting himself into? Although Jay was having trouble believing that Brian could be mixed up in this it was the style he was used to during his college football days. "Brian," said Jay, "I hope that you are not mixed up in this. That Gallagor character that Stone is running against is a bad guy. There are rumors that he is linked with several groups including some retired Soviet military people that came over to work for him after their country's collapse."

"I never heard that," Brian snapped back. "There were never any news stories on that, and you can't tell me that your right wing radio people are a credible source."

Jay shrugged his shoulders and told Brian to just be careful. He did not want to alienate his brother, especially if he is getting himself into trouble.

That night Senator Stone made some phone calls. He had a trusted aid call Tyburg, who was actually on another line trying to call Stone. Stone picked up a secure line and asked, "What the hell happened?"

Tyburg said he didn't know.

"What about your secretary?" Stone asked.

"No way," said Tyburg, "She just called me hysterical herself. Jane's been with the company for 15 years, 7 of which have been as my personal secretary. She works hard, and I pay her very well just to make extra sure that I can trust her. My wife and I have had Jane and her husband over, and I know both of her kids. I will still do all of the expected checks, but right now I just can't believe it's her."

"They were private records," Stone said. "There will be an investigation of just how they were obtained. Perhaps we can learn something there. After all, it was the credit card company, and the hotel records that were infiltrated. Both yours and mine."

Tyburg jumped in, "I never thought of that. My personal records too." The two men signed off. Stone picked up the phone again. He had a friend in the FBI who might be able to help.

It was after dinner, and they were still sitting at the dinner table when Jay looked at his watch. "Time for me to help you with the clean up and get going. I have an early day tomorrow, and I need my sleep."

Brian got up and said, "I can get the dishes. I'm really glad you came over. I only see Julie on the weekends and it gets a little lonely here during the week."

"When are you going to marry that girl?" asked Jay.

Brian just shrugged his shoulders. He knew Julie was a keeper, but had to wait until she finished her masters' degree. "All in good time Jay," was Brian's response. They had been over this before, especially with Jay's wife Rebecca.

After Jay left Brian went upstairs and fired up his computer. He wanted to surf the net and see exactly how much damage Stone's interview cost him. Gallagor was now ahead in the polls by 8 points. Just then the phone rang. "Did you see the latest poll numbers?" asked the voice on the other end.

"Yes I did," replied Brian.

"I need you to check on some other things. Stone is planning a big fund raiser in two weeks and I need to know the following,"

Brian interrupted and said, "Wait a minute while I get something to write this down."

The voice quickly snapped back, "Do not write anything down! No written records and I hope you deleted everything from the last time."

"Yes," mumbled Brian.

"That wasn't a very convincing response."

The two men talked for another 20 minutes. Brian was a little uneasy when he hung up the phone. He went back to his computer and called up his files from the last job. He used the same program he had for years to get the phone records, but getting the credit card records was more difficult. Brian had to find a name to e-mail his computer program or "virus" as the non-computer world calls it, which would automatically e-mail back to Brian the codes required to download the files he was after. This same program had to self-destruct after the information was sent in order to leave no trace as to what happened. It took Brian a year and a half to write, and constantly needs to be updated. He started to erase the files, but the computer junkie inside of him would not allow him to erase them without making a DVD copy first. Brian had a file on every program he wrote in case he needed any part of it again. There was even a copy of some of his more difficult work in a safety deposit box in the local bank. Only Brian knew of its existence. This file needed its own box, perhaps in another bank.

Brian remembered Jay's warning and decided that it was time to implement his latest idea. Brian opened up the paper and turned to the obituary column. His plan was to match up a recently deceased person with his list of Internet accounts he downloaded earlier. A recently deceased person with an Internet account would still be current. It all depended on how long the account was paid up for.

One to three months was the average. When Brian logged onto one of these accounts it would be very difficult for someone to go back at a later date and try to cross reference Internet routers. Unfortunately, tracing the line while Brian was on it is a lot easier. Using his laptop from an open Internet source such as a coffee shop, etc., could solve that problem if he could detect the trace and get away before the cops arrived. Brian now wished he had spent more time on that one.

It was late in the evening and Jim Gallagor was watching the 11:00 news with his top two campaign advisors. Although they were enjoying their increase in the polls the battle was still in the beginning stages. They needed to plan the next move. Mike spoke first. "Do you think that our information source is still secure?"

Jim answered, "So far yes, but we do have someone watching him most of the time. We have a handle on his habits. He works at home and only goes out occasionally, always with the same girl who has checked out by the way. He has a brother who is two years older, and an accountant for a medium sized company. The brother did have a classmate who is now in the FBI, but they don't stay in touch any longer. Our man seems quite dedicated, and his talents are extremely valuable to us. He was worth 8 points tonight."

"I still think we need an exit strategy with this guy, just in case," Allen said, who finally spoke.

"I already have that worked out," Mike said. "We presently have no traceable contact with him. A simple accident before he has a chance to implicate us would clean things up nicely."

Jim looked a little unhappy. Mike asked what was wrong. Jim said, "I think that we should milk this out as long as possible. The information this guy can get for us is extremely valuable. At first I was a little suspicious of a set up but after tonight I don't think so. I'm not saying we should let our guard down, and I do encourage a backup plan."

Mike said. "I will speak to Ivan, and tell him to implement the standard surveillance, but I will tell him no contact without speaking to us first." All three agreed.

"So what's next?" asked Jim.

"I think we will need to run some more campaign adds capitalizing on tonight's achievement," Allen interrupted. "But we are going to need more financing."

Jim guaranteed him the funds. He was meeting with Joe Lang tomorrow and should get a sizable donation.

"Just be careful," Mike added. "You know who Lang can be tied back too."

Jim pointed to Mike and said, "You know who from the press we can invite, just keep the rest away as usual. I will keep it a quiet fund-raiser without saying any good sound bites during the speech. I'll make the good quotable comments during a morning press conference. It's been a successful technique to date."

The three men got up, exchanged their good-byes and called it a night.

Jay pulled into his driveway and hit the remote. As the garage door was opening he was pleased to see his wife's car already in the garage. She was taking a night class at a local college and although there had never been a problem it still made Jay a little nervous knowing that she had to walk back to her car in the dark. Jay pulled into his spot, turned off the car, and hit the remote again. As the door was coming down Jay looked into the rear view mirror and noticed a car driving by a little slower than normal. There was no way to get a license number, and besides, Jay thought, I'm just being paranoid. Nothing exciting ever happens around here.

Jay came into the house to find his wife brushing her teeth in the bathroom. "Hi Hun, how was school tonight?"

Rebecca gave him a puzzled look, finished brushing her teeth and asked, "Where were you tonight?"

"My mother asked me to stop by and check on Brian."

"Well?" asked Rebecca, "How is he?"

"He's doing okay."

"Your facial expression tells me something different. What's wrong?"

Jay hesitated for a couple of seconds, and then spoke. "I think he's working on the Gallagor campaign."

"So, what's wrong with that?" asked Rebecca. "Just because you don't agree with his politics doesn't mean your brother can't have his own opinions."

This was usually enough to get Jay started, but not tonight. "I think Brian is doing one of his information searches for him. You know what I'm referring to. If he were just stuffing envelopes or something I wouldn't have a problem. Gallagor has a reputation for being ruthless."

Rebecca loved her husband, but believed he's a little too suspicious of the world. She responded, "People like Gallagor don't even acknowledge the small fry. I doubt Brian has made any connections like that."

"Yea, you're probably right. Let's just go to bed, I'm tired," Jay said.

"Oh, I almost forgot." Rebecca said suddenly. "You have a class reunion coming up, 15 years."

Jay rolled his eyes and said, "I haven't spoken to anyone in years. Why……, you want to go, don't you."

Rebecca gave a half smile and said, "It would be a night out for us. Between my going to school and your working, we haven't gone out in a while."

"Let me look at the details in the morning and we can discuss it then. I'm too tired to think about it now," Jay said.

Chapter 2

Ivan Spelluchuvik is a tall thin man with huge shoulders. Although the gray marbled in his hair gives away his age, Ivan is still in great physical shape.

After hanging up the phone with Jim Gallagor Ivan sat quietly in the dark. It was late, and Ivan often wondered how much Jim knew about the old Soviet Union's efforts to recruit politicians which Jim was a part of. As Ivan dozed off the old story replayed in his mind:

"I've been working on this for 6 months. I think it's ready for Dr. Vilnius," Kiev said out loud to himself.

Kiev picked up the phone and called his boss. "Hello, Dr. Vilnius, this is Kiev."

"Yes Kiev," interrupted Dr. Vilnius, "I was going to call you this afternoon. You have been working on the Recruitment Program for six months now. Judging by all of the information you've been signing out of the library, you should be ready to sign up half of the American population!"

Kiev thought to himself, isn't there anything the KGB doesn't know? Kiev responded, "Yes Dr. Vilnius, the report is ready for your review. I called to make an appointment to present my findings to you."

Dr. Vilnius responded "Why don't you drop it off for my review."

"With all due respect Dr. Vilius, I would like to present the report to you. Although I really think you will be interested in the findings, I am afraid that I can do a better job with a verbal explanation to go with the written report."

Dr. Vilnius was silent for about 10 seconds, which seemed more like 10 minutes to a nervous Kiev. When Dr. Vilnius finally spoke he sounded a little annoyed, "Very well then. Be in my office in 30 minutes."

The two men hung up the phone, and Kiev quickly collected his folders and headed for Dr. Vilnius's office. It was a fifteen minute walk, but Kiev wanted to swing by the information center one more time to get the latest status on the Vietnam War.

Kiev reached Dr. Vilnius's office 5 minutes early. Dr. Vilnius was on the phone but waved Kiev in to sit down. The phone conversation was not going well judging by Dr. Vilnius's facial expressions, even though he had not spoken yet. Dr. Vilnius rolled his eyes and finally spoke, "Listen, I sent you an outline of how this is to be handled. I want both of them pulled out and flown back to Moscow immediately. You have made your case but the security risk is too high. I will see the three of you in my office in the morning." Dr. Vilnius hung up the phone without waiting for a reply from the other end. Kiev noted Dr. Vilnius's style. He never yells, which can temp one to let their guard down. It's important to remember that his word can be life or death.

Dr. Vilnius held out his hand motioning toward the report in Kiev's hand. Kiev handed it to him without speaking and watched Dr. Vilnius open the report. Kiev sat there without speaking. Fifteen minutes later Dr. Vilnius looked up and spoke, "Do you really think we can recruit them? Aren't they all just a bunch of drugged out misfits?"

"Not all of them," responded Kiev. "Look at the files of some of the names I have highlighted. Start with the guy from Arkansas. He graduated high school with high honors in 1964, graduated from Georgetown University in Washington DC, and is now attending Oxford on a Rhodes scholarship. The second man, named Gallagor, came from an upper middle class family, also attending Oxford. Both men are intelligent, and are very outspoken in their political views while walking around Oxford denouncing their government. We have a man following each of them. In the case of Gallagor, our man has made contact with him on several occasions. If you look in the second chapter, I have proposed a training outline suggesting how we can handle aligning them with us."

Kiev reached across the desk for the report to turn to chapter 2. Dr. Vilnius was somewhat surprised by Kiev's taking charge. He was actually pleased with Kiev's enthusiasm but could never allow himself to show it. Kiev turned to the outline in chapter 2 and said, "This is the outline I put together. Each step is monitored for reaction. We first introduce ourselves and review how the communist ideology works. We blur the distinction between capitalism and communism at first by introducing some monetary rewards for their recruitment. I figure that the greed factor, which is present in all Capitalists, is probably the first thing we can reach for to hook them in. We then gradually progress to more in-depth ideas such as how to win elections, manipulate the media, and once in office how to work people's emotions to get public opinion. I would like to try and keep people isolated from one another. I know individual instruction is much more burdensome but it gives us much greater control. Every project is controlled from our office, without any one of them knowing the full picture."

Kiev looked up and suddenly realized the position he was in. He never took charge like this before, and his boss never sat this still before. Kiev said, "I'm sorry Dr. Vilnius, I got a little carried--"

Dr. Vilnius interrupted Kiev and said, "Please continue, so far I am very impressed. We will need to speak about how you authorized the operation to collect some of your data on these men, and making actual contact with one of the targets can be serious."

Dr. Vilnius had reached a crossroads. He knew if he reprimanded Kiev for allowing the contact with Gallagor now, he might withdraw and not continue, but Dr. Vilnius could not allow a breach of security to go unnoticed. Kiev's face got a little pale.

Dr. Vilnius made his choice and spoke. "Kiev, the security risk can only be made by a Captain or above. As you already know, the risk to our agents goes up by a factor of ten when actual contact is made. I read here that the agent who made the contact is Ivan Spelluchuvik. His undercover name is John Smithe. Has he gone through the appropriate training? If my memory serves me correctly he is a good man but has a problem controlling his Russian accent at times."

Kiev tried to speak but was quickly interrupted. "I am going to put you in for the Captain's promotion. I will need approval of course, but with the promotion comes the great burden of taking charge of this project. The risk of failure is great, but so are the rewards."

The color started to return to Kiev's face. He knew that he was out of trouble for now, but the KGB system was extremely rigid. It seemed like the higher up the ladder one climbed; the easier it was to fall off.

Dr. Vilnius asked, "How do you propose to get the targets together for the training?"

Kiev hesitated for a moment before he spoke. After all, 1968 was a difficult year for American – Soviet relations. "I suggest that we allow some of those Vietnam protests in Moscow. During the protest we make contact, one at a time, with our targets. It can't get any easier on our own soil. We would also get the added benefit of the American news coverage of the protests themselves."

Dr. Vilnius thought for a moment. He looked up at Kiev, then at his phone. "Kiev,"

"Yes Dr. Vilnius?"

"I have to sell the protest idea upstairs. I will call you in a couple of hours. Please leave now. I am impressed." Kiev began to reach for his report but Dr. Vilnius shook his head no. "Please leave the report here."

Please? Thought Kiev to himself. I hope I'm not getting in over my head! Kiev left the office, and as he closed the door he could hear Dr. Vilnius dialing the phone.

Jim Gallagor walked into class and sat in the middle of the second row. Usually he gravitated toward the back, but because it was

14

Oxford, and the heavy English accent of the professor, Jim needed to pay closer attention than usual. Jim recognized John Smithe as he walked in right after him and sat down behind him. Jim considered John a casual acquaintance, someone to talk to during class, but he didn't even know his last name. Jim turned around and the men chatted before class started.

"So Jim, are you ready for the final coming up in a couple of weeks?" asked John.

Jim responded, "I've been spending a lot of time with the Vietnam protests. I can't believe our stupid government is over there! We need to let our government know how we feel, and we need to send that message as loud as possible." Just then the professor walked in.

"Listen Jim," whispered John, "Meet me tonight at Jacobs pub. I have an idea how you can make your message even louder."

Jim turned around with a curious look, and said, "8:00 okay?" John paused a moment pretending to think about it, and nodded yes as the professor started his lecture.

Jacob's Pub was one of your typical English pubs. It was poorly lit, and smelled of beer and tobacco smoke. It was constructed of stone and old wood timbers. Even though Jim had been here many times before, he could not get over how old everything looked. Of course, coming from America, Jim thought to himself, we just don't have the history of a place like this. The plumbing runs around the outside of the walls, a clear indication that the walls were built long before there was plumbing. The knobs on the faucets in the bathroom are considered antiques back home; here they are just used. The beer was brewed in the back, and there was a chalkboard to tell everyone what was available tonight and how much alcohol was in each choice. Jim looked around but did not see John. He remembered seeing him here before, kind of in the background. John never seemed to get involved in any of the heated political debates that sometimes took place. Jim just figured that he didn't really care, and was just there for the social aspect. It was because of this that Jim almost didn't come tonight.

15

He had a lot of studying to do. I guess curiosity got the best of me, thought Jim.

Jim worked his way to the bar and ordered himself a beer. He turned around and saw John over to the left. John waved as Jim began to make his way over. The two men exchanged greetings, and moved to a table against the wall. John sat down and waited for Jim to bring up the protest issue first.

Jim started; "So John, I have to admit I almost didn't come tonight. I have a lot of studying to do and besides, I always took you to be someone who didn't have strong opinions. Please don't take this the wrong way. You seem like a nice enough person, but I just figured your attendance at our protests was more for the social aspect."

John smiled and replied, "I have to admit that I am not as vocal as you are during the protests. I guess that's just not my style. I like to think of myself as an organizer. You know, make connections and get things done behind the scene. But make no mistake about it; I'm just as committed as you are."

"Okay," Jim said, "So, what's your plan?"

John looked around the room before he spoke. "Jim, I have this friend who can get us into Russia to do a protest march there."

"Russia!!" yelled Jim as he almost fell backwards in his chair.

"Shhh shhhh, yes Russia. But you have to be quiet about it or you will scare off my friend's contact," John said.

Jim tried to control his excitement as he asked his next question. "Do you think we can get news coverage? It would not be all that effective without it."

John nodded his head yes and said, "According to my friend's source, the American journalists over there will eat this up. You will get your country's attention over there!"

Jim studied John's face, then gave John a more suspicious look and asked, "What do you get out of this?"

John replied, "Look, I'm actually Scottish. My last name is Smithe spelt with an 'e'. You know how the English treated my ancestors."

Jim replied. "So when do I get to meet this guy, and how can he get us into Russia? I don't want to get stuck there either. I also need to ask how many people we can bring. An effective rally requires numbers."

"Hey, slow down," John said as he waved his hands. "First of all, I don't think that you can meet this guy. The Russians are very careful about that. The problem really isn't getting in. You can go to the Russian embassy here and simply apply. Getting together in Moscow to do the protest is another matter. This is where the contact comes in. We need to clear it with the Russian police. That's really all that I can tell you at this time."

Jim was already dreaming about the protest, and what he would say to the cameras. He was getting excited.

John pulled out a pad and pencil. "Jim, before we go I think we should put together a list of who we should invite. Make sure that its people who are really dedicated to the cause."

Jim was in a daze from all the possible exposure he could get from this. He started rattling off names without thinking about how any of these men might feel about being put on a list. John was writing as fast as he could. When they finished the two men agreed to set up another meeting as soon as John had any information.

It was midnight, and John was walking through a nearby park. Another man appeared and the two began to talk. The other man spoke first, "So, how did it go?"

John smiled and said, "Great. I even got a written list. There are a couple of new names on it." John handed the man a folded up piece of paper.

The other man took the list and asked, "Do you have a copy?"

"Yes," replied John. "I recopied it. You will see an asterisk next to the new names. It's not finalized yet on this end who will be going, but all are involved in rebellious activities. Since firm commitment is difficult with these people we will need to investigate all of them. Most, if not all, just need to be cross-referenced with our current lists. We don't want to invite any government agents."

Jim Gallagor was getting a little tired. He was thankful this was the last connection on his trip to Moscow. Each stop required a re-inspection of his luggage, with this last connection being the most thorough. The plan was to spend a week in Moscow, with 3 protest marches scheduled. What will I do the rest of the time? Jim wondered to himself. Jim was told that his hotel and food would be paid for because he agreed to act as negotiator between America and the Soviet Union on the Vietnam issue. What this meant, he was told, was that he would have to meet with some Soviet officials and listen to their take on the subject. Even though Jim thought the Communist system had some strong merits, he still did not believe in how the Soviet Union ran their government. Jim was going primarily for the personal gain he envisioned was there for him.

The first rally was scheduled for the first full day. Jim met John Smithe in the lobby and the two men walked out together. Jim commented that he wasn't too familiar with the area and not sure exactly where to go. John pulled a hand written map out of his pocket. "What's that?" asked Jim.

John replied, "I couldn't sleep last night so I went down to the bar for a drink. Thought I'd try out some Russian Vodka. I got talking to this guy who claimed to be part of the camera crew for today's march. He drew me a map of where to go and where he thought the cameras might go. He did emphasize that the Russians tend to move the cameras around a lot last minute, so he wasn't guaranteeing their location. At least it would be a good starting point."

"John," said Jim, "you *are* quite good at the networking thing."

When they turned the last corner approaching the rally Jim was surprised by the number of people there. This became a concern since the more people there the less likely Jim would get a chance to make a speech on camera. The two men joined the crowd and began to work toward the spots on John's map. Jim was squeezing his way through the crowd and forgot all about John. This first spot had to be correct judging by all of the people crowding around. When Jim got to the other end of the crowd there were no cameras anywhere. Jim then turned back around to look for John but didn't see him.

Jim looked at his watch. He really wanted to get on camera but John had the map. Jim immediately started to backtrack, but found it much more difficult to squeeze through the crowd. Valuable time is being wasted, Jim thought to himself. Jim found John, who was talking to a pretty girl. Jim grabbed him by the arm and asked to see the map again. John reached into his pocket, pulled out the map and unfolded it. Jim snatched it from his hand and began to read it, looking for the next spot for a camera.

"Its way down at the other end," shouted Jim.

Jim began to walk away when John yelled, "Wait up, I'll go with you." The girl handed John a piece of paper as the two men started to walk away. John nodded, putting it into his pocket.

"What's that?" asked Jim.

"Ohhh nothing," answered John. "It's just her phone number."

Jim added, "She is pretty."

As the two men continued their way through the crowd a lot of commotion started farther up the street. The crowd was starting to move in different directions as if they were told to disperse.

John grabbed Jim's arm and said, "It's time to get out of here."

"Not yet," Jim answered.

John continued, "The other thing I was told at the bar last night was to get out of here when told. Getting arrested by the Russians is totally different than in England or America. It could be months before you even get a trial. Besides, with this crowd somebody had to see it. We can watch the television news and have a beer back at the hotel. Maybe we can get a better idea on how to get noticed in the next march." Jim turned around to get one more look. He could see the Soviet police breaking things up, and reluctantly agreed to leave.

Jim got back to his hotel and decided to take a nap. He was feeling a little down about not getting on television and possibly a little jet lag. The cold wind today did not help either. Jim lay down to sleep and just at the point of dozing off the phone rang. It caught Jim off guard and startled him. When Jim picked up the phone he was still groggy. The voice at the other end began to speak before Jim could even say hello.

"Hello Mr. Gallagor. My name is Kiev Ruskof of the People's Soviet Union. How do you do today Sir?"

Jim answered, "Okay..., what can I do for you?"

Kiev answered "I would like to meet with you to introduce you to our country, and perhaps offer my assistance in your efforts to communicate with your country's leaders."

Jim thought for a moment. Was this the agreed upon meeting? The adrenaline from Jim's sudden wakening was not allowing him to think straight. "What was it that you wanted to discuss?" Jim asked.

Kiev answered, "I thought that we might get together to review your progress to date on the protesting, but if I caught you at a bad time I could call you back later. How about I call you in the morning. Tomorrow we could go for a tour of Moscow, and then we could review some ideas that I had."

"Why do you want to help?" asked Jim.

"That's an easy one," answered Kiev. "In the Soviet Union we want an end to the war in Vietnam just as badly as you do. We are concerned that if America drives the North Vietnam soldiers into China World War Three could start right in our neighborhood! We want peace just as badly as you do. I will call you in the morning. Try to relax tonight."

With that Kiev hung up the phone and turned to Ivan. "Is everything ready for tonight?" Ivan (John Smithe) nodded his head yes.

Jim woke up again several hours later. It was agreed that everyone would meet that evening down at the bar. Jim was a little depressed as he made his way down. The combination of not getting on television and perhaps some leftover jet lag had Jim in a slump, and the last thing he wanted was to be bothered by some Soviet bureaucrat tomorrow.

When Jim entered the bar he was surprised to see everyone there already. John Smithe came over to him and handed him a beer. "Here you are, I've been looking for you," John said. "You have some catching up to do."

"What time is it?" Jim asked.

"It's almost 9:00," answered John. "Where's your watch?"

Jim motioned toward his wrist and said that it had stopped working yesterday. "I guess the clock in my room isn't keeping correct time either."

The two men walked over to the crowd to join in. There were several people that Jim didn't recognize. One man in particular was annoyingly bragging about how much television time he got today. At first this didn't bother Jim too much. It started to get on his nerves when the man began taunting people who were not so fortunate. He worked his way through the crowd and could see that he struck a nerve when he got to Jim. Although he moved on to someone else quickly, Jim was still quite aggravated. Jim turned to John and asked, "Who is that loudmouth anyway? I feel like punching him in the mouth."

John replied, "I'm not sure who he is. Although he is annoying we should remember that we are on the same team."

Jim shrugged his shoulders in reluctant acknowledgment, although that was not what he was thinking. "I got a phone call this afternoon from some Russian Official. He wants to meet with me tomorrow."

"What do you think that's all about?" asked John.

"I'm not sure, but after the disappointing rally and this guy tonight I'm open for other ideas. This guy is proof that these rallies depend on a lot of luck. I could use a backup plan."

John agreed. The two men shared another beer and some dinner before deciding to call it a night.

The next morning Jim was up and ready to go early. He wanted to get breakfast out of the way before the expected phone call. The phone rang just as Jim was finishing up tying his shoes. "Are you ready to go?" Kiev asked on the other end.

"I was just leaving for breakfast," answered Jim. "Can you give me an hour to eat?"

"How about I take you out instead. I know a nice café down the road where the food is much better. They even have a special American style menu."

"Well, okay," responded Jim. "When will you be here to pick me up, and how will I know you?"

Kiev answered, "I'm in the lobby now." Jim's next thought was to look around the room for a camera. What if I slept late? He thought to himself.

The elevator reached the first floor and the door opened with its usual squeal. "I wish someone would oil that door," Jim mumbled out loud. He exited the elevator and made a right toward the lobby.

When Jim entered the lobby there was only one man there. He was sitting reading the newspaper. He wore a gray suit, with a black overcoat laid across the back of the couch next to him. Jim walked toward the man hesitating when he reached the area where the lobby couches make their circle designating the sitting area. Kiev casually looked up, and then began folding up his paper before standing up.

"Are you Kiev?" Jim asked.

Kiev stuck out his hand to shake Jim's and asked, "Jim? My name is Kiev Ruskof. It's a pleasure to meet you."

Jim shook his hand and said, "It's a pleasure to meet you too."

The two men stood there for a few seconds sizing each other up. Jim thought that Kiev looked like your average Russian, with a definite Russian accent. Kiev broke the silence first, "Shall we go? As I mentioned on the phone, I know a nice restaurant nearby that has an excellent American breakfast menu. I think you'll be pleased."

Kiev's car was a small black sedan parked at the curb. Kiev headed for the driver's side and told Jim to jump in. Jim waited a couple of seconds for Kiev to unlock the door before noticing that it was not locked. As Jim got in it took everything he had not to make a sarcastic remark about the small car. Kiev started the car, shifted into first and accelerated into traffic. "Peppy little car," Jim finally said.

"I know that it's not as big as American cars are, but in the city a small car is just easier. Besides, I like to, uhm how do you say it, tinker with the motor. It's just a hobby."

"Is it hard to get parts in Russia?" asked Jim.

"No," answered Kiev. "We have our automobile parts stores same as America." Kiev was trying to make Russian life sound as similar to American life as he could.

They arrived at the café, sat down and were waited on immediately. The waitress seemed to know Kiev. Finally, Jim's young impatience got the best of him. He asked, "So, what did you want to see me about."

Kiev took a very small sip of his obviously hot coffee before answering. "Jim, we Russians are very concerned about the ongoing cold war between your country and ours, and despite our best efforts to work things out the cold war continues. We can understand the ill feelings caused by Stalin's rule, but he is gone now. Since your current leadership cannot forget, we thought maybe we could work with some of the next wave of good men about to join the political ranks in America. Perhaps with some people who can understand our side of the story we can plant the seeds of change. This crazy notion of communist expansion starting with Vietnam is proof of our position. We know this route will take time but we have made a long term commitment."

"Makes sense," responded Jim. "But I haven't even made up my mind to go into politics yet. Besides, how can Russia help anyone in America get elected?"

"Russians have been studying your country for a long time. We believe that you can have a great future in Washington. What you will need to know are some of the basic rules of human nature, how your media works, and even how to handle potentially damaging situations. But before we begin I need a commitment from you for

24

the next two days. You will be meeting with several experts, and their time is valuable. If you are not willing to put in the effort, then we are wasting our time."

"I will miss all of the protest marches," Jim interrupted.

"A future politician in America should not allow himself to be caught on camera here. It's just too easy for a future opponent to misrepresent you five, ten, or more years from now," answered Kiev.

Jim had to take a minute to think about this. He had his heart set on protesting. This was a major change in his plans. "Can you give me some examples of what will be covered?" Jim asked next.

"Of course," answered Kiev. "Are you familiar with the Machiavellian principles?"

Jim shrugged his shoulders. "I have heard the name but am not familiar with his teachings."

Kiev answered, "We have adapted and modernized his 15th century teachings. An example of our improvements is to never give up any ground. Time is your ally. Let's say a news story comes out about you that could hurt you politically. After all, none of us are perfect. The first thing to remember is that people get bored with a story fast in America, so the longer you can stretch out bad news about yourself before reacting the better. One way to do this is to release the details of a negative story bit by bit. This will also lessen the shock of a story compared to the whole thing coming out at once. While the story is getting dragged out, you go on the offensive. We can show you how to put your accuser on the defensive."

Kiev looked up as the waitress brought over their breakfast. Kiev said "Enough talk for now, let's eat."

Jim thought about what he had heard. He figured that once back in America he could use the knowledge offered here any way he liked.

He could also see how the aging politicians back home could have our U.S. – Russian relations all wrong. Perhaps he could help.

Jim leaned across the table and said, "Okay, I'm in."

"Excellent," responded Kiev. "Now enjoy your breakfast, and drink plenty of coffee. You will have lots of information to absorb."

A week later Kiev and Ivan were with Dr. Vilnius in his office celebrating their accomplishments. "Comrade Kiev," said Dr. Vilnius, "Your recruitment plan worked very well. Both of our targets this week responded better than expected."

Ivan sat there quietly listening wondering how they were going to maintain contact when the Americans go back to their country. He was hoping for some kind of promotion and possibly a chance to work undercover in the United States.

Finally, Ivan had to ask, "How will we maintain contact with the Americans once they go back to their home country?"

Kiev's facial expression turned to a cautious stare as he looked over at Dr. Vilnius. Dr. Vilnius nodded his head and said, "Tell him."

Kiev turned to Ivan and said, "For now, we don't stay in contact with them. Our plan was to convince them that we are not their enemy. We gave them tools to get elected. We also picked people with certain characteristics such as a strong self-centeredness, and a lack of loyalty. The people we chose we would never want working for us. We could never trust them not to sell us out. So we put them in a position where they can, and hopefully someday will, sell out their government to us. They know how to contact us, but we do not want them to try until they have something of value for us."

Ivan looked confused, which was really more of an act to hide his disappointment. Kiev said, "I can sum it up this way, if you look at the American government as a giant barrel of apples, our goal is to toss in a few spoiled ones to infest the whole lot."

Chapter 3

Brian had let over two weeks go by before starting his next project for Gallagor. NASA had new images from the Mars rover and Brian was easily sidetracked. Searching for information on someone was boring 90% of the time. It was that rare occasion when you stumble onto something that could make it interesting.

Brian thought to himself. They want me to start searching Senator Stone's past. The request was not as easy as it seemed. Not only are they looking for specific things that could hurt him in the election, they wanted Brian to put similar type behavioral patterns together for predicting future behavior. Brian wanted to organize data as he accumulated it rather than wait until he had a big mess to sort through. "But how do I categorize things? I'm a computer hack, not a psychologist." Brian mumbled out loud. Brian decided to do a web search to learn more about it, and maybe go into a chat room or two.

Brian's first search brought him into Maslow's hierarchy of needs concept. "No, I don't think that's it."

Next Brian found information on what is called personality types. Predicting behavior based on a person's personality. Here is a way to categorize. Brian looked at several different methods to divide people up. He settled on something Hippocrates came up with that had only four categories. Sanguine, which is considered the friendly, outgoing salesman type, Choleric, the natural born leader, Melancholy, the neat and organized person, and finally Phlegmatic, the easy going one. As the theory goes, we are a blend of two out of the four. Also, melancholy and sanguine never mix, and choleric and phlegmatic never mix.

Sounds simple enough, Brian reasoned. I'll make up four file flags, and decide which flag goes on each data point. I can graph the results and have a decent profile perspective in no time.

Brian continued. Let's start with where he grew up. Did Stone play any sports? It seems that he grew up in an average middle class family. His parents never divorced. His father passed away several years ago, and his mother is now in a nursing home. Brian made himself a note page of things to check. On it he typed himself a note to check who is paying for Stone's mother's expenses at the home. If he were getting some kind of special consideration because of his position this could be useful information. Next Brian would get all of the medical records of Stone's children. Hospital security is poor at best so birth records on the kids are easy. Unfortunately, it's much more difficult for people born before 1970. They just didn't computerize records back then. No files to access. Brian then followed Stone through high school and college. Not much here, he thought. Brian looked at his watch. It was getting late, and Brian had to make one of his rare appearances at the main office tomorrow. His boss had a new project to kick off and wanted Brian to be there. Tomorrow he would access Stone's complete credit history.

Senator Stone was in his office when the call came in from Bill Tyburg. "Bill, did you find out anything?"

"Well, yes and no. We traced back to an outgoing e-mail that provided someone the access codes to our files. Although we are still investigating, it appears that this person was able to breach our security through the Internet. I know you said that you had a friend in the FBI. I think we should contact him right away. Apparently this person can access any of our files as he chooses and we can't stop him. We need to bring in the pros. At this point I have to assume there is a professional spy ring involved possibly even foreign agents. We have some good programmers here and they are very impressed to say the least."

"Hang on," answered the Senator. "I will call him now and tie you in on a conference call."

Bill could hear his line click on hold. After a couple of minutes the Senator came back and introduced Jeff Creamore, a senior agent for the FBI.

After the usual introductions Jeff asked, "Tell me what you know so far."

Bill explained, "All we know so far is that someone was able to access our phone records and some of our billing records relating to a business trip we, I mean I, went on."

Senator Stone interrupted, "Listen Jeff, in order to do your job you're going to need to know everything. Bill and I went to Puerto Rico on a seminar together. Although Bill made the arrangements through his company, I paid my own way. Nothing illegal happened, but my opponent in the next election is making an issue out of it, which is to be expected. The reason we are calling you is because someone accessed private records from Jamerson Pharmaceuticals over the Internet."

"Yes," interrupted Bill, "And I'm concerned whoever accomplished this can get any record they want. There are a lot of overseas companies that would want to steal our formulations, accounting records, or any other sensitive information. The level of technology used to infiltrate our company is very impressive, and at this time I can't stop them short of cutting every Internet line in every division."

Jeff spoke next, "Bill, do you have backup files that might help us. Usually we look for the program used to access your files. Most computer programs have a style variation unique to its author."

"That's part of the problem." answered Bill. "The program had an automatic erase function, which didn't leave a trace. We back up twice a day automatically, but these people were in and out in less time than that. We tried to trace where the information was sent but it was lost in the maze of the Internet."

There was a moment of silence, before Jeff spoke. "Senator, in order to launch an investigation of this magnitude I must do it officially. Any findings have to be reported."

Senator Stone answered, "I already know that. We haven't done anything illegal. I do want to ask if we can keep this out of the news for as long as possible. This can be damaging before an election."

Jeff replied, "We never go public with these types of cases until after we catch the hackers. If they find out we are after them they usually stop for a while. Then leads get cold, and it makes it that much more difficult to catch them."

Everyone knew what was implied here. There were to be no favors or no ignoring of evidence regardless of which side is involved.

The Senator spoke next, "Like I said Jeff, I haven't done anything illegal, and I think this is serious enough that it has to be investigated. If there are computer experts out there who can access sensitive data we need to find them."

"I should also tell you," replied Jeff, "If my initial investigation starts to look like what you two are describing the CIA will be called in."

Bill finally spoke up, "Jeff, whoever it was could access any file that they wanted. I am very concerned."

Jeff made arrangements to see Bill at Jamerson first thing the next morning. Bill promised full cooperation, and promised to have several of his top programmers available if needed. Jeff hung up the phone and went right to work. He already knew Senator Stone. He knew of Jim Gallagor but had no details. The FBI keeps records of all politicians so Jeff decided to check out Mr. Gallagor. He asked for the standard search, and entered his computer access code to begin. The file starts when Jim was arrested during a Vietnam protest. His file continued with his studies in Oxford, and into his visit to Moscow. Jeff requested more information on the Moscow trip but was denied access. Due to their sensitive nature he would have to go down to the records department and sign out the files. This doesn't look good, Jeff thought to himself. He looked at the clock on the wall and it was 5:15 PM. Records closed 15 minutes ago. Jeff continued through the standard search for another hour, noticing how there seemed to be things missing. He needed the other files. It was time to go home anyway, so Jeff decided to finish up the night with an e-mail to records requesting they put this file aside for Jeff to pick up after his visit to Jamerson tomorrow. He also copied his boss, followed it up with a voice message requesting to see him after the Jamerson visit. Jeff was a little concerned where this investigation might go and did not want to call in the CIA on his own.

Brian pulled his car up to the gate of Computation Consultants Corporation, CCC for short. He showed his badge to the guard at the gate, and was waved in. The radio in Brian's car started to buzz as he passed the gate, and then went to a steady hum. On top of the fence surrounding the building was an antenna, which was designed to scramble any outgoing signals from the building before anybody on the street could pick them up. With the technology today, Brian knew that it is possible to monitor a computer screen from a car sitting on the street. This system was designed to prevent that. It was quite a security measure. Brian was considering installing something like that around his office at home. This way even the CIA with all of their high tech equipment could not monitor what he was doing. Unfortunately, it also ruins the reception from the local radio stations, which is something that he couldn't explain to his parents.

The elevator doors opened, and Brian stepped out and turned left. Since Brian worked mostly at home he really didn't know any of the other employees very well. Brian was a couple of minutes early for the meeting and decided to wait over by the water cooler with Chuck and Adam. They were discussing the hot senate race between Stone and Gallagor, and Brian decided to listen in. Chuck was talking about Gallagor protesting in the Soviet Union during the Vietnam War, going so far as to accuse him of being a card carrying communist.

Adam asked, "Where did you get your information from? I hope it's not from the right wing radio junk you listen to."

Chuck just stood there looking annoyed. Adam turned to Brian and asked, "Since you work at home I figure you probably hear more news than us. What have you heard?"

31

Brian really did not want to get into this. He didn't want anyone at work to know of his involvement in the campaign. "I haven't heard anything about protesting in Russia."

Chuck asked Brian next, "Where do you get your news from?"

"I don't know," Brian responded. "All the major news networks are about the same."

"Yea, all left wing only," grumbled Chuck. Just then Ed Bell, their boss, opened his door and waived Brian in. Brian was relieved, to say the least. He made a mental note to ask his brother about the Vietnam thing with Gallagor, and maybe his Uncle Steve, who fought in the war, might know something. Brian felt bad for Steve. He lost half of his right foot in that war, and still to this day is obsessed with it.

Brian sat down in Ed's office and Ed shut the door. Ed began speaking as he was walking over to his desk. "The reason I called you in here is because we are trying something new here at CCC. There is a government contract that we are bidding on. The CIA is looking for someone to write new software to code all of their secret messages. There will be two contracts awarded. One for writing the code and another to a different company to try and gain access to it. Both contracts will require us to get government security clearances, which is something we never did before. Brian, do you remember a couple of years ago when you decoded that computer virus we had on our network? We never did prove whether or not that guy we fired had written it. You were able to write a program to access our network overriding the virus. I think we should go for the decoding contract and I want you to run this thing."

Brian interrupted with, "Will I still be able to work from home?"

"Probably not," answered Ed. "The contract rules require a secure area to work on the programs and your house could never be set up for that. It's a promotion, and if we get this contract we will make it worth your while."

Brian knew that the home set up would not last forever, but he still had to act annoyed to get the best deal from Ed. He was more concerned with his involvement with Gallagor. With a security clearance there is the background check, and periodic snooping by the FBI.

Ed got up and said, "We hired someone to be in charge of the new security requirements and I want to bring you to her now. There are a few forms to fill out and she can get you started on them."

As Brian walked down the hall he got to thinking. How was he going to continue collecting information for Gallagor while working on this security thing? He would have to be very careful. Should he quit working for Gallagor? Which is more important? Brian decided to put everything on hold and get more information before making a decision. He would talk to his Uncle Steve and to his brother about Gallagor. Giving up this opportunity was out of the question. This is my dream job, Brian thought. Breaking computer encryption code was what I was born to do. Brian spent the rest of the day filling out the security forms and moving into his new office.

The door to Jim Gallagor's office opened. The secretary was bringing in a fresh pot of coffee. Allen looked up and stopped talking in mid sentence. Although Allen looked a little annoyed at the interruption he was the first to reach for his coffee cup. As soon as the secretary left Allen began again. "Jim, our campaign has gone a little stagnant. I have not heard from our computer whiz in several weeks. According to Ivan he no longer seems to be working at home."

Jim asked, "Do you think he is losing interest in us?"

"Could be," answered Allen. "Maybe we could offer him more money to get his interest back."

Mike replied, "I'm not sure money will do it. We recruited him based on his political ideology."

33

There was a half moment pause before Jim spoke. "Do you think he's checking up on me?"

Allen gave Mike an annoyed look and answered, "I expressed concern about this from the start. If this guy is as good as it appears, he could access files from anywhere. I already removed our book keeping information from our online computers. I have one computer that is not hooked up to the Internet that I keep all of our more sensitive information. What I can't control is any information any of us give or receive using emails or the Internet. We need to be careful."

"Do you think we need to ask Ivan to shut him down?" Jim asked.

"Not yet," Mike interrupted. "I don't think this guy is any threat to us. All kinds of information is out there. Our friend in the FBI raised the classification status of the important parts of your files Jim. This makes them harder to get into. I think we should approach our computer guy again and ask him why we haven't heard from him in a while. I recruited him. I can approach him the same way as before. At least then we'll know for sure what his intentions are. You guys need to remember that most people just don't have our commitment level. It's very possible that something's come up at his work, which requires more of his time. We have already noted his change in work habits. I think the change from working at home to now going into the office everyday is evidence of that. Let me talk to him first."

"Okay," answered Jim, "but if there are any problems you are to get back to us immediately. I don't like our lack of control with this guy."

Jeff arrived about 5 minutes before 8:00 AM. As he walked through the lobby toward the front desk he looked over at the magazine selection on the table. He was expecting to be kept waiting while people do whatever they do during the 15 to 20 minutes it takes to invite him in. "Hi, I'm Jeff Creamore and I'm here to see Bill Tyburg."

34

"You're from the FBI right?" asked the young lady behind the desk. "We've been expecting you. Please sign in." She immediately picked up the phone. "Yes sir, he's here." She hung up the phone as Jeff turned around to go sit down. "Uh, excuse me, Mr. Creamore, right this way sir."

Another woman got up and motioned to Jeff to follow her. "Can I get you a cup of coffee or anything?" she asked.

Jeff's reply was "No thank you" but she persisted. After explaining that he avoided caffeine beverages, joking that he was hyper enough, he finally agreed to a bottled water. Jeff was led to a conference room where three men were waiting for him.

"Hello Mr. Creamore, my name is Bill Tyburg." Bill walked up and shook Jeff's hand. Bill looked around Jeff toward his escort and asked, "Could you get Mr. Creamore some coffee?"

She shook her head and explained that they already went through that, and that she was leaving now to get his water. Bill smiled and replied, "Thanks Jane, I should know better. Could you send in a fresh pot for the rest of us?" Jane nodded and was gone.

Bill introduced Jeff to his programmers. They showed Jeff the outgoing e-mail that contained the access codes for the Jamerson files that were breached. The programmers began explaining how they found this e-mail in the thousands that were sent but were cut short by Bill. "I already know that you guys are good," was his comment.

Jeff asked, "What about the person whose e-mail this was sent out on?"

Bill answered, "We know for a fact that he wasn't here then. I spoke to him and lucky for him he was out of town at a family wedding that week. He does not have remote access. Since everyone's name is coded into his or her email address it's very easy for anyone to get an employee list and figure out how to reach someone. This guy's last name is Miller, which doesn't help either. It could've been a lucky guess."

Jeff wrote down the person's name, and the e-mail address that the files went to. "Hopefully," Jeff said, "we can trace this e-mail address and find our guy."

"We tried that and it came up unlisted on our web search," Bill said. "We even tried to send another e-mail but it came back undeliverable."

Next they reviewed the incoming e-mail. The actual program to figure out the codes and e-mail them back out had a self-erase function. This left no trace of the actual program. "It was obviously written by a pro," commented one of the programmers. "Usually a program like this will damage other programs or erase other data. This one went in, got what it wanted, and was gone without a trace. You government guys should find this one just to sign him up! The CIA would love him."

Bill looked up at Jeff and rolled his eyes without comment. Jeff pretended to be serious but couldn't hold back the smile. He spent about another half hour asking questions and taking notes. As Jeff drove off he made a call to his secretary to give her the email address and asked her to start a trace on it.

While driving back to the office Jeff tried to summarize the visit in his head. It does appear that Jamerson Pharmaceuticals is concerned and is cooperating. It also seems like a good idea to contact the CIA, even if it's just to make the information available to them. All the CIA does is take information; seldom do they give any out.

When Jeff got back to the office his boss, Dave Gillian, and another man were waiting in his office. Dave immediately introduced the other man as Charlie Gurns from the CIA. Jeff knew right away what this meant. The three men sat down and Charlie spoke first. "The reason the CIA is interested in this case is because of Gallagor's involvement with the former Soviet government. Did you get a chance to read the Gallagor files?"

"Part of it," answered Jeff. "Some parts were made classified and taken off the network." Charlie looked over at Dave and gave him a puzzled look.

Dave looked annoyed and said, "Some politicians pull strings to get parts of their past taken off our standard network file. The information is not really classified, but they get insiders to help hide information to make it more difficult to access. They all do it. I will call records and get it straightened out."

Charlie said, "Our concern with Gallagor is that we believe he has hired out of work Soviet operatives after their government's breakup."

Jeff asked, "This may be a tough question to answer, but is he involved in any espionage operations?"

Charlie understood the tone of the question. He knew of the CIA's reputation for being one sided with information flow. Charlie answered, "As you guys know, the CIA has been severely cut back in recent years. We don't have the manpower to handle things like we used to. Everything I tell you on this case, which will be most everything, needs to stay with the three of us. Assuming your question was more than a test of our relationship here, we do know that Gallagor has made contact with representatives from countries we do not consider allies. At this point he really isn't in a position where he could access information valuable to them. We think they're offering him money now hoping he will be elected Senator. If the average American only knew how much money countries like China dump into our elections, they would be shocked."

Jeff was getting a little restless. He asked, "Can't you do something about this besides watch?"

Charlie continued, "Unfortunately, we really can't take much action. We lack the resources, and in a court you need hard evidence, you need to show how you got it, and people to testify. Our surveillance equipment is top secret, our information is usually not gotten legally, and our witnesses are all spies."

Jeff pulled out his notebook. He reviewed what he found with the other men. "My only lead is an e-mail address."

"We don't have anything there either," interrupted Dave. "We traced the email address to an elderly gentleman who passed away 2 weeks before that email was sent. His widow let his Internet account expire one week later. We sent someone out to visit her, just to make sure, but Charlie suspects that someone else was using the account. If you can tap into someone's company records, getting email accounts should be easy."

"So we have nothing," said Jeff.

"Not exactly," answered Dave. "We checked into which local news papers listed his obituary. If our guy is an American he probably lives in the circulation area of that newspaper. Gallagor and his staff do not, so I guess you might say we got our first clue."

Jeff sat there without expression. However, inside he was starting to get that excited feeling when he gets on an interesting case. As far as he was concerned this feeling does not happen often enough.

Charlie got several files out of his briefcase and spread them out on Jeff's desk. "I have Gallagor's file, and a summary of his staff including a retired Soviet spy we know is working for him. Let's start here."

Chapter 4

Brian looked up at the clock. It was 4:00PM on a Friday afternoon. Although it was only his third week at his new position, the routine of getting up and driving in every day was getting a little old. CCC submitted their bid package yesterday, so there wasn't a lot to do. Monday Brian would start on a filler project until the decoding contract was awarded. CCC felt confident they would win the decoding portion of the contract. All of CCC's main competitors only seemed interested in writing the coding programs. Brian was excited about getting started.

Brian had a big weekend planned to celebrate his promotion. He rented a house for the weekend plus Monday at the ocean, and is to meet Julie at his house at 5:00. This required Brian to leave about 45 minutes early. His brother Jay and his wife Rebecca were to meet them at the rental later that evening.

It was about 4:10 and Brian stood up to leave just as his boss walked into his office. Great timing, Brian thought to himself.

"I just wanted to thank you for the work you put into the bid," explained Ed. "We expect to hear something by the end of next week."

Brian nodded and said, "I'm looking forward to getting it." Then with a devilish look added, "I feel sorry for the company that will be writing the scrambling codes. It will be fun to crack their codes." Ed just smiled. He has seen Brian in action several times and doesn't doubt his ability.

Ed sat down, stretched out and said, "Listen Brian, I really don't have anything else to do today so I thought I would just hang out here with you."

Brian was silent. He just wanted to go! Ed started to laugh and said, "I know you want to get out of here to beat the traffic to the beach. I was just busting you. I'll see you on Tuesday."

Brian shook his head, grabbed his briefcase and said, "You think I'd be used to your humor by now. My brother is the same way."

Brian continued on his way. As he left Ed thought to himself, Brian seems to be adjusting well enough to the office life. He seemed less nervous than when he started. Once Brian gets started on the project he should be fine.

Traffic was already heavy as Brian was waiting for an opening to pull out of CCC's parking lot. When Brian finally pulled out he was a little close and angered the driver behind him. The other driver started flashing his lights and tailgating Brian. Just great, Brian thought, now I have some jerk pissed off at me. Behind that car were Ivan and Mike. After a couple of minutes of watching the driver between them Mike shook his head and said to Ivan, "You know, technically our computer whiz still works for us."

"Yes," answered Ivan, "but we will lose him."

"That's okay," Mike said, "I really wanted to contact him this weekend. It will be much easier to make contact somewhere at the beach. Jim was getting a little concerned so I thought if the opportunity presented itself before Jim left tonight I could put his mind at ease."

With that Ivan hit the gas and bumped the irate driver that was harassing Brian. This made the man forget about Brian and start in on Ivan and Mike. Ivan turned on his blinkers to turn right. The angry driver turned right after seeing the blinker. The two cars pulled over on a side street and the angry man jumped out of his car. Ivan stepped out of his car without saying a word as the other man approached him. He started going on about the damage when Ivan asked how you could tell using his best Russian accent. The other driver took this as an insult to his car and threw a roundhouse punch at Ivan with his right. Ivan made a left diagonal step toward the man deflecting his punch with his right hand, while grabbing his wrist. He spun around and elbowed the man in his solar plexus with his left, just hard enough to knock the wind out of him. Ivan then flipped him over his right shoulder. Suddenly the other man found himself flat on his back with Ivan standing over him, one foot on his neck and twisting the man's right arm in a typical Judo control hold.

Next Mike jumped out of the car and started talking to Ivan in some gibberish. If Mike could speak Russian it would have been that. Mike then explained to the man that Ivan was a guest from Russia and that he didn't know how to drive cars made in America. Mike made up a story about the gas and brake pedal locations being reversed in Russian cars, and that he could get into a lot of trouble if his boss found out that his guest was driving. Mike asked that since there was really no damage done could we forget the whole thing. Just before the man could give his answer Ivan tightened his grip a little more.

The man reluctantly grunted out his agreement. As Ivan let the other driver up he moved in such a way to let the man see Ivan's gun that was holstered under his coat. Without another word the man jumped into his car and drove off. Ivan and Mike looked at each other and started to laugh. They got into the car and Mike took out his phone to type in the other car's license number, just in case.

Brian kept looking in his rear view mirror the whole way home. "Why did the other driver disappear so suddenly?" he mumbled to himself. He quickly pulled into the driveway and almost hit Julie, who was standing there waiting for him.

"Hey," Julie yelled, "watch where you're going! I don't need to spend the weekend in the hospital!"

Brian got out of the car, and started to apologize to Julie. She could tell from the expression on his face that something was wrong.

"What happened to you?" she asked.

"Oh, I pulled out of CCC's parking lot and pissed off some jerk. He was really giving me a hard time, and then all of a sudden he was gone. I think he turned off, but with the traffic in front of me to watch I must have missed it. I thought he was going to follow me home."

"You should have run him off the road," was Julie's answer.

"Yea, yea, I know, unfortunately, it's my brother who's the fighter in the family. Maybe it's time to pay for all those years of him watching out for me. I'm the computer geek, remember."

"Well, you're my computer geek," answered Julie, as she walked over to give him a kiss.

Mike walked into Jim's office just as Jim was finishing up a phone call. "Well," asked Jim, "how did it go?"

"It does appear that our computer whiz is no longer working at home. He is still working for a company called Computation Consultants Corporation, so I don't know if this is just a temporary thing or if he will be going in every day from now on."

"I guess that explains his not getting back to us. Did you make contact with him?"

"No," answered Mike. "We had another situation that we had to take care of. We actually had to rescue him from some idiot in another car who was trying to force him off the road. Ivan and I took care of it. We just scared the guy a little."

Jim sat back and thought for a moment. "What if you had let the other guy take care of him for us?"

"This was just an irate idiot," answered Mike. "He was not someone we could expect to do anything except rough him up a little. That would not serve our purpose. Besides, I want to give him one more try."

"You know my concerns," Jim said. "Just make sure this guy can't hurt us."

Jay lifted the last suitcase into the trunk and slammed it shut. "Honestly Rebecca, we'll be back Monday night. How much stuff do we need for 3 days?"

Rebecca was already sitting in the car looking over brochures as Jay climbed in. Without looking up she replied, "If you took me out more often I would have more experience at packing."

Jay started the car and pulled out before answering. "You know, that's really not a fair argument. It's your schooling that's draining our resources the most."

Rebecca finally got her nose out of the brochure and reached over and kissed Jay on the cheek. "Yes I know, and you've been very patient. One more year and I graduate. Then I can get to work, we can catch up on all the bills, and finally start thinking about kids."

"Kids!" Jay pretended to be shocked, but the truth is he is ready to start now.

"Speaking of school," Rebecca said, "I sent in your class reunion forms. It's next month, and I couldn't see how the football star could not be there."

Jay thought for a moment and said, "I can't believe how I haven't kept in touch with anybody, except maybe waving to Fred Milnurg when I see him driving around town. I don't even know where anybody is so I could call them to see if they're going. Besides, it's been so long, I wouldn't know who to call. Let's pull out the yearbook later this week so I can remember who people are."

"We can do that," answered Rebecca, "but I'm sure everything will be fine once you get there."

Jim walked into the restaurant and gave his reservation to the waiter standing behind the podium. Joe Lang was already seated at the bar waiting for Jim. Joe got up, grabbed his drink, and the two men followed the waiter to their table. After exchanging some small talk while ordering dinner, Jim asked, "Joe, what did you want to see me about?"

Joe paused for a few seconds before answering. "My people were interested in how you got your information about Stone's travel arrangements. It took us a few weeks to realize that you must have had someone either on the inside or someone who could breach Jamerson Pharmaceutical's security. We have heard through other sources that the CIA is involved in the investigation. That suggests the security breach might be the more likely scenario. We might be interested in working with him on some other projects."

Jim thought for a moment before answering. He wasn't sure if Mike would be successful with Brian this weekend. He also wanted a cut in the action. If Joe had to go through Jim then he could get his cut. Jim answered, "One of my staff members is handling him. The only information that I have is that he likes his privacy."

Joe thought to himself, do you Americans think I'm stupid. Of course I want to be paying you too. This way I guarantee your silence. American greed is so easy to predict. Joe replied, "Maybe your staff could ask him for us." Jim nodded his head and agreed to get back to Joe in a couple of days.

It was a beautiful summer morning at the beach. Brian was the first one out of bed, showered and ready to go. He turned on the television to get the local forecast for the day. He left the volume up hoping someone else would get up. Finally giving up he decided to go get everyone breakfast. As he was grabbing his keys he saw Jay still half asleep walking into the room. "Where are you going?" Jay asked.

"I was heading out to get everyone some breakfast," answered Brian.

"If you wait a minute, I'll come with you."

Brian said "Okay." He wanted to talk to Jay privately and since Jay and Rebecca didn't get in until late last night he didn't get a chance.

As they walked out Brian said, "I'll drive, you still look half asleep." Jay complained of a headache and slumped down low in the car seat. As they turned off the highway toward the diner Brian remarked how peaceful it was early in the morning before all the traffic of the day starts.

"It appears he is alone," Ivan said to Mike. "Now would be a good chance to talk to him."

"Just follow him for a couple of minutes," Mike answered. "I don't want to force him off the road or anything. Let's not make it look like we are threatening him. This is supposed to be a non-confrontational contact."

Brian was enjoying the salty air not really paying attention to who was following behind. He pulled into the diner and picked a spot along the side. Another car pulled up two spots over leaving a car between them and Mike jumped out. Brian looked over at Jay and decided to let him sleep. Since Jay was not a drinker Brian hoped that he was not getting sick.

Mike met Brian just as Brian closed his car door. Brian looked up and was startled. Mike smiled and said, "Hello Brian, we haven't heard from you for a while."

Brian was caught completely off guard. He had not even thought about Gallagor for a couple of weeks. He just froze. Mike was an expert at this and was in complete control. "Look Brian, we were just worried about you and I wanted to check and see if everything was okay. You're still with us on the election aren't you?"

Brian nodded his head yes. "Good," Mike said. "When can we expect something from you? We could really use your help again."

Brian started to catch his breath. He said, "I've had less time since my promotion at work. I'll have to get back to you."

"Yes," Mike said, "we noticed you haven't been working at home any more. You must have gotten a nice raise too. This is a nice area for a vacation. Maybe while you're lying on the beach you could come up with some new ideas to help us. Jim has us all working overtime to support the election."

Just then Jay opened the other door and climbed out of the car. Mike looked over at Jay and did his best to hide his surprise. He smiled and said, "Hello," to Jay before turning to Brian and saying, "Brian, it was good to see you again. I have to run but I will call you later in the week." Mike walked back to his car, and they drove off.

Across the street, John Hunt, from the FBI's security clearance division was watching the whole thing. This job is so boring, he thought to himself. He wrote down the license plate of the car that was leaving, just in case, but it was probably just a friend or something. John's job is to check up on all new applications for a security clearance. Part of his job is to follow Brian around for a few days to make sure he wasn't a security risk. Except for occasionally finding someone who drinks too much or is cheating on his wife, nothing exciting ever happens. He did have to reject someone who bought some marijuana once.

Jay looked at Brian and said, "What was that all about?"

Brian just looked at him. Jay could tell that he was nervous. Jay asked, "Who were those guys?"

"I know," answered Brian, "I was going to tell you everything this weekend."

Brian turned toward the diner. Jay asked, "Brian, shouldn't we get out of here?"

Brian shook his head no and said, "They told me that they will contact me next week. I don't think I'll hear from them again until then." Jay quickly caught up to Brian. He was falling into his same old habits. Whenever Brian was getting picked on in school his big brother the jock would always come to his defense. Most of the time Brian didn't even know that Jay was right around the corner.

"Listen Brian, I don't know what this is all about, but if that was part of Gallagor's gang you could be in more trouble than you think."

"What do you know about Gallagor anyway?" asked Brian.

Jay groaned and said, "We need to start at the beginning with this. From our dinner last month I assumed you're getting information for them in your usual way."

46

As they entered the diner Brian and Jay knew to stop discussing this until they get outside again. They ordered 4 breakfasts' to go, got back into the car and drove off.

"Brian spoke first while they were driving home. "Here's the story. As you know, I began helping the Gallagor campaign. My job was to get information that Gallagor could use against his opponent. My contact was always Mike; the guy you just met. They would give me leads to follow. I would access files as needed to verify information they had."

"How do you do that anyway?" asked Jay.

Brian said, "It's really very easy. I work through the Internet. Almost all corporations and all government agencies have e-mail and are connected to the Internet. I have written several programs that I email into their company. Then I get a return e-mail with all of their addresses and access codes."

"Don't you worry about them tracing your return e-mail?" asked Jay.

"Got that covered big brother. I start by opening up the local paper looking in the obituary section. I look for a possible professional person who is recently deceased who still might have an active Internet account. I used to have to go through a lot of server accounts to find someone. I have since learned to start with an address and work backwards. The main advantage of a deceased person's account is that I can get the email before the owner. All of my programs self erase so there is no way to analyze them. The only way to get caught is if I'm traced while on the net. I haven't come up with any way to jam a trace yet."

Jay asked, "What about public Internet access such as a coffee shop? You would just need to limit your time. You know, get off and drive away before the cops come."

"I've started on a program to detect a trace when it reaches the modem," responded Brian. "This would tell us of the trace only after

47

they know where we are, but should still leave us some get away time. It would also allow us to stay on longer if we weren't being traced."

Jay interrupted, "Brian, quick, make this right turn on red."

"But this is not the way back," Brian said.

"Just do it! I think we're being followed," Jay answered. Brian made a last minute turn. Jay was leaning forward trying to see behind them using the passenger door rear view mirror. Brian was also watching behind them and slowing down without realizing it.

"Speed up," Jay said. "I'll watch behind us." The light obviously turned green because the traffic started to move again.

"There," said Jay. "The car that just turned was two cars behind us the whole way from the diner. Make another right at this light." Brian started to panic a little and hit the gas as he made the turn.

Jay yelled, "Take it easy. Don't make it look so obvious!" The other car made the next right also.

"Now what?" Brian asked.

"Make another right. Then turn right again onto the main road. If the person following us cares about being obvious we should lose him now." Jay and Brian watched as the car continued straight through the last light instead of following them back onto the main road.

John Hunt picked up the mike of his radio and made a call to his supervisor. "Yea, it looks like they spotted me. I'm going to circle by the rental place and then come back in for another car. I'm curious what the big deal was to lose me, or why they were watching for a tail in the first place."

Brian and Jay pulled into the driveway, grabbed the breakfasts and headed inside. "Brian," Jay said, "this Gallagor thing is turning into a real problem. We need more information. Did you ever do one of your checks on Gallagor?"

"Yes," answered Brian. "I ran a standard FBI check, but it didn't tell me much. There was a lot of information marked at a higher security level than my access code allowed."

The girls were still in bed sleeping. Jay and Brian decided to let them sleep while Brian filled him in. Breakfast, on the other hand could not wait. They decided to eat while they discussed Brian's situation.

Jay continued the conversation with another question. "Where is the report? I want to read it."

Brian gave him a disappointed look. "I didn't save the file. At that point I still thought that he was one of the good guys."

Jay returned the disappointed look as he answered. "I wanted to know more about the trips to Moscow. Can you re-access the files?"

"Of course," said Brian. "After we eat we can drive around and find an open Internet modem. I can download the whole file, and then we can print out copies later." Jay thought to himself, of course he brought a computer with him. What computer geek wouldn't?

"Brian, I need to ask. Why all of a sudden did you change your mind about helping Gallagor?"

"I got a new assignment at work. They want me to head up a new government contract we are working on. I'm supposed to evaluate new encryption technology. Translated that means that I'm suppose to try and break into new protected computer programs as a way of testing them."

The two brothers looked at each other and started to laugh. Brian has been picking apart computer coding for years. "Wow Brian, talk about your dream job!"

"Yes," Brian said, "I'm real excited. It does require my getting a security clearance though. That's why I do not want to get involved with the Gallagor campaign right now. I don't want to screw up this opportunity."

Mike and Ivan drove up to the Gallagor residence in the afternoon. They put their card into the electronic slot to open the gate. As they drove up the driveway Mike would roll down the window about a quarter of the way and torment the two watchdogs. Ivan shook his head and said, "Mike, one of these days one of them is going to get a hold of you. Rottweiler's leave nasty teeth marks."

Mike rolled the window back up as they reached the safe zone. The dogs were fitted with electronic collars, which kept them a safe distance from the house so people could get in and out of their cars. Ivan stopped the car and the two men got out. One of the dogs had gone to lie down. The other one continued to bark at Mike. Ivan pointed at him and said, "That's the one that's going to get you one day. He holds a grudge."

Mike smiled, pulled out his pistol and pointed it at the dog. This made him bark and growl even more. Jim opened the front door and yelled to Mike, "Quit tormenting my dogs, and put that thing away." Jim yelled at the dog to lie down as they walked into the house.

They walked into the study. Allen was already sitting down reading the paper. Jim could not wait for them to sit down before asking. "How did you make out with our Internet hack?"

Mike shrugged his shoulders and said, "I'm not sure yet. We shook him up a bit. Nothing physical just surprised him. I'm supposed to contact him again later in the week. If he has something for us then he's still in. If I get more excuses then it means he's moved on."

Allen asked, "Can we trust him to keep quiet?"

Mike said, "I think that we are assuming too much here. I'm his only contact, and I really haven't told him much. If he were to go to the police he would have done so. If the police were using him to set us up he would not be so hard to get a commitment from, and my last point is technically he was the one breaking the law, not us. Personally, if he decides not to continue then we should just let him go. My guess is that he just decided he can't take the risk or something like that."

Jim spoke next. "We have something new to consider. Last night I had dinner with Joe Lang. He was very interested in this guy, asking a lot of questions. Joe's people would also like to hire him. I worked it so they would have to go through us. We could make a lot of money if we do this right."

Mike said, "I don't think he will go for that. This guy is not motivated enough by money, and I'm not sure if scaring him will work."

Jim interrupted, "I didn't think this guy was that tough to break."

"That's not what I mean," answered Mike. "If we put too much pressure on him he will just break down and not be any good to anyone."

"That's the type that will go to the police," Allen said.

"Then we should get rid of him," Jim said. "I just don't like someone like that hanging around."

"I have another idea," Ivan said. Everyone else was quiet. Ivan rarely spoke up during one of these meetings. "What if the Chinese decide to pick him up?"

Jim said, "I thought we decided that he would never work for them."

Mike answered, "No Jim, I think he means kidnapping." Mike turned to Ivan before continuing. "I thought the Russians hate the Chinese. I'm surprised you would want to help them."

Ivan smiled. "You did say that he could not take the pressure. My guess is he would not be much good to them anyway, and they would take care of him without leaving a trace."

Mike jumped in, "Let me try and talk to him first. The best scenario would be to get him to work for us a while longer and then turn him over after the election."

"That's fine," said Jim. "Now let's get to our other business."

Chapter 5

Jay looked at his watch, and then at Brian. Ordinarily Jay liked to sit under the umbrella on the beach all day and watch the girls in bikinis go by. However, after today's incident in the diner parking lot Jay was preoccupied with his concern for his brother. Rebecca and Julie got up to go swimming. Jay turned to Brian and said, "Do you want to go and get the information on Gallagor now?"

"Yea, I was thinking the same thing," answered Brian. "What should we tell the girls?"

"If we told them we were hungry we wouldn't be lying." Jay got up and walked down to the water to tell the girls they were leaving for a while. Brian gathered their stuff and the two brothers walked back to the house.

"How long will it take?" asked Jay.

"After we find an open Internet access it takes about 2 minutes to hook up and another minute or so to download the information. I thought we could download to a thumb drive right away and sign off. I brought a small ink jet printer if we wanted copies."

Back at the house Brian gathered his computer equipment together as Jay pulled his car around to the front. Brian walked out, locked the front door behind him and got into Jay's car. "Where do you want to do this?" asked Jay.

"Just drive around past the stores downtown until I find an open modem." Brian said while pulling out his computer, and starting it up.

"Slow down," Brian said as he pointed to the coffee shop on the corner. "Pull over along the side of the building without any doors. Shouldn't be any cameras facing this way, but stay on the street in case we need to leave fast."

Jay pulled over to the side but kept the motor running. He gave a nervous look around the parking lot and across the street. "So what's our odds of getting caught?" Jay asked.

Brian continued to type away as he answered, "It's not very likely. The access code I have is actually through the state police hookup. If they realize that it's not legitimate they would then start the tracing process. All of this is assuming that someone is right there paying attention."

"What about someone identifying your computer?" Jay asked.

Brian waited for a break in his typing answering. "I cloned a deceased guy's computer a while back. It's a little hard to explain."

Jay just rolled his eyes and turned to look out the window.

"This is odd," Brian said.

Jay turned to him and asked, "What's wrong?"

"The file size seems much larger than the last time," answered Brian. "There must be additional information. It's going to take a few minutes longer."

"Stupid computers," Jeff mumbled to himself.

Charlie looked over and asked, "What's wrong?"

"The computer has suddenly slowed down. My guess is somebody is doing maintenance on the system."

"Or maybe someone else is accessing the same files," suggested Charlie. "Is there anyone else working on this case?"

Jeff answered, "Not that I'm aware of. We can look it up easily enough." Jeff walked out the door and down the hall. On every floor is a mainframe access station with a monitor and keyboard. Charlie jumped up and followed Jeff, obviously anxious but not saying a word. Jeff stopped about halfway down the hall in front of a small office with a locked door.

Jeff pulled a set of keys out of his pocket looking for the correct one as Charlie pushed his nose against the glass to look inside. "It looks like there are two lines on the screen," Charlie said.

"We need to hurry," answered Jeff while frantically searching for the correct key. "If I don't get in there before whoever is accessing the files is finished their name goes off the screen and I'm not sure how to retrieve it out of the computer history files. I usually ask the secretary for stuff like that."

That was all Charlie needed to hear. The door was an old style with three rows of three small windows with a wood frame around them. Charlie used his elbow and smashed out the window closest to the doorknob. The sound echoed down the hallway. Jeff just shook his head, reached in and unlocked the door from the inside. The two men hurried in and looked at the screen. "Why are the state police involved?" Jeff asked.

Charlie answered, "I'm not sure, but we need to find out. Let's call right away." Just then the screen went blank.

The two men turned to leave just as security guard entered the room. As he walked in the sound of crunching glass could be heard under his foot. "What the hell is all this?" asked a very annoyed guard.

"We needed to get in," answered Charlie.

The guard looked at Jeff and said, "You have a key for this room, couldn't you use that?"

Jeff, trying to defuse the situation said, "I couldn't get it to work and we couldn't find you. Where were you anyway?" Jeff put on his best-annoyed face.

"I was making my rounds," answered the guard. Charlie understood Jeff's plan, but couldn't believe it would work. The guard took his walkie-talkie and called for a maintenance person to take care of the mess.

When they got back to Jeff's office Charlie said, "I can't believe that worked. How did you know?"

Jeff looked up and said, "He has a girlfriend he meets downstairs all the time. I was just playing the odds." Charlie didn't say anything more, but he was beginning to respect Jeff's talents.

Jeff reached for the phone. "Let's see why the state police wanted that file." Jeff dialed the phone, identified himself and asked for someone in records. The phone clicked a couple of times before someone picked up.

"This is Officer Wilkins. Can I help you?"

"Yes, this is Agent Jeff Creamore of the FBI. Approximately 10 minutes ago someone from your office ran a background check on a James Gallagor. I would like to know who that was and why."

The phone was silent for a moment. "How soon do you need this information?" Wilkins asked.

"Why do you ask?" responded Jeff. "Since it was only 10 minutes ago it should be easy to look up. All of your requests around the state go through your central computer."

"That's true," interrupted Wilkins, "however since it is Saturday the people who could access the computer log to look this up will not be in until Monday. If it's an emergency we do have someone on call. Usually they aren't called unless the system goes down, but if this is a time sensitive issue I could get you the information in a couple of hours."

Jeff thought for a moment, and then looked over at Charlie. With a sigh he replied, "Yes, please call him in."

Wilkins said, "I thought so. Leave me a number where I can reach you, preferably a cell phone number so we can make sure to get you the information right away." Jeff got the hint. If Wilkins was going to go to all this trouble, Jeff had better be around to get the information.

Jay pulled into the driveway of the beach house and Brian jumped out of the car first. Jay said, "What's your hurry? I thought you said that you've seen all of this information already."

"I know what I said. I also told you the file size seems much larger this time. I want to see what else is in there," Brian answered.

Brian went in the house and plugged in the computer first. As it was starting up he unpacked the printer. Next he opened the new file and started to read.

Jay came over and started reading over his shoulder. "Stop scrolling so fast." Jay said.

"I saw this part before," answered Brian. "I want to get to the new stuff! I will print everything out so you can read it."

The printer started to work as Brian scrolled down to Gallagor's college years. Meanwhile, Jay decided to get a beer out of the refrigerator.

"Wow, check this out!" yelled Brian. "Gallagor really was in Russia during the Vietnam War! It says here that although he went there to march, most of the time he disappeared during the day. The CIA claims there were people the Soviets recruited. Although they cannot prove it they think Gallagor may have seen some of the training."

"That's great," Jay said. "So you're helping a Russian spy get elected into the U.S. Senate!"

"Well, maybe an ex Russian spy," interrupted Brian. "Remember that the Soviet communist government fell apart. It also says here he has an Ivan Spelluchuvik working for him who they think was part of the KGB. They are quick to point out in this file that none of this can be proven."

Jay plopped down in a chair and with an overwhelmed look said, "Print everything out so we can go through it. We have got to get you out of this thing!"

Brian put more paper into the printer and continued printing. "It will be a while," he said. "The one thing I can't understand is why there's so much more material this time. All of those files that were marked confidential before were suddenly declassified."

Jay stood up. His stare seemed to go right through Brian. "Everything happens for a reason," Jay said. "Either your passwords got you into another security level or something has changed downtown. Maybe the police are investigating Gallagor."

Brian shook his head and said, "The security level I reached was the same as before, and I don't knows about the file access." Jay decided to let it go for now.

"What about the tail?" Brian asked next.

Jay shrugged his shoulders and said, "I don't know. The most obvious answer is to assume it's one of Gallagor's men. Maybe they wanted to see if we would go straight to the police."

Brian replied, "How can I go to the police? If anyone is guilty it's me, and the last thing I want is to lose all my years of work. Do you have any idea how many hours are in all of my programs? I'd be devastated!"

The next thing Brian did was jump out of his chair and pace around the house. This was the first time he thought about the consequences of getting caught. The possibility of it had never been so real before.

Jay said, "It's a little late to panic. We just have to be smart about all this. Let's start with Gallagor's file. I think that we should get to know him as thoroughly as we can. Maybe we should also find out who else besides the KGB agent is working for him. How long until that thing stops printing?"

Brian answered, "I'm not sure. At least another 20 minutes."

Jay spoke next, "The only other question is who was following us? Let's not automatically assume it was one of Gallagor's men. Who else could be following you? Do you think the police are already on to you?"

"I hope not," answered Brian. "If there is a problem I think it would show up in my application for a security clearance at CCC. I'm supposed to hear about that sometime next week. What if they think I'm connected with Gallagor? With his history file there is no way I could get a clearance! This whole thing just keeps getting more complicated!"

John Hunt climbed the stairs back to his office. Although he did look at the Brian Chestburg file and did not find anything unusual, he was thinking that another look was appropriate. John sat down at his desk and dialed the phone. Although he was thinking there was probably not anything to it, he wanted to run the license plate of the other car at the diner anyway. I may be bored with my job, John thought, but at least nobody can say I'm not thorough. A quick phone call revealed the car belongs to a leasing company for government employees. Another step before I get my answer, John thought. It never ends. John looked at his watch. It was 2:00 on a Saturday afternoon. It's time to salvage some of my weekend, he decided. "I'll follow up on this on Monday," he mumbled to himself.

Jeff's cell phone rang. He answered, "Creamore".

"It's Wilkins from the State Police," answered the other side. "We tried to trace back the information you requested, but hit a dead end. What we got was a trace to an open Internet modem at a coffee shop. All of our regular patrolmen were accounted for at that time and it was none of them. It appears to be someone on our staff because they used our local access codes."

Jeff asked, "Can you tell us where the coffee shop is?" Charlie got up to walk over as Jeff began scribbling. Wilkins then told Jeff that he sent a car over to investigate.

"And of course he didn't find anything, right?" Jeff asked.

"Whoever accessed the files was long gone," answered Wilkins.

Jeff hung up the phone and looked at Charlie. Charlie got most of the story listening to Jeff and reading the address of the coffee shop.

Charlie started pacing as he discussed possible scenarios. "Now who else would be accessing Gallagor's files?" Charlie asked. Then Charlie stopped pacing and asked, "Doesn't this appear to be the same kind of computer hack that Jamerson experienced?"

"Maybe, but why would someone on Gallagor's team do a background check on him?" Jeff asked.

"Are there any third party candidates that want to hurt both of them?" Charlie asked.

Jeff thought about it for a moment, and then said, "Although the third party candidate is possible, at this point in the election we should already know who else is running. Only the two main candidates have the finances to hire someone this good at what he does. Another possibility is he was checking to see how much of Gallagor's file was classified, and therefore unavailable to outsiders."

59

"If that's the case," Charlie said, "then this guy would be a close insider and therefore hard to reach. It could also be someone new the Senator hired."

Jeff shrugged his shoulders and said, "Although it's possible, I don't think it's likely. I've known Bob for a while now and it doesn't seem like something he would do."

"Are we going down there?" Charlie asked.

Jeff stood up, grabbed his car keys and said "Yes, let's go. At least there might be a surveillance camera recording we can get."

Brian and Jay were busy reading the section of Gallagor's file on the Russia visit as the girls walked in. "Where were you guys?" a somewhat annoyed Rebecca asked.

"Oh, you know," answered Jay, "we were just talking."

"We were wondering what happened to you guys. We thought you were going to get something to eat and come back. We're getting hungry too."

Jay looked at Brian first, then answered, "We were looking for a place to go to dinner. Found a seafood place about 4 blocks down that looks interesting. How about we get cleaned up and go. I know I'm hungry again."

The truth of the matter was that Jay and Brian never had a chance to eat either. They all agreed to go. Jay and Brian sat down on the couch as the girls walked back toward the bedrooms deciding who would shower first.

Jay turned to Brian and said, "Let's pack all this up for now. We will come up with a way to shake off Gallagor. Meanwhile, just keep an eye on your surroundings."

"What's that suppose to mean?" asked an alarmed Brian.

"I'm sure nothing," answered Jay, "but you know that I like to error on the safe side. That's why I take that self defense class once a week."

"You still doing that?" asked Brian. "You've been at that for years. Is it any good?"

"I like it," answered Jay. "Although I have to admit that after all these years I never had to actually use any of it. Just like nothing will come of this mess either." They both agreed to be careful but not panic.

Jeff pulled into the parking lot of the coffee shop and drove over to the state trooper. Charlie got out of the car first, although neither of them was in much of a hurry. They walked over to introduce themselves to the state trooper, who was getting out of his car as they walked up. Jeff showed his badge, and held out his hand to shake the trooper's. "I'm Jeff Creamore with the FBI, and this is Charlie Gurns of the CIA." The trooper straightened up as Charlie was introduced. You could see he was taking this meeting very seriously. Charlie could see this and wanted to put the trooper at ease without making the situation seem less important.

Charlie asked, "Did you ask around to see if anybody saw anything?"

The trooper pulled out a pad. "I asked around. The general comment was there are cars in and out of here all day, and nobody bothers to notice. I also asked the clerk inside, but he didn't see anything either. I hope you don't mind my poking around in your investigation."

"No," Charlie said, "I'm thankful for your help. You could have found somebody who would have left before we got here."

The trooper continued, "Here's a copy of the surveillance camera for today. They only have one camera facing the front door. "

Jeff interrupted, "Wow, you got two copies that fast?"

"Yes," answered the trooper, "There was a young guy who knew computers working there part time."

Jim was about to wrap up their meeting when the phone rang. Mike was already standing when Jim motioned for him to sit back down. The phone call was quick. Jim hung up the phone and immediately updated Mike, Allen and Ivan on what he just learned, "I had our Mr. Chestburg and his company checked out. Apparently his company is working on a contract to write and test encryption codes. It's all very high tech stuff. It also requires a security clearance, which may be the reason he is suddenly reluctant to work with us. I'm wondering if we should arrange to have him not get his clearance approved. He might come back to us then."

Allen was about to speak but Ivan interrupted him. "I think you should do the opposite. Do you know how much more the Chinese will pay after he gets that clearance?"

Jim turned to Allen. "Allen, can you arrange to get him approved next week?"

"Should not be a problem. I can make a call first thing Monday morning," replied Allen.

Mike spoke up next, "I had planned to meet with him later next week. Should I still meet, or let it drop?"

Jim answered, "We still don't know for sure how much we can get out of him. If he comes back to us after his security clearance approval is behind him that would be good. We can certainly use his talents. We might even be able to gain access to some of the decoding information he is working on."

Mike interrupted, "I doubt that. He doesn't seem to be the type for full-blown espionage."

"Will our Chinese connection still risk grabbing him once he gets started on his company's new contract?" Allen asked. "You know how the FBI likes to follow them around."

Jim answered, "I'm really not sure. There will probably be a point when that will be true. The decoding community is a small circle. They seem to know each other, if only by name and reputation. That's part of what makes our guy so valuable to us. He is still an unknown. So to answer your question Mike, I would say contact him as planned. However, you will need to be more careful. You never know when he could have an FBI tail behind him."

Mike and Ivan looked at each other. "I hope that's not the case already," Ivan said.

Jeff and Charlie were sitting on the hood of Jeff's car each drinking an iced coffee from the coffee shop where the file hack took place. "I really didn't expect it to go this way," Jeff said.

Charlie gave him a surprised look. "What do you mean?"

"What I mean is I figured this was just a simple case of some computer hack moonlighting for a few extra bucks. Now I'm not so sure. We are seeing some strange behavior combined with first rate programming. Whoever this is can access any computer system he wants. If this was your usual hack, by now he would be going after the stock market or something looking to make a fortune."

"Usually that means foreign nationals," Charlie said. "At first I thought the same as you did."

Chapter 6

John got to his office late on Monday. He was feeling a little run down and decided to sleep in. When he got to his desk there was a note for him to see his boss stuck to his computer screen. John was known for the long hours he kept so he was not worried about being a little late today. Before I see him I think I will check and see who is renting the car I saw on Saturday with Chestburg, John thought to himself. John picked up the phone and dialed the number. The girl at the other end was very helpful. "The car is currently assigned to Mr. James Gallagor," she told John. John was aware of the campaign and the election coming up, but he was not real familiar with the candidates.

By now John's computer was logged on to the network. He ran a search for Gallagor's file and went straight to the summary page. John didn't like what he saw. There was a reference to the time Gallagor spent in Russia during the Vietnam War, and some of the possible contacts he currently maintains. John scrolled down and began reading some of the information covering the Russia trip. He then scrolled to the section on current contacts. John didn't like this part. Apparently Gallagor has an occasional contact with a Chinese diplomat named Joe Lang. John also read the list of Gallagor's staff. The name Ivan Spelluchuvik seemed to jump from the page. Although the FBI could never make a positive identification, there is a possibility that Ivan was working in the KGB under the name of John Smithe during Gallagor's Oxford days.

The phone suddenly rang, which brought John out of his deep concentration. "Hello," John said.

"John, are you working on anything right now?" asked Terry Agmore, John's boss.

"Yes," answered John. "I am working on the Brian Chestburg security clearance case. I..."

Terry interrupted and said, "I signed that off earlier this morning. It was on my desk when I came in so I figured you approved it." John began a slow burn. Unfortunately, at least in John's opinion, Terry is more of a bureaucrat than a real FBI investigator. "John, are you there?" Terry asked.

"Yes, I'm here."

"Listen," Terry continued, "it's getting close to lunch now. Can you see me after lunch? I have a new assignment I want you to get started on. Is 1:30 okay with you?"

"I'll see you then," answered John in a flat voice.

John went for the delete button on his computer out of frustration, but just couldn't do it. Instead he copied everything over to a local file on his computer. I'm going to see this one through even if I have to do it on my own time, John thought to himself.

Jim Gallagor pulled his car into the valet parking lot. He handed his keys to the attendant, who looked Chinese, and asked him to park it close to the front so it wouldn't get blocked in. Jim was concerned because it was still only 11:30 and the noon crowd had not arrived yet. He had to leave for a press conference and didn't want to be late. The attendant nodded but Jim wondered if he understood English. The attendant then jumped in the car and drove around the corner into the lot. What Jim didn't see was what the attendant took out of his pocket and stuck way up into the dash.

Jim Gallagor entered the restaurant. He paused for a second to let his eyes adjust to the dim lights. As usual Joe Lang was already at the bar waiting for Jim to arrive. Jim sat down next to Joe and ordered a drink. "How is the campaign going?" asked Joe.

"I think it's going well, especially considering the limited budget we have to work with," answered Jim.

Joe reached into his briefcase and pulled a piece of paper from a notepad. He jotted down some notes, folded the paper in half and handed it to Jim. What was not seen was the envelope that Joe slipped into the folded sheet of paper. Jim folded the paper one more time and slid it into his coat pocket. "Your suggestions will come in handy," was all Jim said.

They decided to eat at the bar instead of waiting for a table. Joe began the conversation asking about the weather but gradually moved the discussion topic he came for. Joe asked, "Have you asked your computer expert if he would like to work with us?"

Jim took a drink from his glass before answering. "Unfortunately he is not part of my regular staff and it's looking like he might be moving on. It's much harder to keep the freelance guys focused."

"What is he moving on to?" asked Joe.

"I'm not sure. He works for a company that's getting involved in cryptic coding for the military. It's all the latest high tech computer stuff. You can see why he was so valuable to us," Jim answered.

On the outside Joe looked as casual as ever. However, on the inside he was doing back flips. "Do you think that he will pose some danger to you?" was Joe's next question.

Jim answered, "We are a little concerned. Someone with his talent walking around with the knowledge of our operations is a risk."

"How much does he know? Does he know about our association?"

Jim paused before answering. He has two options here. He could play it down so as not to panic Joe. His other option was to make the situation sound bad enough for Joe to handle it on his own. Jim decided to play it somewhere down the middle like a true politician. "Being an independent he was not given access to much information. What he has pulled off the computer is another matter. I don't know if

66

any of our emails were intercepted, but I doubt it. We don't communicate that way very often."

Joe interrupted, "All of our emails are encrypted."

Jim gave him a sarcastic look. "That wouldn't stop him, but like I said, I doubt that he has bothered to intercept any of our emails. There is no other evidence available to him."

Joe just shook his head and said, "This is too much risk for me. You cannot allow him to keep walking around."

Jim interrupted, "It's not that simple. He's now working on a government contract. Anything unusual will trigger an investigation."

"Accidents happen all the time," Joe said.

"I know," answered Jim, "but I lack the resources right now to do it properly. If it turns into a problem then I'll do something."

Joe was silent for a minute, and then decided to change the subject. He decided to do something about it now and not wait for it to be too late. Jim felt he knew Joe well enough to be sure he would do it right. The fact that Brian now had that security clearance guaranteed that Joe wouldn't do a sloppy job. It would really look like an accident.

Brian walked into the office Tuesday morning feeling good. The rest of the weekend had been relaxing. When he got to his desk Brian could see that the message light on his phone was flashing. Suddenly he was reminded of the whole Gallagor incident and how it might affect his security clearance. Brian listened to the message right away. It was his boss Ed asking to see him as soon as he got in. Brian took off his jacket, turned on his computer so it could begin booting up while he was away, and left for Ed's office.

Chuck was in with Ed but when he saw Brian he waved him in. Chuck turned to Brian, said hello and left. Ed invited Brian in and asked him to sit. "So how was the beach?" Ed asked. "You look like you got plenty of sun."

Brian said it was "Okay," but was now more interested in the security clearance. "Did you hear anything about the security clearance?"

"Yes," answered Ed. "That came in all approved yesterday afternoon. What also came in was some kind of test. Apparently because we are new at this they want us to prove ourselves." Brian breathed a sigh of relief. At least he was in the clear on that issue.

Ed handed the package to Brian and said, "See what you can do with this. I read through the directions and it seems like some kind of a test. I figure you can handle it. The directions on how to run it are on a separate sheet. They also want you to be logged onto the Internet before starting so I'm assuming they somehow monitor your progress as you go along."

Brian asked, "Do we want to allow them to do that?"

Ed answered, "What do you mean by that?"

Brian did not answer. He was totally absorbed in the project by now. Ed could see the wheels were turning! Brian got up to leave still reading through the directions for any clues on how to break into this whole thing.

Ed rolled his eyes and said, "Just let me know how you make out." Brian waved and was gone.

Back at his desk Brian looked over the materials. There was what looked like two standard DVD's labeled one and two. The directions said to load DVD one first. Brian's first thought was to copy the DVD without writing to it. "Yea right," he mumbled to himself. He next went into his briefcase and began searching through his program DVDs. He had one that allowed copying of a DVD without writing to it. Brian was guessing there was something in the program that would void the disk if it detected it was being tampered with. He had a way to over ride this. He installed his program into his computer and made 3 copies of both DVD's. He then put the originals aside. The next thing Brian did was to physically unplug the network line from his computer. He hit the open command on the first disk. A warning came on telling him to log onto the Internet. When Brian tried to look at some of the files a warning light flashed and the disk erased itself. Brian just smiled.

Brian then reached for the second copy. Before installing it he opened another program he had written to over ride the erase function. This time he could see the disk file folders but couldn't open them. He would need to crack the code first. After studying the code to see if he could recognize it, Brian took out another program he had to look at the binary coding. This would take a while to run so after getting it started he decided to take a walk.

Joe Lang was on a secure phone talking overseas. "I recommend we do a pickup," Joe said. "This guy seems to be quite knowledgeable in computer coding. He does not appear to be on the list yet, but is about to start on a government contract that will probably get him on the list. At that point he will be much more difficult to successfully transfer out."

The voice at the other end said, "We will make the necessary arrangements. Start gathering the intel required. Report back with the final details. You will get final approval then."

Joe hung up the satellite phone and called Jim on his domestic cell phone. Jim's secretary put the call right through. "Joe, what can I do for you?" Jim asked.

"I am making the necessary arrangements per our discussion on yesterday. I will need more information, however. Can you put together a folder for me to pick up later today?"

Jim thought for a moment before responding. "I'm not sure if I can get all the information together today. Can we meet for lunch later in the week?"

Joe answered, "I have other appointments this week. Can I send a courier over later in the week?"

"Yes," answered Jim, "I will call and leave a message with your secretary when it's ready."

They hung up the phone and Jim immediately called Mike. "Mike, this is Jim. There's a change of plans. I've worked out another solution to our computer problem. Don't make contact again, and put together a profile for me. It has to be clean. Can you have it ready in a couple of days?"

"Yes," said Mike, "but can you explain the details?"

"When you get back," answered Jim.

"What's up?" asked Ivan as Mike hung up the phone.

"Jim wants me to put together a profile on our computer geek. He also asked it to be clean, which means generic paper and no fingerprints. We are also not to have any further contact." Mike unbuckled his seatbelt and reached for a digital camera in the back.

"What's the camera for?" Ivan asked.

Mike answered, "I need a picture of him for the file. We can take it as he heads for his car after work. We could also get a couple of him in his car, and even the license plate."

Ivan looked at his watch. "We have some time before he gets out. I assume that you want to get started on the file so I will start heading back to Jim's."

"Okay," answered Mike. "I can also get the rest of the details from Jim."

Brian went back to his desk carrying a cup of coffee. The computer had stopped and on the screen was a message asking if he wanted the code displayed or if he wanted to go straight into the program. Brian decided to get the code first, and copy it to another file. As he surfed through the program he could see the test with the correct answers, and what looks like a subroutine to immediately email the results to a Washington office as the test was in progress. Brian kicked back his chair and thought for a minute. The test itself seemed simple enough, but the coding to get into the program was at a higher level. Brian really wanted this contract and really wanted to make his answers stand out. He looked again at the program itself and found several places where he could shorten it while still making it work. This would leave room for a little extra surprise without making the file any longer. One of the ways to tell if a program has been tampered with is to compare its length with the original. Brian then reached for a thumb drive out of his desk and headed out of his office.

Ed was walking down the hall, and as he passed Brian he said, "Ed, can I borrow your computer for a few minutes?"

"What for?" Ed asked.

"I just need to check something. I will also need your Internet password. It's for the test."

Ed studied Brian's face. He had a weird smirk on his face that made Ed a little curious. Ed also noticed the thumb drive in his hand. Obviously something was up. Ed pulled out a piece of paper and wrote down his Internet password. He handed it to Brian and said, "I'm not sure what you're up to and I'm not sure I want to know. Just don't do anything I'll regret later."

Brian took the piece of paper and said, "Don't worry boss, I just want to make sure we get that contract."

About an hour later Brian returned to his desk with his thumb drive in hand. By now he was totally engrossed in what he was doing and forgot about the time. Adam and Chuck were walking out to lunch

71

and stopped in. "Hey Brian," asked Adam, "What are you doing for lunch?"

Brian looked at his watch before answering. "I guess I forgot about the time. I really need to finish this before I go anywhere."

"I understand," replied Adam. "Can we at least bring you something? We're going over to the new chicken place down the street."

Brian said yes and handed Adam 10 dollars. "Thanks Adam, I appreciate that."

"No problem," answered Adam, "just remember me when you staff up for that new project."

Brian just smiled and said, "You *and* Chuck."

Brian worked on the project for the next two days. The program he had contained several links to another program. He was very careful to make sure his program rewrites would not interfere with the other program. This meant that anywhere he changed the location of a sub program there was a line of computer code telling the program where to find what it was looking for. Since Brian didn't have the other program he did not know what other sub programs might be called out so he had to include the same go-to program codes on all sub programs or data files he moved. Since his goal was to shorten the program this meant changing almost everything.

"Finally," Brian mumbled to himself.

Ed, who was waiting down the hall for a while now, heard Brian and walked in. Brian looked up, and then at his watch. It was another late night. "What are you doing here?" Brian asked as he bent down to hook up the network line to his computer. Ed was hanging around because he wanted to support Brian. He knew his future, as well as the whole company's would be heavily influenced by whether or not CCC gets this contract.

Ed answered, "I was just coming to see how you were doing." As Ed reached down to help Brian untangle the disconnected network line he asked, "What are you doing? The way I read the instructions you were suppose to already be on line when you began taking the test."

They both paused for a second and Brian started to chuckle. Ed said, "I'm afraid to ask how you're doing on the project."

Brian answered, "I just finished it now. I'm sending the file, and they should have it first thing in the morning."

Ed, who knew that Brian didn't do it by the book rolled his eyes and said, "I hope you didn't go too far."

Brian said, "I just made a few small changes to help us get noticed a little more. I was very careful not to mess up their main program. If they really want to know who's the best they will analyze my changes to their program."

"I hope you know what you're doing. Are you ready to head out?"

"Not yet," answered Brian. "I have to finish sending the test."

Ed put down his briefcase and coat and sat down. He decided not to even ask Brian if he wanted company. He really didn't like Brian not following the rules on this one, and although he did not authorize it he still knew about it before it was too late to change things. That sort of made him part of it, which he was a little uneasy about. Brian, however, was totally absorbed in the project and had no idea how Ed felt, and did not even think to worry about it.

Brian finished up and shut down his computer for the night. He looked at Ed and asked, "What's wrong? You look kind of tired."

Ed could tell that Brian was coming back down to Earth. He actually noticed something, Ed thought. "I'm okay. It's been a long day and I'm just a little tired," Ed answered.

The truth of the matter is that the CEO was in today and asked Ed a lot of questions about this project. Ed felt it was his responsibility to handle this part of the job without involving his programmers as much as possible. They did a better job if they didn't have to worry about what the boys from mahogany row were doing. Mahogany row was the nickname for the corporate executives who sat upstairs in the nicer offices with the wood furniture.

The two men walked out of the building and into their cars. The guard at the gate was getting used to seeing Brian. He was a young man who was almost hoping for a little excitement. Ed was ahead of Brian as they pulled up to the gate. Ed just waved and drove through. Brian rolled down his window and said, "Are you still reading those spy novels?"

The guard smiled and said, "Yes I am. Maybe someday we will get a little excitement around here."

"Don't count on it," answered Brian.

Across the street Mike was getting ready with the camera. Adjusting the zoom lens he began taking pictures of Brian as he drove out of the parking lot. Brian pulled out into the street and as he began driving Mike stepped out of the car to take another photograph of Brian's license plate. This caught the attention of the guard, who immediately reached for his walkie-talkie. "Yea central? This is Ryan at the main gate. Across the street is a car taking pictures of some of our guys as they leave. I'm going to go check it out."

"Mike, I think the guard across the street spotted you taking pictures. Get in the car so we can leave before he gets here."

Mike looked across the street at the guard walking down the driveway toward them. "He doesn't even have a gun," replied Mike. Mike then waved to the guard as he got into the car. "Who cares about some dumb rent a cop?"

"Sometimes you are not careful enough," Ivan said.

Mike watched the guard turn around and start walking back as they drove away. "He's not in too big a hurry to get back, and he is not writing anything down. I think we are safe."

"AKY-395, AKY-395, AKY-395," mumbled Ryan to himself. When he got back to his station he wrote down the license plate number in the back of his book. "Central, this is Ryan again at the main gate. The car left before I got over there. They drove off when they saw me coming."

"Did you get a license number?"

"Yes, it's AKY-395."

"Okay Ryan, thanks. We will check it out."

A few weeks earlier when the FBI came through to check out CCC's security Ryan approached one of the agents. His long term goal is to be an FBI agent, but his high school grades were not the best. For now Ryan is taking courses on his own at the local community college, but he knows he will need an inside contact someday.

Ryan put down the walkie-talkie and thought for a moment. He pulled out his wallet and looked for the card the FBI agent gave him a couple of days ago.

Ryan picked up the phone and dialed the number. "You have reached the desk of John Hunt of the FBI. Please leave your name and number and I will get back to you as soon as I can."

"Mr. Hunt, this is Ryan McWilliams. I'm the evening security guard for CCC. We met when you were touring CCC, I mean Computation Consultants Corporation. Something happened today I think you should know about. I will try and call you back tomorrow." Ryan hung up the phone by pushing down on the button with his finger. With the receiver still in his hand he debated whether or not to call back and leave the license plate number on the message, but Ryan really wanted someone from the FBI to call him back.

With a bit of a depressed look on his face Ryan hung up the receiver. He sat and stared out at the street for a while, then got up to start his rounds.

John Hunt was sitting down with his family for dinner. He was still wearing his cell phone, which goes off when someone leaves a message on his answering machine at work. His wife Tara gave him that look. "Can't you wait until after dinner?" she asked.

John shrugged his shoulders and reluctantly agreed. He hated to admit it, but his career was slowly winding down. John looked across at his 2 children. His oldest was 15. It wouldn't be too many more years and she would be off to college. She was your typical first child at 15. She was studying John, waiting for him to get up and check that message. She couldn't wait to jump in and lecture her father, sounding just like her mom. The youngest was only 9. Being the younger brother, he would be happy enough just to escape the wrath of his older sister.

Tara got up to clear the table off before serving dessert. John got up to try and sneak off for a moment when he heard: "Mom, Dad's going to check his phone now!"

Tara looked at her husband. John said, "I'm just going to check the message; it'll only take a minute." John also followed his reply with an angry look on his face. Tara wasn't fazed by the look. But she also knew that for the past several years something has been missing for John.

Several years ago John and Tara had agreed for the sake of the children John would take a safer position. Five years earlier John was grazed in the shoulder by a convicted felon on the run. It was not a serious wound, and didn't leave much of a scar, but it got them thinking more about the risks. Another couple of inches and he would have been dead. John was always a calm person who could work his

76

way out of a dangerous situation. It was not the first time he was wounded, just the first time since he had a family. Tara is well aware of what John gave up for them. Finally Tara yelled from the kitchen to her daughter in the dining room, "Just mind your own business and start clearing off the table. We have a few minutes before I can serve dessert anyway."

John got his message and as he was listening he thought to himself, some details would've been nice. John searched through his wallet for the number to CCC where he could reach Ryan. "Hello, can I speak to Ryan McWilliams please?"

"May I ask who is calling?" replied the CCC operator.

"Yes this is John Hunt returning his phone call."

The voice at the other end paused for a moment. John could tell that they wanted more information but John preferred to keep a lower profile. "Hold on a moment please," the voice at the other end finally said.

After about a 5 minute wait Ryan came on the phone. During that time John didn't see Tara when she looked in to check on him. She decided to go a little slower with the cleanup. "Hello, Mr. Hunt? This is Ryan McWilliams."

"Hi Ryan, I got your message. What happened?"

Ryan went through the whole story just as he saw it, including the license number and description of the car. "I'm sorry that I don't have much else," Ryan said.

"Actually," answered John, "you did very well. I have a lot to go on here. The only thing I ask is that you don't let people know we talked. I didn't tell the guard who answered the phone that I was from the FBI. I don't want to scare them off."

"Whatever you say Mr. Hunt. I don't think these guys cared if I saw them judging by the way they waved to me. You should also know that I already gave the license plate number to my supervisor."

"That's fine," John said. "I'm not asking you to go behind your boss's back or anything. It's just that it's hard to determine who is involved sometimes."

Ryan was thrilled to be involved. "Is there anything else I can do?" he asked.

"Yes there is. Keep working as you normally do, except keep an eye on Mr. Chestburg. Just don't make it obvious! This is a true test of a really good FBI agent." Ryan was really excited now, and agreed to be discreet. As far as he was concerned, he was on special assignment for the FBI!

Chapter 7

In the contract office Dok Rhee's computer was downloading the test from Computer Consultants Corporation. Dok ran the download through the standard scan, looking for hidden executable files, which would suggest a virus, and checked the program length. Everything seemed okay. He hit the run button and sat back.

Suddenly his computer screen went blank. Dok jumped up to push the escape key on his computer. It had no effect. Next what appeared to be a commercial came on for CCC except that the 3 Stooges were doing it. When that finished the answers to the test flashed up on the screen, with an apology at the bottom of the screen for the graphics not being as sharp as Brian would have liked. That was one of the ways Brian kept the file size just right.

Dok was doing a slow burn when the program ended. He called up his supervisor Sam Pellinger but had to leave a message. He told him to cross CCC off of the list. "They tried to be cute by altering the program. I hope they didn't mess up the rest of my system with their little surprise," was the message he left. Dok thought about the last time someone tried the same kind of stunt. The program was not very well written and did not work correctly with his main system program. Several files were changed and it took Dok two days to straighten it all out.

Dok grabbed a blank DVD and downloaded the CCC file to it. The last time he actually had to take the vendor's program apart to figure out what it did. He next ran a check file through his program, which he made after the last time. After several minutes it came back showing no errors. Dok was a little more optimistic but not yet convinced. He called up another company's response that he received and reviewed yesterday and reran that. It ran smoothly without any problems.

Dok put the CCC disk back in and tried to open up the file. Up popped a one page tutorial explaining what was altered in the program. Dok began reading it and felt a little offended. He mumbled, "What do you mean you cut out a lot of wasted steps to make your addition fit. What wasted steps?"

Dok continued to go through the tutorial moving back and forth between the actual program and the tutorial page. He hated to admit it, but whoever did this did a nice job and should be considered further.

Dok picked up the phone to his boss again. This time Sam picked up. "Sam, this is Dok again. Remember that message I left about the CCC proposal?"

"Yes," said Sam. "I have the paperwork here."

"Hold up on it. This time I got a program that is definitely better than most. I will need some time to go through it but we might actually have some talent here."

"What do you want to do next?" asked Sam.

"I was thinking. I once got a virus program that locked up my computer without going into the company mainframe. I could add a time limit to it that would extend 24 hours past a given deadline. That way I will know if they got past it. What do you think?"

"And what if they get past it?" asked Sam. "Do they get the contract?"

"I would have to say yes," answered Dok.

"You're on your own," Sam said. "Just keep me up to date."

Mike called Jim from the office. "Jim, I got the package together. How are you delivering it to them?"

"They want to send a courier to pick it up. I'm still assessing our risk, and how much I think it should be worth." Mike thought for a moment. He didn't want to tell Jim he was seen taking the pictures, but he also wanted to let him know about all the risk he and Ivan took during the several contacts.

Finally Mike said, "Remember we did make several contacts as well as all the times we followed him around. We also had to get close yesterday to take the pictures."

Mike braced himself. Jim knew him all too well. "Did anyone see you?" Jim asked excitedly.

"There was a guard that started to walk over to us, but I doubt he knew exactly what we were taking pictures of. We drove off before he could cross the street."

"Great," Jim said sarcastically.

"I watched him go back and he didn't seem to be in any hurry to get back. I don't think he put much importance in us," Mike added.

"I hope you're right. I think I should hand deliver this myself," Jim said.

"Remember, you wanted it to be clean," Mike said. "If you handle it you will lose that."

Jim said, "Good point. Put it in an envelope and mail it Federal Express. Drop it off across town. I don't want our secretary to handle it either. I will let them know its coming. Mike, one last thing. Turn in the car you guys are using and get another. It's been seen too many places."

John Hunt had waited until the next morning to run the license plate. On his way into the office he couldn't help but think that the plate sounded familiar. Before calling it in he would check his files. Getting to his desk, John began looking through his files before even taking off his jacket. John was really bothered by how quickly Brian got his security clearance. Look at this, John thought to himself. It's the same car that was following him around at the beach.

John looked up to see his boss Terry standing next to his desk. He looked down to see the name on the file. Terry asked "What are you doing John? I thought the Chestburg security case was done?"

John got an uneasy feeling. Why was Terry so interested in this case being over, he thought to himself. "I'm just gathering up some miscellaneous notes I had to put in the file."

"At least take off your jacket and stay a while," Terry said as he walked to his office.

John finally took off his jacket and hung it up. He then sat back in his chair to think. John knew Terry to be more worried about politics then policing, but John never thought him to be dishonest. What was the big deal about this case? John unlocked his desk. Although John always carried a gun he stopped carrying a backup piece strapped on an ankle holster. John stopped carrying it when he transferred to his current position. He didn't think he would need it anymore. Although it was not what he promised to Tara, John couldn't walk away from the uneasy feelings he had about this case. He also knew he needed to get out from under Terry's watchful eye, if only temporarily.

Dave Gillian's phone rang. It rang a couple of times before he answered it. "Hello Dave? This is John Hunt."

"John, how are you? Are you bored yet and ready to come back to work for me? We have a couple of interesting cases going on and could use some help."

John continued, "To be honest Dave, I need a favor. I really need some cover for a couple of weeks so I can follow something here. Can we meet somewhere so I can give you the details?"

Dave leaned forward in his chair and picked up a flattened bullet he keeps on his desk. Finally he spoke. "John, I have always trusted your instincts. Can you guess what I have in my hands now?"

John hesitated for no more than a second before asking, "When are you going to throw that dumb bullet out?"

It was about six years ago. Dave and his partner were in a shootout in an abandoned warehouse. Both of them were out of ammo, and Dave's partner was trying to stop the bleeding from the bullet Dave took in the hip. They thought that they were done for sure. It was only a matter of moments before the men they were up against would figure out their situation. They heard a couple more shots, and then looked up to see John's smiling face standing over them. It was another example of John's reputation for unexpectedly showing up at the last minute to save the day.

Dave's wound left him needing a cane to walk. He was "promoted" to a desk job. Dave now does his best to satisfy his craving for adventure by recruiting the maverick type investigators and working the system to keep the bureaucrats away from them so they can do their job. Dave was like the middleman between the field investigators that sometimes had to bend the rules and the bureaucrats who were always waiting to pounce on them.

"So John, how about we meet for lunch and you can fill me in then?"

"Is the usual place still there?" John asked.

"Yes, I'll see you there at noon," answered Dave.

John hung up the phone. He knew he lacked any hard evidence that something was wrong. The other problem was Terry. How was he going to convince Terry he wasn't working on the Chestburg case without really saying so? John looked at the file, and then the copy machine. He decided to quietly make a copy of everything and then make a big deal about turning the information over to the central file.

Jim picked up the phone and called Joe Lang on his private phone. "Hello?" Joe answered.

"Joe, this is Jim. The package you requested is on its way. It contains the usual information plus some extra photographs. It will arrive to you tomorrow Federal Express."

"Why didn't you have my courier pick it up?" Joe asked.

"I want to start paying more attention to my exposure. This is one way to limit that," answered Jim.

"Is there something new developing that I should know about?" asked Joe.

"No," answered Jim. "It's just that we had to increase our exposure to get the pictures. Even an accident is going to bring some attention."

Joe thought for a second before speaking. It was obvious that Jim didn't know it was going to be a pickup. "I understand," answered Joe. "We were thinking that a disappearance might be better." Jim didn't like the idea, but knew he couldn't stop it.

"It's your call Joe, but I'm not convinced that's a good idea just in case they do link us."

Joe wanted to tell Jim that he really didn't care about him, but instead said, "Not to worry Jim, we have it all planned out."

Charlie got a text message and looked a little concerned as he read it. He looked over at Jeff and asked if there is a secure phone line he could use. Jeff got up and reached for his keys again.

Charlie said, "Will you be able to find the right one this time?"

Jeff struggled to keep a straight face as he handed Charlie the right key and said, "Spare me the comments. Down the hall to the right is an office with a small desk and a phone. Use lines two or three."

"Thanks, I'll be back in a couple of minutes."

Charlie came back after about ten minutes and handed the keys back. "Jeff, I'm getting switched to another assignment. We have reached a dead end on this for now anyway."

"What's the other assignment?" Jeff asked.

"Well, I'm really not supposed to say."

"Don't give me that crap" interrupted Jeff. "I thought we agreed to cooperate!"

"Okay relax," answered Charlie. "Here is what I know so far. There are two Chinese men from an elite task force sitting on a plane right now heading for the U.S. We have traced their flight arrangements to this location."

"What kind of task force?" Jeff asked.

"They are a specialty group that does difficult assassinations, kidnapping, etc. We happened to get lucky. We had one of our guys on a return trip and spotted them on the plane."

"How did he get word out to you guys if they are still on the plane?" Jeff asked.

"Never mind that," answered Charlie. "For these two guys to be coming over something big is happening. Now that you know the details, I could use some help. These guys will be more difficult to follow once they get off the plane. We will have them bugged when they leave the plane, but it's normally good for about two days max."

"What happens after that?" Jeff asked sarcastically.

"Our bug gets flushed down the toilet," Charlie answered with a grin. Jeff cringed. He didn't even want to know how they get them to swallow the tracking devices.

Brian walked into Ed's office. "Have you heard anything at all?"

Ed reached for an overnight package he received about an hour ago. Brian picked up the envelope. "Hey, it's already opened," Brian said.

Ed looked at Brian and his face turned a little red as he spoke. "There were no real directions in the package so I tried to see what was on the disk. Now I can't get my computer to run. The return address is the same one as before, but it must have had a bug on it."

Brian smiled. "I wonder if this is supposed to be another test." Brian walked around Ed's desk to the computer and tapped a couple of keys. "Did you try and reboot?"

"Yes," answered Ed, "twice. Whatever it was, they locked it up big time."

Brian picked up the disk and began to walk out. He was so intrigued by the possibilities that he forgot to say goodbye to Ed.

"Hey," Ed yelled as Brian got to the door, "what about my computer?"

"I will fix that as soon as I figure out what they did. This must be the test," answered Brian. Ed sat back in his chair. Brian was totally absorbed in the task and there wasn't any point in trying to talk to him anymore.

Brian got back to his desk to hear his phone ring. "Hello?"

"Brian this is Jay."

"Who?"

"It's Jay, remember, your brother Jay?"

"Oh hi Jay, what's up?" "Well, Rebecca and I haven't seen you for a while. We were wondering what you were doing tonight."

"I think I'll be working late tonight."

"Oh?" answered Jay. "Did you get that big contract yet?"

"No, not yet. We got another package today, which I think is supposed to be part two of the testing. In fact," Brian said with a chuckle, "Ed locked up his computer this morning."

"Why is that so funny?" asked Jay.

"Long story, but I think there was a little surprise in it that was meant for me. I think it's a good sign. It shows I got their interest."

"Well, good luck then," Jay said.

"I should be free for the weekend," Brian added.

"Now you're talking," Jay said in a more upbeat voice. "Does a Saturday barbecue sound good?"

"Sounds like a plan," answered Brian.

As they hung up Jay wanted to ask Brian if he heard from any of Gallagor's men lately. Brian sounded really upbeat. I hope he's not so distracted that he's not looking over his shoulder, Jay thought.

Two Chinese tourists got off the plane and into the terminal. After waiting for their luggage they took the shuttle bus to their hotel. It was still before noon and their rooms were not ready yet. The hotel manager offered to lock up their luggage if they wanted to go out anywhere. They agreed, and the hotel manager called for a cab.

Around the block Jeff and Charlie sat watching a monitor. On the screen were two flashing lights. They had the speaker turned down low but Jeff could still hear a lot of gurgling sounds. Any speech was tougher to hear. All sounds were being recorded, and a computer will isolate and remove the unimportant background noises. Jeff turned up the volume a little. "I can't believe how noisy their stomachs are," he said.

Charlie just smiled. "You would not believe how noisy your stomach and intestines are," Charlie said. "We once had a guy with a lot of gas. I don't think I ever heard anything so noisy. He was so bad we missed some very important information."

"Do you think they will make contact?" Jeff asked.

"I would be surprised," answered Charlie. "Usually they will wait a day or two to see if anybody is on to them. Eventually they will make contact and go underground. Hey wait a minute. Look at this!"

The cab stopped in front of a Chinese restaurant. The two men got out and went inside. The cab waited for them outside. About five minutes later two men got back in the cab and drove off. Charlie started to follow after them.

"Hey wait a minute," Jeff said. "According to the tracking screen, they are still inside. Do you think they found the bugs?"

"If they did there is no way for them to get them out now." Charlie said as he got on the radio. There is an observation helicopter overhead and another car around the block. He told the other driver to follow the cab. Charlie talked to the team in the helicopter. They confirmed that a car with two men in it is leaving out the back.

Charlie looked over at Jeff. "They used a decoy to try and lose us. Let's use the helicopter more and stay back a bit. We aren't really sure if we were spotted, or if this is a standard thing."

John was a little late as he walked into the restaurant. Dave was already sitting down reading a menu. As soon as Dave spotted John he stood up and shook his hand. "John, it's good to see you again. As I said before, we could really use your help on a couple of cases we're working on."

"I know Dave, believe me I miss the action, it's just that I promised Tara and the kids."

"Hey, I understand. How can I help you today?" Dave asked.

John pulled out the Brian Chestburg file and opened it up as he slid it across the table. "John, you know that you're not supposed to be carrying that file outside the office. This must be serious for you to be breaking the rules."

John looked up at Dave and said. "Like you should be telling anyone about the rules."

John then went through the whole story with Dave. He told him about the Gallagor contact, and the unusual way that Chestburg's security clearance got approved. "Well, there isn't much to go on here John, but I'm not going to start doubting your instincts now. Here's what I can do. I know Terry is your boss. His boss owes me a favor. I will give him a call and get you transferred back as a temporary thing. Right now I have a CIA man following around one of my agents. I can use that to appear short staffed and get you back."

"Thanks Dave, I really appreciate it."

"It will be my pleasure. Who knows, maybe you will want to stay," Dave said.

Brian got out his notebook computer, plugged it in and turned it on. He didn't want to risk locking up his main computer. His notebook computer was highly modified. It had a huge amount of RAM, and a switch on the side to actually shut off the hard drive once he installed his program. This tricked the computer into thinking his plug in external drive was the hard drive. This way any computer virus picked up would infect the external drive, which was simply unplugged and erased. The computer then could be restarted using its internal hard drive so critical data was never lost. The switch on the side to turn off the internal hard drive was simply a backup to guarantee its safety.

Brian next loaded another program he had written to review the disk without allowing any information from it to be downloaded. He could see the virus program and the next test. Brian knew he should do the test first but decided to analyze the virus program instead. It was a simple hacker program that attacked the operating system but Brian did find a newer subroutine. He took a look at that, and found the time limit feature. Brian smiled and picked up the phone.

"Hello Ed? This is Brian. I have some good news. It looks like the virus has a time limit, after which your computer should start working again."

"So how long do I have to wait?"

"That's the bad part," answered Brian. "It will be the day after tomorrow."

"What?" asked an excited Ed. "Is there anything else you can do? I really need my computer."

"I can take a look at the virus program if you want me too. Maybe I can figure out another way to disarm it."

Ed tapped a few more keys on his computer before answering. "I think you should do whatever they want you to do on the disk first. I'll bet that getting past the virus before a time limit is part of the test."

"That's right," Brian said. "Let me get that out right away and get back to you."

Brian looked at the rest of the information on the disk. He opened it carefully just in case there was another surprise waiting for him. In it was a form asking for the time and date, and congratulations for getting past the virus. Brian emailed out the form.

Brian spent the rest of the day analyzing the virus program and unlocking Ed's computer. When he finally looked at his watch it was past 6:00 PM again, and decided to go home. Ed was already gone so Brian walked out to his car alone. Although Brian didn't know it, Ryan was in high gear watching Brian every night. As Brian drove through the gate he waved to Ryan.

Across the street two men were in a van. Removing the contents from an envelope they compared the pictures they had of Brian as he drove off. They followed behind. As they drove the men recorded the route and times past landmarks, intersections etc. When Brian made the final turn into the development where he lives they drove past, then suddenly u-turned.

"Watch out," Charlie yelled as the blue van they were following suddenly u-turned. "Keep driving or they'll notice us."

"What about who they were following? We didn't get a license plate number so we still don't know who they were following," replied Jeff.

"I know," answered Charlie, "but if they spot us we will never know what is going down." Jeff reluctantly drove on, watching his rearview mirror as they went.

"We will just have to wait until they get back to their hotel," Charlie said. "Sometimes it goes that way."

Jeff continued down the road. A 7-11 store was on the left and Jeff suddenly pulled in. "I thought we were going back to the hotel to wait for them," Charlie said. "Remember that we lost our internal bugs yesterday and we don't want to spook them by turning back and getting spotted."

"I know," answered Jeff. "I think we should try and find out who they are interested in. We got a look at the car, maybe we can go back for a license number."

"Give it a try," said Charlie, "but don't get your hopes up. We will probably find a couple of similar cars in that development. Let's also hope that the one we are looking for is not in the garage!"

They turned around, and as they were driving toward the development they saw the blue van driving off. They pulled into the development and started driving around the streets. Jeff read off plate numbers of possible cars as Charlie wrote them down.

"Oh great," Jeff said in an annoyed voice. "Charlie, look behind you. This is attention we do not need!"

Charlie turned around to see the flashing lights of the local police following behind them. Charlie then quickly got on the radio. He called into the central dispatch and asked for the frequency used by the local police. Meanwhile, Jeff could see that Charlie was not getting a quick enough response and decided to stop. He reached in his pocket for his badge, and got out of the car while holding it up. The local officer could see the badge but pulled out his gun and kept it out of sight just in case it was a fake.

Jeff walked up to the car and introduced himself. The officer got out of the car with his gun behind him and looked at Jeff's identification. The officer gave an embarrassing smile and holstered his gun. Jeff looked down at the gun, and gave an understanding nod. "Can't be too careful," the officer said.

"Hey, I understand. Can you shut off those stupid lights?" asked Jeff. "We are supposed to be undercover here." Jeff could see the officer was just doing his job so he decided to ease up a bit.

Jeff said. "We are investigating some computers that disappeared. How well do you know this neighborhood?"

The officer thought for a moment. "The only person I know who has any real computer knowledge is a guy who lives over on Hickory Street. He used to work out of his house, but now works for some company downtown. I doubt that he would be involved."

"Why not?" asked Jeff.

"I know the guy and he isn't the type. We went to high school together, and we still talk occasionally. He's a genius when it comes to programming," answered the officer.

"I think you're probably right," answered Jeff as he struggled to contain his excitement. "We are looking for a rougher type of crowd. We are going to make a couple of more laps around and then call it a night. Maybe we should drive past your friend on Hickory Street. If he has a lot of equipment he could be a target."

"Do you think I should keep an eye on his place?" asked the officer.

"It couldn't hurt, but I would do him a favor and not mention him to anybody else. You know how attracting attention to him could turn him into a target if he isn't already. Also, if you see anything suspicious, make sure to give me a call in addition to calling it into your dispatcher." Jeff reached into his pocket and pulled out a business card. "Leave a detailed message if nobody answers." The officer agreed and drove off.

Jeff got into the car. "I got a possible lead," Jeff said to Charlie. "Let's circle around on Hickory Street."

As they drove by Charlie copied down the license plate of a car that matched what they were looking for. "I have a good feeling about this one," Jeff said.

"Me too," answered Charlie. "Turn around again so I can make sure I copied it down right." Jeff turned the car around, and they drove past again.

"Let's drive past our friends in the blue van and make sure they got in okay, and then call it a night," Jeff said. Charlie just nodded as they drove off.

Chapter 8

Dok got in a little early the next morning. It was Friday, and he was hoping to get out a little early. After getting settled in, which includes a fresh cup of coffee; Dok's first official act was to check his email messages. Scanning through the list of incoming messages he spotted one from CCC Corporation.

Although Dok was beginning to respect the programmer working on the project from CCC he still checked the file size of the incoming message before opening it. The one page document that was supposed to be sent back was very small in size. There was really no room for any extras to be added on without noticeably increasing the file size. Dok then opened the document, only to find his one page document filled out as requested.

Dok picked up his phone and dialed his boss Sam. "Hello?"

"Sam, this is Dok. Well, guess what. Remember that company that I sent the second disk to with the little surprise?"

"Have they responded already?" asked Sam.

"Yes they did."

"Remember what you said," interrupted Sam. "Do you still think we should award them the contract?"

"It looks like we should," answered Dok. "But I would like to meet their staff first. I want to find out who is behind their success. They don't have anybody on the official list, and if there is someone new out there who belongs on the list I want to get that person on it before something happens. You know how our foreign enemies are always looking for new talent."

"Do you really think you found another one with the gift?" Sam asked.

Dok answered, "Maybe, and if he is, after he gets some recognition from this contract he could be in some danger if he doesn't get the protection we give everybody on the list."

Sam said, "I will set it up today for early next week."

Charlie walked into the FBI office and headed directly to Jeff's desk. The office staff was getting used to seeing him around and had stopped asking him for ID. Jeff was already at his desk running the license plates from the list of similar cars to the one the Chinese were following. Charlie looked around for Jeff's coffee cup and found nothing on his desk.

"Can I get you coffee or anything?" Charlie asked. "I think they just brewed a pot of decaf if you're interested."

Charlie knew that Jeff prefers to avoid the caffeine. Jeff looked up and said, "Only if you're already getting yourself a cup."

"I'm on my way now, only mine will be regular."

"By the time you come back I should have the list of names for all the license plates we wrote down."

Ed walked down the hall looking for Brian. He was doing his best to try and hide his excitement. He stuck his head into Brian's office and found him there talking to Chuck. "Brian, am I interrupting something?"

"Not really," answered Brian. "Chuck and I were just strategizing." Brian looked over at Chuck while fighting a smile.

Chuck stood up and said, "I'll let you guys talk."

Ed said, "It's okay if you stay. This might affect you too."

The truth was that Ed knew why Chuck was there. He was working on Brian trying to get on the new project.

Chuck sat back down. Ed took another seat and sat down. He deliberately hesitated before speaking. "I just got a phone call. It looks like we may have won the contract. The Contract Administrating Officer asked to meet with us on Monday morning. His name is Sam Pellinger, and he is bringing someone named Dok Rhee."

"How do you want us to prepare?" asked a very happy Brian.

"I'm not sure. I think they just want to meet us, and have a look around. I also gave them your name, Brian. My guess is that Dok is another programmer so I will let you handle any technical questions."

Brian thought for a moment before asking. "How much are we allowed to show them?"

"That's a good question," answered Ed. "Being from the government they're not suppose to ever be a competitor. The downside is they are people first and can always quit and go to a competitor. So I guess we can show them more than the usual tour but not all of our secrets."

Brian gave Ed a confused look. Ed looked at him and said, "Just play it by ear. If they get too nosy let me know."

"Okay," was all Brian said.

Ed stood up and said. "I think it's time for celebration here. Lunch is on me today. I will meet everyone at noon. Can one of you tell Adam?"

Ed paused for a second then turned to speak directly to Brian. "Brian, this is your project. You let me know who you need to help you with it." Ed then walked out.

Brian already knew this was his project. Although Brian was thankful Ed made it clear he was in charge he still wasn't comfortable with it. Brian was a programmer, not a boss. Chuck looked over at Brian.

"I'm sure I'll need help," Brian said. "I just don't know how much until after the work scope comes in and I have time to go over it. So just don't bug me, and I will get you and Adam involved as much as I can."

"Fair enough," answered Chuck. "I'm sorry if I'm becoming a pest. I just want to get involved in the interesting stuff."

"I think I understand where you're coming from," Brian said. "This should be fun once we get going, and I'm sure I can work you in."

Chuck was actually thinking that Brian probably didn't need any help. He wanted to tell him that but figured it would just sound like he was sucking up. "I'll see you at lunch," Chuck said as he walked out.

Charlie came back with the coffee to an empty desk. Normally he would walk around and sit at whoever's desk he was working with but Jeff has definitely earned his respect. Charlie sat down on a side chair just as Jeff turned the corner. "I got a lead on who they were following," Jeff said.

Charlie adjusted himself in his chair and said, "You can tell me while you drink your coffee."

Jeff walked over and handed Charlie the report instead. Charlie read through it as Jeff picked up his coffee and took a sip.

Charlie pointed to the list. "It looks like Brian Chestburg could be our guy. Did you do a file search on him yet?"

Jeff answered, "It's printing now. Give it a couple more minutes."

Brian picked up the phone and decided to call his brother and give him the news. Jay picked up the ringing phone, "Jay Chestburg."

"Jay, this is Brian. It looks like we won the contract!" Jay said, "Congratulations."

"What's the matter Jay? You don't seem too enthusiastic." Jay crunched down on his desk with the phone and started to whisper.

"It looks like I get another boss starting next week."

"Is that good or bad?" asked Brian.

"Who knows? At the very least it will mean having to prove myself all over again," Jay said.

"Jay, have you ever thought of a career change? You never seemed like the accounting type anyway."

"I've thought about it," answered Jay, "but I don't know what else to do. Besides, Rebecca has not finished her schooling yet. Maybe after that I can start looking around. That's assuming she doesn't want kids right away! Anyway, I appreciate you letting me whine a little."

"No problem big brother. We're still on for a barbecue tomorrow right?"

"Looking forward to it," Jay said.

Jeff pulled the file on Brian Chestburg off of the printer, made a copy and handed the copy to Charlie. "Not much here," Charlie said.

Jeff pointed to the bottom of the last page. "It looks like he just got approved for a security clearance."

"Do you know who John Hunt is?" Charlie asked.

"Yes," answered Jeff. "He used to work in our department. If he approved Chestburg's clearance, then he has to be clean. John is very thorough. In fact he saved my boss's life once years back."

Charlie asked, "Do you think we should talk to him anyway?"

"It couldn't hurt," answered Jeff as he reached for his phone directory. Jeff dialed the phone but got John's answering machine. "John, this is Jeff Creamore. I have some questions about a security clearance you approved for a Brian Chestburg. Could you pull your file and give me a call? Thanks."

John Hunt was sitting in Terry Agmore's office. "John, I got a strange call from my boss. He wants me to temporarily transfer you back to your old position. Apparently they are working on a couple of important cases and need another body."

It's just like this guy to make it sound like this is no big deal and anybody would do, John thought to himself. Terry continued, "I tried to get them to pick someone else but they thought that you would settle in faster because you came from there. If you want, I can really press the issue if you would rather stay."

That was clever, John thought. The only reason Terry would offer to help is to see whether or not this was my idea, or how much I already knew. He's probably bluffing anyway. I need to handle it just right. After a brief hesitation, John asked, "How long did you say it would be for?"

Terry leaned back in his chair before answering, "I don't know, they didn't say."

John could see that Terry was studying his face looking for some clue as to what's up. John continued to look directly at Terry with his best possible blank stare. After several seconds pause, which seemed like minutes, John shrugged his shoulders and asked, "What do you think I should do?"

Terry could see he was not going to get any information out of John, and since there wasn't really anything he could do to change things, he decided to take John's opportunity to save face. "You should go," Terry finally said. "It will be good for your career to be a team player."

"Okay," John answered as calmly as he could. John started to stand up. Terry sprang quickly to his feet to be the first one up. He then reached to shake John's hand.

John asked, "When do I go?"

"They want you Monday morning."

"Wow," John said, trying to act surprised.

As John walked out Terry said, "I will try and find out how long it will be for."

"Thanks," John said as he walked out the door.

Brian was following Ed back up the stairs after lunch as Ed turned around. "You might as well go home early," Ed said. "You already put in enough hours this week."

Brian looked up at Ed, then at his watch. It was 1:30, and Julie would still be at work until 3:30. Sometimes on Fridays she would have to stay later and help the cashiers at the bank. With the number of people going to direct deposit it was less often than it used to be so he hoped she would be on time today. Brian looked at Ed and said, "Okay, let me get my things out of my desk and make a quick call."

Ed said, "I'll see you Monday. Don't forget about our new customer visit."

Brian just waved as he left and said, "I'm ready, see you Monday."

Brian went back to his desk to shut down his computer. He considered calling Julie just to let her know he was stopping by but decided to just show up instead. Brian gathered his things together and headed out. He felt a little awkward leaving before quitting time just as anyone leaving early usually does, but nobody really seemed to notice.

As Brian walked outside the sun was shining bright. It had been a while since he got out early. He jumped into his car and as he drove through the guard gate he missed Ryan's familiar wave. He wouldn't be starting his shift for another hour or two. It was also a lot easier to pull out into traffic since the rush hour volume had not started yet. I wonder if I could talk Ed into letting me change my hours so I could leave earlier, Brian thought. Of course that would never work since Brian had a habit of staying late. It would just mean less sleep from coming in early and getting out the same time anyway.

When John got back to his desk he decided to get some boxes before getting his phone messages. It was about an hour later when he heard Jeff's message. I'm really going to look bad if I'm wrong about this Chestburg case, he thought to himself. Not only will I be wasting my time, but it looks like Dave has asked Jeff Creamore to spend some time on it too. John picked up the phone and called Jeff. John also had to leave a message. As John hung up he looked over his shoulder. He had a funny feeling about this, and wanted to call Dave. John didn't feel comfortable talking about it here and decided to wait and call Dave on his cell phone outside. John then proceeded to quickly pack a box of his things to carry out to his car. This way it would not look like he was going out just to make a call.

Jeff and Charlie decided to pass by CCC on their way to stake out their two Chinese guests. They happened to catch Brian just as he was pulling out. Jeff was driving, and Charlie looked over at him and said, "It looks like he's messing up the schedule today."

Jeff said, "I wish I knew how this whole thing fits together. Is this guy an informant, or has he been bugged, or are they really going to try and grab him."

"I know," answered Charlie. "This is one part of the job that isn't fun. I just hope this is not a hit."

Jeff took a quick look over at Charlie. "You're not joking are you?"

"No," answered Charlie. "This is the bad part about waiting for them to make the first move. If it's a bullet for him we will be too late."

"What could they possibly want with this guy, and how did they even find him?" Jeff asked.

Charlie just shrugged his shoulders. "There's a link here somewhere, and when we find it at least some of our questions will be answered."

John carried out the first box and put it in the trunk of his car. He decided to make the call from inside his car to be less obvious. Dave picked up the phone on the second ring. "Dave this is John."

"Hey John, how did it go with your *old* boss?"

"Very funny. Did they give you any problems at your end?"

"No," answered Dave. "All I had to do was ask."

Actually, Dave had to really push to get John back. There is always a concern when someone leaves a field position because of concerns about the danger. Everyone knew that John left because of his family. The distractions caused by worrying about a family can really interfere with making sound judgments under stress. Dave personally witnessed John keep his cool while being shot at. He could not imagine him any other way. Dave's fight to get John back is one of those things John will never know about.

"Dave, the reason I called you is because of the call I got from Jeff Creamore. Is he also going to be working on this case?"

Dave thought for a moment before answering. "No John, in fact I did not mention anything to the others. I figured you would want some time to work on this one on your own. I thought you might want to work out of your car for a while. This way, if nothing comes of this you could slip back, assuming that you'll want to go back."

"You sure do know how to lay it on thick," John said. "But I do appreciate your approach on this. I will really owe you on this one."

"I don't keep score with you John, remember? Jeff is the one working with that CIA guy that I told you about. They are off following what they think are some Chinese spies. Do you want me to contact Jeff for you and see what he wants?"

"No Dave, I'll talk to him. I have to admit that I'm really curious now."

"Let me give you his cell phone number, and make sure you guys keep me informed! I'm beginning to wonder where this is going."

"I promise Dave. I will also drop a hint to Jeff to check in with you," John said.

"Who do we follow today?" Jeff asked.

"Let's see where Chestburg goes, then double back to see if our guests notice if he has left yet," Charlie answered.

"That works for me," answered Jeff. "I will stay back a little so as not to be seen."

Brian pulled into the bank parking lot. Jeff pulled in across the street. Julie saw Brian through the window and waved. Charlie then looked at Jeff. He reached behind the seat and got out the binoculars. As Charlie looked through them he said, "Jeff, quick, write down this name. First name is Julie. The last name is spelled V-A -L-I-S-K-I."

"Got it," Jeff said.

Charlie replied. "Sometimes it comes easy, just a matter of reading a name tag!"

"We can check her out," Jeff said. "My guess is she's his girlfriend."

As Brian walked into the bank, Julie met him at the door. "What are you doing here at this time of day?" she asked.

"I finished up early. What time can you get off?"

Julie turned to look at the clock. "I've got another hour."

Brian said, "I could stop at the store and get us a couple of steaks for tonight."

"Aren't we going to your brother's for a barbecue tomorrow?" Brian nodded his head yes.

"Then in that case you can take me out for dinner tonight. How about you go home and change, then come back and pick me up."

"Okay boss," Brian said as he pretended to be annoyed.

Outside in the car across the street Charlie looked at his watch. "Hey Jeff, how about we get going and check up on our Chinese guests." Jeff started the car and they drove off.

Inside the apartment the Chinese were packing two large black duffel bags. Inside were several pistols, a bottle of chlorophyll, which can be poured into a rag and held over the nose and mouth to put someone to sleep, and a hypodermic needle already filled with a drug used to put a man to sleep. There were also some overalls large enough to slip over someone in clothes. They didn't speak much but went to work as if they had done this many times before. One of them looked at his watch and said, "We had better get going."

"I hope they realize we have not established his patterns well enough yet," said one of the Chinese.

"I know, but after Monday he will be on the list and the added security will not make this possible."

Jeff pulled the car around the corner and into a convenience store parking lot. "Uh oh," Charlie said. "They never carried out any bags before. If today is supposed to be the day, we won't have to mess things up since Chestburg already left for the day."

Jeff sat up in his seat and reached for his phone. "I'm going to call in. I'm overdue anyway, and I want some backup standing by in case we need some help."

"If you're going to call in, how about I drive?" asked Charlie.

Just then the two Chinese jumped into the van and drove off. "No time," Jeff said as he handed the phone to Charlie. "How about you make the call? Just unlock it and hit speed dial 02."

As soon as the phone rang Charlie handed it to Jeff. Jeff told Charlie to put it on speaker and just hold it up. "Hello Dave? This is Jeff. We are following the two Chinese. We watched them carry out a couple of duffel bags and their luggage. Our guess at this point is that they are going to make their move today."

"Did John Hunt call you back yet?" Dave asked.

"I haven't checked my messages for a while, why?"

"What is your involvement with Brian Chestburg?" Dave asked.

"He is the guy that the two Chinese have been following around. I called John because his name was on the file for Chestburg's security clearance. That's all I know so far."

Dave took a moment to try and put this together. "I guess John was right on this after all."

"Right about what?" Jeff asked.

"I think that you and John need to get together on this right away. John called me earlier this week about a security clearance. There is a lot more to this story. The politician Gallagor might also be tied into this."

"You're kidding me," Jeff said.

"Dave," Jeff continued, "we are still not sure if the Chinese are going to grab Chestburg, or try to make an informant out of him." "Or kill him," Charlie added.

"Right," continued Jeff, "or kill him."

"Where are you now?" asked Dave.

"We are following the two Chinese to Chestburg's work, just like every other day this week. The only problem, at least for them, is that he already left about an hour ago. It looks like he got off early today."

"If you think they plan to grab him today they must have a backup place to do it. Does he have a family?"

"No," answered Jeff. "He has a girlfriend that we saw today."

"Then Friday would be the perfect day. His disappearance would not be noticed right away. Possibly not even until Monday. They will be long gone by then," replied Dave.

"I have a suggestion," Jeff continued. "How about we pick him up at his house for questioning on the Gallagor case we were working on. He is a computer programmer and is really starting to look like the Internet hack we have been looking for. Assuming that he is, it would make sense for the Chinese to want him. They might use the information to blackmail him, or maybe they really will grab him. What information do we have on a possible Gallagor Chinese relationship?"

"I can look that up and get back to you," answered Dave.

"What about John?" Jeff asked.

"I will call him too. For now, try to find Chestburg before the Chinese do. I like your plan about picking him up before they do, but don't do it yet. We really need to find out their true intentions."

Jeff hung up the phone and looked at Charlie. "Dave thinks we should stick with Chestburg. Let's see if he's still at the bank."

"Wait a minute," Charlie said. "We are almost to his work now, and I want to check something."

"Check what?" Jeff asked.

Charlie answered, "I want to see if they stop, or if they can tell if he left yet."

"Do you think they have someone on the inside?"

"No," answered Charlie. "I have some information on a new bug they might have used on his car."

"Charlie, after all we've been through you're still holding out on me?"

"No, not really. The Chinese are just now starting to get in the electronic age. I just want to see what happens."

"Doesn't CCC have that security fence with the electronic scrambler antenna along the top?" Jeff asked.

"Yes," answered Charlie. "But there is a new electronic bug that works at a much lower frequency. It should be able to work through the fence. The down side is that the range is not very good."

The van slowed up as it approached CCC. They found a spot across the street and parked. Jeff passed by them and turned down the next block. He pulled over and Charlie jumped out. Jeff waited with the car running as Charlie walked to the corner to watch the Chinese. The van was there less than a minute before they started to leave. Charlie ran back to the car and jumped in. "They're leaving now," Charlie said. "They must know he's not there."

"What do we do?" Jeff asked.

"My guess is they are heading back to his house to wait," answered Charlie.

"Do we try and intercept Chestburg at the bank or follow them."

"I say that we follow them," answered Charlie. "If we miss him at the bank, they might get him before we do."

Brian had some extra time to kill before Julie got off work, so he decided to call Jay and see if there was anything special he could bring over tomorrow. "Hello," answered Jay.

"Jay this is Brian. I was wondering if there was anything special I could bring over tomorrow."

"Where are you?" Jay asked. "I tried to call you earlier but they said that you left early today."

"Right now I'm on my way home. I was going to stop at the store and pick something up for tomorrow."

Jay said, "I need to stop by and pick up Mom's punch bowl set. When do you think you'll get back to the house?"

Brian looked at the clock on his dashboard. "I need about an hour. What if you stop by about 4:00?"

"Sounds good to me," Jay said. "I will see you then."

Jeff and Charlie followed the van as it pulled past Chestburg's house and around the corner. They turned the van around and stopped about two houses away from the Chestburg house. Jeff and Charlie pulled around the block. After about 15 minutes a cable TV truck pulled up and blocked the entrance to the driveway. It seemed to take about five minutes for anyone to get out of the truck. Finally someone got out. He pulled a ladder off the truck and seemed to take forever to set it up against the pole.

Charlie looked over as Jeff said. "This cable TV truck looks suspicious to me."

Charlie then reached behind the seat and pulled out the binoculars. As Charlie looked through them he said, "The guy in the cable TV truck looks Chinese to me."

"What do you think his role will be?" Jeff asked.

"I'm not sure," answered Charlie. "They have the driveway blocked. Maybe they intend to jump in his car and drive off with him."

"What advantage do you think that would have?" Jeff asked.

"It could buy them some time if they hide the car well enough. The police would be so busy looking for him in his car they might not start anything else. It's all about getting enough time to sneak him out before the all out search begins." Jeff looked at his watch. It was 3:40 PM.

Chapter 9

Ryan arrived about 20 minutes before his 3:00 PM shift starts. While walking from his car to the time clock to punch in he noticed that Brian's parking slot was empty. I wonder if I should call John and let him know, Ryan thought to himself. Ryan was concerned about looking foolish if he called John with information that was not really of any value. Brian could simply have left early today.

As Brian turned onto his street he could see the cable truck in front of his house. When he got closer he noticed that the truck was blocking the driveway. He then stopped next to the truck and rolled down his window. "How long are you guys going to be?" Brian asked. The cable worker just nodded and walked over to the car.

Jeff and Charlie jumped out of their car and started to run toward the truck. Brian noticed them first and started to panic. He assumed they were after him. As he started to roll forward the cable TV worker produced a hypodermic needle and stuck it into Brian's arm. Brian hit the gas and the needle pulled back out of his arm only administering half of its dose.

The two men in the van jumped out and one of them fired at Jeff, hitting him in the chest. Jeff took two more steps before going down. Charlie fired back as the first Chinese took cover. The second Chinese ran behind the van and Charlie dove behind a small fence. They exchanged gunfire until Charlie ran out of ammo. Charlie rolled backwards to reload his gun with a fresh clip. Something caught his eye and he looked up.

Jay drove around the corner and saw the man standing behind the van. He was not aware of anything going on. He pulled his car over to the side and got out. The Chinese standing behind the van quickly holstered his gun as he looked Jay over sizing him up. Jay was still in his suit from work minus his tie. The Chinese said nothing as Jay walked up to him. Jay pointed to the cable truck and started to ask about it. The Chinese just looked at him. He had Jay figured for an easy kill. Suddenly the Chinese went to strike Jay in the throat using

110

a bear claw fist. Instinctively Jay moved to his left as he tried to block the punch. Since he caught Jay off guard Jay only half blocked the punch and it glanced off his neck. Suddenly there was a gunshot in the background.

As Charlie looked up he froze. Standing over him was another Chinese with his gun pointing right at his head. Charlie glanced over at Jeff, who looked like he was still breathing but not moving. Jeff's gun was about two feet behind him. Charlie started to lower his gun to the ground. He thought about going for it. Maybe he could roll on his side, finish loading his gun, and shoot the man standing in front of him. He figured he was dead anyway and should try something. He closed his eyes, and then heard a shot. The sound of the shot made Charlie's eyes clamp shut even tighter. At least death doesn't hurt, he thought to himself.

Charlie then felt something touch his arm. He opened his eyes and looked up. "Who are you?" Charlie asked.

"John Hunt, FBI."

Charlie stood up, and looked at the Chinese man lying on the ground. He then turned to look at Jeff lying to his right. "Jeff!" Charlie shouted as he leaped to his side. Charlie opened up Jeff's blood soaked jacket and reached in to apply pressure to the wound.

The gunshot in the distance made the Chinese man in front of Jay hesitate for a second. He turned back and went to kick Jay with a roundhouse kick. Jay's mind seemed to split in two. His conscience mind could not believe what was happening, but his sub-conscience seemed to take over his body.

Jay immediately stepped back letting the kick go past him, even giving the kicking foot an extra push. This unexpectedly spun the Chinese man around. When his back was to him, Jay punched him in the back at his eighth vertebrae, which shocked the Chinese man's heart while he kept spinning around to deliver a back fist. Jay easily blocked the back fist, which lost most of its energy when the Chinese

111

man's heart fluttered for a brief second. After blocking the punch, Jay grabbed the Chinese man's arm, lifted it up to expose his ribs, stepped in, and delivered an elbow to the Chinese ribs followed by a back fist to his nose. He then flipped the Chinese over his back slamming him to the pavement while still holding onto the same arm.

The Chinese man was flat on his back, with Jay's knee holding his elbow straight and twisting his wrist to put him in a Judo hold. The man was gasping from his broken ribs, but out of the corner of his eye Jay noticed the Chinese pull a gun out of his belt. Jay was still on autopilot as he stepped on the Chinese man's throat snapping his neck and instantly killing him. The gun fell to the ground and went off.

John Hunt spun around pointing his gun at Jay, who was standing over the Chinese man down the road. Jay had not even seen them yet. As Jay reached over to pick up the gun John fired a shot that hit near the gun and kicked up some asphalt on the road. Jay jumped back and looked up. When he saw John pointing a gun at him he immediately put his arms up. John walked over to Jay who just stood there with his arms up.

"Who are you?" John asked.

The adrenaline was still running through Jay. He immediately got angry as he replied, "None of your damn business. Who the hell are you?"

John reached into his jacket pocket and pulled out his badge. "John Hunt, FBI," was his reply.

"My name is Jay Chestburg."

"You're Brian's brother?" John asked as he put his gun and badge away.

"Yes," answered Jay.

"Well, you can put your arms down now," John said next. Jay was so hyped up that he didn't even notice that his arms were still up.

John walked over to the Chinese as Jay slowly turned around. He bent over to feel a pulse, and then noticed that his throat was crushed, and his neck was broken. "Did you do this?" John asked.

"He had a gun and was about to shoot me!" Jay quickly responded.

John stood up, still looking at the body on the ground. He noticed the caved in ribs, and his bloody nose. "Do you know who this guy was?" John asked.

Jay shook his head and said, "No."

"Well," answered John, "he was from an elite Chinese military group and you kicked his ass!" Jay was still waiting for John to arrest him and said nothing.

"Hey," yelled Charlie, "I need an ambulance over here."

John pulled out his phone and dialed 911, but was told that one was on its way. One of the neighbors' already called the police, and asked for an ambulance. John identified himself to the 911 operator and asked her to hurry on the ambulance, telling her that an officer was down.

John went over to Charlie and Jeff. Charlie had Jeff's shirt opened up and was desperately trying to stop the bleeding. Jeff was semi-conscious as he looked over at John. "It looks like you did it again," Jeff said.

Charlie looked up at John. "I heard about your reputation for showing up at the right time. I want to thank you for saving my life. I really thought I was done back there."

Before John could reply another car quickly turned down the block and skidded to a stop. It was a beat up Camaro from the 80's and it sounded like there was extensive engine work done. John reached for his gun while looking for Jay. Jay's adrenaline rush was wearing off and John could see that he was going to throw up. "Jay," John called out, "you have to shake it off. It's not over yet."

As the car skidded to a stop and the dust that was kicked up started to thin out the car door swung open and Ryan jumped out. He started to jog over to the group as John called out "Ryan you idiot! You almost got shot!" John's comment didn't even register with Ryan. The dead Chinese next to the van caught his eye, and he slowed his pace as he walked by.

Jay got up and started to walk over to John. "Hey Jay," Charlie said, "how about picking up my gun on the way over."

Jay reached down and picked up the gun and both the empty clip and the full clip. Not thinking what he was doing Jay inserted the full clip and pressed the slide release lever which snapped the slide closed. He then applied the safety before reaching down to hand it butt first to Charlie. Charlie looked over to John who nodded to him. John was thinking this guy knows how to fight and knows guns. How did I miss this? "On second thought why don't you hang onto it," Charlie said. "I'm kind of busy here trying to plug a leak."

"Not funny," Jeff said. "This really hurts!"

John turned to Jay. "Have you ever shot a gun before?" John asked.

"Yes," answered Jay. "I don't have a permit for this thing. Should I be carrying it?"

"The fact of the matter is I need your help," John replied. "I don't have time to fill you in on everything. If you want to keep your brother alive you're going to have to trust me."

Jay just nodded so John continued, "We have two possible scenarios here. Your brother drove off, alone as I can tell, when the shooting started. If you look over to your left there is a hypodermic needle on the ground. It looks to be about half empty. I watched the other half go into your brother's arm. It's probably something to make him sleep during the kidnapping. The guy who stuck him ran off, so he is still out there. We have to find your brother before they do."

"That's only one scenario," Jay said. "What's the second?"

Charlie spoke next. "Let me answer that. The other possibility is that they already have him. We will need to act fast before they can get him out of the country."

"You're kidding right?" Jay asked. John just looked at Jay and shook his head no.

"We're going to have to split up," John continued. "Jay, do you have a cell phone?"

Jay reached in his coat pocket and pulled out his phone. Jay read off the number to John who quickly programmed it into his phone. John then called Jay's phone. "Okay great, it works. Now Jay, use your caller ID to program my number in your phone." A couple of keystrokes later it was set.

Charlie called them over as the ambulance was pulling up. He was still kneeling next to Jeff applying pressure to his wound. Charlie then reached into his pocket with his free hand and pulled out his identification. As he handed it to Jay he said, "There is a toll free number on the other side. If you get into any trouble you call that number, and I mean anything from getting in a shootout to getting picked up by the local police for speeding. Most things can be forgiven. Just don't hurt any innocents."

"All I'm going to do is help find my brother. I'm not sure if I really need this or the gun," Jay said.

"Jay," John interrupted, "there is still one guy from this mess who is unaccounted for. He ran off as the shooting started. Please do it our way."

The ambulance followed by two police cars came to a stop next to the Chinese lying next to the van. "He's dead," yelled Charlie. "One of ours is over here and needs attention."

"Charlie, are you going with us now that the ambulance is here?" John asked.

"No," answered Charlie. "I'm going to ride in the ambulance and see this through. I will catch up with you later."

John turned to Jay and said, "Let's get going. Can you take your car?"

Jay nodded and said, "Yes, I'll be fine."

As they turned to leave Ryan said, "Hey, what can I do?"

Jay ignored him as he hustled to his car. John looked at Ryan and said, "What do you mean what can you do? You're driving."

Ryan nodded as they jumped into his car. One of the police officers walked up to their car, as they were about to pull away. John got back out and handed him a card and explained that they had to leave and to call that number to contact his office.

As the officer started to protest Charlie called out, "Let them go. I will help you fill out the paperwork." With that John jumped back in the car and drove off.

Since Ryan had parked close to the end of the street he made a U-turn and drove off. Ryan was excited about being involved, and the tires squealed some as he drove off. "Take it easy," John said.

Ryan was a little embarrassed but said nothing. John pulled out his phone to call his boss Dave. "Dave, this is John. It just went down about ten minutes ago."

"Do they have Chestburg?"

"I don't know. He drove off when the shooting started, so unless they caught him down the road he might have gotten away."

"Is everybody okay?"

"No. Jeff Creamore took one high in the chest but is still alive. He should be riding the ambulance right now. Two of the Chinese are dead, and one ran off on foot. My guess is he is long gone by now."

"Do the local police know about him?"

"No Dave, I'm sorry. These guys are highly trained killers and I was afraid the local guys might get hurt if they found him."

"I will send some of our guys to look around just in case," Dave said.

"There is one other thing I have to tell you," John continued. "Brian Chestburg's brother showed up during all of this."

"Oh no," Dave said. "How bad is it?"

"Dave you're not going to believe it. I don't know what kind of training this guy has but he took out one of the Chinese in a hand to hand fight! This guy beat him up real bad, and then when the Chinese pulled out a gun Chestburg killed him. I think it was his first kill."

"You're kidding me," Dave said. "Where is he now?"

"I sent him out to help look for his brother. We gave him a gun, and Charlie gave him his identification."

"You did what?" Dave said in an excited tone.

John responded, "He picked up Charlie's gun and without thinking he knew how to load it, and work the safety. He obviously has some experience there too."

117

Dave couldn't believe what he was hearing. "Did you ever run a background check on him?"

"No," answered John. "His name is Jay Chestburg. Can you run it and call me back?"

"No problem," answered Dave. "Where are you headed next?"
"There is a private airstrip a couple of miles from here. I got a tip a private jet is there owned by a company that is a front for the Chinese. I'm figuring if they did grab him they might bring him there. We have to stop that plane."

"Why don't I just send some people over there to seize the plane now?" Dave asked.

"I don't think that's a good idea. If we seize the plane before they get there with him they'll probably just kill him and dump the body somewhere. Then they will disappear. I would like to get him back alive, if possible."

Dave thought for a moment. "How about I get a couple of our guys in there undercover. I'll think of some way to get them in unnoticed."

"The help would be appreciated," John said. "Oh Dave, before you hang up there is one more thing. I'm with the security guard at CCC. He showed up right after the shoot out. I took him with me to keep him away from the local police until we can find Chestburg."

"Just keep him away from the action," Dave said. "There are too many civilians in this already."

Jay got into his car and started it up. He looked at himself in the rear view mirror. "I cannot believe what just happened," he mumbled to himself. As he pulled away, Jay took one more look at all the flashing lights behind him. What am I going to tell Rebecca? Jay thought to himself. As Jay drove down the street he took the first left, which would be the inner loop in the development. Going straight would go around the outer loop. The outer loop bordered a large area of state owned land where Jay and Brian used to play in as kids.

Jay drove slowly and pulled out his cell phone. He had to tell Rebecca he would be late, but decided against giving her any details. He didn't think she would believe him anyway.

"Hello," answered Rebecca.

"Hi, it's me. I'm going to be a little late."

"Is everything okay? Your voice sounds off. Is something wrong?"

How does she do that? Jay thought to himself. "No, everything is fine. I just need to help Brian with something. Did you know he got that contract?" Jay asked trying to distract her.

"Congratulations Brian. Can I talk to him?"

"He's not here. I'm in my car running an errand for him. You can talk to him tomorrow at the barbecue," (hopefully, Jay thought). "Rebecca I'll call you before I get home. Go ahead and have dinner. I will explain everything when I get home."

"Something is wrong. Are your parents okay?"

"They're fine," Jay answered. Jay came to a stop at the stop sign at the end of the inner loop road. "Listen Rebecca, I've got to go and I'll talk to you later. I love you."

"Love you too," Rebecca answered as she quietly hung up the phone.

Jay pulled out onto the road which makes the inner loop heading out of the development. As he accelerated he looked in the rear view mirror again and hit the brakes. If Brian was hurt or groggy from a partial injection he might take the outer loop and go up to the lake they used to fish as kids. In the rocks behind the lake is a hidden cave they used to play in. Jay quickly made a U-turn and drove down the outer loop. For the first time he was thankful he drove a small car that can U-turn on a narrow street.

Ming Chow, the third and final Chinese was hiding in the woods along the outer loop. He dialed his cell phone. "This is Chow. The operation failed."

"What do you mean you failed?" yelled the other voice in the phone.

"There must have been a leak somewhere. They were waiting for us. The other two are dead."

Ming Chow crouched down in the bushes as Jay slowly drove by. "One of them is passing now," he whispered into the phone. "According to our information this road loops around some wooded area and heads back up. I'm going to hike down and see if I can find out what he's looking for."

"Just make sure it's not you," the voice in the phone told Chow.

"What are my orders now?" Ming asked. "Eliminate him if you can, then call back for a pickup."

Jay drove along the outer loop slowing down when the paved section ended. It would be a gravel road until it started to turn back away from the woods. Jay turned the last corner at the bottom section and spotted Brian's car parked on the side. It was off on an angle with the right front corner in a ditch. Jay skidded to a stop and jumped out. The driver's side door was open and as Jay ran up to it he could hear the chime telling him that the keys were still in the ignition. Jay reached in and pulled them out and turned to lean on the car.

Okay, Jay thought to himself. Remain calm. He reached into his pocket and pulled out his cell phone. "Hello John? This is Jay Chestburg. I found Brian's car a couple of blocks from the house. The way it was parked, with the driver's door still open and the keys still in the ignition it looks like they must have grabbed him."

"Good job Jay, but I would not give up hope yet. I'm on my way to a private airstrip close by where I got a tip there is a plane waiting. We won't let that plane take off."

"Is there anything more I can do?" Jay asked.

"Not really," answered Dave. "We're almost there and hope to wrap this up soon. Maybe you should go on home. I will call you as soon as I know anything."

Jay closed up his phone, and grabbed Brian's computer and briefcase out of the back. He then closed and locked up Brian's car, and started walking toward his car. This must be a dream, Jay thought as he got in his car and started to drive away. Ming Chow was hiding in some thick bushes as Jay drove toward him. Ming cocked his gun and took aim as Jay got closer. Jay took one more look in the rear view mirror and suddenly slammed on his brakes. Ming ducked down a little lower as Jay started to back up. Ming's plan was only to shoot Jay if it was an easy shot. His reason was revenge. Ming watched as Jay backed up and got out of his car.

Jay walked over to his trunk and opened it up. I should have a flashlight here somewhere, he thought. Although it was a long shot, Jay thought that maybe Brian was hiding out in the cave by the lake. Jay figured he had nothing to lose by checking it out. Ming watched as Jay started out into the woods and decided to follow.

Ryan pulled into the airport parking lot and per John's instructions drove through the parking lot and right up to the gate, which leads to the airplane hangars. The guard at the gate took one look at Ryan's 1985 Camaro with the primer patch on the rear corner panel and knew right away that he didn't belong here. The guard jumped in front of Ryan's car and told him to stop. Unfortunately for Ryan he was going a little too fast on the gravel road and had to skid to a stop to keep from hitting the guard. He missed by about two inches, even after the guard jumped back a couple of feet.

121

Ryan rolled down the window as the guard came storming up. Ryan turned to John who was on the phone again. He was on a conference call with his boss Dave and the control tower. John was in the middle of explaining to the tower that the private jet taxiing out now must not take off.

"What do you want me to tell them?" asked the air traffic controller in the tower.

"Tell him you see smoke from one of his engines, and he has to come in and get it serviced," answered John.

"What? I can't do that," said the controller.

"Just do it," ordered Dave Gillian.

At this time the guard was standing on Ryan's side of the car and screaming in the window. John put his hand over the phone and reached in for his badge. He flashed his badge at the guard and told him to shut up. "I don't care who you are," yelled the guard, "you idiots almost killed me."

John was pressed for time and didn't have any to waste arguing with some hot head. The guard had his head in the window and was yelling across at John. Since John knew that the guard was unarmed, he pulled out his pistol and stuck the barrel on the guards nose. The guard looked cross eyed at the gun and finally stopped yelling. "Now quietly go back to your guard house and call your boss. He's going to have plenty to say to you," John said.

As the guard pulled away a black ring was left around the tip of his nose from the barrel of John's gun. Ryan noticed it first and it took all he had to keep from bursting into laughter. By the time John got back on the phone the plane was already on its way back to the hangar. A fire truck was on its way over to the plane, which stopped in front of the hangar. John put his phone back up to his ear and said, "Hello?"

"Your boss hung up already, but our instructions are as follows. Our firemen will quickly clear everyone off of the plane. If you pull over to the right we will escort everybody past your car. Just stay inside and look for your man. If he's not there you can search the plane after everyone is off," said the controller.

"Make sure none of your men go in first," John said. "If he's in there they will leave somebody behind who will be armed."

The firemen jumped out of the truck and sprayed the right engine with a fire extinguisher. This made the engine smoke and look like it was on fire. "Nice touch," John said to the controller.

"Thanks," was the reply. The pilot was the first to jump out of the plane, and when he saw the smoke he immediately yelled to the others to get out.

Several Chinese men jumped out in business suits along with the pilot and copilot. They were escorted to the hangar past Ryan's car. "None of them are who we are looking for," John said.

John then got out of the car and boarded the plane. As soon as John was in the plane out of sight of the people in the hangar he pulled out his gun. John searched the entire plane and found nothing.

John pulled out his phone as he sat down inside the plane. There were two other FBI agents dressed as firemen still searching inside the plane. "Hello Dave, this is John again. We have searched the entire plane but didn't find him. I have to admit that I don't know where to go from here."

"John, what exactly did you tell his brother to do?" Dave asked.

"I told him to go home," John answered. "Why do you ask?"

"I got a call from one of our agents still at the house. He told me that the local police found his brother's car parked next to Brian's on a side road two blocks down from his house."

"I don't know what his brother Jay is up to," John said.

"I suggest we set up a conference call with him right now," Dave said. "Hold on the line while I call him."

When the ambulance pulled up to the hospital, Charlie jumped out first and moved out of the way. Jeff had lost a lot of blood but was still awake. He looked up at Charlie as they wheeled him past. Jeff pulled off the oxygen mask and called over to Charlie. "Hey, I'll be fine now. Go get back in the game."

"Are you sure you'll be okay?" Charlie asked hesitantly.

"Just go rescue that kid," Jeff said as the intern put his oxygen mask back on and wheeled him away.

Chapter 10

Jay looked at his watch as he hiked further into the woods. He had about another twenty minutes of a thirty-minute walk to get to the cave. Jay jumped at the sound of his ringing phone. "Hello?" Jay answered.

"Jay this is Dave Gillian from the FBI. Hold on a second while I tie in John Hunt."

"Okay," was all Jay could say. This whole thing was still a bit overwhelming for him. Jay heard the phone click again.

"Jay? This is John Hunt. Where are you? The police found your car next to your brothers."

"Did you find him?" Jay asked.

"No, I'm afraid not. Where are you going?" John asked.

"It may just be wishful thinking, but there's a lake back here where we used to play as kids. On the other side is a cave up in the rocks. I thought I might at least take a look. You did say he could be partially drugged. I thought I might as well do something."

"Jay listen to me very carefully. Your brother was not in the airplane as we thought. He may just be where you think. The other concern is that one of the Chinese escaped by running in that direction. Do not go to the cave until we get some more men in there. If you see the Chinese before we get there kill him if you can."

"What?" Jay interrupted.

"Jay this is not the movies. He's a trained killer and if you get lucky for a second time you must take him out. I'm sure by now he has made contact with his people and they have changed his mission. Either way as soon as he thinks you have led him to your brother he will kill both of you."

Jay got a shiver down his spine and turned to look down the path he came from. "Whatever you do don't start turning around looking for him," Dave said.

"Too late for that," Jay answered back.

"Just keep walking Jay. Maybe make a turn somewhere until we get there."

Dave interrupted again, "I'm going to send in the regular police since they are closest to you."

"It's going to take me about twenty minutes to get there," John said.

Jay thought for a minute. "I'm heading for a small lake. Can you get a helicopter that can land on water? It's the only place to land in the woods here."

John looked around the airport and did not see any helicopters around. "I don't see any here, and I can't wait around to look. I'm going to start back now," John said.

"Are you going to let that crazy kid drive you back?" Dave asked.
"Yes I am," answered John. "And I'm going to tell him to step on it. I just hope he doesn't kill us."

"If this guy is following me," Jay asked, "how far back would he be?"

"Dave I'm going to let you take this. I will call you back as soon as I'm in the car," John said.

"Just stay on the line," Dave answered. "You can put it back to your ear as soon as you get going."

"Jay this is how these guys are trained," Dave began. "He will stay close enough to maintain a visual contact, but stay far enough back to be able to duck behind a tree or rock if you turn around. He probably wasn't trained to follow your trail."

"Okay," Jay said. "Let me think this through. When the woods get thicker he would have to get closer, and if they opened up to a field he would have to drop back."

"In theory that's true," answered Dave, "but remember if you toy with him he will probably just kill you."

"You guys sure do put everything in perspective," Jay said. "I have an idea but I will have to call you back," Jay continued.

"Wait a minute," Dave yelled into the phone. "Just keep walking and let the police handle it."

"That idea would work except that he would probably just shoot me and take off as soon as he saw the police coming," answered Jay.

There was silence at the other end of the phone. "Hello?" Jay finally said.

"Yes," answered Dave. "I will not lie to you. There is a possibility that he might try and shoot you before he got out of there. He would only do it if he thought that he could get away afterwards."

"That's all I need to hear," Jay said. "I may go to jail for this but I'm going to get him first," Jay said angrily as he snapped the phone closed. Jay started to wind up to throw the phone but stopped himself. Instead he just shut it off and slipped it back into his pocket.

John ran over to Ryan's car and jumped in. As he was buckling in he said, "Everything's changed Ryan. We need to get back to Brian's house as soon as possible. Turn on your lights and your flashers and don't get us killed."

Ryan opened his mouth but no words came out. He could not believe what he heard. Finally he asked, "As fast as I can go?"

"As fast as you can go and not kill anybody," answered John.

Ryan started his car up and shifted into first. He hit the gas, which started the tires spinning in the gravel. He pushed in the clutch and quickly shifted to second, and the wheels started spinning even more. The car was fish tailing as he drove through the guard's gate. Ryan looked into his rear view mirror to watch gravel hit the guard shack as he shot by. The guard inside never even came out.

John got back on the phone with Dave. After filling John in on his conversation with Jay, Dave said "I hope he doesn't get himself killed."

"Me too," answered John. "Although, somehow I think he just might pull it off."

"John I hope you're right. We just can't get anyone there fast enough to help him."

"Did you try and call him back?" asked John.

"Of course!" answered Dave. "I think he shut the phone off. What concerns me most is that Jay still thinks he'll get into trouble for shooting the Chinese militant. That can cause a second of hesitation which could get him killed."

"God help him," is all John could say.

Jay made a slight right turn that took him off of the well-established trail and up a hill. When he got to the top he stopped to look around. The sun was setting now but there was still enough light to see. Jay leaned up against a tall tree, thinking to himself that although he could not hide behind it at least he would make it more difficult for someone behind him to shoot him.

Jay stood there motionless straining to hear any sounds in the woods. There it is! Jay thought to himself. He heard a slight crack of a branch when someone steps on it behind him. He estimated it to be about thirty to forty yards away. Jay stepped out from behind the tree and started to walk down the far side of the hill, heading toward another smaller hill with several large rocks on top of it. In between the two hills was a small clearing. Jay figured that between the downhill he was currently on and the clearing ahead the Chinese would have to drop back a little more which would give Jay more time to hide.

This is where I can get him, Jay thought to himself. He reached for the gun that was stuck in his belt in front of him, being careful not to make it obvious to anyone behind him. He pulled back on the slide just enough to verify that a bullet was in the chamber. Jay then pulled out the magazine and could see it was full, minus the one round that was in the chamber. He then put the gun back in his belt and continued to walk.

Ryan pulled up to a light just as it was turning red. There were no other cars coming so he hit the gas, running the red light. Ryan looked over at John, who was on the phone with his boss. John gave no indication whether or not he approved of going through the light. Ryan then cut over to the right to enter the freeway.

Out of nowhere there was a police car behind them with his lights flashing. Ryan looked down at his speedometer. He was going about 80 miles per hour, and started to slow down. John stopped talking on the phone and looked over at Ryan. "What are you doing?"

"There's a cop behind us," answered Ryan.

"So what," yelled John as he turned around to look. "You just get me there. I will worry about him."

Ryan gave a nervous smile and said nothing. John continued on the phone, "There is a state trooper behind us trying to get us to pull over. Can you make a call and get him to understand who we are?"
"Okay," answered Dave. "I'll call you back."

John looked over at the speedometer as he hung up the phone. They were going about 85 miles per hour. "Is this as fast as this thing can go?" asked John.

"You told me not to kill anyone," answered Ryan.

"Yes I did say that didn't I." John turned around again as he continued to talk. "I wish that idiot behind me would shut off his siren. It's giving me a headache."

Ryan smiled. "How about I try and lose him?"

"Just don't crash or kill anybody," John said. Ryan sped up a little more but he knew that John wasn't really serious about losing the trooper behind them.

A few seconds later the siren shut off, but the lights were still flashing. "It looks like Dave got through," John said. John reached for his phone as it began to ring. "Hello," John said.

"John this is Dave again. The trooper in the car behind you wants to know if you want him to lead."

John turned to Ryan and asked, "The trooper behind you wants to know if you want him to lead."

Ryan shrugged his shoulders but didn't take his eyes off of the road. "You're kidding me right?" Ryan asked.

"I'm being a little sarcastic," replied John, "but we will need someone to help us get through the lights when we get off the highway." Ryan nodded and lifted his foot off the gas pedal. "Tell him to come around," John said into the phone.

Jay cleared the first hill and crossed the small field. He wished the field was wider but he had to make it work. Passing between two boulders Jay looked quickly on both sides. He chose to go to the right, and then quickly ducked down. He crawled down around the rocks and behind a large tree that grew up next to the boulder on the right. Looking around him Jay wished there was a better place to hide, one that would protect him from all sides. He then looked down at his white shirt. Why is white the standard color of the business world? Jay thought to himself. It's a good shirt too, but it seems to glow in the low light of dusk right after sunset and had to go.

Ming Chow watched as Jay turned to the right after walking between the boulders. Ming felt uncomfortable about losing sight of Jay so he decided to pick up the pace some. It was starting to get dark but Ming didn't want to walk through the middle of the clearing. He followed along the right edge, which is the direction Jay last turned.

As Ming approached the two boulders he decided to go around them instead of in between them. Since he was approaching from the right he decided that was the side he would go around.

Jay heard some leaves rustling and crouched down lower next to the rock. It was getting a little darker now, and only light colors could be seen contrasting in front of the darker background. Jay was motionless as Ming walked by.

As Ming came around to the backside of the boulder something white to his left caught his eye. I can't believe he hid behind the rock, Ming thought to himself. He decided to keep walking to put some space between them. As he was walking Ming also reached for his gun.

Jay let him get about ten feet past him and yelled, "Hold it right there."

Ming stopped but didn't turn around. Jay sat there frozen with his gun aimed at Ming. Suddenly, Ming dove to his left, spun around and fired two shots. Jay fired one shot as Ming was turning but missed. Ming was lying on the ground on his stomach with his gun pointed toward the only thing he could see which was the faint outline of Jay's white shirt. Ming studied the white glow wondering if he missed or if Jay was lying on the boulder dead. He took careful aim and shot again. There was no way he missed this time so Ming

131

decided his enemy must have fallen against the rock, and that was holding him up.

As Ming stood up he felt the sting of a bullet hit him in the center of his chest. He fell backwards and rolled down the hill as he lost consciousness for the last time. Jay stood up and carefully looked down the hill. In the fading light he could just make out the Chinese who had been following him. Jay could see where the ground was covered with blood and figured the Chinese man following him was now dead.

Jay turned and walked over to where he hung his shirt in the tree. There were two bullet holes in it, one of them breaking the stick he put in it to make the shoulders stand up straight. As he sat down on a log to pick the splinters out of his shirt Jay decided to call John and let him know what has happened. He pulled the phone out of his pocket and turned it back on. The setting sun was making it cooler out and Jay was getting eager to get his shirt back on.

As Ryan made the last turn on the dirt road he could see three police cars parked haphazardly along both sides of the road. "Hey look," Ryan said. "Isn't that Charlie the CIA guy? I hope your friend Jeff is okay."

John was on the phone with Dave and just nodded. "There isn't an ambulance here yet," John told Dave. "Can you get one over here right away? If Brian Chestburg is here, we will need to get him to the hospital right away. I think they only gave him half a dose, so there's still hope of finding him in time."

"In time for what?" Ryan asked as he was shutting off his engine.

John turned to him and started to explain when he got a beep indicating he had another call. John turned his attention to the phone. "Dave I have another call coming through. I'll call you back." John hit the pound key, which switched to the other line. "Hello?" John said.

"John this Jay Chestburg. You guys were right about the last Chinese guy following me. I'm afraid I had to shoot him."

"Is he dead? Because if he isn't don't take your eyes off of him," John said.

"He rolled down a hill, and judging by all of the blood splattered on the trees where I shot him I would say he's dead. He left me no choice." Jay took a deep breath and asked, "Do you know a good lawyer?"

"For what?" John asked. "You still don't get it, do you? You're representing the FBI now, or maybe the CIA since you're using Charlie's gun."

"I have killed twice today. How can you make light of it?" Jay interrupted.

"Because they were the enemy!" John said. "Don't go soft on me now Jay! You haven't found your brother yet. Stay focused on the mission!"

Jay heard the sound of leaves rustling behind him. He started to turn around, then he heard, "Freeze, police, don't turn around or I'll shoot."

Jay dropped the phone and froze where he was. "Now put your hands up over your head but don't turn around."

John could hear what was going on in the background. He quickly hung up the phone and called Dave back. "Dave, this is John. Some local cop is in the process of arresting Jay Chestburg. Call down there and tell them to back off, will you?"

"I'm on it," Dave replied. "I'll call you back."

John looked over at Ryan as he started to get out of the car. "Thanks for the ride Ryan," John said. "You did great."

"Do you need anything else?" Ryan asked.

"I'm not really sure, but at this point you might as well come with us just in case we need help carrying Brian out. If he's here we'll need to get him to the hospital quickly."

Jay raised his hands over his head and the cop handcuffed him. Jay was then frisked and the cop pulled Jay's gun out of his belt, and his wallet out of his pocket. It was now too dark to read the officers nametag, and the flashlight shining in his eyes didn't help either. "How about getting that light out of my face," Jay said.

"Nothing doing," replied the cop. "I have one man dead, and I overheard you saying you killed him. Until I know what's going on you just stay there."

The officer took out his portable radio and called his dispatcher. Jay could hear both sides of the conversation. "Dispatch, this is Officer Blackfeld. I have a Jay Chestburg in custody."

"Stand by Officer Blackfeld," was the reply from dispatch. As both men waited, the next thirty seconds seemed like ten minutes. Jay was starting to realize that he was getting tired and decided to sit down on a rock that was about three feet to his left.

"Officer Blackfeld this is dispatch. You are to release Inspector Chestburg immediately. From now on you are to follow his orders." Jay started to smile and had to look away. Inspector Chestburg? Jay thought. For now he would say nothing and just go with it.

"Dispatch, please repeat," Blackfeld said.

"Release Inspector Chestburg *now*. He is currently in charge and you are to assist him as he requires."

"Hey," Jay yelled. "You heard them. Now get these handcuffs off of me. We are wasting time and a life depends on us."

The officer walked over and immediately removed the handcuffs. He began apologizing but Jay held up his hand and interrupted him. "Look, just forget it. We don't have time. Now will you help me find my phone? I dropped it somewhere over in the leaves." The officer switched on his flashlight as both men dug around in the leaves where Jay was sitting. Jay found it first and opened it up to answer it.

"Hello," Jay said. There was no one on the line but the phone rang again right after Jay hung up.

"Jay this is John. Is the officer still within hearing range?"

"Yes," Jay said.

"Then just listen. This is your show. Make no mistake about it; until I get there you are in charge, so you will need to act like it. Did he give you your gun back?"

"No," answered Jay.

"As soon as I finish here demand it back. Don't take no for an answer. You guys need to get over to where you think your brother might be as quickly as you can. I'm starting to walk into the woods now. How far away do you think I am?"

"About thirty minutes," answered Jay.

John continued, "We also have a helicopter coming with a spotlight. He's about ten minutes out, so watch for him. Let's hang up so you can make better time. Call me if you see anything."

Jay hung up the phone and turned to the officer. "You have my gun." The officer pulled Jay's gun out of his belt and handed it to Jay without saying anything. The officer began to apologize again but Jay interrupted him. "Forget it. We need to start fresh. Let's get going, and I will explain what is happening along the way."

135

The two men began walking. Jay continued, "The fact is we are looking for my brother. When we were kids we used to play in a cave near here. I'm hoping we find him hiding there."

"Who is the guy you killed back there?"

"All I know is he's from the Chinese military. I'm hoping to get the rest of the details after this is over."

Jay stopped for a moment. He reached into his pocket and hit the speed dial on his phone. "John, this is Jay. When is that helicopter going to get here?"

"Any minute now, why, what's wrong?"

"Well, I turned off the trail to steer the Chinese away from the cave, and it's a lot darker now," Jay said reluctantly, "I'm having trouble finding my way again."

"Are you lost?" John asked.

"That's another way to put it," Jay said sarcastically.

"Inspector Chestburg, I think I've found the trail again," yelled Officer Blackfeld.

Jay had his ear to the phone. "Wait, I think we found it," Jay told John. "Hold on a second."

Jay moved the phone from his ear and called back to Blackfeld, "That's great. Hold up the flashlight, I'm coming." Jay put the phone back to his ear. "It looks like he found the trail again. We are on our way. Give me about ten minutes and I will call you back."

"Maybe you should just stay on the line," John said.

"I'm worried about my battery," answered Jay. "I have to admit I'm a little lax at keeping it fully charged."

John hung up the phone as Charlie was walking over to him. "How about an update?" Charlie asked.

"Jay Chestburg is on his way to a spot he and his brother used to play as kids. We are hoping Brian is there. If he isn't, then we don't know where he is."

Charlie looked off into the distance. "Remember," Charlie said, "there was still one more Chinese soldier who got away."

John smiled and said "Chestburg handled him already."

"Wow, which one of us is going to sign him up," Charlie asked.

"That depends on whether he wants to work on domestic or foreign issues," John answered.

John looked at his watch. He could hear a siren in the distance. "I hope that's the ambulance," John said.

"Are you worried about what they put in his arm?" Charlie asked.

"Should I be?" John asked.

Charlie shook his head yes and said, "They have been known to mix in a slow working poison just in case the target gets rescued. Without the antidote, which is delivered at the other end, he dies anyway. This way if they can't have him, at least he is silenced."

John leaned against a tree at the beginning of the trail into the woods. He was really getting angry now. John is usually very even tempered, but he also hates to lose. Charlie could sense the anger, and was misreading it to be directed at him. "Getting pissed at me isn't going to help now," Charlie finally said.

"I'm angry," John replied, "but not at you, at least not yet. Can you think of anything we can do now? Remember that Chestburg did only get about half of the shot."

"How do you know that?" Charlie shot back quickly.

"I saw the needle lying on--"

"On the ground!" Charlie interrupted. "I'll go get it."

"No, wait," John said. "Let me get it. I remember where I saw it, and I can rush it to an FBI lab close by."

"Fair enough," Charlie said. "I will work on getting Chestburg to the hospital."

John looked over to Ryan, who was leaning against his car. The state trooper who followed them in was talking to Ryan. John pointed to the trooper's car and told them both to get in. "What's up?" asked the trooper.

"I'll explain in the car," answered John.

"Well, my name is Ed Jones."

John paused for a second. "I apologize for my rudeness. My name is John Hunt, and this is Ryan McWilliams." John reached out to shake the trooper's hand.

"Ryan and I already met," Ed said.

Charlie watched the three of them pull away as the ambulance pulled up. The ambulance slid to a stop and the first paramedic jumped out. Charlie was already on his way to greet them. "Hi, my name is Charlie Gurns."

The paramedic, who was beginning to unload some of his equipment, turned to shake Charlie's hand. "I'm Phil Decker, and my partner is

George Bilk. Nice to meet you Charlie. Can you tell us what's going on here?"

"I think so," answered Charlie. "We have a guy in the woods, about thirty minutes in. He isn't quite there yet but we believe he will find a man who will need medical attention."

"Are you trying to tell me you're not even sure he's there?" Phil asked.

"To be honest, no," answered Charlie.

George came around from the back of the ambulance. He had heard enough of the conversation to ask, "What do you want us to do? Wait here until your man finds him?"

"No. We need to get started now. If he finds him and we wait, there may not be enough time to save him," answered Charlie.

Phil gave Charlie a strange look. "What exactly will be wrong with him?"

Charlie took a deep breath before answering. "He will probably be poisoned."

"Poisoned!" Phil shouted. "We will need to know what it is. Is there an antidote?"

"Get your stuff and I will explain it as we go," Charlie said.

Jay was moving slowly in the dark. It had been many years since he was in these woods, and the dark made finding his way even more difficult. As they came up to the lake Jay got excited and picked up his pace. "The cave is just on the other side of the lake," Jay said as he pointed across the lake.

"Which way around is the fastest?" Officer Blackfeld asked.

"We should turn to the right and follow it around. Unless things have changed over the years the path will start to fade away half way around."

The trooper drove them back to Brian's house and weaved past the clean-up crews. He pulled up where John pointed to, leaving his engine running and the headlights on. John explained what he was looking for to Ryan and Ed. It was a short ride, so John did not have time to explain much else. "It doesn't look like the cleanup crew has gotten very far," John said. "If you guys don't mind, start looking over there, and I'm going to ask the crew if they found the needle."

Ryan and Ed both said, "Okay," and Ed handed Ryan a flashlight.

Charlie looked up as the helicopter began to hover over them. Charlie waved his arms and motioned to the pilot to go into the woods. "Why did you do that?" George asked.

"The guys already in the woods are going to need the light more than we will," answered Charlie.

John got halfway down the road to the cleanup crew when Ryan shouted, "I found it."

John spun around to run back as his phone started to ring. "Hello," John said.

"John this is Jay. We found Brian!"

Chapter 11

"John," Jay said, "He doesn't look that good."

"Tell me what's wrong," John, requested.

"He's groggy, which we would expect from the shot, but he's complaining that he's having trouble breathing. What do you think is wrong?"

"Jay, you have to listen to me. There is a possibility that Brian was also poisoned."

"Poisoned," Jay said, "that doesn't make any sense. Why would they poison him if they were going to kidnap him?"

John answered, "I found out from Charlie that sometimes they mix a slow working poison into the sedative. They have an antidote waiting at the other end. If the mission fails, then the target dies."

"You mean my brother dies," Jay said.

"That's their plan but it's not going to happen that way this time. I'm in front of your house with the needle in my hands now. We are going to rush it to a local lab and get it analyzed. Charlie is on his way in with the paramedics. You make sure Brian gets to the hospital as quickly as possible."

Jay looked up as the helicopter appeared. The spot light was almost blinding as Jay's eyes tried to adjust to the bright light shining through a hole at the top of the cave. "John I can barely hear you. The helicopter is too noisy."

Officer Blackfeld was feeling helpless waiting outside the cave but from listening in to Jay's half of the conversation finally found a way to contribute. He pulled out his radio and called dispatch. "Dispatch this is Officer Blackfeld. Patch into the helicopter and ask them to fly up another 500 feet. Inspector Chestburg needs to hear what's being said on his phone." After about a two-minute delay the helicopter rose about 500 feet as requested.

"Okay that's better," Jay said. "How far out did you say the paramedics are?"

"They were just pulling up as I was leaving. How far in did you say you were?"

"About a half hours walk, and that's in the daytime without a stretcher," answered Jay.

John was silent so Jay asked, "Are you also adding up the time? The way I figure it we are looking at a minimal of an hour before we get Brian to the ambulance, then whatever time it will take to drive him to the hospital. John I think we need another plan."

Officer Blackfeld could hear Jay's half of the conversation, which is all he really needed. He called dispatch again. "Dispatch this is Blackfeld again. Can you patch me into the helicopter pilot?" "One moment," answered dispatch.

Blackfeld's radio began to roar with the sound of the helicopter on it, which caught Jay's attention. "John, can I call you back, I want to hear this," Jay said as he listened in on Blackfeld's conversation.

"This is Officer Blackfeld on the ground below you. We have a man down here that isn't going to make it unless we get him some help right away. Can you hover that thing over the water?"

"Yes I can," answered the pilot, "but you guys aren't going to be able to breathe in the spray that will be kicked up, and we do not have a cable to lift you up."

"Ask him about the clearing where we met," Jay yelled from inside the cave.

142

Blackfeld nodded and said, "There is a clearing to our south. Can you set down there, or is there anywhere else you can see from up there to touch down at?"

"Let me look around and get back to you," answered the pilot.

Officer Blackfeld walked over to the mouth of the cave, and crouched down at the entrance. "How's he doing?"

"Not good," answered Jay. "He seems to be having trouble breathing."

"Jay," Brian said in barely a whisper, "what happened? Who was it that did this and why?"

Jay shrugged his shoulders and said, "I wish I knew, but whatever is going on at least you're in good hands now. We got the FBI and the CIA taking care of business for us."

Brian looked away and did not answer. Jay wondered if Brian understood what he said, or if Brian was thinking the same thing he was.

Brian turned back to Jay with a tear in his eye. "I'm sorry I got you into this big brother. If I don't make it just tell them it was all my fault. No sense in you going to jail." Brian turned away again noisily struggling for each breath.

"You have it all wrong," Jay said. "These guys have been working their asses off to save you! Trust me, you have no idea what's happened today."

Blackfeld's radio roared to life echoing in the cave for everyone to hear. "Officer Blackfeld, this is chopper AX-1. That's a negative on landing in any field close enough to save any time. There is a road however that would be passable if someone could get through the first fifty feet. There is a locked gate, and then about fifty feet of deep

143

mud. After that it's a pretty easy ride. I am currently over the paramedics hiking to you now."

"I copy that, thanks anyway," replied Blackfeld. Officer Blackfeld wanted to look over and say he was sorry to Jay but just couldn't.

"I have an idea," Jay said as he quickly picked up his phone and began dialing. "Rebecca, this is Jay."

Rebecca snapped back, "Where are you? Julie is over here and she is worried sick about Brian. He was supposed to take her out to dinner tonight."

"I don't have time to explain," Jay said. I need Fred Milnurg's phone number." Officer Blackfeld got out a pen and his ticket book of all things to write on the back of.

"Jay what is going on," Rebecca demanded.

"Rebecca you wouldn't believe me if I told you. I need Fred's number as quick as you can get it. I will explain everything later. For now just sit by the phone with Julie and wait for my call."

"You know you are frightening me with all of this. It had better be good," Rebecca snapped back.

"Trust me Rebecca, now how about the number?" Rebecca read off the number, which Jay repeated out loud, and Blackfeld wrote down. "Thanks, and I love you Rebecca, now wait for my call, which should be in about an hour."

Jay hung up the phone and dialed Fred. "Fred this is Jay Chestburg."

"Jay, how ya doing?"

"Not good Fred. Remember the lake we used to play in as kids. I'm with Brian and we need you to drive up here and get us."

"Are you guys okay?" Fred asked. "I'm okay but Brian is hurt. You still have that Chevy Suburban with the big tires and 4 wheel drive right?"

"You know I do, but there is a gate across the access road, and besides I could lose my truck if I get caught."

"What if I promise you a police escort complete with a helicopter to light your way?" Jay asked next.

Fred got up to put on his jacket and look for his keys. "I did see a helicopter flying over my house about ten minutes ago. Was that you?"

"Sort of," Jay answered. "Listen Fred, I couldn't be more serious. Smash through the gate if you have to, blast the lock with a shotgun, I don't care how you do it, just get up here as quick as you can."

"Okay," answered Fred. "I will see you in about twenty minutes."

Officer Blackfeld got back on his radio. "Chopper AX-1, this is Officer Blackfeld again. We have someone coming up the trail any minute now. Can you help him see his way through the gate?" "Officer Blackfeld this is chopper AX-1, affirmative, we are on our way."

"Dispatch, did you copy that?"

"Affirmative Officer Blackfeld. We have a state trooper in the area to assist."

"He will need a key to the gate," Blackfeld said.

Charlie looked up as the chopper flew away again. "Damn, we can make a lot better time when we can see where we're going," Charlie said. It suddenly occurred to Charlie that maybe something happened to Brian and he felt bad. He decided to call Jay and find out.

"Hello," Jay said when his phone rang. "Jay this is Charlie. We can see the moonlight on the lake ahead, how far away are we?"

"We are on the other side of the lake. It's easier if you turn to your right to follow the lake around counter clockwise to the other side."

"How is Brian doing?"

"Not good. He is having trouble breathing."

"We brought up a portable oxygen tank and a stretcher. The oxygen should help him breathe easier until we get him to the hospital."

"You guys are making great time considering the equipment you're bringing," Jay said.

"Don't thank me. You would not believe the shape these two paramedics are in. But Jay, I have to tell you. We do not have any extra time here. Brian's breathing will slowly get worse until we can get him back to the hospital and get the antidote in him."

"I figured that," answered Jay. "I have a friend with a 4 wheel drive truck coming up from the other side of the lake. He's trying to get through an old road now."

"Excellent idea Jay, good to see you thinking," Charlie said making no effort to hide how impressed he was.

Fred pulled up to the locked gate along the side of the road and skidded to a stop. He turned his truck so his headlights would light up the gate, and hopped out of his truck carrying a sledgehammer across his shoulder. The lock was encased in a metal pipe and Fred could see that he would not be able to get a good hit on it. Just then a state trooper pulled up with his lights flashing, and at the same time the helicopter showed up to light up the area. Fred got a little nervous and felt like he was busted. He hoped this was not some kind of a setup or something.

The trooper jumped out of his car and said, "Did you get it."

"Get what?" Fred asked without even thinking.

"Did you bust the lock open yet?" asked the trooper, obviously a little excited.

If there was any doubt about the seriousness of what was going on in Fred's mind before, it was definitely gone now. "The lock has a piece of pipe welded around it. I can't get a clean hit with my hammer," Fred said.

The trooper looked at the lock, and pulled out his gun. "I don't think I could shoot it off either. Whoever made this gate knew what they were doing."

Fred looked over at the winch on his truck. "I've got an idea," he said. Fred pulled out the cable to his winch and hooked it to the gate near the top, figuring he could bend it over some to make it easier to pull out. He jumped back in his truck and started pulling with the winch. The gate started to bend some but then started dragging the truck. The trooper saw this and signaled for Fred to stop. He then got back in his car, pulling it up close to the fence along side of Fred's truck. In the trunk the trooper pulled out two straps, which he tied to the gate and then the brush bar that was bolted to his front bumper. Both men started to pull on the fence and it finally came out of the ground.

Fred jumped out of his truck and started to help the trooper untie his car. The trooper went straight to Fred's truck and said, "I can untie the car, we need you to get going right away."

Fred felt bad leaving him. The brush guard was bent badly and the weight of the gate will make it difficult to untie it from the car.

Fred reeled in the cable to his winch and was on his way. He hit the mud and almost bogged down, but kept the motor revs up to keep from getting stuck. Mud was flying everywhere, and it was nice to

147

have the helicopter's spot light above him so he could see where he was going. When Fred got to the other side he looked in the rear view mirror. The grooves he cut in the mud would make it even more difficult to go through again on the way back.

Charlie could see the light from Officer Blackfeld's flashlight. As he got closer Charlie could not resist picking up his pace, which separated him from the paramedics. Blackfeld was standing outside of the cave. Jay was inside with his brother. "How is he doing?" Charlie asked.

"There hasn't been any change in a while," answered Officer Blackfeld. Holding out the flashlight, Blackfeld said, "Here take this. I'm going to help the paramedics carry up their equipment."

Charlie ducked down and went into the cave. Jay looked up but could not see who it was. He knew that it wasn't Blackfeld. Charlie heard the sound of a gun cocking and immediately said, "Jay, its Charlie Gurns, CIA."

"Okay," answered Jay. Charlie could then hear a snap as the safety was applied to the gun, which also decocked it.

"Maybe I should take my gun back," Charlie said next in a joking manner.

"Here, take it now," Jay answered in a very flat tone.

Charlie ignored Jay's last statement. He could see that Jay was extremely concerned about his brother, and trying to lighten up the situation a little would be lost on him now.

Charlie could hear a slight gasping sound with each breath Brian took. "How is he doing?" Charlie asked.

Jay answered, "He's still having trouble breathing, although it hasn't gotten any worse in a while now."

148

Charlie responded, "Remember that he only got about half a dose. I have seen symptoms like this before. I think if we keep him still until we get to the hospital he should be fine."

"Do you think so?" Brian whispered.

"You're awake!" Charlie said. "That's excellent."

Outside, a light shining into the cave followed the sound of clanging metal. "I'm afraid your batteries will not last much longer," Charlie said to Blackfeld as he handed back the flashlight.

The paramedics crawled in and went to work. Brian was examined and hooked up to the oxygen. The cave was starting to get a little crowded, so Jay and Charlie decided to crawl out and wait outside.

Charlie pointed to the helicopter light off in the distance. "It looks like your friend is coming through," Charlie said.

"He lives for an excuse to get his truck dirty," Jay answered. Jay's phone rang: "Hello?"

"Jay, this is John, how is it going?"

"John, I'm sorry I didn't call you back."

"Jay don't even waste time thinking about it."

"Okay," Jay said. "The paramedics are working on Brian now. I called a friend with a four-wheel drive truck to come and pick us up. We can see the helicopter off in the distance so I assume he's under it and getting close now."

"I heard about your friend Jay. That was good thinking. If the truck is road worthy I suggest you go straight to the hospital instead of going back to the ambulance. The paramedics will protest but you and Charlie can handle them."

149

"Is timing that critical?" Jay asked.

"No, it's not that," answered John. "The press are staked out at the ambulance now, and I want to save your brother from the unnecessary publicity. It will also be easier to find out who is behind this if the press doesn't blab about Brian's rescue."

"I already know the bastard behind this," Jay growled into the phone. "It's that Gallagor creep running for the senate."

Charlie's ears perked up when he heard that. John froze for a second. Finally John said, "Jay you have to promise me something. No vigilante crap here. We will get him, but you have to trust us and do it our way. You promise?"

Jay looked over at Charlie but could only see the outline of his face in the dark. "Okay, I promise. But will you include me in it somehow, at least in some small way?"

"I think I can promise that," John answered.

"Jay, can I talk to Charlie?" John asked next.

Jay handed the phone to Charlie. "Here, John wants to talk to you."

Charlie took the phone and said, "Yes John, what's up?"

"Charlie I know you can't answer me now, but do you think Brian Chestburg is the guy you and Jeff were looking for?"

"Yes, I think Brian will make it," Charlie answered. John knew Charlie was trying to answer his questions without letting Jay know the actual subject.

"Do you think Jay will let us handle this?" John asked next. "I don't want him to go after Gallagor himself."

"I think the paramedics have Brian stable," Charlie answered. The word stable was the answer to John's question.

Next John asked, "Does he still have your gun?"

"Yes," Charlie answered.

Charlie continued, "John, how are you making out with the antidote?"

"I'm at the lab now. It shouldn't be much longer."

"That's good," Charlie said. "John I don't think we should check Brian in under his real name."

"You're probably right," answered John. "I will call my boss Dave Gillian and have him set it up."

"That's good," Charlie said. "Have your boss call us at this number so we know what name to use."

Charlie hung up the phone and handed it back to Jay. Jay said "Shouldn't you hold onto it since you are expecting a phone call?"

"*We* are expecting a phone call," answered Charlie.

Jay reached around to pull the gun out of his belt and hand it to Charlie. "What's this?" Charlie asked.

"I know you guys are afraid that I will go after Gallagor. I was thinking you might want your gun back."

Charlie answered, "Jay you did promise not to. Like it or not you are now part of the team, and all our lives depend on everybody on our team being good to their word."

Jay hesitated and did not say anything. Charlie could sense that Jay was unsure but because of the darkness could not see the confused look on his face. After a couple of seconds pause Charlie said, "After

151

we get your brother to safety we will sit down and talk, but for now I will take my wallet back."

After Fred cleared the mud the road was very bumpy but passable. It was a little narrow in some spots, and Fred broke a headlight on a small tree he ran over. He was sure glad that the helicopter was lighting the way. It had been a long time since he was up this way and Fred was hoping he didn't make any wrong turns.

"I wonder how long we'll be waiting here." Ryan asked.

Trooper Ed Jones shrugged his shoulders and said, "I'm not sure. You would think the lobby of an FBI lab would have better magazines to read." Ryan just shrugged as he stood up to look out the window.

John was inside working with the lab chemist Zac Gentale. "How much longer before we know what it is?" John asked.

"I think we are going to get lucky here," answered Zac. "According to our data base the Chinese are only using a couple of different types. I tried an old favorite of theirs first and it looks like it will match up. My only concern is he is probably near death by now. I doubt that you will get it to him in time."

"Even though he only got about half the dose?" John asked.

Zac turned around to face John. "Can you check how he's doing right now?" asked Zac.

"Yes, but why?" answered John.

Zac went back to his testing of the poison before answering, "There is a possibility that he may not need the antidote if he got a small enough dose. Giving him too much antidote could make things worse. If he didn't get enough of the poison to die the best thing to do is let him ride it out."

John picked up the phone and dialed Jay's phone. "Hello," Jay answered.

"Jay this is John again. How is Brian doing?"

"He's actually doing a little better since they put him on the oxygen. How is the antidote coming?"

"We almost have it," answered John. "But Jay, the lab technician is telling me that if Brian starts to get better on his own, he would be better off just riding this thing out without the antidote. What's saving him is that he didn't get a full dose."

"I will let the paramedics know," answered Jay. "What if he doesn't get better, and how long until we know for sure?"

"Hold on a second," answered John. Jay could hear John talking to the lab technician, but couldn't hear his answers. John got back on the phone, "A couple more hours," he said. "I will meet you at the hospital with the antidote just in case he needs it."

Jay's phone beeped signaling that he has another call. "John, I have another call coming through, can you hold on?"

"It's probably my boss Dave with the name for you to use at the hospital. I will hang up and see you there," answered John.

Jay switched over to the other call. "Hello Jay, this is Dave Gillian. Sign Brian in under the name Will Smith."

"Will Smith, it's not very creative," answered Jay.

"I know but it will do," Dave said. "How's Brian doing?"

"He seems to be doing a little better since they put him on the oxygen. Dave, can I call you back later? Our ride is pulling up now."

"That's fine," Dave said. "I will meet you guys at the hospital later."

Fred could see a flashlight waving in the air about thirty yards to his right. The road he was on continued past the light, but there was no road to them. Fred stopped his truck and got out. With the light of the helicopter above him, Fred studied the terrain trying to decide if he should make his own road the rest of the way.

Charlie turned to Jay and said, "It looks like your friend has gone as far as he can. Let's go down to greet him."

George turned to Phil and said, "It sounds like our ride is here. I'm going out to check it out."

Phil nodded and said, "I'll stay here and monitor the oxygen." George crawled out and called to Jay and Charlie, who were already halfway to the truck. George figured Jay and Charlie couldn't hear him since they didn't turn around.

Fred walked into the woods looking for a way in. "Fred," Jay called out, "thanks for coming to help!"

Fred looked up and smiled. The two men shook hands. Fred could not help his reaction to Jay's appearance. Jay's white dress shirt was soiled, and had two bullet holes in it. It was still obvious through the dirt that his dark blue pants were part of a business suit. His dress shoes were also ruined. There was a black smudge around the gun stuck in his belt suggesting that not only was he carrying a gun, but it had been fired too. Finally Fred nervously asked, "What's going on Jay?"

Jay forced a smile, which was an attempt to put Fred at ease. "Fred, you wouldn't believe it if I told you. Do you remember that cave we used to play in as kids?" Fred nodded his head yes. "The quick story is that Brian is in there now, he was poisoned, and we need to get him to the hospital as quickly as we can. I'm sorry to leave you hanging and I promise to give you the details later. Right now we need to get Brian to the hospital."

"You're not in any trouble are you?" Fred asked.

Charlie reached for his wallet and spoke up before Jay could answer. "Hi Fred, my name is Charlie Gurns, CIA."

Charlie extended his hand and shook Fred's, then showed his identification to Fred. "As you can see," Charlie continued, "Jay is working with us on this."

Fred paused for a second, and then said to Jay, "I thought you were an accountant."

Jay answered, "I am."

"But he is currently interviewing with us," Charlie quickly said next.

George walked up to the group, which refocused their attention on him. "Is that our ride?" George asked as he walked over to Fred's truck.

Fred followed George over to the truck. Jay started to follow but Charlie grabbed his arm as Jay took his first step. "I know you have to tell your friend something," Charlie said, "but for his safety you should keep the details to a minimal."

Jay nodded and said, "I think I've seen enough to understand what you're saying. Oh, before I forget, what do you mean by interviewing with you?"

Charlie chuckled and started to walk to the truck without answering. Jay followed a few steps behind and said, "This has been the roughest interview I was ever on!"

"Open up the back," George said to Fred.

Fred opened up the back of his truck, which were two vertical swinging doors. There were three rows of seats. "Can you fold down the third seat so Brian can lie flat?" George asked.

155

Fred nodded his head yes and climbed inside to ready the truck. George turned to Jay and Charlie and said, "Come with me to help bring Brian and our equipment down."

Officer Blackfeld looked out of the cave opening. The light from the helicopter caught his attention. "It looks like your ride is here," Blackfeld said to Brian.

Brian nodded his head and started to pull off the oxygen mask to speak but Phil stopped him. "You can talk all you want after we get you to the hospital," Phil said.

Brian rolled his eyes. Although he was feeling better with the oxygen, Brian was not about to argue with the paramedic.

Zac came out of the back and handed a small bottle to John. "Here is the antidote. The poison used is similar to a time-release bee sting. The throat starts to close off choking the victim to death. This was also mixed with something to make him sleep so theoretically he would quietly choke to death while asleep."

"So all Brian needs is one of those bee sting kits?" John asked.

"Not exactly. The chemicals used are different, so the antidote is required if he got enough of it. However, he would benefit from an antihistamine similar to any allergic reaction."

"Thanks for your help," John said as he ran out of the lab door. Moving through the lobby John signaled Ryan and Trooper Jones to follow him.

Jay's phone rang as they were carrying Brian through the woods to the truck. "Jay this is John. We have the antidote and we are on our way to the hospital. How is Brian doing?"

"He seems okay just as long as we keep the oxygen going. We had to disconnect it momentarily while we got him out of the cave and he was complaining about shortness of breath."

"That goes along with the lab technician's description of the poison. Apparently it works similar to a time-release bee sting. He told me to tell you that a regular antihistamine will help. Ask the paramedics what they have. Have you told the paramedics they aren't going back to the ambulance first?"

"No," answered Jay. "I will pull aside Fred and Charlie first, and let them know on the way out of here."

"That works for me," answered John.

"Have you called any family yet?" John asked next.

"Yes I called my wife a while ago," answered Jay. "Unfortunately I think I just scared her more than anything."

"Jay, since we are ahead of you, would you like us to swing by and pick her up?"

"She's with Brian's girl friend," Jay answered.

"That's okay, we can bring her too," John said.

"I guess it will be all right," Jay answered. "But I should call her first so you guys don't scare them any more than they already are. Do you want the address?"

John laughed. "Jay, what kind of FBI agent would I be if I needed you to give me your address?"

"Very funny," Jay said sarcastically. "We will see you there."

Chapter 12

Jim Gallagor was watching the local news when his phone rang. "Hello Jim, this is Joe Lang. Have you seen the local news yet?"

"I'm watching it now," Jim answered. "I'm surprised to hear from you on this line." That was Jim's way of telling Joe they were not on a secure line.

"From the reports I'm getting, it doesn't look like the kidnappers were successful," Joe said.

Up until now Jim had no way of knowing this mess was the Chinese attempt to grab Brian Chestburg. That explains the strong police presence and the lack of information available on TV. Jim was starting to get angry, but still had to choose his words wisely. This was creating some hesitation and choppiness in his voice. "Is there any reason to be concerned?" Jim finally asked.

"It's still too early to tell. The last connection is late checking in, and his status is unknown."

"What about the rescue going on in the woods," Jim asked next.

"Unknown at this time," Joe answered.

As soon as Jim hung up the phone he immediately called Mike. "Mike this is Jim. Can you round up Ivan and Allen and come up to see me?"

"Jim I'm sitting in a little pub all the way across town, what's up?"

"Is Ivan with you?" Jim asked.

"I'm looking right at him," Mike said.

"Ask Ivan if he still has that security attachment for the phone in the car."

Jim could hear Mike asking Ivan in the background. "He says yes. We will call you back when we hook it up."

Mike and Ivan paid their tab and walked out to the car. Ivan reached into his pocket, pulled out the keys and opened the trunk. "What exactly is this thing anyway?" Mike asked.

"It's a voice scrambler for the telephone. It works sort of like a fax machine. You speak into it, and it will convert your voice to coded beeps similar to what you hear from a fax machine. At the other end is another machine which will unscramble the voice. There are about fifty different codes, and the machines will change and resynchronize every sixty seconds. The technology is getting a little old now, but should still be effective for our use."

"I'm assuming Jim has one too," Mike asked next.

Ivan answered, "Yes, I was able to get a set of two when I left the KGB to work for Jim. Something must really be wrong for him to want to use them."

Mike picked up the box and carried it into the car. The machine was modified to accept a cell phone. It is painted green on the outside, and if you look close you can see where the red Russian star was painted over on the sides of the box. Mike hooked up the phone and called Jim. "Hello Jim? Can you hear me?" The sound was a little tinny but clear enough to understand.

"Hi, Mike, I'm here. Have you seen the local news tonight?"

"No," answered Mike.

"It looks like the Chinese have screwed up grabbing your computer friend."

"What do you want me to do?" Mike asked next.

"We don't have any details about what happened. I want you to drive by his house, and find out what you can. We need to know if he survived," answered Jim.

"Is there anything you want us to do if things didn't turn out right?" Mike asked next.

Jim thought for a moment. "I'm not sure what you'll be able to do. Security will be tight. I doubt that you'll get anywhere near him."

Mike turned to Ivan and said, "Jim wants us to go by Chestburg's house and check it out." Ivan just nodded as he started the car and drove off.

"So Jim," Mike continued, "what do you think happened?"

"All I know is Joe's men were not successful. What I want you to do is find out how bad it is. Hopefully there aren't any dead bodies left or any other evidence that might point to who is behind it. Look for things that could point to us."

Mike asked, "Can this be made to look like they went after him because of his job?"

"In my opinion yes," Jim answered, "that would work best if he didn't survive. If he figures out that somehow we were involved, we would need to know and prepare for it as quickly as possible."

"They might be able to connect Joe's people to what happened tonight, and connect us to our computer friend, but that third leg in the triangle of connecting us to Joe seems unlikely," Mike said.

"That's true," Jim said, "but if we had to go through a grueling audit it would be hard to account for every dollar."

"I understand," Mike said. "Jim, I should hang up and put the scrambler away. We're getting close to the house."

"Mike, just remember to keep a low profile, and report back as soon as you find out something."

Ivan turned the last corner to drive down Brian's street. A police barricade prevented them from going any further. Mike reached behind the seat and got the binoculars. "Look at all of the police and rescue people," Mike said.

"Uh oh," Mike continued, "I see at least two dead bodies. They have a sheet over them, and they don't appear to be in a hurry to move them. That might suggest they are Chinese and the locals are waiting for the FBI to take them."

Ivan nodded and said, "That seems like a possibility to me. Where should we go next?"

Mike thought for a moment. "Maybe we can circle around to the other side of the block and get a better look."

Ivan backed up the car and started to drive around the block taking the longest loop around. The road turned to dirt. Ivan looked over to Mike. "Let's keep going," Mike said.

They went around the corner and were surprised to see another ambulance, along with one police car and several other cars.

"Is that Brian's car off to the side?" Ivan asked.

Mike looked through the binoculars and answered, "Yes, that's his car. But look at this, there are only two cops and a news reporter there, and they are just standing around. I would like to know where everybody else is."

Mike opened up the glove box of his car and pulled out a book of business cards. "Who should I represent today?" Mike sarcastically asked Ivan.

"Do you think this is a good idea?" Ivan asked.

"I'm just going to ask a few questions and leave. This is a quick and easy way to get the latest news." Ivan just shook his head as Mike got out of the car.

Mike took his time walking over to the three men. He had two business cards, one in each pocket. His plan was to try and quickly figure out whether the reporter standing next to the policemen was a local reporter or someone from one of the national networks. The policemen appeared to be local, which was a big help. As Mike got within listening range he could hear them talking about the local little league schedule this year.

Mike walked up to the group but did not speak first. The three of them turned to greet Mike, and one of the policemen spoke first. "Can I help you?"

"Hi, seems like a lot of action going on tonight," Mike said. All three men nodded but did not say anything. "Can you fill me in on the latest?" Mike asked next.

One of the officers replied, "Can we ask who you are?"

Mike pulled out a business card and held it up for the officer to read. "I'm a reporter for the ABS network," Mike said.

The local reporter looked over to Mike and asked, "How do you national guys find this stuff out so fast?"

Mike took his business card back and put it into his pocket as he answered the question. "We were in the middle of another assignment when we got a call on this. We saw bodies lying on the road around the block, but we hear this is a rescue operation. Can you clear up the confusion?"

The two officers nervously shuffled their feet and looked away. The local reporter spoke next, "There hasn't been a lot of information available." The reporter pointed in the air over the woods as he continued, "I'm watching for the helicopter and when it gets close enough I'm suppose to call in the camera crew around the block. Maybe then we can find out who it is they are supposed to be rescuing."

Mike nodded thoughtfully. He was observing the police officer's behavior. They knew something the reporter didn't. Mike could also see the helicopter moving away from them deeper into the woods. If the rescue workers were really coming back this way, it was obvious it would be a while. Mike looked at his watch and yawned. "Well, please don't take this the wrong way, but it doesn't look like this will be a story requiring immediate national exposure. Besides, it's been a long day for me already. I'll let my boss read about it on the AP wire if he's interested. Nice to meet all of you."

The three men waved to Mike as he started to walk away. As they watched Mike get back into the car one of the officers spun around to write down the license plate without letting the reporter in the group see him.

Mike got back into the car. "What did you find out," Ivan asked as he began to pull away.

Mike answered, "There is definitely something going on. The two police officers got real nervous when I started asking questions."

"One of them also wrote down our license number," Ivan added.

Mike looked annoyed when he heard that. "I didn't see that," he said.

As they drove out of the development toward the main road Mike said, "Take a right here."

"We really should get back," Ivan said. "It won't take them long to run our license plate and find out who we are."

"Yea I know," Mike answered, "but I have a hunch they are taking him out another way. I wanted to see if we could circle around and maybe figure out where."

"We could do that," Ivan said, "but why don't we just hang out at the hospital. We have an advantage over the regular press. We can identify him if we see him."

"The only problem with your idea is he can also identify us," Mike answered. "But," Mike continued, "I guess we could try to stay out of sight while we wait." Ivan turned to the right and headed for the hospital.

While watching the television news Jim had tried to call Allen Bismark several times. Finally Jim's phone rang. "Jim, this is Allen. I got your messages, what's up?"

"Have you seen the local news tonight?"

"No," answered Allen. "I've been out."

"It looks like someone tried to grab our computer friend and failed."

"How is he doing, I mean, did he make it?"

Jim answered, "We're not sure yet what the status is and I'm concerned about how vulnerable we are over the Internet."

"We have a web site posted, but until we go on line to download emails or access the sight we are not in any danger. I have set up a single computer dedicated to only the Internet, so there is no way to access any of our records or private files."

"How long will you need to set all this up?" Jim asked.

"Jim, I already set this up a while ago. Remember, I'm the one who didn't like this arrangement from the start. The only computer with our financial records does not have an Internet hook up."

"Good," Jim said. "I guess I'm finally starting to understand now. Is there anything else I should know?"

"Yes Jim, just one more thing. Do not send any emails that could come back to you in any way."

"I've been careful all along," Jim said.

Fred looked in his rear view mirror right after hitting a bump. They were cruising along the freeway now with a police car in front and another one behind them on their way to the hospital. Fred was watching the dirt fall from his truck and bounce along the road behind him. He couldn't help but smirk a little. Charlie was sitting next to him and noticed his smile. "What's so funny?" Charlie asked.

"Oh, it's nothing," Fred said. "It's just that I feel sorry for the officer behind me. The rocks and dirt falling off my truck have got to be a little rough on his windshield." Charlie turned around to see for himself.

Jay was in the second row turned around to watch Brian. The two paramedics were scrunched in next to Brian, who was lying down comfortably and trying to talk to Jay. Brian was actually starting to feel better but still kept the oxygen mask on. "Only a couple more miles before we get to the hospital," Jay said to Brian.

Jay could see the improvement in Brian and was starting to relax finally. Brian asked, "Did you call Rebecca and Julie and let them know where we are?"

Jay started to laugh a little. "Yes I called Rebecca, and Julie went there after you disappeared. They are getting a ride from John. I wish I could have seen her face when I told her the FBI was going to give her and Julie a ride to the hospital."

Jay looked down at Brian and could see he was missing the humor in it. "Aren't you worried when she sees what you did to your new suit?" Brian asked.

"After the day I had," Jay answered, "I will be looking forward to a little scolding from her."

George looked over at Jay and said, "You know he's right. You are a mess." George reached into his medical kit and handed Jay a package of pre-moistened towels. "Here, at least clean off your face and arms."

As Jay opened the package and began cleaning himself off Phil reached into his bag and pulled out a white overcoat. "Here, put this on after you clean off," Phil said.

Charlie knew Jay had been through a lot tonight and was doing his best to keep Jay from knowing he was watching. Jay put on the white overcoat, which made him look like a doctor. He then started to tuck in his shirt, which reminded him of the gun tucked in his belt. He pulled it out and tapped Charlie on the shoulder. Jay said, "Here, take this," as he handed the gun to Charlie.

"Why don't you just keep it?" Charlie asked.

"I would prefer not to. I look bad enough, and if my wife sees a gun shoved in my belt before I can explain it might freak her out."

Charlie reached back to take the gun and said, "Okay, but I would prefer that you take it back before you go home tonight."

"Now you're making me nervous," Jay said.

Charlie wanted to explain but knew he couldn't now because they were pulling into the hospital driveway. "That's not my intention Jay. I will explain it all later."

They pulled around back to the emergency entrance, and Fred backed up to the door. The two police escort cars parked on either side of the truck and jumped out. Mike and Ivan were parked in another lot about forty yards away. Mike was looking through the binoculars and said, "With all of the people standing around it's difficult to see who it is."

"We should not stick around long," Ivan said. "The police are starting to patrol the parking lots as part of their security."

"Okay I guess we can…no wait, there he is. Thank you Chestburg for sitting up. I can see him now. It also looks like his brother is with him," Mike said.

"Brian you're supposed to be lying down," George said.

"I know it but I'm feeling better, and I didn't want to freak out my girlfriend."

Charlie ran over and grabbed Brian's shoulder pulling him back down. "Just stay down until we get you inside," Charlie said.

Brian looked over at Jay, who just shrugged his shoulders. Jay was about to ask Charlie to explain but before he knew it they were inside.

Jay looked over to his right and saw Rebecca and Julie running over. Julie was speechless. Rebecca stopped about two feet short of Jay and asked, "What in the world happened to you?"

Jay just looked at her and said, "It's a long story, most of which you probably aren't going to believe anyway." The adrenaline flowing through Jay earlier was just about worn off, and Rebecca could see he was tired.

Standing behind Rebecca was John Hunt. John leaned forward and said, "Let's get your brother up to his room and I will help you explain." Jay and Rebecca just nodded as they turned to follow everybody heading up to Brian's room.

167

Ivan started up the car as Mike reached for the phone scrambler in the back. "I think you should wait until we exit the parking lot to use that," Ivan said.

Mike sat back down and said, "I'm wondering if they will be able to link this back to us."

Ivan looked in the rear view mirror as he pulled away from the hospital and said, "I think you can make your call now." Mike got the phone scrambler out from behind the seat and dialed Jim.

When Jim picked up the phone he heard a loud screeching sound. Jim knew it meant he had to hook up the scrambling device to his phone. "Well Mike, what have you found out?"

Mike answered, "It was Chestburg they tried to grab. It also looks like he got away without serious injury. He was awake and sitting up when they wheeled him into the hospital."

"Was there a lot of security around him?" Jim asked.

"Yes definitely. No way can we get near him now. It also looks like his brother was somehow involved. He rode in the truck with him."

Jim asked, "How did he get there? The television is still reporting that nobody has come out of the woods yet."

"I don't know," Mike answered. "They came in a big four wheel drive Suburban. It was covered in mud, so maybe they used the truck to get him out at another location."

"I spoke to Allen a little while ago, and he seems to feel that our sensitive files are safe for now," Jim said.

"I hope he's right," Mike said.

"There isn't anything else you can do tonight, but I want to get together tomorrow morning and go over this again. I want to make sure we didn't miss anything," Jim said.

The hospital elevator could not fit everyone, so Jay, Charlie, and John decided to stay behind and wait for the next one. Charlie stepped over to Jay and spoke as he lifted Jay's coat to look at his shirt. "Jay, I've been meaning to ask you how you got two bullet holes through your shirt without even a scratch."

Jay looked down at his shirt and said. "It was dusk, and I was afraid that my white shirt would be too easy to spot, so I hung it in a tree while I hid behind some rocks waiting for the last Chinese to go by. I gave him a chance to surrender, but as you can see from the holes in my shirt he wasn't interested."

John spoke next. "I asked my boss Dave Gillian to check you out. He told me that you are an accountant, but he couldn't find any information on where you learned to fight like that."

"I've been taking a martial arts class for years. It's just something I enjoy doing." Jay took a deep breath before continuing. "All I can tell you is that when the first guy went to hit me I just reacted. I also think that last gunshot from you guys distracted him enough for me get the edge."

Finally the elevator door opened. There were two other people already inside when the three men stepped inside. When the doors closed Jay asked, "What happens next?"

John gave him a funny look and said, "Just the usual paperwork that you've done before."

Done before? Jay thought to himself. He looked over at Charlie who gave him the same look as John, which of course meant they really couldn't talk further with the other people standing in the elevator next to them.

169

"Of course," Jay said, letting them know he understood.

Brian was wheeled into a corner room on the top floor of the hospital. Julie and Rebecca were walking along side of him, followed by a doctor and a nurse, Ryan McWilliams, state trooper Ed Jones, and Officer Blackfeld.

Brian turned to look back at the crowd and asked, "Where's Jay?"

"I think they had to catch the next elevator," answered Officer Jones.

As they approached the door to the room Dr. Hatlmer asked everyone to wait outside the room while he examines Brian. Officer Jones glanced at Officer Blackfeld who shook his head no. "Sorry Doc, but we have our orders to stay close," Officer Jones said.

The doctor shrugged his shoulders and said, "Fine, I'm in no mood to argue."

It was a double room and on the window side was another man with two visitors. They were a man with a cane and a woman. He was hooked up to a heart monitor, oxygen, and an IV but was awake. Officer Jones, who was told by John Hunt to guard Brian, positioned himself in the center of the room between the unknown people and Brian. The man with the cane started to walk over to Brian and Officer Jones stepped in front of him.

The man looked at Jones's name tag on his uniform and holding out his hand said, "It's okay Officer Jones, my name is Dave Gillian. I've been on the phone with John while you were driving him around."

Dave also reached in his pocket and showed Ed his identification. Ed read it quickly and shook his hand. "Sorry about that," Ed said.

Dave answered, "No need to apologize. I'm glad to see that Brian's in good hands."

Brian, who was watching this whole thing, had no clue what was going on. Just as Brian was about to ask Dave who he was Jay walked in with Charlie and John. Dave, then John introduced themselves to Brian, who was now directing his puzzled look to Jay. Jay knew his brother well and could see his confused look. "I'll explain everything later," Jay whispered in Brian's ear.

Rebecca was on her way over to Jay and heard his comment. "I'd like to hear your explanation too," she said.

Dave, who was watching the reunion, spoke next. "I apologize to everyone but I have to talk to Brian and Jay alone. John and Charlie can stay, but everyone else must leave."

Rebecca looked annoyed and said, "This is a free country and I'm staying."

Jay looked at Dave and said, "Let me talk to her."

Jay gently grabbed Rebecca by the arm and spoke softly to her. "Hun, I promise to fill you in on everything just as soon as I find out myself. Let's just do it his way for now." Rebecca was still annoyed, but reluctantly agreed.

As everyone asked to leave walked out, the door behind them closed. "Now what do we do?" Rebecca asked.

The doctor told them about the lounge downstairs where they could get something to eat or a cup of coffee. As the group started to leave trooper Jones said, "I think I will stay behind and guard the door."

"Suit yourself," someone in the crowd said as they walked down the hall.

Dave waited a couple of minutes for the group to walk down the hall before he began. Dave looked over to Brian first. "You're probably wondering what happened." Brian just nodded. Dave continued, "To sum it up in one sentence, the Chinese government tried to kidnap you. What we don't fully understand yet is why. At first we thought it was because of the contract your company just won, but we have some problems with that theory. For one thing, you are relatively unknown in the computer programming field."

"What do you mean unknown?" Jay asked.

Dave turned to Jay as he answered, "We keep a list of our top computer programmers in the country. We also keep an eye on them as a way of offering protection for them and their families. Most of them are not even aware of the service we provide."

"You must have known something about me," Brian said.

"Actually it was the Chinese militants we were tracking who led Jeff and me to you," Charlie said.

John spoke next, "I got involved from a different direction. I was originally in charge of investigating you for your security clearance. I came in one day and was told that you were approved, and I was to start on another case. I wanted to know what happened, so I started investigating on my own."

Brian looked over at Jay. "Just tell them," Jay said.

Brian looked down at the bed before he began. "I think I can tell you the rest. I was working for Gallagor helping with the campaign. My job was to dig up information on Senator Stone."

"So you are the guy who hacked into Jamerson Pharmaceuticals!" Jeff yelled from behind the curtain.

Dave walked over and opened the curtain. "I thought you were sleeping!"

"Never mind," Jeff said, "so tell us how you did it."

"It's a little complicated," Brian answered.

"He's amazing when it comes to a computer and the Internet," Jay said.

"We figured that," Dave said. "But let's get back to the Gallagor connection. If you were working for him, why do you and your brother blame him for the kidnapping?"

Brian continued, "When it looked like my company, CCC, was going to win the decoding contract I didn't want to work for Gallagor anymore. I thought it was Gallagor trying to make sure I didn't pose a threat to him. We know about his connection to the old Soviet Union."

"How could you know about that?" Dave asked. "They are confidential FBI records."

Brian got suddenly quiet. "Don't tell me you have access to our files too," Dave said.

"Only your lower level confidential records," Brian said.

Dave just rolled his eyes in disbelief. Charlie, who was taking all of this in, spoke next. "Do you think there is a possible connection between Gallagor and the Chinese?"

"I'm not sure," Brian answered. "Jay and I might be just assuming that based on Gallagor's Soviet Union connection during college. I just want to say that I didn't know any of this when I agreed to help him. I'm not unpatriotic or anything."

"Nobody is accusing you of that," Charlie said trying to get Brian to relax.

"Now that you know what I did there must be a way to stop him." Brian said.

"It's a lot harder than you think," Charlie said. "Most of the politicians with foreign connections are from the same party, but there are a few in the other party. Because of that we get no support."

"This is still America," Brian said. "There must be something we can do."

"The official position of the FBI is not to get involved in the outcome of any political election," Dave said.

"Yea right, and I also suppose it's not an official position to give a civilian a gun to shoot Chinese militants either," Jay said obviously a little annoyed.

"I'm sure that the bullet found in the dead Chinese will match Charlie's gun, so it must have been Charlie who shot him," Dave said.

Jay gave Dave a shocked look but could not get any words out.

"Hey slow down," Brian interrupted. "Listen guys, my brother and I *want* to help. We are asking. We know you hold all the cards here."

There was about thirty seconds of silence. To Jay and Brian it seemed like thirty minutes.

"That's great," Dave said. "We were working on putting together a small task force to handle some of these situations. It would have to be a small group of people who all know and trust each other. John, Jeff, and I go way back. Charlie you have only been associated with us for a few weeks but you seem to have gained Jeff's respect."

"If you are asking me what I think you are asking me, I'm in," Charlie said. "I'm just as disgusted with the CIA bureaucracy."

Suddenly the door opened and Officer Ed Jones walked in. "I'm in too, if you will allow it," he said.

"How long have you been out there?" Dave asked.

"Long enough," Ed answered. "I have seen Inspector Hunt handle himself, and if the rest of you guys are the same I'd like to help if I can."

"You might as well come in and close the door," Dave said.

Dave turned to the group and continued, "I haven't worked out all of the details yet. My first decision is what to do with you Jay. How do you like accounting?"

"It's okay," Jay said.

"Bullcrap!" Brian yelled out. "Jay you hate accounting and you know it."

"Why do you ask?" Jay asked Dave while appearing to ignore Brian.

"From what we saw today, the FBI could use you."

"Unless you would prefer to work on foreign issues instead," Charlie said. "Do you know any other languages?"

Dave gave Charlie a sarcastic look, which everyone caught.

"No I don't," Jay said to Charlie, "although I am flattered by both of you. Dave, can I get back to you? I should really think about it and also talk to my wife. I don't think she would go for the foreign travel though."

"I understand," Charlie said.

Dave reached down for his briefcase and put it on the bed next to Brian's feet. He opened it up and pulled out a gun with a shoulder holster and handed it to Jay. "I didn't say yes yet," Jay said.

"We know that, but just in case you do, you will need this." Dave also handed Jay a temporary identification card, a badge, and a list of

175

phone numbers. "I have to be honest with you Jay," Dave said. "You showed some rare talent today. I cannot in good conscience let you go without trying. Please think about it and call me on Monday. As for the rest of you, Brian you get some rest tonight, Charlie, John, and I will be in my office for a few hours tomorrow morning to start figuring out how to put together our group. Ed if you can make it you're also invited."

Dave walked over to Jeff. "How are you doing?"

"I'm scheduled for surgery tomorrow morning, but fortunately the bullet is not in a critical spot. They tell me it went in just above my right lung, and after they take it out I should only need a couple of months to recuperate."

"I will see you after the surgery then," Dave said.

They shook hands, and as Dave opened up the door to leave the room Rebecca and Julie walked in. "Well?" Rebecca asked. "Do I get my explanation now?"

Dave started to laugh. "Come on guys, let's leave the Chestburgs alone for now," Dave said.

"What about security?" Ed asked.

"It's already taken care of. This is a secure wing," answered Dave.

Chapter 13

Jay woke up early the next morning. He looked over at his alarm clock and couldn't believe it was only 5 AM. He had been up late explaining everything that happened to Rebecca; so he was surprised to find himself wide awake so early. He also wasn't sure if she believed it all or not. He was pleased she promised to support him if he decided to join the FBI.

Jay went down to the kitchen to make some coffee. On the counter was the temporary identification paperwork that Dave Gillian gave him last night. Jay picked it up and started to examine it again for about the tenth time.

"What are you doing up," Rebecca asked a startled Jay.

"Don't sneak up on me like that," Jay said.

Rebecca looked deep into his eyes and said, "You aren't going to start weirding out on me now are you?"

"What do you mean?" Jay asked.

"What I mean is you were through a lot last night. We have all heard stories about people who break down after going through a war like experience."

"I'm fine Rebecca, really." Then after some pause Jay said, "That's not it."

"Well what is it then? You were also given what might be the chance of a lifetime. You know that you hate accounting. I'm personally worried about how an FBI agent who might get shot someday could raise a family or have a normal life, but I told you I won't talk you out of it either."

Jay walked over to hug her. "Thanks for that," he said.

Jay paused for a moment and said, "I think I'll try to sneak into the hospital and have breakfast with Brian. Would you like to come?"

Rebecca yawned, and then said, "No thanks, I'm going back to bed."

The IV hooked up to Brian caused him have to get up and go to the bathroom several times through the night. He was told the more he went to the bathroom the faster the poison would work its way out of his body. Now it was 6 AM and it was all the commotion next to him that was keeping him up. They were prepping Jeff for surgery, which Brian overheard was scheduled for 6:30.

Jay pulled into the hospital parking lot and looked at his watch. It was only about 6:15 AM. Jay felt the gun in his shoulder holster. He was still not used to the weight of it. I shouldn't need it in the hospital, Jay thought. He took off his windbreaker jacket and the shoulder holster and wrapped the gun in the jacket. He then put the wrapped bundle in the trunk of his car.

As Jay walked into the lobby he tried to look at natural as possible. He nodded politely to the receptionist and walked straight to the elevator. Jay knew it wasn't even close to visiting time and was trying to bluff his way in. "Can I help you?" asked the receptionist in a stern tone.

"No thanks," answered Jay, "I know where I'm going."

"Well I'm happy for you. The only problem is it's my job to also know where you're going."

"Sorry," Jay said as he reached for the badge he was given last night.

"I'm here to see Brian, I mean Will Smith."

The receptionist really looked annoyed now. "Can't you guys let the poor man get some sleep before you question him, Mr." -the receptionist paused for a moment as she read the name on the identification – "uh - Chestburg. Wait, your name is Chestburg too?"

"Excuse me?" Jay said.

"I mean Mr. Smith," the receptionist said as she started to blush. "Any relation?" she whispered.

"Yes mam," Jay whispered back, "he's my brother."

The receptionist sat back in her chair and Jay could see her whole mood change. "That changes everything Mr. Chestburg. Of course you can go see him."

Jay immediately returned her change in tone with his most polite tone. "I'm thankful to see he's in good hands. Do you have any information on how he's doing?"

The receptionist punched some numbers in her computer. "It looks like he will be discharged later this morning. Since there's no other information, I'm assuming that's good."

Jay smiled and said, "I think so, and thank you."

Jay walked into Brian's room as quietly as he could. Brian was lying there with his eyes closed, so Jay assumed he was sleeping. "Who is it now?" Brian asked in an annoyed tone.

"It's your brother Jay." Brian immediately sat up and looked surprised.

"Jay you have to get me out of here."

"Why, what's the matter?" Jay asked.

"I've been up all night. They just took the IV tube out of my arm about twenty minutes ago. I think I was up every half hour all night going to the bathroom. I need some sleep."

Jay just sat back and laughed. "They told me at the front desk you'll be leaving later this morning." Jay then noticed the empty bed on the other side. "Where's your roommate?"

"They took him to surgery earlier this morning. We should check on him before we go. He got shot trying to rescue me, remember?"

"Oh I remember all right, after all I was there for the whole thing."

"Did you see him get shot?" Brian asked.

Jay got up from his chair so he could speak in a lower voice to Brian. "We never did get to talk about what happened. There is something else you need to know." Brian just sat there motionless as Jay continued. "I killed two of those Chinese guys last night."

"What do you mean killed them?" Brian asked.

"Killed as in dead. The first one pulled out a gun while we were fighting and I had no choice. The second one shot at me so I shot back."

"Where did you get the gun?" Brian asked.

"Charlie gave me his when he went to the hospital with Jeff." Brian took a few seconds to let everything soak in.

"No way," Brian finally said. "How could they give you a gun when you had no formal training?"

Jay shrugged his shoulders. "I don't know. It was after I killed the first one. I think the weirdest part is their attitude about my killing them. They took it as no big deal."

"That's where I think you got it wrong big brother. I overheard them talking about you last night. They were very impressed with how you handled yourself, especially under pressure. I think they really want you to join them."

"I wonder what would happen if I said no," Jay said next.

"My guess is nothing. They really want you, but one of them said it would have to be your choice. If fact, now that I think about it, it must have been the CIA guy Charlie talking to John from the FBI. They promised each other not to fight over you. It would have to be your choice."

"What should I do Brian?"

"What did Rebecca say?" Brian asked.

"She said it was my decision and she would work with me either way." Jay answered.

"You've been taking martial arts classes and exercising for years. You've obviously been training for something, maybe you found it. Besides, you told me again just the other day how you hated accounting. I think it would be kind of cool to have a big shot in the family."

"What about you?" Jay asked. "Have they made you any offers?"

"No," Brian answered, "which is fine with me. I'm looking forward to working on that contract my company just won. Maybe I could work undercover gathering information for you. I would be Joe average guy going to work every day, and turn into espionage extraordinaire at night gathering information for your latest case!"

Jay paused for a second, and then they both laughed. "Do you think we should clear it with Dave Gillian first?" Jay asked as they both laughed again.

"Jay, I do have another question. Where's my car? My computer and all of my information were in my car."

"Your car was towed back to your house, but I have your briefcase with your computer in the trunk of my car. I took it out before I went into the woods looking for you."

Brian leaned back obviously relieved. "Thanks again big brother."

"Hey wait a minute," Brian said. "Didn't they say they were getting together this morning? Where are my clothes? We should talk to them about our idea."

Jay looked around and finally found Brian's clothes hanging in the closet. "How did you keep them so clean?" Jay asked.

"They sent them downstairs and cleaned them for me overnight," Brian said. "I have to say they really treated me first class in here, at least when I wasn't going to the bathroom!"

Jay pulled Brian's clothes off the hangers and tossed them to him. "I'll wait outside while you get dressed trying to think of a way to sneak you out of here."

"You're going to sneak me to breakfast first big brother, I'm hungry. It will be my treat."

Brian was tying his shoes as the doctor walked in. Jay was behind him. "Can I ask what you are doing Mr. Smith?"

"I'm supposed to check out today. I was going to find you and ask if I could go a little early," Brian answered.

"Yea sure you were going to find me, and how did you know you were going to check out today?"

"Inspector Chestburg standing behind you said so."

The doctor turned to Jay and asked, "Can I see some identification?" Jay pulled out his new identification card and handed it to the doctor. The doctor opened up his chart and whispered "any relation?"

"We're brothers," Jay whispered back, "but I have to ask, what kind of a secret is it if everybody here knows his real name?"

The doctor laughed and said, "We have to know for medical reasons. We just play along with you guys to keep the press out of here. They can be quite disruptive."

The doctor then filled out a form and handed it to Jay. "Take this over to the nurse behind the desk on this floor and she will dismiss Mr. Smith."

"Thanks doc," they both said.

Dave Gillian was the last to enter the conference room and closed the door behind him. Sitting at the conference table in the center of the room were John Hunt, Charlie Gurns, and Ed Jones. All of the men were dressed more casually than usual, which was the only hint it was a Saturday. Dave handed out folders to each of the men. "Before we get into the specifics, I think we will need to go over some ground rules," Dave said.

The beeping of John's cell phone interrupted Dave. John looked at the display on the phone and said, "I'd better take this."

"Yes, yes, can you escort them up? Thanks." John smiled as he hung up the phone. "The Chestburgs are on their way up," John said enthusiastically.

"Both of them?" Charlie asked.

John nodded his head yes as Dave said "I got a phone call early this morning before 7:00. Jay was there signing Brian out. Although I didn't send Jay there I thought it was a good idea. They will be long gone before the press gets there watching the usual 10:00 AM sign outs."

"I have to ask this," Charlie interrupted, "and nobody take this the wrong way, but do you think Jay knew this or was it more dumb luck?"

All the men looked at each other and shrugged their shoulders. "I'll try and find out," Dave finally said. "Why don't we break for some coffee and wait for the Chestburgs."

There was a knock on the door. Dave got up to open the door as the others stood up and also moved toward the door. Jay came in first followed by Brian. "Welcome," Dave said as he shook hands with Jay and Brian. They continued into the conference room and shook hands with Charlie, John and Ed. Both Jay and Brian were a little overwhelmed by the warm reception.

"It's good to see you up and about," Charlie said to Brian.

"Thanks to you guys," Brian said.

Meanwhile, as John was shaking hands with Jay he opened up Jay's jacket. "Where's your gun?" John asked.

"I had it on earlier, but I took it off before I went into the hospital. I didn't think I was allowed to wear it in here."

John looked over at Dave, who shook his head no to John. Dave then interrupted, "We can cover that later. We are glad you guys came."

As they all sat down around the conference room table, Dave handed Jay and Brian each a packet of information. "Like I was saying," Dave said, "I want to start this meeting laying out the ground rules. First of all, we will not be a vigilante group. We were brought together last night because of a problem that's been building for a while now. Politics are controling everything. Even the FBI and CIA are influenced by politicians who are more interested in their party than right and wrong. What I'm proposing here is we team together to do the investigative work required to bring these people to justice without hinderence from the politicians."

184

John asked, "How are we going to do that when they pull us off certain cases before we've collected enough data to convict somebody? As you already know Dave that's how I ended up with you now. Brian got his security clearance before I finished my investigation, and I just had a feeling that something was up."

Everyone looked across the table for Brian's reaction. "It's no reflection on you Brian," Dave said, "but it does give you an indication how far some politicians can reach."

"Here's how I'm invisioning this," Dave continued. "If one of us turns something up that might warrant further investigation we should get together as a group to discuss it. If we agree there is something to it we can then decide how to divide up the investigation. The plan at first will be to keep the investigation just among ourselves, which should help prevent getting reassigned. At the same time we should always have another project to work on in case anybody asks."

"What about gaining access to data files?" Charlie asked. "That always gets the attention of the higher ups."

"That will be a weak point we will have to deal with," Dave said. "I will try to cover that up as best I can."

"Can I interupt for a moment?" Brian asked. Everyone got silent so Brian continued. "I think I can help. If you just tell me what information you need and have some idea where it is, I can go get it."

Dave looked at Brian and said, "That's quite a statement Brian but--"

"Just give him a chance. He's the best computer hack you've ever seen," Jay said. "After all, he did get into Jamerson's accounting records, and was able to access your FBI files on Gallagor through the state police."

Dave sat down in his chair. "Okay Brian, maybe you could give us a demonstration of what we can expect." Brian pulled out his laptop and started it up. He looked around the room for a network wall jack. He then reached into his computer case for a bag of adapters and a cable, plugging the wire into his computer. A few seconds later the computer was buzzing, then he was disconnected.

"What's the matter?" Charlie asked.

Brian answered, "The Internet account I was using has expired. Does anybody have yesterday's or today's local paper?"

Dave reached into his briefcase and pulled out this mornings paper. Brian opened it up to the obituary section. Jay moved over next to him as they both looked through it. "What about this one? He looks like the computer type," Jay said.

"I will give him a try," Brian answered.

Brian signed back onto the Internet using his own account. He then pulled out a disk and let it run as he sat back. "What are you doing now?" Charlie asked.

"What I'm doing now," Brian answered, "is looking for this man's email address, which I will use to get his access code for the Internet. The program I wrote starts with the email version of the phonebook. From the address I can determine which of the major Internet providers he's using. I then go into their account records, get his password codes and log in as him. If anybody tries to trace it back they will hit a deadend since this man was deceased before today."

Charlie got up from his chair and walked around behind Brian. He stood there silently watching the screen. "How did you get the initial access codes to get this information?"

"I'm using a program I wrote years ago. All programmers put in a back door in case they get locked out of their own operating system. It's better than losing years of programming time because of a crash or mistake. They all follow a similar pattern which I access with a program I've developed."

When the computer signaled it was done, Brian logged off the Internet and back in using the new codes. "Check it out," Brian said as he pointed to the screen, "I can see all of his emails if I want. I already have the FBI access codes but I can show you how I get them if you like."

"We can see that later," Charlie said. "Let's see just how much access you really have. Can you pull up the Gallagor FBI file?"

"Yes, no problem," answered Brian.

Within a couple of minutes the complete Gallagor file came on the screen. Brian looked over at Charlie and said, "Anything else you want to see?"

Charlie reached for his pocket size notebook and began flipping through the pages. "How about this one. Can you look up Ivan Spelluchuvik?"

Brian typed in the name and within a few minutes the file started to download. Brian was reading through the text while his picture, which always takes a little longer, downloads. Brian looked at the picture when it finally downloaded. "Hey, that's one of Gallagor's drivers."

"It's a long story," Charlie said, "but basically we think they met some time during Gallagor's college days."

"You mean when Gallagor went over to Russia to get his training," Jay said.

Charlie looked shocked. "How do you know about that?" he asked.

"We already downloaded Gallagor's file and read through it a while ago," Brian said.

"I don't suppose that was on a Saturday about a week ago from a coffee shop near the beach, was it?" Charlie asked.

Brian's face turned red. "How did you know that?" he asked.

"Let's just say you got away with that one," Charlie said.

Dave decided to get the meeting back on track. While walking away from Brian's computer and back to his chair Dave said, "Okay Brian, I think that you made your point. Although we should definitely see what else you have and maybe review how you do it, we need to postpone that for now. Besides, it's all over my head anyway. We will have to be careful how and when we use Brian. Remember, we will not commit any illegal activities. That will get us caught. And we will not play favorites to any political party. We can't take it to the other extreme and worry about keeping things even either. Just find out who is dirty and prove it. Are we in agreement?"

Everybody nodded their head yes.

Dave continued, "This is the way I'm envisioning this. We will all keep our current positions, except for Jay if he will join us. Brian I would like you to be back at work on Monday. I would prefer to provide you with a secure Internet access when we need your help. I will have to set that up and get back to you. Ed, is there any problem with you staying where you are for now?"

Ed shook his head no.

"Good, we also need to set up a way to contact you while you are on the road. There may be times where you as a state trooper are the only person out there I can call for a quick response to an emergency. Charlie, I don't expect you to be going anywhere."

"My current position in the CIA with my established contacts is where I would be of most value to us," Charlie said. "Dave, you also mentioned getting phones for all of us. I would like to handle that.

The CIA has the latest security technology and I think I can get my hands on what we need."

"That would be great," Dave said.

Dave looked over at John next. "Well John, what will happen with you? Are you going back, or would you like to stay with us?"

John looked down at his feet without saying anything. The rest of the group silently looked at John. "We can discuss it in private if you wish," Dave said, "but I think some of the others might benefit if we fill them in."

John looked over at Dave and nodded. "I'll tell them," John said. "A few years back I switched out of Dave's group to another area. I did it for my family. We were raising two children and one day their father comes home after getting shot by an escaped felon on the loose. I was only grazed, but my wife was quite upset. We decided for the sake of the children I would take the transfer. It was safer, but definitely boring."

"I'm thankful you got involved," Charlie said. "I'd be dead if you didn't."

"I owe John my life too," Dave said. "I was wounded and they were moving in for the kill when John showed up."

"I appreciate all this male bonding guys," John said jokingly, "but I was just in the right place at the right time."

Jay spoke up next, "My wife has some of the same safety concerns. We don't have a family yet, but she is concerned about how it will all work."

John turned to Jay and continued, "I think my wife is coming around. She seemed to have no objection to my transferring back. I even overheard her telling my 15 year old daughter to not say anything. When I told her about last night she was unusually supportive. She knows how bad the last couple of years out of the action have been for me. I will talk to her over the weekend and get back to you officially on Monday, but I think I would like to stay."

Dave nodded without saying anything, but you could see how pleased he was.

"I think that about does it," Dave said.

"Wait!" Brian said. "What about Jay?"

Dave was trying his best to sound neutral, even to the point of sounding uninterested. "Jay has until Monday to decide what he wants to do." Brian frowned at Dave's uninterested appearance, but Jay was not affected by it.

"How would it work if I said yes?" Jay asked.

Dave stopped packing up his briefcase to answer. "The first thing you would do is get trained. I know what you went through, and how well you handled things, but we would treat you almost the same as a new recruit. You would get all the weapons, security, procedural, etc., training. That would take several weeks. Then you would come to us, and for the next year you'll work with John and maybe Jeff when he gets back."

Jay said, "What about my current job? Normally I would give two weeks' notice, but I don't really want to tell them where I'm going."

"So don't," Dave said.

Jay continued, "When that happens they will assume I'm working for a competitor and will escort me out right away."

"Then we will see you on Tuesday, unless you want some time off first," Dave answered.

"Tuesday it is then," Jay said.

Dave couldn't hold back his excitement any longer and smiled from ear to ear. He walked around the table to Jay, shook his hand and said, "Welcome aboard. I know you'll be one of the great ones."

Charlie and John got up and also shook his hand. Dave reached into his briefcase and took out an official FBI shield and identification. He handed it to Jay and said, "Here, I had it made up this morning, just in case. This replaces the temporary identification I gave you yesterday."

Everybody laughed. "Now wear that gun and don't be bashful about it," Dave said.

As they were driving home, Brian turned to Jay and said, "A lot has happened in the last 24 hours."

"I'll say. If someone else were to tell me a story like this I wouldn't believe a word of it," Jay answered.

Brian thought for a moment. "Why did you come over yesterday anyway?"

"I was supposed to pick up mom's punch bowl set for the barbecue today."

Brian chuckled and asked, "Are we still on for the barbecue?"

Jay looked over at Brian and they both laughed. "Should we invite Fred and his wife?" Brian asked. "We do owe him an explanation."

Chapter 14

Mike and Ivan were the last to arrive at Jim Gallagor's home on Saturday morning. Allen was already sitting down drinking a cup of coffee. He looked annoyed as ever. "I told you bringing in an outsider wasn't a good idea," Allen said.

"Couldn't you at least wait until I get in the door and get my coffee before you start whining," Mike replied.

Jim interrupted, "I hope you two are finished. Although we don't know yet how much this will hurt us, we do know we got some good information at a critical time. Without it I don't know if our campaign would have really gotten going like it has. I think what we need to do now is keep the momentum going into the home stretch."

Mike got up and walked to the other side of the room to get some coffee as Jim continued. "Our goal here is to get me elected. As a United States Senator it will be almost impossible for anyone to conduct an investigation for several reasons." Jim could see the puzzled look in Ivan's face. "For starters," Jim continued, "any investigation of a Senator cannot be kept quiet. There will be enough leaks for us to be one step ahead, and even steer them in some frustrating directions. The other reason is something we might want to implement now."

"Now?" Mike asked as he sat back down.

Jim continued, "Yes Mike now. Any reference to illegally collected information we simply dismiss as a partisan attack. It was a news media outlet that broke the story about the soon to be ex Senator Stone's vacation. My guess is there just isn't enough proof for them to come after us, regardless of what our computer friend tells them."

"Have you talked to any of your contacts at the FBI yet?" Mike asked.

"Yes but they didn't have much information," Jim answered. "There is a maverick named Dave Gillian running the rescue and investigation. Gillian has until Monday to submit his report, and he is the type to wait until the last minute. My contact was not sure if that was deliberate or just sloppy work."

Ivan interrupted, "Can he be bought?"

Jim shrugged his shoulders. "I don't think so. It sounds like his maverick attitude will only work against us. It also appears that Chestburg's older brother is joining the FBI."

"That seems unusual," Mike said. "What's the story behind that?"

"From what my source said he might have had something to do with taking out at least one of the Chinese, possibly in a hand to hand fight."

"I'm not impressed," Ivan said. "At least in the old Soviet Union we did not think much of the Chinese in combat. I think the only thing that kept us out of their country was there were so many of them."

Jim smiled. "I don't think you'll get a chance at him Ivan. Chestburg will be just starting his training, which should carry him through the election."

"Oh well, maybe next time," Mike said to Ivan in a sarcastic tone.

"What about our contact with Joe Lang?" Allen asked.

"Unfortunately," Jim answered, "it looks like we will have to stay away from Lang for a while. If they decide to watch us we cannot risk it. We need to start looking for other sources for our funding. Allen, can you put together a list of companies in the state that may be looking for favors from a newly elected Senator? Find anyone Stone may have voted against. At this stage of the game I don't care what we have to promise them."

"What about the chicken processing plant that was looking for waste water disposal relief? Before you answer remember it's our party that is supposed to be standing up to big business on environmental issues," Allen said.

"Put them at the top of the list," Jim answered. "We really need funding."

As Jeff was recovering from the surgery in the intensive care area, Senator Stone was sitting quietly in the waiting room. He was alone, and held the magazine he was reading up in front of his face. He was hoping nobody would recognize him. The nurse at the desk said Jeff's surgery went well, and he would be out of intensive care and into a regular room in another hour. It would mean the Senator would not have much time to visit, but he wanted to at least wish Jeff well.

Dave Gillian walked into the waiting room and immediately recognized the Senator. He sat next to him and quietly introduced himself. "I didn't get to read any official reports yet," the Senator said, "what exactly happened?"

Dave answered, "It's looking like he was shot by Chinese kidnappers trying to grab one of our computer programmers."

"Jeff was working on the Jamerson pharmaceutical case. Is there a connection?"

Dave hesitated for a moment. Although he might need the Senator's help in his planned investigation of Gallagor, he definitely didn't want the Senator to know about his newly assembled team. Dave answered carefully, "We don't have enough information yet to know, but we are investigating."

"Cut the crap Dave. Everybody knows about my opponent's connections to several communist countries. What's your best guess?"

"We're looking for a connection, but have nothing yet. But Senator, I have to ask. If you know so much about your opponents illegal connections, why don't you use them in your campaign?"

Senator Stone looked around the room. There was another person across the room from them, but nobody else. The Senator lowered his voice as he answered. "There are several reasons which combined prevent us from working this issue. The first is the general lack of patriotism currently running through our country. So many people just don't get outraged about these things anymore. The second reason is the cold war is over, and unfortunately not enough people remember how serious it used to be. The third reason is the bias in the mainstream news media today. They are always preaching tolerance, which for some reason translates into sympathy for our enemies. It's just not politically correct to be a patriotic American. The media doesn't report a story like that anymore."

Dave sat back in his chair. "Wow Senator, I never heard a politician answer a question so directly and to the point before. Please don't take offense, but isn't there any way you can work this issue into your campaign somehow?"

"Most of the answer to that question is in my last explanation, but I would like to add that it's too difficult to get my explanation into a thirty second sound bite. What is really needed is an actual investigation that I could comment on as an outsider." Dave looked at the Senator and they both chuckled.

"So now let me ask you," Senator Stone said, "why doesn't the FBI go after politicians taking money from foreign governments?"

Dave answered, "You know why Senator. It takes time and money to build a case, and halfway into it somebody pulls the plug on the operation, and the evidence collected is sealed and filed away. I always blame it on some politician, either the person being investigated or someone else from their party. Every one of you guys have your inside connections. Both sides are equally good at circling the wagons to protect their own."

195

The Senator looked down at his feet as he spoke. "Politics is a winner takes all business. There is no second place, and the rewards are significant enough for some to justify almost anything. Just between you and me Dave, I don't think I'd be too disappointed if I lost."

Dave was beginning to get excited. "Senator, you can't let someone who is paid off by the Chinese government to get elected!"

The Senator snapped his head up in surprise to look Dave in the eyes. "Are you saying you have proof of actual payoffs?"

"No, not yet," Dave answered, "but I am putting a plan together to get the proof we need."

"I wish you luck, but how far do you think you will get before the election? You know both sides will be watching every move you make in your investigation."

"I'm currently working out a way to prevent interference," Dave said.

"Off the record I wish you luck and will answer any questions you have, but I think you will be much better off if you don't tell me or any other politician about it."

Dave nodded and said, "I understand."

Before they could say anything else the nurse came in to tell them Jeff was ready for visitors. As the two men stood up Charlie Gurns, who just walked in, met them.

Later that afternoon as Jay was standing in front of his grill turning over a steak; he could see Fred Milnurg pull up with his wife Katie. As they walked up Jay yelled out, "Hey, how about washing that truck!"

Fred smiled and said, "No way, I earned that mud last night and I'm going to leave it there for a while!"

"Yea but did you have to park on my grass?"

"Sorry Jay, but you know my truck hates blacktop."

Katie shook her head in disgust. "You wouldn't believe the crazy story he told me when he got home last night. He would have slept on the couch if he didn't sound so convincing, but I still have my doubts."

"We'll sit down and explain the whole thing over dinner," Jay assured her.

As Fred and Katie walked onto the deck, Brian walked out with a beer. "I just can't believe you recovered so fast," Fred said to Brian.

"From what I understand," Brian said, "the poison is not supposed to last long. I wouldn't be much good to them if the drugs they used took a long time to wear off."

"Doesn't that creep you out?" Fred asked next.

Brian shrugged his shoulders, but Jay said, "It pisses me off."

Fred turned to Jay and asked, "What about you? I thought you were an accountant. Don't tell me accounting is just a cover and you're really a secret agent or something."

Jay looked at Brian and they laughed. "Actually," Jay said, "as of Friday I was just an accountant. Because of what happened last night the FBI has offered me a job. I give my notice on Monday. I'm hoping they won't want me to stick around for two weeks so I can start my training on Tuesday."

"I have to admit I'm a little jealous," Fred said. "It sounds like you're starting on a really great adventure. Just remember if you need any help, you know who to call."

"Thanks Fred, I appreciate that, of course I already knew that last night."

Sunday morning Brian was up early. Although it was usually his brother Jay who's the one to get angry, Brian could not shake off the anger that was building inside of him. How dare they try to kidnap him? Was Gallagor involved, and if he was, what about the help Brian already gave him? Was he angry that I left, or is he just heartless like the characters seen on all those mafia movies on television? Brian wondered if Gallagor actually tried to sell him to the Chinese. The more he thought about it, the angrier he got.

Brian sat down with the Sunday paper, and turned to the latest coverage of the coming election. There was an article on Senator Stone's voting record, and another on how the labor union is getting ready to endorse Gallagor. I wonder how much money Gallagor is getting from the labor union, Brian thought. I'm going to try and get that information, but should probably wait until Dave Gillian gets me secure Internet connection. Brian decided to get out a pad of paper and take some notes. In the middle of his first sentence he crumpled up the paper and threw it across the room. There is no good reason to wait, Brian thought to himself. He then stood up, got himself some more coffee and went upstairs to his computer.

Brian went over to one of the web sites to review Senator Stone's voting record. Although these sights request you to sign up and pay a nominal fee, Brian had hacked his way in while working for Gallagor. At the time he thought it was better to remain anonymous. He decided to use the same passwords again.

Most of the bills that went through the Senate in the last several years were not specific enough to their area to make them local issues, except two. The first was a wastewater treatment relief bill a local chicken processing plant had lobbied hard for. It was a close vote, but it was defeated. Senator Stone voted against it, and was quoted as saying his priority was a small town down river of the plant. "The town was on the shore of a lake the river fed into and was a major tourist attraction in the area. Although the waste is considered biodegradable, too much of it would increase algae growth eventually choking the lake." There was a time when Brian would have expected the environmentalists to rally behind the Senator after his vote, but he has learned party loyalty doesn't make any sense sometimes.

Brian paused for a moment, thinking he heard the doorbell. Outside at the front door Charlie Gurns looked at his watch and rang the doorbell again. This time Brian was sure that he heard it and ran down the stairs. He looked out the dining room window to see who was at the door before opening it. Brian then walked around the dining room table and into the hallway to open the door.

"I hope you looked to see who it was before you opened the door," Charlie said.

"Of course I looked first," answered Brian. "Hi Charlie, come on in, how are you doing?"

Charlie wiped off his feet and stepped inside. Brian closed and locked the door behind him. "Can I get you something to eat or drink?"

"I smell coffee," Charlie said, "is there any left?"

"Follow me into the kitchen and I'll pour us both a cup."

Charlie sat down at the kitchen table as Brian poured the coffee. As Brian sat down across from Charlie he asked, "So what brings you out this way?"

Charlie took a sip of his coffee before answering, "I was just wondering how you were doing. We really didn't get to spend much time with you after what happened Friday night. Sometimes in the interest of keeping things quiet we tend to neglect the person who went through the trauma."

Brian responded: "You know, I really appreciate that. I don't think I'm feeling traumatized. If anything, I'm really starting to feel pissed off. How dare they treat me like an object they can just steal away if they wish too."

"Anger is a normal response. Just don't let it make you do something dumb," Charlie said.

Charlie looked around before continuing. "I thought this was your parent's house. Are they around?"

"No, and I'm thankful for that. They are on a cruise and won't be back for a couple of weeks. I couldn't imagine having to explain to them what happened Friday night."

Things got quiet for a moment as they drank their coffee. Finally Brian asked, "Is this the only reason you stopped over?"

"Well, yes and no," Charlie answered. "I was concerned about how you were doing. The getting angry thing is pretty normal. I have to admit I'm very interested in how you break into the company sights. I guess you could say it's part of my CIA thinking, but just imagine how much damage could be done with this kind of knowledge. I'm looking to see just how much you can do, and just how easy it is to do."

Brian perked up. Now was an opportunity to show off what he does best. "I will admit it took me a couple of years to perfect the initial programs I use. Now it's much easier to keep up with the incremental improvements others make in their protection programs by improving my programs. In fact, as computers get faster, and more people switch to digital cable, it gets even easier to break a code."

Charlie tried to appear as calm as possible. Inside he was still a little skeptical, but was also excited at the possibilities. Unfortunately, that excitement was not necessarily a positive thing. He wondered how many other people out there were capable of the same thing. Finally,

Charlie asked, "You were cut short at yesterday's meeting. Is there any way I can see a real demonstration?"

"Yes," Brian said. "I can show you some of what's out there now." As they walked upstairs to the computer room Brian continued, "I was looking up some things about our friend Gallagor when you arrived."

"I hope you were not logged into a place where you could be traced back to here," Charlie said. "Remember, Dave Gillian is supposed to set you up with an untraceable line."

"I remember," Brian said, "but I still think I'll be okay. I'm working on a way to tell when someone is trying to trace my line so I can shut down before they can lock onto me."

"That's fine," Charlie said, "but there is something else that maybe you should know." Charlie waved Brian over to an upstairs window. As they were looking out Charlie said, "Do you see that blue van parked across the street?"

Brian looked at Charlie but did not answer, so Charlie continued. "They work for the FBI, but not under Dave Gillian. They are here for two reasons. The first is for your protection. The second reason is to monitor what you're doing. I looked inside while talking to them before I knocked on your door. We, meaning the government, now have equipment sensitive enough to pick up and monitor what is displayed on your computer screen. They can actually watch whatever you have up on your screen. I'm sure you've noticed how your car radio stops working when you get inside the front gate of your company. They actually run an antenna wire in the fence, which puts out a signal meant to scramble any outgoing signals. It also works for incoming signals like those for your radio."

"I've heard of the technology," Brian said, "but I didn't know how portable or effective it was." Brian hesitated for a moment while he thought. "You mentioned they do not work under Dave Gillian. Who do they work for and why are they here?"

"Your attempted kidnapping got a lot of attention. Dave thought he could take control of it sooner, but it will take him a couple more days to work the politics. The contract your company won has all of our security people in high gear. The big boys down at the Pentagon are really paying a lot of attention to the whole encryption issue. They would have been watching you anyway, but after Friday night you can almost guarantee you'll have a small army following you around for a while."

"It sounds like a two edged sword," Brian said. "They aren't just watching out for me, they are also spying on me."

Charlie nodded, "This is where Dave can hopefully help us. If he can take charge of your case then we can let you do your thing for us without detection."

"Should I just shut down until that happens?"

"Not yet," Charlie answered, "they were hungry when I stopped to visit them so I told them to take a break. They shouldn't be back for about another hour."

Brian laughed. "I'm glad I'm on your side," Brian said. "Shall we get started?"

Charlie nodded his head yes. Brian continued, "I was looking up Senator Stone's voting record. I wanted to see if there were any companies in the area who might be unhappy with how he voted on some of the bills that came through."

"That's a good idea," Charlie said, "I think you should look at the bigger companies first. Gallagor probably knows we will be watching him, and if we can cut off his Chinese cash it will force him to look elsewhere."

Brian called up the wastewater relief bill that didn't pass, and noted how it hurt the chicken processing plant. Charlie got out a pen to write down the company president's name. "I can look him up in our files and see who he is," Charlie said.

"I could search the FBI files now if you want," Brian offered.

Charlie shook his head no. "I would rather you wait until Dave Gillian gets you that secure line."

After what seemed like ten minutes but was closer to an hour, Charlie looked at his watch. "Wow, where did the time go? It looks like the guys in the van will be back soon. You might want to consider shutting down now."

"This is going to drive me nuts," Brian said. "Is there any way to jam their equipment?"

Charlie looked around the room. "I have heard of some people turning on several televisions and putting them around the computer, but the positioning has to be just right. If they move to another spot you would have to reposition the televisions again."

"Can't you just tell them to go home, or at least stop monitoring?" Brian asked next.

Charlie shook his head no. "Anything I say will just get them curious and make it harder for Dave Gillian."

Charlie could see that Brian was getting frustrated. "You know Brian, I have already confided in you more than what's normal. We obviously checked you and your brother out and feel you can be trusted to do the right thing. Asking you to join the team is no small thing."

"Yes I know," Brian said, "it's just that I want to get started right away." Brian paused for a moment to think. "Do you think we'll be able to get this guy?"

"I don't know Brian. It's hard to predict what motivates voters. There are also a lot of people who actually believe the communist ideology would be better. I've seen my share of it. Most of them do not actually have any subversive ties to any enemy nations. The best we can do is catch Gallagor doing something illegal, expose it, and hope for the best."

"You don't sound very optimistic," Brian said.

"I have to confess that I'm not. I've lost more of these than I've won."

Brian shut down his computer and looked at Charlie. "Well," Charlie said, "I'll go back and talk to Dave again and see if he can speed things. Unfortunately the CIA has been neglected for several years now and there isn't much I can accomplish going up my management chain. My recommendation for you is to go to work and get started on that decoding contract. The ease at which you seem to be able to break into company records is rather scary, and quite frankly our country can benefit from your experience. That would have a greater effect than any one Senator could."

Charlie continued, "The only other suggestion I could make is for you to go to the library and do some reading on our election process. Learn about the mechanics of how money is raised, how each candidate puts their message together, and even how the media plays its part. This will help you with your research."

Brian thanked Charlie as he left. Brian watched from a window as Charlie walked across the street to the van and knocked on the back door. He saw two men get out. They talked for a couple of minutes, and then Charlie got in his car and drove off. They got back in their van but did not leave.

Chapter 15

Jay was up early on Monday morning. He was showered, dressed, and sitting in the kitchen drinking a cup of coffee when Rebecca got up. She walked into the kitchen and said, "Aren't you up early, running on a little nervous energy perhaps?"

Jay shrugged his shoulders. "I hope I'm doing the right thing," he said.

Rebecca rolled her eyes and said in a sarcastic tone, "I think we've been through this already. If it doesn't work out you can always go back to accounting. You can go back to sitting at a desk in front of your computer working on spreadsheets all day every day for the rest of your life. Doesn't that sound like fun?"

Jay smiled. "Okay, I get your point. I'll even go in early, which will make me look like a dedicated employee. I can use the time to type out my resignation letter."

Brian walked out of his house, locked the door behind him and walked to his car. He tried to pretend that he didn't notice, but out of the corner of his eye he could see two men sitting in a car across the street. As he pulled out of the driveway, he waved to them as he drove by. Watching them from his rear view mirror, Brian noticed there was a lot of white smoke coming out of their exhaust, just like his car. This told Brian their car was not warmed up, which meant that they had been sitting in front of his house for most of the night. Brian wondered if his brother Jay would be doing a lot of similar things when he joins the FBI. Rebecca is going to love that, he thought. They continued to follow Brian all the way to his work.

Jay walked through the building to his desk. The first thing he did was turn on his computer and log on, just like every other morning. One of his coworkers walked by and reminded him of the staff meeting in fifteen minutes. With all that happened this weekend Jay forgot his new boss had scheduled a staff meeting a half hour before normal work time. The purpose of the early time, he was told, is to get everyone up to date before the actual work day started. Jay chuckled to himself. It always seemed like every new boss did the same thing when they first get started. Jay was not a clock-watcher, but it still didn't seem right to call a meeting before the assigned work hours. So much for getting his resignation letter done before anyone got in.

Jay's briefcase was empty. His plan is to pack up his personal belongings, family pictures etc., in it. He started on his resignation letter but didn't finish before the staff meeting. Jay stopped by the coffee pot and poured himself a cup, which made him a few minutes late to the meeting. It was a small way for him to be defiant one last time. Jay quietly walked into the conference room and had to stand with two other last minute arrivals. There was one chair left in the back, but since the meeting already started nobody had the nerve to walk across the room and sit there.

The meeting started with Jay's new boss introducing himself. He then continued with the same story Jay has heard so many times before. Profits were down, more of the companies who use their accounting firm are cutting back, and they will have to concentrate on being more efficient. Jay took another sip of his coffee and looked around the room. Many of his coworkers were doing their best to conceal their look of concern. Nobody likes to get laid off. At least, Jay thought, his quitting might help keep someone else employed.

The meeting ended, and Jay was one of the first out. As he was walking back to his desk one of his coworkers made a comment how Jay looked very relaxed after the bad news. The truth was, Jay thought, after Friday night this was not a big deal even if he didn't have another opportunity.

Jay finally arrived at his cubicle. His computer screen had the screen saver on, but it suddenly occurred to him that he might have left the resignation letter on the screen when he left. What an idiot, Jay mumbled to himself. He typed in his password to unlock his screen saver and sure enough, the half done letter was there. Jay finished the letter and before hitting the print button decided to gather up his personal things. It would look too obvious to put everything into his briefcase so he decided to just put everything into a single drawer. Jay then hit the print button and walked over to the printer. He would stand there and wait for his letter to print.

As Jay was waiting, he looked around the office one last time. He had a couple of friends he would miss, but overall he was glad to get out. Finally his letter started to print. As it was coming out Jay looked over his shoulder. Since it was early, nobody was in line behind him to look over his shoulder. Jay reread the letter, signed it, and headed toward his boss's office.

Although Brian pulled into his parking place exactly the same way as every other time, something felt different. It also seemed like a long time ago, although it was only the weekend. A lot happened over this past weekend, and somehow Brian felt a connection he never experienced before. He put his car into park, but didn't shut off the motor.

Brian looked around the parking lot. Brian used to talk to Ryan McWilliams, the second shift guard sometimes. He never talked to the morning guard except when the guard was exerting his authority for no apparent reason. Brian hated the harassment, but always complied. Brian pulled out of his parking spot and decided to back in. The guard hated that for some reason Brian never understood. Brian would watch the guard call some of the younger guys out of their office just to turn their cars around. Today would be his day for a little fun.

As Brian got out of his car he carefully looked around without being too obvious. This should be fun, Brian thought. Let's see that guard try and pull me out of a meeting while I'm with the government reps on one of our company's biggest contracts ever. Brian turned around one more time before turning the corner.

Brian walked into his office and hung up his coat. Ed Bell walked in as Brian was unpacking his computer. "I hope you had a nice, relaxing weekend Brian."

Brian laughed and said, "Not to worry, I got plenty of rest." If he only knew, Brian thought.

Ed looked at his watch and said, "Good, they should be here in about an hour. Maybe take a walk through and review your presentation before they arrive. I want everything to go as smoothly as possible."

Jay walked to the door leading to his boss's office and looked inside. The office was empty. It figures, he thought. This guy will be just as inaccessible as the last one. Jay started slowly back to his desk, thinking about what to do next. He could email his resignation, but decided instead to just email his boss a request for time to talk to him.

Jay sat down at his desk, but before he could send the email to his new boss, the phone rang. It was Dave Gillian. "Hi Dave, what's up?"

"Jay, I have your paperwork in front of me and I wasn't sure what day to put on your start date."

Jay hesitated a second before answering. "I have the letter typed up and in my hands. I'm still looking for the boss to give it to him. I should know as soon as I find him."

"That's great Jay. I didn't mean to put any pressure on you. Take your time."

"It's okay," Jay said. "It's good to hear a friendly voice if you know what I mean."

"Jay I understand. I will hold onto the paperwork until you get back to me. You still have my number right?"

Jay pulled out his cell phone and scrolled through the saved numbers. "Yes Dave, I have it here in front of me now. Before I forget, how's Jeff doing?"

"He's doing well. They got the bullet out, and he's recovering. The bad part is he will be out of commission for a while. The good part is the bullet was only a .32 caliber and didn't do a lot of damage."

"That's good to hear," Jay said. "Dave, I've got to go, my new boss just walked by so let me catch him now."

"Good luck Jay!" Dave said.

Jay grabbed his letter and quickly walked to his boss's office. He knocked on the door and walked in. His boss was on the phone and looked up as Jay walked in. Jay could tell he was just checking his messages because he was just pushing buttons and not speaking into the phone. "How do you erase old messages?" Jay's boss asked.

"Dialing 7 will erase them," answered Jay. Jay waited a couple more minutes before the boss hung up the phone.

"What can I do for you?" His new boss asked.

Jay laid down his letter and said "I wish to give my resignation."

"I'm sorry to hear that." Jay's boss looked at the bottom of the letter for Jay's name, and then opened up a folder on his desk. It was a new organizational chart, and Jay watched as he circled his name on the chart.

"Can I ask where you're going?"

"Actually," Jay answered, "I would rather not say."

Jay's boss sighed before he spoke next. "If you're looking to avoid the two weeks' notice just say so. We were going to have to cut back later this month anyway, and although I'm not saying you were on that list, from my point of view giving you two weeks pay is still cheaper than a severance package to whoever the unfortunate person might be. I think we can work something out. Is it a competitor?"

Jay sat down before answering. "No it's not. It's something totally unrelated. But I do need to get going to get into their next training session as soon as I can."

"That sound fair enough. You can finish out the day if you like, or leave at lunch. The only thing I ask is you don't disturb or bring down the office morale any more than it is now."

Jay nodded his head and said, "Thanks for your candor. I will quietly leave at lunch."

"I will make a call to personnel and let them know what we discussed, and if you could go there about 11:30 to sign whatever paperwork they require I would appreciate it." Both men stood up and shook hands, and Jay walked out.

Jay walked straight back to his desk and called Dave Gillian. "Okay Dave, it's done!"

"That's great Jay. How do you feel?"

"I guess a little relieved and nervous at the same time."

"That sounds pretty normal to me. Come straight to my office tomorrow. Your training is going to be handled differently than a new recruit. Come in a jacket and tie, but also bring a set of workout clothes, a towel, and your gun. You're going to get the crash course since you already passed the survival test Friday night."

"Okay Dave, I will see you then."

Sam Pellinger and Dok Rhee arrived at CCC at approximately 9:00AM. The receptionist was extra careful about signing them in per the new security procedures implemented a couple of weeks ago. Ed passed by Brian's office on his way to greet the guests. "They're here," Ed said to Brian.

"Great," answered Brian. "I have everything set up in the main conference room." Ed already knew that since he has been checking up on everything this morning. He had a lot of nervous energy to burn.

Brian followed Ed down to the lobby to greet their guests. As they entered the lobby Brian took special notice of the weight of the computer Dok was carrying. The strap appeared to be pulling extra hard on his shoulder.

Everyone introduced themselves as they were walking into the conference room. Dok couldn't wait any longer to ask, "So, which one of you is responsible for the test results?"

"That would be me," answered Brian.

"I have to admit your first response almost cost you the contract," Dok said.

"You didn't like it?" Brian asked with a slight sarcastic tone. Ed tried to give Brian a look to get him to cool it but Brian was not looking his way.

"It's not that I didn't like it," answered Dok. "It's just the last person who tried something like that messed up my main program and it took me a week to fix everything."

Brian gave Dok a puzzled look and said, "You shouldn't have experienced any problems with my changes, did you?"

"No, I didn't. I guess you could say that's one of the reasons we're here today is to make sure it wasn't just good fortune on your part."

"Dumb luck?" Brian asked in a somewhat annoyed tone. "I can assure you that was not the case. I was very careful about how I rearranged all of your subroutines so your main program could still find them. I also had to write a couple of new subroutines to shorten up the program enough to fit in the extras. All of the new subroutines

211

included new go to lines in the main program so everything would work as before. I explained everything in the text page I added."

"I apologize if I offended you," Dok said. "It's just that I've had some bad experiences in the past. I would also like to know how you knew how my main program worked. Perhaps after we get through our presentations we could sit down and go over that."

"I would be happy to," Brian said.

Ed looked over at Sam with a distressed look on his face. Sam looked back at Ed and rolled his eyes, then whispered so only Ed could hear, "Must be something with these computer guys, but don't worry, they'll be fine." Ed just nodded in agreement.

Jim Gallagor was in his office with Mike, Ivan and Allen. Jim began, "I got off the phone a little while ago with the national representatives for our party. They are telling me that since we are still down about five points in this weekend's latest polls they are going to start diverting their limited funds to some of the other, closer races. Without more funding for additional commercials I'm afraid we will need a miracle to win now."

Allen looked down at his feet. Mike hesitated a few seconds before speaking. "Where do we go from here?"

Jim answered, "There are two more weeks before the election. We should still plug away as before. Continue to raise funding where we can. I'm not saying we should give up."

Jim looked over at Ivan. He was sitting there and returned Jim's glance. As he did Jim shifted his position so as to lean on his phone. This was an old signal Jim and Ivan had used a long time ago. Jim was hoping Ivan still remembers it.

Jim stood up and said, "That's about it. I wanted you to know where we stand."

As they got up to leave Ivan said to Mike, "You go on today without me. I have some questions for Jim about my visa status, and will probably need some time to work on it."

"Okay," was all Mike said. He was still feeling the disappointment from the bad news.

After the others left Ivan went back into Jim's office and closed the door. "I can't believe you used that old signal," Ivan said.

"I can't believe you still remembered it!" Jim shot back.

Ivan sat back down in a chair in front of Jim's desk. From where he sat he could watch Mike get in the car and drive off.

Ivan looked back at Jim and shrugged his shoulders. "What's on your mind?" he asked.

"Ivan, I'm going to need you for something a little different. Remember my comment about needing a miracle?"

Ivan just nodded as Jim continued, "I have an idea, but I'm not sure how to execute it. There was an election about ten years ago where the politician leading the election was tragically killed less than two weeks before the election. Although he still got a lot of sympathy vote, enough of the undecided were more worried about throwing away their votes and went with the surviving candidate. That, combined with a lot of people on the other side who just stayed home, the surviving person won. In fact, he's been winning re-election ever since."

Ivan leaned forward in his chair and said, "You realize I'm really pressed for time here. We need time to study his habits, and come up with a plan. This takes time."

"I understand," Jim said, "but I have some information that might help. As part of his campaign strategy the Senator has a chartered plane standing by ready for his use. It's from a private donor and it's always the same plane. The question now is what can you do with the information?"

"I will need a car, and will have to get back to you," Ivan said.

"You should rent a car yourself under an alias, so it can't be traced back. Let's go now and I'll take you."

As they walked out Jim said to Ivan. "If this goes as planned, you'll have to leave for a while."

"How long were you thinking?" Ivan asked.

"I'm not sure, but you should disappear back in your country for several months at least."

Ivan nodded in agreement. "I have some connections who can help me out," Ivan, said.

John Hunt was sitting in a car down the street from Gallagor's place. He was on the phone with Dave Gillian. "So Dave, what should I do? I can see Gallagor pulling out in his car now, and it looks like he might have Ivan Spelluchuvik with him. I'm not sure if I should follow them."

"Probably not," answered Dave. "They might see you."

"Hey Dave, check this out," interrupted John. "It looks like Gallagor already has a tail. They look Chinese, but what I want to know is how come they don't appear to be concerned about staying in visual contact in order to follow Gallagor."

"John, go ahead and follow the Chinese. I'm going to try and get a chopper in the air. I don't suppose you have any scanning equipment in your car, do you?"

"Sorry Dave, but no I don't. I had to give most of my gadgets back when I transferred out of your department," John said.

"I'm going to fix that," answered Dave. "They might have Gallagor's car bugged, and it would be convenient if we could also pick up on their frequency."

John followed the Chinese, who were following Gallagor, for several miles. He remained on the phone with Dave. "It looks like Gallagor is dropping Ivan off to rent a car," John said.

"How about I stick around and get a license plate number on his car."

"Sounds like a good idea to me," answered Dave. "Who did the Chinese decide to go with?" John looked back in his rearview mirror. "It looks like they are going back with Gallagor."

After lunch Sam and Ed went off to meet the new security officer at CCC and review the security plan. Brian and Dok stayed behind in the conference room. They sat there silently for a moment. It was one of those situations that happen when two computer geeks get together and don't know what to say.

Finally Chuck walked in and introduces himself to Dok. "Brian," Chuck asked, "did you get a chance to show Dok any of your virus cracking programs yet?"

"No I haven't," answered Brian. "How about we go back to my office where I keep my DVD's."

Brian figured it shouldn't be any harm in showing Dok how they work. He would just have to make sure that Dok doesn't see the actual program. As Brian and Dok stood up to leave the conference room Chuck said, "It was nice to meet you Dok."

Chuck then turned and left the room. As he headed to his office he could see Ed down the hall right outside the new security office. Chuck gave Ed a subtle signal his mission was accomplished. What Brian didn't know was Ed sent Chuck in the conference room to make his suggestion. Although Ed thought highly of Brian's computer skills, he knew Brian needed some help with the social skills at times.

It was a little early for the second shift to start when Ryan arrived. He stepped into the guardhouse just as the day shift guard was getting up to leave. "Hey McWilliams, I'm glad you're here. I have to go up and straighten out some joker who decided to back his car into his spot."

Ryan turned around and could see it was Brian's car. He rolled his eyes, and then looked over at the car in the visitors parking area. "Who are the visitors," Ryan asked.

"They are some new customers, and I think they might be from the government."

"In that case I wouldn't go up there," Ryan said. "I know the guy who owns that car and I guarantee he is with them."

The other guard stopped and gave Ryan an annoyed look. He then looked at his watch. Ryan continued, "I know you get off soon. I can go tell him to turn his car around after they leave."

"Okay," said the other guard. "Just make sure you tell him." Ryan nodded, and then looked the other way. After Brian's weekend, Ryan was not about to bother him over something so stupid.

John was parked at the far end of the rental car lot. He got out of his car to look in the trunk. He pulled out what looked like a small can of spray paint and slipped it into his pocket. Just then Charlie drove up and parked next to him. John walked over to Charlie's car as Charlie rolled down the window. "How's it going?" Charlie asked.

"Boy am I glad to see you. I need your help. Ivan is in there renting a car. I want to mark his rental car with phosphorus paint."

John then showed him the can. Charlie knew the paint would go on clear, but will glow at night with a special light they use in a pursuit helicopter. "You better hope he doesn't smell it when he gets in," Charlie said.

"It's a risk I'll have to take," John answered.

John walked in the rental office and back out the door leading to the rental cars. He was moving slowly and trying not to look suspicious. Charlie went into the office and looked for Ivan. He was at the counter and was already getting his paperwork processed. Charlie walked over and stood in line behind him. There was another service counter without a line but Charlie tried not to look over that way. He was hoping the girl behind the counter would not call him over.

After several seconds of trying to figure out why he wasn't noticing that she was open, the girl behind the counter finally called Charlie over. At least he was still in ear range of Ivan. Charlie started going through his coat pockets pretending to look for his wallet. Finally the girl waiting on Ivan handed him his ticket. She told him that his car was a blue Chevy parked at location G687. That was all Charlie needed to hear. He gave the girl at the counter an embarrassing smile and told her he would be right back. He then turned around and took out his phone. Charlie texted "G687" to John.

Charlie then threw some papers down on the ground where Ivan was standing. "Excuse me sir," Charlie yelled out. At first Ivan didn't turn around. Charlie scooped up the papers and ran over to Ivan. "Excuse me sir, are these your papers?"

Ivan turned around and looked at the papers. "No," was all Ivan said.

Ivan then looked up at Charlie, who quickly spun around and said, "Sorry to bother you." Charlie didn't want to give Ivan time to study his face. Ivan slowly turned back and headed out to his car. Charlie was hoping it was enough of a delay for John.

Meanwhile, John raced over to spot G687. A blue four door Chevy was parked there. John quickly walked by it and ran his arm across the top. Inside his sleeve was the can of paint. John painted a long streak across the top trying to stay closer to the passenger's side. He knew there was time for only one pass. John continued to walk and put his hands in his coat pockets. This allowed the spray can to drop into his pocket. John quickly walked over several rows and made the same arm motion over the tops of the other cars, this time without the spray can.

A suspicious employee from the rental car company was watching John. Finally he walked over to John and asked, "Can I help you?"

John waved his arm for the employee to follow him. "As a matter of fact you can," John said. "I bought a car similar to one of your rental cars and I noticed the paint on my roof doesn't look right. I was driving by and wanted to look at your cars."

The employee looked at John and said, "Sir I'm going to have to ask you to leave."

"I'm sorry," John said, and he turned around and walked out.

Ivan didn't even notice John as he found his car and started it up. John walked back to the parking lot toward Charlie. "Well, did you get it painted?" Charlie asked.

"Are you busy?" John asked without answering his question. Charlie knew John wanted help tailing Ivan.

"No, and I'll help," Charlie said without waiting for John to ask. "But we need to hurry." Charlie nodded his head over toward the exit. Ivan was pulling up to the final gate before pulling out of the parking lot.

Chapter 16

John was in his car about five car lengths behind Ivan. He picked up his phone and spoke to Charlie. "I think it's time I dropped back. I know this next exit off the freeway. It's easy to get back on, and that should put me out of sight behind him. You can pick up the tail from here for a while."

"Got it," was all Charlie said.

John got off the intersection as planned. He had four cloverleaves to circle around to put him back on the highway. He was just about to start the fourth and final loop when Charlie spoke. "John, it looks like he's getting off at the next exit. Where do you think he's going?"

"I don't know. We'll just have to wait and see," John answered.

Ivan drove down the main road that runs along the airport noting all of the exits. There were two separate ways to get in. One was the main entrance, which led to the parking area. The second entrance was a service entrance and had a guard shack with a guard controlling traffic in and out. Parked behind the guard shack were the planes. Private planes were to the left, and a hangar for the charter planes was to the right. The doors to the hangar were open and Ivan could see two charter planes inside.

Ivan continued past the airport and suddenly pulled over. Charlie picked up his phone but was careful not to lift it up enough to be seen if someone was looking at him in the car. "John, it looks like he's about to U-turn so I'm going to keep driving."

"Okay," answered John. "I'll pull into the airport parking lot and try to blend in."

John parked in between two other cars about three quarters of the way down the parking lot. It was a small airport, not one for the commercial airlines, so everything was at a smaller scale. John slumped down in this seat as Ivan slowly drove past.

219

Ivan thought to himself, I really need a reason to be wandering around. He pulled into an empty spot at the end of the lot and shut off the car. He picked up his phone and dialed. "Jim, this is Ivan. I am in the lot now. I can see the hangar where the plane would be, but there are rental cops all over. I will need a way to get in there." Ivan turned around and noticed another building that was behind the hangars. "I think I might have an idea," continued Ivan.

"Well, what is it?" asked Jim.

"Did you know there is a mechanics school in here?"

"No I didn't," answered Jim.

Ivan said, "I'm going to check it out and call you later."

"Just let me know what you come up with," answered Jim.

They hung up the phone. Ivan got out of his car and walked over to the mechanics school office. John picked up his cell phone. "Hey Charlie, where are you?"

"I'm parked outside the airport across the street. Where are you?"

"I'm sitting in the parking lot watching Ivan go into the mechanics school," John answered.

"That could make a good cover," Charlie replied.

As Ivan opened the door and stepped inside, he carefully looked around. It was an old building. The desks were obviously older too, and there was little formal order to things. The whole building was one large room with several desks and filing cabinets organized in separate groups. There were no partitions anywhere, and from any desk one could see who was in the room. This is perfect, Ivan thought. I'm clearly not dealing with one of the well-organized national chains.

Ivan stood there a couple of minutes looking around. Finally, someone came over to him. He was in his late twenties or early thirties. "Can I help you?" He asked.

"Yes," answered Ivan. "I was looking for some information on getting certified as an airplane engine mechanic."

"Do you have any experience?"

Ivan thought for a moment. He wasn't sure how to play this. Showing experience might get him into the hangar faster, but how does he do that without triggering an extensive background check?

"I have a lot of mechanical experience, but very little formal certification," Ivan said.

"My name is Eric," Eric said as he reached out to shake Ivan's hand. Eric was struggling to keep his flight school open, and was eager to get all the new students he could. Ivan was careful not to give out his name unless specifically asked. He still wasn't sure what alias he was going to use.

"If you have the aptitude I wouldn't worry about the formal training. That's what our school is here to handle. How soon can you start?" Eric continued.

"Right away, if that's possible," answered Ivan.

Eric went over to his desk and pulled out some papers. He walked back over to Ivan. "Here, fill out these forms and bring them back with you tomorrow with a down payment. If you want to you can also start tomorrow. Come in at 7:00 AM."

Ivan smiled. "7:00 AM it is then."

As Ivan stepped out of the building, he tried to casually walk over to the hangar. A guard patrolling the area stopped him. John watched the whole thing from inside his car. He carefully looked through the binoculars, and could see Ivan showing the guard some papers. The guard shook his head, and Ivan shrugged his shoulders, turned around and walked away. John slumped down in his car again as Ivan walked to his car about two rows away. John watched as Ivan drove away. He then got back on the phone with Charlie. "Do you think we should follow him?" Charlie asked.

John looked at his watch first. "No, let him go. Why don't you come in and we can look around."

Charlie waited until Ivan drove off and out of sight. He then drove in and parked next to John. John explained everything he had seen to Charlie, who just looked around silently as John spoke. "Hey," Charlie interrupted. "Aren't the guards from the same security company as the guards from CCC?"

John picked up his binoculars to look. "I think you're right. I wonder if Ryan McWilliams could transfer over. It would be handy to get someone on the inside without raising any suspicion."

John looked at his watch, and then pulled out his cell phone. He already had the phone at CCC security programmed into his phone. "Can I speak to Ryan McWilliams please?"

"Ryan is on duty now. Can I take a message?"

"Yes," answered John. "Can you tell him his Uncle John called, and his cousin Charlie had another seizure and was asking for him."

Charlie looked over at John and rolled his eyes, then looked away before John could see him smile. There was some hesitation on the phone. Then the voice said "Hold on, I will try to find him."

"Hello, Uncle John?" Ryan said when he picked up the phone.

"Hi Ryan, do you know who this is?" John asked.

"Yea I know. The message I got was easy enough to figure out, very funny."

"I hope you're not getting tired of hearing from me?"

"No sir," Ryan quickly replied. "I am honored that you called."

"Ryan, I need your help again. I am over at the Regional Airport and it looks like your company also guards this place. How hard is it to get yourself transferred over here?"

"It's not hard at all. I started out working there. The hard part is getting transferred out of there. It's not the most popular place to work."

"Why not?" John asked.

"There's a lot more patrolling required, and the buildings where the planes are kept are not heated. The middle of winter can be nasty."

"I'm sorry to ask you this Ryan, but we need someone we can trust on the inside over here. Can you help us?"

"You know I want to help," Ryan answered without hesitation. "Are you working on a new case?"

"It's part of the same case, and you'll need to wear a wire," John answered.

"Do I get a gun?" Ryan asked.

"A gun?" John repeated while looking over at Charlie. Charlie returned a look that told John he didn't think it was a good idea.

"I'm not sure that would be a good idea," John said. "You'll need training first. Besides, we will have someone close to you at all times on this one."

"Well okay," Ryan said reluctantly.

"How soon do you think you could get transferred over there?"

Ryan answered, "We get a weekly email at work with a list of locations with openings and there are two at the airport now. I could probably start there tomorrow."

John looked over at Charlie as he hung up the phone. "I'm going to owe that kid when this is over," John said. "Maybe we could help him get into college so he could join the FBI."

"Can you get him some kind of scholarship?" Charlie asked.

"I don't know, but I will speak to Dave Gillian when this is over."

When Jay got home Rebecca was already there. He walked into the kitchen and tossed his keys on the counter. "Well?" Rebecca finally asked.

"It's done," Jay said. "I start tomorrow morning. They told me to bring workout clothes and wear a jacket and tie."

"You don't seem too happy," Rebecca said curiously.

"I am," Jay answered, "but I guess I'm still a little nervous. Remember that was some action packed night. I just hope I'm not pushing my luck."

"You'll do fine. They were eager to sign you up for a reason," Rebecca said.

Ivan drove back to his apartment, and gave Jim a call. "It looks like I have a way in."

"Great," Jim said. "Do you need anything from me?"

"Yes Jim I do. I'm going to join a small mechanics school at the airport. This should give me access to the hangar. I will need some identification, and it needs to be able to pass a first level background test. At least with enough background to keep them satisfied for a few days. If they discover more later it will not matter. I should be gone by then."

"What about your John Smithe cover? You could point them to your old Oxford records, and that should give you the couple of days you need."

"I thought about that," Ivan answered, "but that would give your government a possible link to me in the future if they dig deep enough."

"I know, but with us so short on time I can't get you set up any other way. After your vacation back home we will set you up with new identification. A United States Senator should be able to do that easy enough."

"If that's our best option," Ivan said. They hung up the phone and Ivan began filling out the forms they gave him at the mechanics school.

When John Hunt walked into his house, he was still on the phone with Dave. "I think I may have discovered a connection," Dave said. "Senator Stone charters a jet out of that airport."

"Do you think they are planning sabotage?" John asked.

"It's a possibility," Dave answered. "I sure would like to come up with a way to set them up."

John thought for a moment. "What if we let them do whatever they are planning, and catch them in the act?"

"Sure," Dave answered, "that would catch Ivan, but how does that tie him back to Gallagor? We couldn't let the Senator fly in that plane."

"What if we just let Gallagor believe he did?" John asked.

"I don't know," Dave answered. "I'm not sure how that might influence the election outcome. If we don't make an immediate arrest, it could look like the Senator faked the whole thing. He could end up losing. Plus we would have to crash a plane."

John continued, "I asked our security guard Ryan McWilliams to transfer over to the airport. His company guards over there too."

"How much does he know?" Dave asked.

"He has most of the details. I will give him a wire and show him how to wear it and operate it," John said.

Dave didn't like the idea but it was too late to stop it now, "Just make sure he doesn't take any unnecessary risks. We're talking about professional killers here."

"I know," John said. "I think he'll be okay. We are going to owe this kid when this is over."

"I think you like that part," Dave answered.

John was standing in his kitchen talking to Dave as Tara walked in. "Dinner is ready," she said.

"Dave I have to go. I don't think he'll do anything else tonight. I will call you tomorrow and give you the latest after I confirm everything with McWilliams."

When John walked into the dining room Tara and the kids were already sitting down and waiting for him. "About time Dad," his daughter said. Tara gave her a kick in the shin from under the table. Not enough to hurt, but to get her attention. Although Tara didn't like the idea of John working for Dave Gillian again, she could see how much happier he was to be involved in something more interesting. For now she would quietly support him – and pray.

Since Ryan McWilliams worked the afternoon shift, he had to call his supervisor at home. "I can't believe you want to go back to the airport Ryan. Is everything okay at CCC? I know you disappeared last Friday."

"Everything is fine," Ryan answered. "I just need the extra money from the overtime I can get at the airport."

"You know I'm shorthanded there, so if you want to you can start tomorrow. I just hope you're not going to change your mind again in a couple of weeks."

Ryan thought about that for a couple of seconds. He was hoping John Hunt might be able to get him into the FBI somehow.

"Not to worry," was all Ryan said.

After they hung up, Ryan looked at his watch. He wanted to call John and let him know he was all set for tomorrow. He decided to wait another hour, figuring John might be eating dinner now.

Ivan was up and ready to go early the next morning. He knew there's usually a certain amount of confusion before the first shift of the day starts. He felt if he could get there at about 6:30 AM, he might be able to wander around the hangar some and get a better idea how to approach the plane.

John Hunt was also up early, and about to get in his car when his cell phone began to ring. "Hello John, this is Charlie. I'm out in front of Ivan's place and it looks like he's already heading out. I thought I would call you and save you a trip over here."

"Thanks Charlie, I appreciate it. My guess is he's heading toward the airport."

"What I can do is follow him out toward that direction just to verify which way he's going, then drop off before he actually gets there," Charlie said.

"Sounds like a good idea to me. I'm in my car now and can be at the airport before he gets there. I will park in the back somewhere away from the mechanics school area."

"Okay," Charlie answered. "I will meet you there about twenty minutes later. This will give him time to get inside and not see me pull in, just in case he notices me tailing him."

Ivan looked in his rear view mirror again as he got off the main highway toward the airport. Ivan spotted Charlie's car and was watching him, not really sure if he was indeed following him. Ivan was in the middle lane and didn't leave much time before he went over to the right lane to exit. This would require the car following him to move over suddenly making it more obvious he was being followed. Ivan could see the car blinker go on, except that it was to move over to the left lane. Maybe he wasn't following me after all, Ivan thought.

The exit ramp went up a hill to meet an overpass above it. Although the airport was on the right, Ivan made a left and parked on the shoulder of the bridge going over the highway. From there he could see if the car following him was going to get off at the next exit and double back. As Charlie continued to drive on, he watched Ivan pull over on the bridge. That's an old trick, Charlie thought. He decided to continue on for a couple more exits, and just to be sure he would double back using a side road he knew of to get to the airport.

When Ivan was satisfied he was not being followed, he continued to the airport. John was sitting in his car in the back of the parking lot on the phone with Charlie as Ivan drove in. "Here he comes now," John said. "I checked the sign on the mechanics school door and it says that they don't open until 7:00 AM. My guess is Ivan is here early to walk around a little to check things out."

Ivan got out of his car and walked over to the mechanics school door. He made a big show of noticing it was locked, and began to look around. He then turned around and headed for the hangar where Senator Stone's plane was parked. He got within twenty feet of the hangar door before he was stopped.

"Can I help you?" asked the guard that intercepted Ivan.

Ivan answered, "I'm enrolling in the mechanics school and was a little early. I thought maybe I could look around a little until they open."

"Ordinarily I could let you inside the hangar, but the plane over there is the Senator's private jet and he's expected any minute."

"Wow, really? Do you think we will get a chance to meet him?" Ivan asked. Ivan knew he would never be allowed anywhere near the Senator, but wanted to put on a show for the guard.

The guard shook his head no and said, "I never get to meet him so I doubt you'd be able to. In fact," the guard continued as he pointed past Ivan, "here he comes now. You will have to move back."

Ivan turned around to look at the limousine driving through the parking lot. "Okay," Ivan said, "I think I'll head back to the flight school and wait there out of the way."

The guard just nodded, but was thankful Ivan was leaving on his own. As Ivan was walking away he made some mental notes. Apparently the security here makes a show of it when the Senator shows up, but was somewhat lax otherwise. They also had access to his schedule, and geared up accordingly.

John was still on the phone with Charlie and said, "You'll never guess who just pulled up!"

"Who?" Charlie asked.

"Senator Stone," answered John.

"Where is Ivan now?" Charlie asked.

"He's walking away from the hangar."

"Watch him," Charlie cautioned, "just in case Ivan is planning a hit."

"I doubt that," John said. "An assassination would not look good for Gallagor. Ivan is heading in the opposite direction out in the open. He doesn't look to be in a hurry. Hey, here is something interesting. Ivan just turned and is walking toward the flight tower."

As Ivan walked back toward the mechanics school he had to pass near the tower. Maybe I could get information on when the Senator's plane will be returning, he thought. As soon as Ivan walked in another guard at a desk greeted him. "Can I help you?" the guard asked.

Ivan gave him the same explanation he gave the other guard about joining the mechanics school. This guard seemed much easier to talk to. "What would you like to know?" the guard asked.

"Oh, nothing in particular. Who is the guy in the limo?"

The guard looked at his chart. "That's Senator Stone. He is scheduled to fly out this morning and return sometime late this afternoon."

Great Ivan thought. His plane would be back tonight, and with a little luck someone will have started on the post flight inspection before they leave. Ivan was hoping to find an inspection cover off in the hot section of at least one of the engines. This would allow him access to the turbine blades.

Ivan looked at his watch. It was approximately 6:45. "I better get going. The mechanics school is about to start and I don't want to be late. Nice meeting you." The guard just waved as Ivan walked out.

"Ivan just walked into the mechanics school," John said. "How about I meet you down the block. If Ivan stopped on the bridge to watch you drive by we should keep your car out of sight."

"Good idea," Charlie said. "You can meet me at the diner down the road in about five minutes."

As Ivan walked into the mechanics school a woman who looked to be in her late thirties greeted him. Although she had several rings on her fingers, Ivan noticed she didn't have a wedding band. She is of medium build and about five and a half feet tall. Dressed somewhat casual, her hair and makeup were done up to the max. Even her nails were perfect, and the nail color was a bright red.

"Hi, my name is Janice," she said as she took his application paperwork. Ivan followed Janice over to her desk. He took a careful look over the desk. Her desk was neat and orderly, which was in sharp contrast to every other desk in the room. Janice had several pictures on her desk of a small boy Ivan guessed was her son. There was one small picture with Eric in it. It didn't fit the pattern of the other pictures, which made Ivan wonder if Eric was her husband or a relative.

"I spoke with Eric Beesely yesterday. He gave me the forms to fill out, and told me to come back this morning," Ivan said.

Janice began reading the application. "You have no next of kin listed," Janice said.

"Yes I know. My family is over in a remote part of Scotland, and I didn't think contacting them in an emergency would be of any value."

Janice looked up at him and smiled. "I see your point," she said.

"So I guess you're not married either?" Ivan thought for a moment. What he was really looking for was a way to gain her sympathy without looking weak. If she was truly single and possibly looking

231

for a husband as Ivan suspected, letting her believe he was available could work to his advantage.

"No, I'm not married. My dream has always been to come to America and settle down here."

Janice nodded. She continued to read through his application. If I struck a nerve, Ivan thought, she's doing a good job of hiding it. Finally she looked up and said, "Okay Mr. Smithe the background check usually takes about a week. Normally we ask the applicant to wait until that process is completed before they begin."

"I was hoping to start right away," Ivan gently interrupted. "Oh, and please call me John."

Janice smiled again, and Ivan couldn't tell if he saw a little extra color in her face. "Okay, John, I would have to get my brother's permission, but I think we could let you start right away with some of the introductory stuff as we do the background check."

"I would really be in your debt," Ivan said. Ivan hesitated for a second before continuing. "Is Eric your brother?" Janice nodded her head yes. "Oh I'm sorry. I was looking at your pictures on the desk. I thought he was your husband."

"No, actually I'm single," answered Janice.

"If it's okay with you, maybe I could treat you to lunch some time," Ivan said.

"That would be nice," answered Janice.

Just then Ivan heard the door open. It was Eric walking in. He immediately noticed Ivan and walked over to them. Ivan stood up as Eric extended his hand. As they shook hands Eric said, "It's nice to see you again. I see you have met the boss."

Janice just rolled her eyes. Eric then turned to Janice and said, "Is he ready to start?"

"All the forms are filled out, but I still need to do the background check, and get a deposit."

"I have the deposit money right here," Ivan interrupted as he reached for his wallet. "I did not get time to open up a bank account, so I hope you can accept cash. I believe it was $550, right?"

Eric just watched as Ivan pulled out five one hundred dollar bills, then two twenties and a ten. Eric was trying to show no emotion, but owning a business with several overdue bills made getting some cash in his hands a welcome sight. Although Eric was speaking to Ivan, he looked at Janice. "I don't really see any reason why we couldn't get you started while the background check goes through. Janice why don't you issue Mr. Smithe his hangar pass. I need about a half hour to schedule a post flight maintenance that has to start later this afternoon."

"Are you talking about the plane that just took off this morning?" Janice asked as Eric started to walk away.

"Yes, that's the one, and of course he is in a hurry to get it done as usual."

Eric walked out the door as Ivan turned to Janice and shrugged his shoulders, but said nothing. Janice said, "It's Senator Stone's plane. He likes to have it ready to go at all times. It seems to be worse around election time. Eric threatened to ground the plane once when they gave him a hard time about doing an engine overhaul which was overdue."

Ivan gave her his surprised look and said, "You think someone as important as a United States Senator would be really meticulous about his plane's maintenance."

"I don't think it's the Senator as much as some of his aids keeping his schedule. I met the Senator once. It was raining and he came in here for a cup of coffee while they got his plane ready. At first I didn't know who he was. We were making small talk until one of his aids came in to get him. He seemed like a nice enough person to me."

Ivan didn't answer her. He was deep in thought. This whole thing was turning out unbelievably well. Not only would the plane be ready for him tonight, but also there was a history of incomplete maintenance that could be leaked to the press. This could cover up his plan until the final FAA investigation was published, which would be long after the election. He couldn't wait to call Gallagor and fill him in. Maybe Jim could use the information to his advantage somehow to score a few points.

As John pulled into the diner he spotted Charlie's car on the right. He pulled into an open spot next to Charlie and rolled down his car window. Charlie had to turn his car on before he could lower the passenger side car window to talk to John. "Do you think there is any need to get back right away?" Charlie asked.

"Not really," John answered. "The Senator just took off in his plane and will not be back until this afternoon. I don't think anything will happen until then. Why, what did you have in mind?"

Charlie looked over at the diner. "How about some breakfast, my treat."

"I am kind of hungry," John answered.

Chapter 17

Jay drove into the FBI parking lot and parked in the visitor's section. I know I shouldn't be this nervous, Jay thought, but the butterflies in his stomach were still uncomfortable. As Jay stepped out of his car and stood up, he shifted the gun holster under his jacket. It would be a while before he would get used to wearing it. Walking around to his trunk he debated whether or not to bring his duffle bag with his workout clothes in it. Deciding that he might as well, Jay closed the trunk lid and headed toward the lobby door.

Walking inside the lobby door, Jay noticed how the glass seemed a little thicker than normal. I'll bet its bulletproof glass, he thought. Across the lobby was a receptionist who was already looking at Jay when he noticed her. She smiled as he walked over to her.

"Hi, I'm here to see Dave Gillian," Jay said.

"He is on his way down Mr. Chestburg, would you have a seat?"

How did she know my name, Jay wondered. "Thank you," was all he said.

Before Jay started to walk away he saw a red light flash on her desk. Behind him he heard someone else walk into the lobby. The receptionist leaned over to look past Jay. The man who walked in waved to her and continued to their left across the lobby. She then hit a switch to turn off the light. Jay gave her a curious look. She shrugged her shoulders and said, "It's just the metal detector. Things can get exciting if it goes off and I don't recognize who it is."

Jay shifted his shoulders around again to change slightly how the weight of the gun was pulling on him. That explains how I could walk in with this thing, he thought.

Jay turned around to sit in the lobby, but got no further than a couple of steps when he heard his name echo through the lobby. He turned to see Dave Gillian's smiling face heading toward him. Jay knew he had a limp but it seemed worse today. Even with the limp, Jay noted, he can still move quickly across the slippery lobby floor.

The two men shook hands as Dave said, "It's good to see you." Dave then lifted Jay's sports jacket slightly exposing his gun. Dave nodded and said, "That's good. Might as well start dressing like an agent right from the start. Follow me and I will review our plan to get you off on the right foot." Jay just nodded, picked up his duffle bag and followed Dave.

When they entered Dave's office Jay immediately saw the desk across the room. To his right was a small conference table, which Dave immediately headed for. "Please sit," Dave said, "can I get you some coffee or anything?"

"No thanks, I'm fine," answered Jay.

Dave sat down across from Jay and opened the file that was sitting on the table. "Jay, we plan to handle you differently. You're a little older than most of our new recruits, and benefit from the maturity that comes from that. You already have the survival instinct. I was very impressed with how you hung your shirt in that tree to distract your opponent, and according to John and Charlie, you can fight too."

Jay just nodded again and gave a weak smile. As pleased as he was about the compliment, Jay was also fighting some nervousness as well as the memory of actually taking two lives.

Dave continued, "We plan to give you all of the same classroom training. This will prepare you for all of the legal issues that could come up."

"Like when John and Charlie decided to give me a gun Friday night?" Jay asked.

"As you will find out, not every answer is neatly packaged in a text book. Sometimes in the field we must go with what seems like the best trade off. We wrestled with that one for a while that night, but we also had to find your brother with no time to spare. We were in a battle, and like it or not you stepped into it too. It turned out to be the right decision."

Jay looked at his feet before speaking. "I haven't talked about what actually happened that night to anybody. I gave my wife some of the details, but I still can't believe it all myself. I killed two people like it was nothing."

Dave quickly interrupted, "I wouldn't say you treated it like nothing. You were definitely stressing about it over the phone when I was talking to you." Dave then leaned over his desk to really grab Jay's attention before continuing. "The important part as far as I'm concerned is even though you were going through all of the normal guilt and shock associated with having to take a life, you stayed focused on finding your brother. Remember, you even arranged to get your friend with the four wheel drive truck in there."

Jay looked up at Dave. "I'm worried I may not be able to get used to shooting someone, even if they are supposed to be the bad guys."

"Jay I'm going to tell you a little secret. The day you do get used to it is the day I start worrying. You did all the right things, and that's why you're here. Now, if you're ready, why don't we go out to the shooting range first, and see how you do."

After breakfast, John and Charlie walked over to John's car. "I guess we should leave my car here," Charlie said.

John had another idea. "I was thinking, what if I went first to see if Ivan is around. If he's inside, you could probably get away with parking your car way in the back. This way if we need it we will have it."

"That sounds like a good idea to me," Charlie answered as he turned to walk towards his car.

Dave Gillian asked Jay to drive Dave's car, and as soon as they were out of the parking lot Dave took out his cell phone. Jay glanced over as Dave hit his speed dial. John Hunt's phone rang as he was driving toward the airport. He looked at the caller ID and knew who it was. "Hi Dave, what's up?"

"I just wanted a status report. What is our friend Ivan up to now?"

John started thinking maybe breaking for breakfast wasn't the best idea. "As of about 45 minutes ago we left him in the mechanics school. My guess is he'll be there for the day."

Dave had several questions, and wasn't sure which one to ask first. "You said we, is Charlie there with you?"

"He's following about five minutes behind. It's a long story. We were worried Ivan might have spotted his car, so we were originally going to leave it behind."

Dave thought for a moment. He could see where this was going. "What changed your minds?"

"Oh, about 45 minutes for breakfast. We are going to hide his car in the back if the coast is clear."

Dave interrupted. "Where is Ivan now, and who is watching the Senator's plane?"

John wanted to give a smart-ass answer, not because he thought Dave was out of line, but because he felt he had everything under control and wanted to let Dave know it. Finally John answered, "The Senator is watching his plane. He left early this morning. According to the flight plan his pilots filed they'll be back about mid afternoon. If Ivan's plan was a simple assassination he had a clear shot this morning. I'm guessing our original idea about him going after the plane seems most likely, and the next couple of days will be a waiting game while he puts a plan together."

"We will need 24 hour coverage," Dave said. "I know you mentioned getting that kid that drove you around on Friday involved, but I think we need an agent."

John interrupted, "Dave, I understand, but I don't want to make it obvious we're watching the airport. If Ivan suspects anything he'll just disappear. It would be much better if we can somehow catch him in the act."

"I still think we should get at least one of our guys in there," Dave insisted.

"I was already planning on wiring the security guard Ryan McWilliams. Can you get someone to sit in the parking lot and cover the night shift? I'll cover the days as planned," John asked.

Dave understood John's concern about involving the security company directly on this. Unfortunately there would be little chance the security company could be trusted to keep things quiet. Dave finally answered, "I will make a phone call and get someone in to relieve you this evening. Just make sure McWilliams wears his wire and doesn't try to be a hero." John agreed before hanging up with Dave.

Dave looked over at Jay before dialing again. Jay got the second half of the story listening to Dave explain things to the person he arranged as John's evening replacement over the phone. Jay could feel a little excitement building as he pieced together the operation. As Dave hung up the phone and slipped it back into his pocket he looked over at Jay. "Are you sure you know what you're getting into?" Dave asked Jay.

"Jay answered, "I do know this sure beats accounting!"

John turned into the parking lot of the airport and pulled into an empty spot about halfway between the hangar and the flight school. He was also about halfway back in the lot, and had a good view of both buildings. Just as John reached into his pocket to get his phone to call Charlie a tap on the driver's side door window startled him. He looked over and saw it was Charlie. He rolled down the window and said, "You scared the crap out of me! I thought you were going to wait for my call."

Charlie began to laugh as he walked over to the other side of the car. John hit the button to unlock the car and Charlie got in. "I know I was supposed to wait for your call, but when we made that plan I forgot about the back entrance. I tried to call but you didn't pick up."

"I was on the line with my boss," John answered. "He wanted to put an agent in under cover. I talked him out of it. I'm afraid Ivan wouldn't be fooled."

Charlie nodded his head in agreement. "So what did you two finally agree to?"

"Dave will send down another agent this evening to relieve us. He was also concerned about getting McWilliams's involved." John hesitated before continuing. "Charlie, you are supposed to be the expert on this. Do you think Ivan would go to the trouble to take out McWilliams if he was cornered?"

Charlie shrugged his shoulders and said, "Maybe. Remember, Ivan comes from the old Soviet Union. They definitely think differently. If he is planning to leave the country right after this he might not hesitate. If he plans to hide out somewhere in the States then I would say no. The hunt for him would start immediately if he killed someone. I'm sure his plan is to get away clean and take his time hiding before the plane crashes."

Jay pulled into the parking lot of the shooting range. As soon as Jay put the car into park Dave reached over to shut off the motor and take the keys. Without saying anything he got out of the car and opened up the trunk. Jay got out of the car and walked around to the trunk.

"Wow," was all Jay could say as he looked over the collection of guns in the trunk. He saw a rack with two different rifles and a shotgun individually mounted. There was a high-powered rifle with scope. Next to that was an AR-15, then the shotgun with a folding stock.

On the right side of the rack was another box Dave had already opened. Inside were two pistols and about ten boxes of different ammunition. Dave looked over at Jay and grinned. "I come from the old school," Dave said. "I like to have enough fire power on hand."

"It's a little hard to carry the rifles concealed," Jay said. I can't believe I said that, Jay thought to himself.

Dave laughed. "You'll get a chance to shoot everything in here soon enough. Today all we have time for is the pistols. They are the hardest to shoot accurately." Jay just nodded as Dave continued to fill a duffle bag with both pistols and several boxes of ammunition.

Dave didn't say much as Jay followed him into the shooting range. He just waved to the man behind the counter as he walked past. "We have two lanes reserved in the back," Dave told Jay.

Dave handed Jay a pair of earmuffs before opening the door into the shooting range. "Here, turn on the switch on the side and put these on."

Jay looked around for the switch and turned them on as instructed. As they walked around the other shooters Jay was amazed at how well the earmuffs worked. He could hear normal conversation better than without them yet the sound of a gun going off was only a mild pop.

Jay watched as Dave clipped a target to his lane first, then the other. Dave pointed and said, "Push that button there and send your target out to twenty five yards."

Jay did as instructed. As he watched the target go out, he studied it. It was a silhouette of a man, with different rings designating points for how far out from the center of the target hits would be. The center ring was ten points.

Dave loaded the first gun he brought and handed it to Jay. It was a nine-millimeter Ruger. It had a three-dot sight, and was easy to see. "Aim for the center of the body for the first five shots," Dave said.

Jay carefully aimed and squeezed the target. He did this five times and stopped. "Good," Dave said. "Now squeeze off five head shots."

"Can we see how I did first?" Jay asked.

"There will be plenty of time for that," Dave answered.

Dave could see Jay was a little nervous. Although Dave was very interested in how good a shot Jay was, he didn't need him to be nervous. That might affect his score. "Relax Jay. Today we are here just to show you the guns. Before the test I'll make you an expert shot. You'll probably be sick of all the practice by then."

Jay nodded and began to shoot his next five. When he was done he put the gun down on the table and turned to Dave. "Be careful," Dave said. "The gun still has another six rounds in it."

"It must be an older gun," Jay commented.

Dave said, "The FBI version has a few more rounds in the clip."

Jay nodded and said, "I should have thought of that."

"Push the button to bring your target up so we can see how you did," Dave said next.

Jay turned, and pushed the button bringing his target up to the front. Dave reached over and pulled it from the clip. He spent a minute or so looking it over before handing it to Jay. "How did I do?" Jay asked.

"Not bad," Dave answered.

Jay looked over the target. All of the body shots hit the target. He got two in the nine ring, one in the seven ring, one in the six ring and one in the five ring. The headshots only had four hits. One in the nine ring, two in the eight ring, and one in the six ring. "It looks like I had one miss on the head shot," Jay said as he handed the target back to Dave.

"Don't sweat it Jay. That's not bad for a weekend shooter."

"How is it for FBI standards?" Jay asked.

Dave always believed it's important to tell it like it is, but he wanted to go easy on Jay on his first day. "We do have some work to do, but that's okay. That's what we're here for."

"Okay," was all Jay said as Dave clipped up another target.

Dave then handed Jay the box of ammunition and said "Speaking of practice, how about burning up this box while I shoot some over here." Jay nodded as Dave turned to walk to his lane.

Ivan looked at his watch as he felt his stomach growl. It had been a long morning filling out all of the release forms, and then sitting through the typical orientation and safety classes before he would be allowed to begin. It's almost 11:30 now and time for lunch. Earlier Ivan noticed a maintenance schedule on Janice's desk, and he was thinking he might have to buy her lunch before he could see it. He wanted to know exactly what was to be done to the Senator's plane. It was critical to what he had planned.

When 11:30 finally arrived everyone got up and headed for the door. Ivan got up a little slower to give the others a chance to get ahead of him. He walked past Janice's desk but didn't see her. The maintenance schedule was there on the desk. He looked around the room again but didn't see anyone watching him. He picked up the schedule and noticed it was a short list. The Senator's plane was next in line. The inspection was to be the typical filter changes and inspections. They are scheduled to visually inspect the turbine blades

243

only. Unless they found something, they would not be replacing any blades at this time. This is perfect Ivan thought. I can strike tonight, and be out of the country by early tomorrow morning. Ivan kept reading the schedule, and read the note at the bottom of the schedule. Apparently the Senator will need his plane again tomorrow afternoon. This is even better he thought. They will be in a hurry to accommodate the Senator and will never notice his handiwork tonight.

Suddenly the door opened behind Ivan. He slowly put down the clipboard so as not to give the appearance he was doing anything wrong. When he turned around Janice was heading toward him with a puzzled look on her face.

Ivan watched her walking toward him and he smiled. "So where does someone get a bite to eat around here?" he asked.

Janice didn't like anyone touching things on her desk, but Ivan seemed so calm about it, which helped to put her at ease. Ivan spoke as she picked up the clipboard, "I hope it was okay for me to look at the schedule. It was mentioned in class this morning and I wanted to get a look at the real thing. I'm hungry. Do you want to go to lunch?"

Janice put down the clipboard. "Just don't let anyone see you looking at that yet. Ever since Senator Stone started keeping his plane here some people have been getting sensitive about anything to do with the security of his plane."

"Oh," Ivan said. "That never occurred to me, but now that you mention it I can see their point. I don't want to cause any trouble, or worse yet, get you into trouble."

Janice appreciated the concern for her. "It's okay," she said. "You asked about lunch. There's a diner down the road that's not too bad. How about we go there?"

"Sounds good to me," Ivan answered.

John nudged Charlie, who was dozing off. "Look at this," John said. "Ivan's got himself a girlfriend."

"He sure knows how to operate," answered Charlie.

John reached for the key to start his car. "I wouldn't bother to follow him," Charlie said. "My guess is he's on his way to lunch and will be back in about an hour."

"Well, what about you?" John said. "Are you hungry?"

"Not really," answered Charlie. "I'm still full from breakfast."

"Me too, but I do need to walk around a little. I need a break from sitting in this car all morning."

John and Charlie got out of the car and casually headed for a grassy area. It was under a tree near a taxi runway for planes to get from the hangar to the main runway. "What do you think he wants?" asked John as he pointed to the right.

Charlie looked over and saw a security guard obviously hurrying up to meet them under the tree. "What story should we give him?" John asked next.

Charlie answered, "I don't want him to know I'm from the CIA. I suggest we tell him we're part of a routine security watch waiting for the Senator's plane to come back. Let's give him some story about not wanting to upset the Senator so we are hanging back and trying to stay out of sight. Just have your identification ready so I don't have to reach for mine."

"Sounds like a plan," answered John.

John and Charlie got to the tree first, and turned to greet the security guard who was a couple of seconds behind them. "I'm sorry gentlemen, this is a restricted area," the unarmed security guard said nervously.

John stepped forward slightly in front of Charlie before speaking. "It's okay. We're from the FBI on a routine security watch for the Senator."

John then pulled out his identification. The security guard looked it over and breathed a sigh of relief. "I have to tell you," said the security guard, "we were watching you guys in the car for about two hours now and wondering what was going on."

The security guard then unclipped his walkie-talkie from his belt and spoke, "All clear. They're from the FBI watching for the Senator's plane to return."

John waved to get his attention. When the guard looked over John says, "Tell him it's just routine. We don't want to upset the Senator."

The guard nodded his head and repeated what John told him to say. He then re-clipped his walkie-talkie back to his belt.

"Hey do us a favor," John said next. "The only reason we're here is to do a routine review of the area. The Senator doesn't know about us and we really don't need to upset him. We are counting on you guys to keep things quiet. If we draw a lot of attention the Senator will get upset, which will get us in trouble with our bosses."

"Is anything wrong?" asked the guard.

"No," answered John. "We do this type of thing before every election, just in case. Of course we never find anything. We just don't need the six o'clock news here, that's all."

"I understand," answered the guard. "When I get back I will speak to my boss. I know he doesn't want the news cameras either."

"We appreciate it," answered Charlie. They all shook hands and the guard walked back.

They watched the guard walk away, and when it looked like he was out of hearing range Charlie turned to John and said, "That's all we need."

John answered, "You realize when we come back tomorrow he will stop believing our claims that this is just routine, especially if the Senator doesn't fly out again."

"I know," Charlie said. "We are going to have to come up with another idea tomorrow."

After a long silence Charlie looked at his watch and said, "What time does McWilliams start?"

"He said his shift starts at 4:00, but we are supposed to meet him at 3:30 around the corner."

"I hope he can keep a secret. If Ivan finds out we are here, we will lose him for sure."

John just shrugged his shoulders and said, "All we can do is our best."

"Although I appreciate the chance to be out in the fresh air," John said, "I think maybe we should start heading back to the car now. Ivan should be back soon."

John got up from the bench he was sitting at and looked over toward the entrance to the parking lot. John took two steps and said, "Oh great. Look who's coming, and we don't have anywhere to hide."

Charlie looked over and saw Janice and Ivan driving right toward them. Charlie sat back down on the bench and said, "Just lean against the tree and don't face them. Make it look like we're waiting for the Senator's plane. Ivan should expect to see some security around."

"Who are those guys?" Ivan asked.

Janice answered, "My guess is they are some of the Senator's body guards. His plane is expected back soon. These guys always show up ahead of time and hang around for a while."

"I forgot about that," Ivan said. Janice didn't say anything but she's starting to wonder about Mr. Smithe. How could he forget about the Senator's plane after they talked about it several times, and the last time was right before lunch?

Ivan drove past Charlie and John, trying to watch them without Janice noticing. He could tell his last statement aroused some suspicion in her, and he wasn't sure how to undo the damage. He knew he couldn't turn around to look at them again and had to pretend he didn't care. He must strike tonight. It's obvious he couldn't wait any longer.

Charlie watched out of the corner of his eye as Ivan got out of the car. "Well?" asked John. "What do you think?"

"I'm not sure," answered Charlie. "He didn't even look at us when he got out of the car."

"Just playing it cool," John said. "I think we should wait here another fifteen minutes or so just to make it look good."

Charlie stretched out on the bench to lie down. "I could really use a nap," he said.

John just laughed and said, "You go ahead. I'll take the first watch."

Ivan took another look around before heading back into class. If they are here because of me I guess they would be doing a better job of hiding, he thought. Still, he wished he had his binoculars so he could see their faces. "Mr. Smithe, are you coming?" It was Eric, calling Ivan back to class. Ivan turned around and headed back without saying a word.

Chapter 18

"Stop squirming," John said.

"I can't help it," answered Ryan. "You're tickling me. Besides, is this wire really necessary? Why can't I just call you or something?"

John looked up at Charlie, who just rolled his eyes and looked away. "You need the wire because we want to be sure we can get to you if you need us."

"Do you think there will be trouble?" Ryan asked next.

"I don't think so," John answered, "I like to error on the side of safety, that's all."

"There, you can put your shirt back on before we test it," John said.

While Ryan put his shirt on John could tell he was deep in thought. John turned on the receiver and stepped out of the car and walked across the parking lot. Ryan put the earphone in his ear and said, "Can you hear me?"

"Loud and clear," answered John.

John then walked back to the car and got in the front drivers side to drive back to the airport. Charlie was still sitting on the passenger's side, but stayed turned around to face Ryan.

"Remember," Charlie said to Ryan, "we all would rather have ten false alarms tonight than see you take any unnecessary chances."

John jumped in and said, "That's right. I know the agents who will be with you tonight and they are good guys. The plan is for them to stay out of sight so don't be surprised if you don't even see them if things stay quiet all night."

"I understand," answered Ryan. "I promise no hero stuff."

"There is one more thing," John said next. John spoke as he handed back a small black box with a white button in the center. It was the size of a pager. John couldn't turn around because he was still driving. "As another back up just push the button. It will leave a message on my phone. Just remember it's more important to call in your backup before you need them."

"I got it," Ryan answered in a half sarcastic tone.

John turned into the parking lot of the airport and pulled into a spot next to Ryan's car. Ryan got out of the car and John got out with him. Charlie stayed in the car. John spoke first. "Listen Ryan, we really appreciate your help here."

"Yea, yea I know. Just tell me. How do I ever get to be an FBI agent?"

John stared for a moment, but finally could not hold back a smile. "I've been working on that. You'll need to go to college first, but you just never know who is ready to help you. Get good grades and I think you will be accepted in the academy. When this is over we can discuss the details."

Ryan face lit up with an ear-to-ear smile. He now knew a door was finally opening up that could lead him to his dream. "I won't let you down," was all he could say.

"I already know that," answered John.

Ryan turned to walk in the airplane hangar to clock in. "One more thing," John yelled out. "Our guys will get here about 6:00. Turn on your wire then and wait for them to call you. Remember, don't take any unnecessary chances!" Ryan just waved back as he headed into the building.

John got back in the car and looked over at Charlie before speaking. "I know I shouldn't be this worried, but I just have a funny feeling," John said.

"I've heard about your funny feelings," answered Charlie, "but I think we have him covered."

John started his car and backed out of the parking spot. "Since Ivan's first day of school ended about an hour ago let's call it a day too."

"Sounds good to me," answered Charlie. "Can you drop me off by my car?"

Ivan walked into his apartment and tossed the keys on the counter. He looked at the clock over the stove and noted it was 4:00. If he was to get back up by midnight he should try and get some sleep first. His clothes were already packed for his departure tomorrow. He just needed to make one more phone call.

Jim Gallagor's private phone began to ring. He picked up right away. "Jim this is Ivan. I've decided tonight will be the night, but I will need one more thing. I'm concerned I might have someone watching me, so I will need another car waiting for me around the block before midnight. Can you arrange it?"

Jim paused for a moment to absorb the news. "Sure, I can have Mike meet you."

"That would be fine, except you need to make it clear Mike will have to take a taxi home. I can drop him off somewhere, but he can't come. And no questions either."

"I understand," Jim said. "But you know Mike. This will not be easy for him."

"I know. That's why it has to come from you. I don't even want to be asked," Ivan said.

Ivan's tone to Jim was stern, but he was really mad at himself. Ivan had grown to like and trust Mike, and was annoyed at himself for letting that influence his judgment. This is the mission, Ivan thought, and he could not allow himself to go soft. "I will talk to Mike," Jim said. "You take care and let me know where you are as soon as you can."

"I will be in touch," Ivan said as he hung up the phone.

Ivan went into his bedroom and pulled out an air rifle. He had bought it a couple of days ago and had to unwrap it. Reading the instructions, he noted that it took ten pumps to achieve its maximum advertised velocity. He set up an empty coffee can at the furthest distance he could in his apartment. Pumping it up five times per shot, it only took him three shots to zero in the sights. He then opened up his bedroom window, which faced to the rear of his building. His plan was to carefully and quietly shoot out two lights in the courtyard area behind his building.

Ivan set himself up in the middle of the room about five feet from the open window. This way most of the sound from the already quiet air gun would stay in the room. Pumping up the rifle to eleven pumps, Ivan loaded a copper coated steel BB instead of a lead pellet. He was counting on better penetration with the BB. Aiming for the first lamp, Ivan hit it in the aluminum housing above the glass cover. This would break the bulb inside without shattering the glass cover and attracting attention. He waited a couple of minutes to make sure nobody heard the first shot. Confident the coast was clear he shot out the second light in the same way. Smiling as he closed his window, it was now time to get some sleep.

Ivan closed the specially made blinds he had on his bedroom windows. They made the room dark even during the brightest part of the day. He got undressed, set his alarm and crawled into bed. From his training in the Soviet Union he was able to get to sleep in a few minutes. Tonight would be an important night and he would need some rest.

Jay pulled Dave's car into his spot. His first day was nearly over. As he put the car in park and shut off the key Dave asked, "How about you and your wife meet me for dinner tonight?"

"Dinner?" Jay asked in a surprised tone. "Sure, I think my wife would appreciate that, but I'll have to call her."

Dave said. "It will give your wife a chance to get used to the idea of your new job. I'm sure she has questions, and my wife has a lot of experience in answering them."

"Dave I really appreciate the offer."

"Are you familiar with the Italian restaurant Luigi's in the downtown section?" Dave asked.

Jay nodded his head yes.

"My wife and I will be there around 7:30, just give me a call and let me know if you can make it."

"Okay," answered Jay as he got out of the car. Jay held the car door open as Dave got out of his side and walked around the car. "Dave I just want to thank you for all of the personal attention you're giving me. I just want to let you know how much I appreciate it."

Dave smiled and said, "You're welcome Jay, but believe me when I say you'll be worth it. You'll see."

The two men shook hands. Jay then turned to walk to his car. It had been an interesting first day. He knew he had a lot to learn and was humbled by the fact that Dave was helping him so much. Jay unlocked his car and sat inside. He watched Dave drive around and out of the parking lot before starting his car. He suddenly realized he left his duffle bag with his workout clothes in Dave's trunk. Hopefully Rebecca will be able to go tonight and he can get them then.

John walked into his kitchen and went into the refrigerator for a cold drink. He looked at his wife Tara. She said, "You look tired. How was your day today?"

"It was okay. We spent the day in the car at a stake out."

"You've done that before," Tara answered. "There must be more to the story than that."

John looked at her for a few seconds before answering. "You are way too good at reading me. Do you remember that kid I told you about that drove us around on Friday?" Tara shook her head yes without saying anything. "We now have him wired and patrolling the Senator's plane. I'm just a little concerned, that's all."

Tara loved her husband, and although she was just as concerned about him as he was for McWilliams, she also knew he didn't need to also worry about her. It was explained to her a long time ago by Dave's wife that her husband's mind must be clear for him to stay safest. She said, "I think I understand. Dinner will be ready in about fifteen minutes. Afterwards you can go on upstairs and go right to sleep. I'll keep the kids quiet. This way if you get a call tonight you'll have had some rest."

John smiled and walked over to kiss his wife. "As usual you're taking care of me. My cell will go off if I'm needed."

John walked out of the kitchen to go see what his kids were doing. He had a little time before dinner to spend with them.

Jay looked at his watch. Rebecca should be home by now. He wanted to catch her before she started dinner. He took out his cell phone and dialed his home number. "Hello Rebecca?"

"Hi Jay, how was your first day?" Rebecca asked.

"It was good. Hey, did you start dinner yet?"

"Not yet," she said sarcastically. "I wanted to get changed first."

"Forget dinner and don't get changed. My new boss and his wife invited us out for dinner tonight. Do you want to go?"

Rebecca hesitated for a second before answering. "It's a little short notice, but I guess so. Whatever you want to do."

"I think we should go," Jay said. "I'll be home in about twenty minutes, but we don't have to be at the restaurant until 7:30. I will fill you in on my day when I get home."

"Okay, I'll see you then," Rebecca said as she hung up the phone.

Ryan McWilliams stood and watched as the maintenance crew packed up their tool for the evening. "Working a little late," Ryan said to one of the mechanics.

"Yea, the Senator wants his plane ready for tomorrow afternoon, so we're in a hurry."

"It looks like you still have a ways to go," Ryan answered.

The mechanic nodded as he turned to look at the engine he had apart. "I've completed my inspections. All I have to do tomorrow morning is put the cover back on and go through a systems check. The hardest part is already done."

"If you say so," Ryan answered.

The last thing the mechanic did was fold up his ladder and lay it down under the plane. "Do me a favor and make sure nobody borrows my ladder tonight. I don't need to waste time looking for it tomorrow morning."

"I'll do what I can," Ryan said.

The mechanic thanked him, and left after locking up his toolbox.

Jay and Rebecca pulled into the restaurant parking lot and Jay spotted Dave's car. "I hope we're not late," Jay said.

Rebecca looked at her watch. "No, I've got 7:25, so by the time we get inside we should be right on-time."

"Let's hurry inside anyway," Jay said.

Jay walked in first and walked up to the greeter. "We are here to meet Dave Gillian and his wife," Jay said.

The greeter just nodded, grabbed two menus and said, "Follow me."

Jay turned to Rebecca and motioned for her to follow. When they turned the first corner Dave spotted Jay about the same time Jay saw them. Jay saw Dave motion to his wife who immediately got up with Dave. Dave spoke first, "Hi Jay and Rebecca. Thanks for coming. This is my wife Jamie."

Jamie smiled and shook Jay's hand first, then quickly went over to Rebecca who was standing behind Jay. "Hi Rebecca, I'm Jamie. It's nice to meet you. What do you think of all this?"

Rebecca rolled her eyes and said, "There have been a lot of changes."

"I know what you mean. We wives like to stick together. Just wait until you meet some of the others."

They all sat down. Jay could see Dave's plan. Getting Rebecca plugged in with some of the other wives will be very helpful for those long days that are sure to come.

Ivan woke up around 11:30 and looked at his clock. The alarm was set for midnight, but his adrenaline levels were beginning to rise and he couldn't sleep any more. He got up, showered, and got dressed. Looking in the refrigerator, Ivan noted how he wished he hadn't emptied it in anticipation of his leaving. Looking at his watch, Ivan decided to pack his bags and leave them all at the door except for one. If something happened, and he couldn't come back here, he would at least have one bag with some essential items in it for his long trip home.

Ivan turned all of the lights out except for one in the kitchen. He looked out a front window, which faced the main parking on the street. He studied all of the cars parked within sight, but didn't see any that were new to him. Unfortunately he couldn't see down the block without going outside.

He looked out the back next, which was pitch dark as expected. Ivan opened up the sliding door onto his patio and stepped outside. He was dressed in black overalls, with black gloves and hat. He closed the sliding door but forgot that he could not lock it. He took inventory of his things to make sure he had everything before opening the sliding door back up. Carefully leaning a wooden pole behind the sliding door, Ivan set it to fall down in the track as he closed the door again. When he tried to open this door this time, it would only open about two inches before the pole stopped it. It was too dark to see why it opened that far, but it had to be good enough.

Ivan grabbed his bag but hesitated when he heard a rustling noise in the bushes on his right. His eyes were still adjusting to the darkness but some things were getting in focus. Suddenly from the left someone said, "Hold it," and forcefully grabbed his arm. On his right someone else appeared. Ivan caught the flash of a knife.

Ivan watched one of the neighbor kids turn into a real troublemaker the past several months and guessed it was his turn. The first man released his grip while the second waved the knife in Ivan's face. I really don't have time for this crap, Ivan thought.

Suddenly without warning Ivan released his bag and curled both hands into a fist, palms up. In a split second one fist hit the knife hand on the back of his hand, and the other fist hit his wrist just below his palm. This collapsed the mugger's hand at the wrist and sent the knife flying into the bushes. Ivan then transferred his weight to his left and roundhouse kicked the other kid, who was unarmed, in the chest. That sent him flying back. At the same time he was kicking that kid Ivan grabbed the wrist of the knife wielding kid, which was numb from Ivan's first strike, and pulled the kid toward him while punching him on his right cheek. Ivan then spun around and flipped him over his back. The kid hit the concrete with a thud. Ivan then grabbed the foot of the kicked kid and dragged them together. Both kids were laying face down groaning slightly as Ivan sat on both of them. He grabbed them by the hair, picked up their heads and said, "If I ever see you two around again I will kill you, and remember I will be looking for you. Now go home." Ivan got up, grabbed his bag and was gone before either of them could look up.

The adrenaline was now flowing through Ivan's veins. It took everything he had to keep from killing those kids. The only reason he didn't was because he didn't need the attention from the police. "I hope the rest of my night goes better than this," he mumbled to himself.

Ivan cut through a vacant field behind his apartment complex and down an alley. At the end of the alley he turned right on a side street. He could see Mike parked on the left waiting for him. Mike was out of the car and leaning on the driver's side front fender. Mike looked up and nodded as soon as Ivan stepped out of the shadows. As Ivan got closer he could see Mike's expression change. "Are you okay?" Mike asked Ivan.

"Yea, I'm okay. Would you believe my stupid neighbor's kid and his friend tried to rob me?"

Mike paused before answering, "You didn't kill them did you?"

Ivan looked up at Mike and said, "Does it look like I did?"

"Well, yes it does. You look pissed," Mike replied.

"I am pissed," Ivan answered, "but no, I didn't kill them. I just smacked him and his buddy around a little bit. You know I don't need the added heat that would generate. I just hope they get up and out of there. It happened right behind my apartment. Now, get in. You can drive until we get around the corner. I want you to drive past the front of my apartment so I can see if anyone is watching me."

"Okay," was all Mike said as they got in the car.

Mike started the car and drove off. He went around the block and as he drove past the apartment Mike turned on his high beams. If there was anybody there the high beam lights would make them easier to see in their car as well as blind them so they couldn't see Mike or Ivan as they drove by. Ivan slouched down in his seat anyway. "Is that who you're looking for?" Mike said as he pointed to two men in a gray sedan. Ivan just nodded. He still had that look in his eyes that he gets when things get serious.

They drove a few more blocks before Ivan said, "Pull over at the diner on your right up ahead. I will let you out and you can call a cab from there."

Mike just nodded and did as instructed. Mike climbed out and Ivan slid over behind the wheel. Before closing the door Mike said, "Good luck. I'm going to miss you."

Ivan looked at Mike and tried to force a smile. "I'm sure we will meet again someday my friend."

Mike nodded and shut the car door. He stood outside as Ivan drove off.

When Ivan was out of sight Mike reached into his pocket and pulled out his cell phone. He hit the speed dial button to call Jim. "Jim, this is Mike. Wherever he's going, he's on his way. It's been a while since I've seen him this serious."

"Not to worry Mike. Just call yourself a cab as planned and go home. Get some sleep and I will see you tomorrow." Mike hung up the phone and walked into the diner to get himself a cup of coffee while he waited for the cab.

Ivan glanced at the clock in the car as he drove. It was 12:45 AM. In a couple of minutes he should arrive at the airport. Ivan made several loops to see if he was being followed. Everything seemed clear.

Parking on the side of the road across from the airport fence, Ivan pulled the car about ten feet off the road between some bushes. Unless someone driving by looked directly in between the bushes they would not notice his car.

Grabbing his bag before he left, Ivan waited for a long break in the traffic before running across the street. Coming up to the fence, Ivan pulled out a pair of heavy-duty wire cutters and cut a small hole in the fence just big enough to crawl through. Along the inside of the fence was a drainage ditch. This was nothing more than a low spot to channel excessive water away from the runway. There was no water for most of the year and had grass growing in it. It was just low enough for Ivan to duck down into if anybody drove by. Ivan was able to follow it right up to the backside of the airport hangar.

When he arrived at the hangar, Ivan forced open a window and crawled inside. There was one light on in the hangar at the other end. The plane cast a shadow that made Ivan hard to see. Unfortunately, the part of the plane he planned to work on was right under the light.

Ivan opened his bag and pulled out a mini torch and a lighter. The torch had a warning label cautioning about an advertised flame temperature of 2500 degrees F. Ivan's plan was to heat up a couple of the blades in the hot section of the plane's turbine engine. This would cause tiny stress cracks that would not be visible to the eye, but as the engine ran, these cracks would slowly grow until the blades break off. This should cause an engine failure sometime in flight. It is also common knowledge the FAA will take years to figure it out, and by that time Jim Gallagor should be the new Senator.

Ivan cautiously walked around to the front of the plane. He debated turning out the light, but if someone saw it go out Ivan could have company in a couple of minutes. Walking out from the shadows Ivan spotted the ladder. As quietly as he could, Ivan picked up the ladder and set it up so he could reach the engine. Just as he got to the top of the ladder he heard a noise outside. Quickly climbing down Ivan heard the sound of a door opening echoing through the hangar. No time to take down the ladder, he thought as he ran behind the plane.

Ivan watched from behind the plane as a guard walked into the hangar. Although Ivan had already shut off his torch, it was still hot and smoking slightly. The guard continued to walk through the hangar seemingly unaware that anything was wrong. It was a large hangar, and Ivan was trying to calculate how far away the guard was and how long it would take him to get to the guard if he had too.

The guard went around to the other side of the hangar and checked the door on the other side. On his way back he stopped suddenly. Ivan was crouched behind one of the landing gear wheels. The guard cautiously walked over to the ladder. That damned ladder, Ivan thought. The guard reached for his flashlight as he moved closer to where Ivan was hiding.

Carefully and quietly Ivan pulled out a knife he carried in a sheath under his jacket. He watched, as the guard got closer, hoping he would turn away. The guard seemed to be focusing his efforts on the back of the hangar and not where Ivan was hiding. This was a good thing, Ivan thought. From where Ivan was hiding, he could watch the light from the guards' flashlight sweeping across the back of the hangar.

Suddenly the guard's flashlight stopped sweeping and stayed fixed. Oh great, Ivan thought, he spotted my bag over by the window. "Hey guys, I think you might want to get over here. I think I found something."

Who's he talking too? Ivan wondered. Suddenly it occurred to him the guard must be wired. It was time for Ivan to get out of here. As the guard walked around the plane past him Ivan knew he had to act.

Ivan waited until the guard took his third step past him before lunging toward the guard. Wrapping his left arm around the guard's neck and pulling back to arch the guard's back, Ivan plunged his knife in just above the guard's collar bone down to his heart. With a twist of his knife Ivan cut his heart in two. The guard was dead before he hit the ground.

As he fell Ivan grabbed his shirt which ripped it open. So he was wired, Ivan thought as he bent over to get a closer look. Ivan also noticed he pulled out one of the wires as the guard fell. Ivan looked up at the plane behind him and decided there was no time to continue. Whoever was listening in on the other end will be here in a few minutes.

Ivan grabbed his things and climbed back through the window. He took the time to carefully close it before leaving.

Meanwhile inside the car parked on the other side of the parking lot a frantic agent was starting the car and jamming it into drive. The second agent said. "I just heard a grunt, and then static. Our guy's wire doesn't seem to be working any more. I think he's in trouble."

"I'm moving as fast as I can," answered the first agent. "And don't forget to call John Hunt. He was very insistent that we call him at the first sign of trouble."

Chapter 19

"John, John wake up." John rolled over with a grunt. His wife Tara was standing over him holding his cell phone. "You have a phone call." John rubbed his eyes and looked at the clock. The digital clock said 2:18, but John couldn't remember exactly how many minutes fast his wife had set it. He looked up at his wife, but all he could see was her silhouette made by the hallway light behind her. John took the phone and Tara walked out of the room, but left the door open.

"John, this is Dave. I got a call from our guys watching the airport. I think you need to get down there."

"What happened Dave? Why didn't they call me direct?"

"I'm sorry John. I don't have all of the details, but McWilliams didn't make it."

John hesitated for a moment. Suddenly he was wide-awake. "You mean he's dead?" John asked. "What happened?"

"I don't have all the details John. Just get dressed and get down there."

As John hung up the phone he heard his wife Tara start walking down the hall toward the room at the other end. He knew she was standing in the hallway listening. Using the light coming in from the hallway, John looked at his phone. Ryan was supposed to call me if he needed me. John punched a wall in disgust.

Tara was in the room down the hall sitting in a chair. She watched her husband walk toward her. She noticed his eyes were red and there was a single tear running down his left cheek. "I'm sorry," she said.

John said nothing and just stood there, so Tara continued, "Why don't you take a quick shower, and I'll have your clothes ironed and on the bed when you get out. Do you want me to fix you something to eat?"

"I'm not hungry," John answered as he turned and headed for the bathroom.

A car pulled in behind the sedan parked in front of Ivan's apartment. The two men in the first sedan got out and greeted the second car, which also contained two men. They spoke briefly before the second two men went around to the back of the apartment. The first two men went up to the front door and knocked. They waited for only a moment or two before kicking the door in. One of the men reached around for a light switch. Both men had their guns drawn. Just then a police car with its lights flashing pulled up. The two agents stepped over the bags Ivan had packed and went through the apartment room by room. When they got to the back they opened up the back door to let their partners in. Only one came in. The other agent decided to stay out to look around for a few more minutes. One of them pulled out a cell phone and dialed.

Ivan was about halfway to the commercial airport when he pulled into a rest stop. He decided it would be too risky to go back to his apartment. At this early hour the rest stop was almost empty. He grabbed his bag from the back seat and went into the bathroom. Checking all the stalls for other people he was relieved to see the bathroom was empty. Ivan walked back to the door and locked it.

Going to the sink with the best mirror, Ivan searched his bag. "I wish I had my other bags," he mumbled to himself. He took out a bottle of hair coloring, and he had a fake moustache. If he had his other bags, he could have added much more. He combed in the hair coloring, which added gray streaks. Using half the bottle, he now was mostly gray instead of his normal brown with only a few gray streaks.

Next he glued on the moustache, and then applied some more gray to it. Finally he dug out a pair of thick-rimmed glasses. Looking himself over in the mirror, he wished he could change his nose and add some more wrinkles. This will have to be enough, he thought. The last thing he did was change his shirt. He had a western style shirt. His plan was to try and pass himself off as someone from Texas.

When John pulled into the airport parking lot he could see the lights flashing from two police cars and one ambulance. He parked his car on the grass, showed his badge and walked straight in. As he walked over to the body, his eyes started to fill up again. They had a sheet over McWilliams's body, but his legs and arms were not covered. He walked over, knelt down, and pulled the sheet back. The color was already out of his face. John also looked at the entrance wound. He knew exactly what happened.

As John stood up again, without thinking he picked up the flashlight lying next to the body. He glanced toward the back of the hangar and noticed the lights outside through the window. "It looks like he came in through a window in the back," one of the officers's said to John.

John turned to the officer but said nothing. Without thinking, John threw the flashlight across the hangar. It smashed through the window startling everyone outside. The officer stood there in shock for a second, and then answered a call on his walkie-talkie. The person at the other end was screaming at the officer who became visibly upset.

John turned to walk away when the officer said, "Excuse me, but my captain wants to talk to you."

When John ignored him the officer reached to grab John's arm. It was obvious to everyone standing around that the captain wanted to chew John out about the flashlight through the window. Before the officer could grab John's arm Charlie stepped in between them. John kept walking either unaware or not caring. Charlie said to the officer, "Let me handle this. He was close to the kid, and quite honestly so was I."

"That's no excuse to be a hothead," answered the officer.

"Maybe not, but let me talk to him," Charlie replied. The officer just nodded and walked away.

Charlie turned toward John, who was leaving the hangar. Charlie ran after him. John was so angry Charlie was afraid he might shoot the captain if he didn't get there first.

By the time Charlie stepped out of the hangar, John was about to get into his car. Charlie started running after him, and tried the passengers' side door just as John started the car. It was locked so Charlie banged on the window. John looked out the window and hit the button to unlock the car. Charlie jumped in the car but said nothing.

Several minutes went by before John spoke. "It's all my fault. I should have never asked the kid to do this. What was I thinking?"

"I'm the one at fault," Charlie answered. "I'm the one who should have known if he was in danger. I should have been able to predict Ivan's behavior. The CIA has been dealing with his type for years."

John looked at Charlie. Charlie could see the pain in his face, and was a little worried about him. This is the kind of thing that could impair John's judgment and get him killed.

"We need to get that bastard," John said next.

Charlie answered, "Yes we do, but you need to clear your head first. You cannot afford to get yourself killed too."

"How are we going to get him?" John asked next, seeming to ignore Charlie's last comment. "He could be on any flight under a dozen different aliases."

Charlie thought for a moment before answering. "What we need is a way to search all of the outgoing flights. There must be something that would make him stand out. Maybe his ticket will be bought last minute. Maybe he will pay cash. There has to be something. Unfortunately, I don't know of a way to search all of the airline bookings that fast."

John looked up at Charlie and said, "I think I know a way."

John pulled out his cell phone and called Dave. "Hello Dave, this is John."

"Where are you?" Dave asked.

"I'm at the airport next to the senator's plane. I need you to help me. Charlie and I are trying to find a way to locate Ivan. We are guessing he must be flying out on a commercial flight back to Russia."

"We are covering all the flights with connections to Russia now," interrupted Dave.

"But what if he takes a flight somewhere else first? He could buy another ticket from anywhere. What we need is for someone to go through all of the flights and look for a something unusual, maybe someone buying his tickets in person without reservations. He may even be paying cash."

"He would probably not have any luggage either," interrupted Dave again.

"What did you say?" John asked.

Dave answered, "We went to his apartment tonight. He wasn't there but he had his bags packed at the door. It looked like he was coming back to get them. We have the place staked out now, but I doubt he will show. The point is he is leaving without his luggage."

"That's another data point for a computer search," John said.

"I think I get your point. Let me call our computer guy you rescued last week. If what he says is true, he should be able to hack into the flight records faster than we can go through all the right channels."

Charlie, who also had his ear to the phone, nodded his head in agreement. He was also glad to see John thinking clearly. Since he didn't think of it himself, Charlie was starting to wonder if he was not thinking straight!

"I will take care of it from here John." Dave said.

"Meanwhile, I will get to the commercial airport as soon as I can, and just so you know, I've got Charlie with me, so we will need two tickets."

"I didn't say I was going to send you," Dave interrupted. "I plan to let the local FBI handle it wherever he is heading."

"I'm going," John snapped back, "even if I have to pay for my own ticket!"

Dave knew it was pointless to argue. It was the price he had to pay for collecting all of the mavericks. Besides, under the circumstances there would be no way to stop him. "Okay John, I will call you when I get more information," Dave said.

Ivan got to the airport and parked the rental car in the long-term parking lot. It would be several weeks before they would find the car, and he would be long gone. Ivan walked up to the outgoing monitors and reviewed his choices. Instead of flying east, I think I will go west. There will be less people looking that way, he thought. Ivan then noticed a flight headed toward Portland, Oregon. From there he could go either to Alaska or straight to Russia.

Ivan walked up to the ticket counter and purchased a ticket to Portland. He used his John Smithe identification and credit card. "Do you have any bags to check?" The attendant behind the counter asked.

Ivan answered in his best southern drawl. "No ma'm. I just have one carry on. My boss told me not to get a round trip ticket. He wasn't sure yet if I could come back tomorrow or the next day."

"Oh I see," she said. Ivan got a nervous twinge. He wasn't sure if she believed his story or not.

Boarding was not for another forty minutes, so Ivan decided to see if he could get another change of clothing. There were a couple of stores in the airport, and another shirt and pants would be a good idea. Ivan found his size quickly, but really had no time to try anything on. Passing a second store something caught his eye. Inside in the back were cowboy hats, and on one side were canes. Ivan slowed down as he headed into the store, faking a slight limp. He purchased a cane and cowboy hat. Part of his plan was to tilt his hat to hide his face if necessary.

Brian Chestburg jumped when his phone rang. Although he was in a sound sleep, he was a little more jumpy since his attempted kidnapping. A quick look at his alarm clock told him it was 3:10 AM. He took a quick glance out of the window before answering the phone. The van he was used to seeing was still there. Brian answered his phone with a groggy "Hello."

"Turn on the cell phone I gave you," was all the voice on the other end said.

Brian then heard the person at the other end hang up. Brian turned on the light in his room, and walked over to his desk where he had the cell phone plugged in charging. Dave had given him a special phone he said used a scrambled signal to prevent interception. Quite honestly, Brian didn't take it too seriously.

About ten seconds after Brian turned it on it rang. Brian answered it in the first ring. "Brian, this is Dave Gillian. I'm sorry to disturb you but we need your help."

Brian got excited. He knew that his chance would come to prove himself, but he didn't think it would be so soon. "Of course Dave, what do you need?"

Dave continued, "Remember Brian, what I tell you is classified information, and the information you provide to us will be the same."

"I understand. Remember, we went through that already." Brian was still not fully awake, and was therefore a little blunter than he normally would be.

Dave continued, "First I need to give you the bad news. Do you remember the young man Ryan McWilliams who helped out that Friday?"

"We've said hello at work and made some small talk. He seems like a good guy."

"I'm sorry to say he was killed tonight. We think it was one of Gallagor's men, possibly the Russian Ivan Spelluchuvik. We also think he might be trying to flee the country. Our problem is we don't know what name he will be using, and what route he will be taking. We are guessing that eventually he will be going back to Russia. How many connecting flights he will make is anybody's guess. That's where you come in. We need you to start searching the airlines computer systems and find possible profile matches."

"That's going to be like finding a needle in a hay stack," Brian said.

Dave answered, "I know. We think he will be flying without any reservations, maybe paying cash or credit card, and probably not have any checked luggage."

Brian walked over to the window and looked out again. "What about the guys outside? I still don't have the secure line set up yet." Brian asked.

Dave was silent for a moment before answering. "I will have to handle that. Let me call you back. For now, turn out any lights you might have turned on, and leave your computer off until I call you back. Make it look like you're still sleeping. You might want to make yourself some coffee."

Dave looked up Ed Jones's number and dialed the phone. Ed was in the middle of a traffic stop when his private phone rang. "Hello Ed, this is Dave Gillian. How are you?"

"I'm doing okay Dave, what can I do for you?"

"Ed we need your help. Do you remember the young man Ryan McWilliams from the night they tried to kidnap Brian?"

"Yes of course. He is a good kid."

"Well I don't know how to say this, but he was killed tonight."

"Oh no!" Ed said. "What can I do to help?"

Dave continued, "We think it was one Gallagor's men. We think he's trying to fly back to Russia, but we need Chestburg's computer skills to track down his flight. Right now there is a van parked across the street from Chestburg's house. They are also FBI, but they don't work for me. Unfortunately they are there to monitor Chestburg's computer activities so you see our problem."

"I'm not sure what I can do," Ed said next.

"What I need you to do is interrupt them for a couple of hours. They will be running a generator to power all of their electronics. I need you to cut their gas or electrical lines or something. Now here is the hard part. They will have all of the proper identification, but I need you to stop them anyway. Make something up about complaints from the neighbors or something."

"You do realize I can get written up for this," Ed said.

"Yes I know," answered Dave. "The best I can offer is that the complaint will die in our office in a couple of days, but there will still be a day or two of trouble for you."

Ed was really down about what happened to McWilliams, and gave a sigh before answering, "I really thought McWilliams had potential. I will be glad to help you catch the bastard who killed him. I will call you back when the coast is clear."

Ed got out of his car and walked back to the driver he had pulled over. "I will let you go with a warning this time, but slow down from now on," Ed said as he tossed the man's driver's license back in the car window to him and ran back to his police car.

The man looked at his wife and said, "This never happened to me before. I think I'll put an extra thank you in my prayers tonight."

Ivan watched out of the window of the plane as it taxied away from the terminal. He breathed a sigh of relief, knowing that the hardest part of getting away is over. If they haven't figured him out yet, it becomes increasingly difficult with each successive flight. After they were in the air, his plan is to get some sleep. The next day or two will be tiring as he hops from flight to flight.

Jay's phone rang and Rebecca answered. "Hello," she said half asleep.

"Rebecca? This is Brian. Can I talk to Jay?"

"Yea, sure, is everything okay?"

"Fine, I just need to ask my brother something."

Rebecca turned on a light, nudged Jay and said, "It's your brother. He wants to talk to you."

Jay rolled over with a moan. He took the phone and said, "This had better be good."

"It is Jay. Let me tell you about the phone call I just got."

Brian explained the whole story to Jay, who seemed gradually go from groggy sleep to fully alert as Brian told him the story. Finally, when Brian was finished Jay said, "I wonder what I should do. Technically I'm still in training."

"I'm not sure big brother. My guess is if I locate Ivan, someone will be going after him."

Jay was still waking up when he asked, "I wonder if I should call Dave Gillian?"

"Jay, why don't you get dressed and pack a bag. I will call you back as soon as I find out anything. This way, you can meet them at the airport," Brian said.

Jay agreed and they hung up the phone. Jay turned to Rebecca and explained the whole thing to her.

Ed Jones turned the last corner onto Brian's street. Parked on the side of the road was the van Dave told him would be there. Ed turned out his lights and pulled in behind them. He rolled down his window, and could hear the generator running. As quietly as he could he got out of his car and walked over to the van. The generator was mounted underneath the van.

Ed crawled under the van, and using a small flashlight and a pocketknife, he cut the fuel line at the base of the tank. As quickly as he could, Ed got back into his car and turned on his flashing lights. This caught the attention of the two men inside. Just as they were opening the door the generator quit. Ed was still sitting in the police car and was on the phone with Dave Gillian. "Okay Dave, you can tell Brian to get started. I will hold them up as long as I can."

The two men jumped out of the van with their identification out. They looked over at Brian's house and since the lights were off, decided not to worry yet. Ed got out of the car as the three men talked.

273

Ed said, "I saw some kid under your van, maybe looking to steal your gas. I think I chased him off before anything happened."

Both FBI agents looked under the van and noticed the small puddle of gas. Ed just stood there as the two men started to panic.

Brian's phone rang as he was looking out the window watching. "You're clear to get started," was the first thing Dave said.

"I will call you back as soon as I find something out," answered Brian.

Brian turned on his computer and dug through his DVD's while it booted up. He had accessed the airline's personal logs before trying to get the best flights for his parents. This would save him a lot of time because he already had all of the access codes. He wrote a quick filter program to search the passenger list based on the conditions Dave had given him. He wished he had a destination, or even a single airline to focus on.

After about twenty minutes, Brian had a list of about 125 names. He called Dave on the phone. "Dave this is Brian. I have about 125 names that meet all of your criteria. Would you believe there are over 200 people traveling without any checked bags tonight?"

"Tell me again. What filters did you use?" Dave asked.

Brian answered, "The three criteria were no earlier reservations, paying cash or credit card, and no checked bags. Oh wait Dave. I just thought of something, although it's a long shot."

Brian ran into the other room still on the phone with Dave. "I'm going to run a word check comparing the list with all of the Gallagor files. I think I will use last names only."

"How long will it take?" Dave asked. "I'm not sure. I guess about ten to fifteen minutes."

"Brian I have John Hunt and Charlie Gurns waiting at the airport. Let me call them and then call you back."

Brian hung up the phone and quickly called his brother. "Jay, I just found out John Hunt and Charlie Gurns are at the airport waiting for me to tell them where to go. Why don't you meet them there?"

Jay looked at his watch before answering, "I could be there in about twenty minutes. Do you think I will make it?"

"Yes, go for it. If they get on a flight I can easily get you a ticket. All you will have to do is check in at the gate. It will be prepaid and everything."

"I'm on my way," Jay said as he hung up the phone. Jay turned to Rebecca, gave her a kiss before turning toward the door.

"Just be careful," she said as she closed the door behind him.

Ivan woke up when he heard the landing gear lower. He was happy to get this first fight over with. Sitting quietly, it seemed to take forever for the plane to land, and then taxi to the terminal. Ivan got out, and started to walk away from the hub he arrived at. He had to go to the bathroom, but didn't want to stay around the same hub his plane just arrived at.

Brian walked down and got another cup of coffee as the computer ran through the cross-reference. He was careful not to turn on any lights that would attract the attention of the agents in the van. On his way up the stairs he heard the computer finish up. One name came up on his cross-reference list. It was Smithe. Brian checked over the list for a first name. John Smithe sounded familiar, he thought.

Brian wanted to review the FBI file on Gallagor, but decided to call Dave first. Dave finally answered on the third ring. "I think I have something," Brian said. "Does the name John Smithe mean anything to you?"

"Yes!" Dave said. "That was Ivan's undercover name in England."

"It says here he took a flight to Portland Oregon. He landed about ten minutes ago."

"Brian, thank you. You are everything you said you were. I can take it from here."

"Dave wait. What are you going to do? I can book Charlie and John a flight from here if you want. The next flight leaves in an hour."

Dave was puzzled and didn't know what Brian meant. "Brian I would like to say yes, but I don't want any records of you paying for the flights. I cannot have you traced to us."

Brian laughed. "Dave, payment is just a perceived electronic transfer of cash. I can make it look like anything I want, including free frequent flyer tickets or anything else."

Dave thought about it, and finally said: "Okay Brian, do it. I will try to get some of our Portland guys to pick him up, but if they miss him I will send our guys."

"Okay," Brian said. "It's all set. Just call me back if you change your mind."

Dave thanked Brian, and then flashed back to John, who was holding on the other line. Dave explained the situation to John. "Even if they get him," John said, "we will still need someone to bring him back."

"That's true," Dave said. "You and Charlie have prepaid tickets waiting for you now. Call me back right before you get in the air."

Ivan found a bathroom down near the other end of the terminal. On his way out he noticed four men in suits without luggage moving quickly toward the gate he just came from. He stood there watching them until they were out of sight. It looks like I will have to drive to

Canada before I can keep going he thought. He then shifted his hold on his bag and headed out to catch a taxi.

Jay felt his cell phone vibrate as he turned off the highway for the airport. "Jay this is Brian. I have you booked on a flight to Portland Oregon that leaves in about 45 minutes. Can you make it?"

"I'm about ten minutes from the airport," Jay answered. "I should make it no problem."

"Good, and I got you a seat across the aisle from John and Charlie. Is there any way you can take a picture of their faces when they see you?"

"Very funny," answered Jay. "I'm only doing this because of what he did to McWilliams."

"I know that. I just hope Dave doesn't get too mad at us."

"I guess we will find out," Jay said before hanging up.

Chapter 20

Jay parked his car in the short-term lot of the airport terminal. He was afraid if he used the long-term lot he would not make his flight. As Jay entered the terminal he pulled out his phone again. "Brian, this is Jay. I forgot to ask. What about my *gun*?"

"You don't have to whisper about your gun," Brian answered with a laugh. "They're already expecting you. Just show them your badge. You're going as a special guest of the airline. I already cleared it for you. Just get to your plane!" Jay hung up the phone and had to smile. Typical Brian, he thought. Got everything covered.

Jay walked up to the metal detector and headed straight to the guard standing on the side. Jay showed him his badge. The guard picked up his clipboard just as another guard came rushing over with a piece of paper in his hands. Both guards looked at Jay's badge one more time and after comparing it to the piece of paper just printed, waved Jay through.

Once past the security checkpoint, another guard waved Jay over. "We have to hurry, Mr. Chestburg, your flight is about to leave." Jay just nodded as the guard headed for one of the electric carts. The two men got in and sped off.

John turned to look at Charlie as he walked through the airplane isle way. "I think these are first class tickets," John said. "Dave never sprang for these before."

Charlie shrugged his shoulders and said, "Don't look at me. We don't fly first class either."

Charlie and John sat down on the left. John had the aisle seat. Everyone looked to be seated, but the stewardess was still standing at the door. Finally Jay walks through the door, down the aisle, and sits across from John. At first John just stares at him in shock. Finally Charlie gives John a nudge. "How did you get here?" John finally asks Jay.

Jay felt a little awkward and buckled his seatbelt without answering. John leaned over the isle and whispered, "Does Dave know you're here?"

"Not yet," answered Jay. Jay tried to think of an appropriate comeback. Finally he said, "So, do you like the tickets my brother got you?"

John turned to Charlie and rolled his eyes. "What do we do?" John whispered to Charlie.

Charlie was much more relaxed about the whole thing. "I say we bring him. We already know he can take care of himself, and this stunt tells me he's working with the right group. None of you guys listen to good advice." John struggled not to laugh.

Nothing more was said until they got into the air. John pulled out his cell phone but the plane was too high to get a signal. He turned to Charlie and said, "Dave should know about Jay coming along."

Without speaking Charlie reached into his carry-on bag and pulled out a satellite phone. He handed it to John and said, "You'll have to slide over to the window seat to use it."

John switched seats with Charlie so he could sit near the window before turning on the satellite phone. When he got a signal he dialed. "Dave, this is John. We all made it on the plane."

"That's good," Dave said kind of sarcastically. Dave was thinking what's the big deal?

"No Dave, I don't think you understand. We are *all* here," John said again, this time really emphasizing the word all.

Dave thought for a moment. "Oh no, is Jay Chestburg there with you?"

"How did you guess that?" John asked sarcastically.

"Listen John, you take good care of him. He may be able to fight hand to hand, but he's only an average shot at best. And he still doesn't have any real battle experience."

John interrupted, "I would have to argue the last point. I've seen him battle, but Charlie and I will take care of him. Do you want to talk to him?"

John motioned for Jay to come over and take the phone without listening to Dave's answer to his last question. "Hello," Jay said a little timidly.

"Chestburg if you survive this I'm going to kill you!" Dave shouted in the phone. "You make sure you keep your head down and follow John's every instruction. Ivan was one of the old Soviet Union's best. Do not mess with him alone. Do you hear me?"

"Yes I hear you," Jay answered.

John looked over at Charlie with a big grin on his face. Charlie whispered, "You are a sick man. You're enjoying this too much."

John whispered back, "I went through the same thing years ago, only my boss at the time was a whole lot less understanding. And would you believe it was Dave who snuck out with me? Watch this."

John leaned over to Jay and tapped him on the shoulder. He knew that Dave was in the middle of his lecture to Jay. "Ask Dave if we should handle this like the Las Vegas case."

Jay looked at John, who was motioning for him to ask. Jay finally interrupted Dave's lecture, "John wants me to ask you about the Las Vegas case. Should we handle it the same?"

There was a long pause at the other end. Finally Dave spoke. "Jay, you are going to make a great agent. Just be very careful. I really wanted you to get more training before you went on an assignment like this. John is in charge and he's a good man. Ask him to call me when you guys get on the ground. Your brother is still monitoring the airlines in case Ivan gets on another flight."

Jay hung up the phone and handed it back to John. "What was the Las Vegas case?" Jay asked.

John answered, "It's a long story, but basically Dave and I did the same thing you're doing a long time ago."

"Jay answered, "It sure got Dave to stop yelling at me."

John looked over at Charlie, who just shook his head in disbelief.

Watching out of the window of the taxi, Ivan asked the driver about a rental car. "Why didn't you get a car at the airport?" The taxi driver asked.

Ivan didn't immediately answer. He was thinking of a good excuse. Finally, he thought of something. "I'm looking to rent a truck. I wanted to spend some time up in the mountains and wanted to make sure I could rent something that wouldn't get me stuck."

The driver looked in the rear view mirror. "I know of a place where you can rent a good truck for that. It won't be a new one; he rents mostly to hunters who tend to beat the trucks up a bit. Is that what you're looking for?"

"That would be perfect," answered Ivan.

"Are you a hunter?" The taxi driver asked next. Ivan thought to himself: this guy asks too many questions. How could I be a hunter without a gun? "No," Ivan answered. "I'm an amateur photographer just taking a little vacation. Besides, it's not hunting season, right?"

The taxi driver didn't answer. He knew Ivan was on to him by the tone of his last question. The driver headed west toward the mountains on route 26. They were well beyond the city limits and starting to head toward Mount Hood when the taxi driver finally pulled into the rental truck parking lot. Ivan quickly looked over the trucks before getting out of the taxi. What a beat up pile of junk, he thought.

Ivan paid the taxi driver and sent him off, although he debated about asking him to stay. He walked toward the office, which was nothing more than a shack with a crude looking chimney pipe sticking out of the side and running up to the roof. It reminded Ivan of a large out house. Since he had to pass a couple of the trucks to get to the office, Ivan decided to get a better look at the trucks. There were only about five of them, and they were all in pretty rough shape. A couple of them had tires that were almost flat, and they all looked like they had been sitting for a while.

As Ivan opened up the door to one of them a man came out of the office. He wore a flannel shirt and jeans, and looked like he hadn't bathed in a couple of days. "Can I help you?" the man asked.

"I'm here to rent a truck. The taxi driver who dropped me off said you rent trucks for people to use up in the mountains."

"That's true, except this is really the off-season. Hunting season is still several months away and I usually start getting my trucks ready in a couple of weeks. If you want one now I will have to go through them to see what I got."

Oh great, Ivan thought to himself. Not only do his trucks look like junk, but he is also trying to make it look like he is doing me a favor by letting me rent one. "Are you saying I can't rent one?" Ivan asked.

"No, no, I'm not saying that. It's just that some of them might have some problems and I will need to go through them. Why don't you wait here and I will get some keys. We can see which ones start, and you can pick from them. My name is Gary Turner." Gary then held out his hand, and Ivan reluctantly shook it.

As Gary ran back into his office Ivan just rolled his eyes. He could not believe the situation. Gary came back out with several sets of keys. He went over to one truck but turned away when he noticed the flat tire in the back. The second truck he went towards looked a little better. The door was not locked, and Gary jumped in. The motor cranked slowly, but started up anyway. A big cloud of blue smoke bellowed out of the exhaust pipe, and the wind carried it back toward them. Gary yelled out, "A little smoke is good for the mosquitoes," and then started to laugh. Ivan wasn't amused, but thought it best to hide his frustration.

Ivan watched as Gary jumped out of the truck. The motor was still running as the two of them headed back into the office. Inside immediately to the left was a counter. Behind that on the wall was a map of Mount Hood and the surrounding area. Ivan studied the map noting the location of all of the logging roads in the area. It appeared to be possible to cross over to the other side into the town of Dalles. From there Ivan could cut up through Washington State into Canada. He doubted the authorities in Canada would be looking for him, so he could fly back to Russia from there.

Ivan turned again to look at the truck outside. If the truck would get him to Washington, he could rent something better to get him to Canada. "How good are the roads on that map?" Ivan asked.

Gary turned to the map before answering. "Although the roads are dirt, they are very good. The loggers need to keep them up to get their trucks through. If you're going to use them just be careful. The truckers have schedules to keep and their trucks are not easy to stop when full."

Ivan continued to look at the map while answering, "That's good advice, thanks. Do you have a copy of the map?"

"Yes," answered Gary. "It's in a packet of information I will give you. Just be aware that a road or two will change occasionally."

Ivan continued to look around the room. He spotted a rifle in the corner in the back. "How long will you want the truck, and what credit card will you be putting the rental on?" Gary asked next.

Ivan answered, "Can I just pay cash?"

"I prefer a credit card for insurance reasons. What I can do is take cash, and an impression of the card. I won't call the card in, and when you get back I can just rip up the credit card impression." Ivan reluctantly agreed and handed over the card. Gary ran it through one of the older hand held credit card machines that uses multiple carbon copies and put it in a folder.

Ivan took his credit card back, and pulled out some cash. As much as he didn't want to deplete his cash he was more worried about someone tracing his credit card to here. "One more thing," Ivan said. "Are there any bears to worry about?"

Gary started to laugh. "There are some, but since it's getting toward the end of summer they are getting fat and lazy by now."

"Should I rent a rifle anyway?" Ivan asked.

Gary was standing behind the counter, and Ivan watched as his right hand dropped out of sight behind the counter. Ivan could see Gary had stopped smiling and was very serious. "I'm sorry Mr. Smithe, but I could lose my license if I rent you a gun. Besides, what you really want is a shotgun. They are much more effective at close range, and I don't have one of those." Ivan decided not to push the issue any further. He thought about just killing Gary and taking what he wanted, but leaving a trail of bodies behind him was not a good idea.

"Okay, just a dumb idea I guess," Ivan said next.

As they were walking out to the truck Ivan made a comment about the truck overheating if left to idle too long. "Not to worry," answered Gary, "all of my trucks have an extra large radiator to handle the heat. You can leave that thing running all day in the hot sun and it will never overheat. Now, can you pull it over to the pump on your left and I will fill up the tanks. With both tanks full you will have a little over fifty gallons of gasoline. That should last you a while. There is also a CB radio if you get into any trouble. The park rangers monitor it, and so do I. From up in the mountains you should get good range." Ivan pulled the truck up as instructed. Gary filled him up, and he drove off.

Gary walked back to his office to count his money. A cash customer was very rare these days. Maybe I should run the credit card through just in case, he thought.

Jay managed to doze off a little during the flight. He was still groggy while the plane taxied to the gate. Jay had stored his jacket in the overhead compartment and stood up to get it as soon as the plane came to a stop. He felt around for his phone, and turned it back on. Looking at the display he could see three separate messages from his brother Brian.

The plane started to unload as Jay said to John, "It looks like my brother tried to call me during the flight." John turned to him and said, "Hurry up and call him back." Jay hit the speed dial button for Brian as they walked through the gate and into the terminal.

"Brian, this is Jay, what's up?"

"Jay, I've been trying to call you. I got a lead on Ivan. It looks like he might have tried to rent a truck on the east side of Portland."

"What do you mean tried to rent?" Jay asked. "Well, a small local truck rental put his credit card through but without an amount," answered Brian.

Jay said, "That's weird. Either he rented a truck there or he didn't. Did you tell Dave Gillian about it yet?"

Brian answered, "Dave knows all about it. They are sending someone to pick you guys up, and take you there first. What did you wear Jay?

It looks like you may be hiking through the mountains before the day is out."

Jay looked over his clothes. He was wearing slacks, a sports jacket, a new white shirt and tie, and the new shoes he had to get to replace the ones ruined during Brian's rescue. "Not good Brian. I got my new shoes on that you still owe me for. I'm not dressed for a hike."

"Where do you think he's headed?" Jay asked.

Brian answered, "After talking to Dave, I checked out the area east of Portland. You have Mount Hood, and all around it is federal land the logging companies use. There a lot of logging roads that zigzag all through the area."

"Do the logging roads go anywhere?" Jay asked.

"I'm still looking at that," Brian answered. "I'm guessing that Ivan might be trying to cut across to the east before heading either north or south."

Jay looked over at John, who was looking a little impatient. "Listen Brian, I'd better go. Find out about those logging roads and call me back."

Jay hung up the phone and explained everything to John and Charlie. John looked at Charlie and said, "Are you thinking what I'm thinking?" Charlie shrugged his shoulders without answering, so John continued. "Come on Jay, let's get out of here."

The three men walked quickly out of the terminal and over to the rental car counter. John walked up to the counter, but Charlie stepped in front of him. "Let me do this," Charlie said. John knew Charlie was trying to keep him out of as much trouble as he could for ditching the local agents.

Charlie got the last four-wheel drive truck. As they walked out Jay asked, "Why didn't you show them your badge?"

Charlie answered, "I was afraid they wouldn't rent me a truck. Let's face it; the odds of them getting it back in one piece are only about fifty-fifty with us."

Jay was walking between them trying to keep up so he could hear. He chuckled when he heard Charlie's answer, which amused John.

"What are we going to do about clothes? We aren't dressed to go hiking in the woods," Jay asked next.

John answered, "That's the main reason we aren't waiting for the local agents. If we went with them now they would just make us sit in the car. If we show up dressed for a hike in the woods they will take our request to go with them much more seriously. And after what Ivan did to McWilliams I'm going to make sure he doesn't get away." Jay followed quietly the rest of the way to the car.

The car they got into was a Cadillac all wheel drive Escalade. Charlie got into the driver's seat and John got in the front passenger's side. Jay got in the back and looked around. "Is that a GPS system?" Jay asked.

"No," answered Charlie. "I think it's that Onstar system they advertise about."

Jay sat back and thought for a moment. John turned around and studied the look on Jay's face. "What's the matter," John asked.

"I have an idea," Jay said as he pulled out his phone. John just listened without comment. "Brian? This is Jay. Hey, I have an idea. We are sitting in a Cadillac with the Onstar feature. They have a locating system as part of that. Is there any way you can tap into it? We can use your help getting us around those logging roads."

John now knew what Jay was up to. He looked at Charlie and said, "Great idea, if Brian can do it."

Jay read off the serial number of the vehicle to Brian. As Jay hung up the phone he leaned forward and said, "Brian said he will call us back when he's hacked into the Onstar system. Hopefully he can locate and start tracking us."

"How long will that take?" Charlie asked.

"Brian didn't know," answered Jay.

"In the mean time let's get our hiking clothes," John added.

Ivan studied the map of the logging road as he drove. The roads crossed the mountainside. There appeared to be no direct way across, but Ivan was convinced it was his best hope of getting out of the area undetected.

By now Ivan was well out of the city, and had not seen any houses for several miles. As he continued up the road he noticed another pickup truck pulled over on the other side of the road with its hood up. Ivan was not going to stop, except that something caught his eye. Through the back window of the truck he could see a rifle, which was something he wanted. Ivan turned around, pulled over after passing the truck, and backed up to it. Ivan shut off his motor and climbed out of his truck.

"Can I help you?" Ivan said as he approached the driver of the other truck.

The hood was up, and the other driver was leaning over the passenger side fender. He looked up at Ivan and said, "My radiator hose broke. I'm trying to tape it up, but it's not holding."

"Do you live far from here?" Ivan asked.

"I'm about 40 miles south of here. I went up in the mountains to zero in a new scope on my rifle and was just heading back." Ivan just nodded as the other man continued. "You look like you're carrying some supplies. There's a stream at the bottom of the hill behind us where I can get water to refill my radiator. Do you have a bucket?"

Ivan turned around to look down the hill that dropped off after the shoulder of the road. It dropped off about one hundred feet with a small stream below. "Why don't you keep taping, and I'll go look for a bucket," Ivan said.

As the other man turned around to work on his truck Ivan reached around from behind to grab his chin and jerked his head first to the left, then suddenly to the right snapping his neck. Ivan quickly carried him over to his truck and sat him up behind the steering wheel. Ivan then grabbed the rifle out of the truck. He looked around and found a box of ammo in the glove box. When he picked it up he noticed how light it was. Opening the box Ivan saw a box of mostly empty shells, with only three loaded rounds left. He must have been saving the brass to reload his own ammo, Ivan thought.

Ivan then checked the rifle. It was an old single shot rifle. Ivan remembered reading about a style from the old west called a rolling block. Taking a closer look at one of the rounds, it was a caliber Ivan was not familiar with. It was a .50-70, which had been discontinued many years ago. "Oh great, three rounds and a rifle I can't buy ammo for," he mumbled out loud. Ivan then noticed the man's wallet sitting on the car seat. Going through it, Ivan took forty of his last fifty bucks and a credit card. Although Ivan needed the cash, he didn't want it to look like a robbery if they find the body.

Ivan loaded the gun, and put the other two rounds in his pocket. He then ran over to his truck, and put the gun behind the seat. Next he ran back to the other truck and started it up. From outside the truck reaching through the driver's side window, he put it into drive and steered it off the shoulder and down the hill. Ivan stood there watching the truck pick up speed as it headed to the bottom. At the bottom of the hill is the stream, and a sharp climb up the other side. The truck jumped across the stream and slammed into the bank on the other side. The man's body crashed through the windshield and landed on the hood before rolling in front of the truck. That should make it look like an accident, Ivan thought, as he turned to get back into his truck.

Pulling out his map again, Ivan started up the truck, made another U-turn, and continued up the road. He was nearing his first turn off of the highway onto the logging roads. He still had almost half the day's light left and was hoping to get to the other side before night. If he could get into Washington State around nightfall, he could get a good night's sleep, then rent a car tomorrow and drive up to Canada from there.

John pointed to a mall off to the right as Charlie drove down the highway. Charlie just nodded as he slowed down to exit the highway. They pulled into the mall parking lot in front of a Sears's department store. John and Charlie jumped out of the truck and Jay followed them into the store. Heading into the men's department John went straight for a clerk.

"Can I help you?" asked the clerk.

John showed him his badge and said, "Yes, my partners and I need to buy some hiking clothes. We will each need a pair of jeans, two warm shirts, a light jacket, thick socks, and hiking boots. We will also be wearing the clothes out of the store." John then pulled a credit card out of his wallet. "Collect the tags as they get removed from the clothes and charge them to this credit card."

The clerk took the credit card and said, "I should get my manager."

"Well then get him!" John said in a curse voice. "We're in a hurry and need your help."

The clerk turned and walked away as the three men began to look for their sizes on the clothes racks. It was only a couple of minutes later when the clerk and two other men came over to John.

"We're sorry for the delay sir. There are three of us now and we can split up and help all of you get what you need."

The manager shook hands with John as John said, "Thank you for your help. I can't really get into the specifics, but we need clothes suitable for hiking in the mountains this time of the year."

The manager nodded and said, "Follow me and we will hook you up."

Twenty minutes later Charlie, John, and Jay walked out of the department store. Not much was said as they headed for the truck. Jay felt a little silly since it was obvious to him everything they had on looked brand new.

Charlie looked in the rear view mirror at Jay and said, "Hey Jay, why don't you call your brother back and see if he can at least tell us how to get to the truck rental place Ivan was at."

"Okay," was all he said as he reached for his phone. "Brian, this is Jay. Can you tell us how to get to the truck rental place?"

"Sure Jay. I can see you guys are on the move again. Keep heading east on route 84 for another five miles. Get off on route 26 heading east, and I will tell you when you get there."

Jay held the phone down and gave the directions to Charlie and John. "He's tracking us already? I thought we needed to call in," Charlie asked.

Jay smiled and just said "Yes."

"Now I'm impressed," Charlie said as he looked at John.

Chapter 21

Ivan turned off of route 26 onto the logging road. He had several different ways to go, but none of them were a direct route. He drove several miles before getting to the first bridge. As he drove over it, Ivan could not believe how good it was. It could pass for any highway bridge, except it was located out in the middle of nowhere. As Ivan continued his drive, he was amazed at how good the dirt roads were. He was starting to pick up speed, almost letting the truck slide a little around some of the curves. Maybe I'll get across much faster than I originally thought, Ivan mumbled to himself.

Charlie pulled into the truck rental place as John commented on all of the police cars there. There were two Oregon state trooper cars, one local police car, and another obviously unmarked car. John pointed at the unmarked car and said, "My guess is that will be the local FBI." John then turned to Jay and said, "Just let me do the talking. One of the first things they are going to ask is why we didn't wait for their guys to bring us. I will talk to them and try to smooth things over."

John got out of the truck as soon as it stopped. Charlie and Jay got out a little slower. John walked over past the uniformed officers while holding up his badge. They said nothing as he walked by. John went into the office and was greeted by someone dressed in jeans and hiking boots similar to how he was dressed. John guessed he was the local FBI agent in charge. The man behind the counter said nothing.

"Can I help you?" the man said as he studied John's badge.

"Yes sir," John answered. "We're the FBI agents who followed Ivan out here."

"Aren't you the boys I sent my agent to pick up at the airport about an hour ago?"

John shrugged his shoulders before answering. "There must have been some kind of mix up, because we missed your man."

The local agent quickly interrupted, "Look, if we're going to find this guy you're after you're going to have to cut the crap. Our guy talked to one of the security guards who saw you hustle on out of there. You ain't hurting my feelings any if you wanted to go buy some hiking clothes first, but I can't work with a bunch sneaky political types."

John thought for a second and did his best to not start smiling. He was beginning to like this guy. "Can we start again?" John asked. "My name is John Hunt. My two partners out there are Charlie Gurns and Jay Chestburg. And yes, we did stop for a change of clothes."

The other agent's facial expression softened a little. He was considerably older than John. His face was more weathered, but somehow John could sense he was still a tough character.

"My name is Hank Deminkoski, but my friends call me Demmy."

Demmy then held out his hand to shake John's. John tried not to show it, but Demmy's handshake was crushing his hand. John said, "Sorry about the confusion. If you figured out about the change of clothes I'm assuming you already know why. The bastard we're after killed a personal friend of mine. I want to personally make sure he doesn't escape."

Charlie and Jay walked into the office. It was starting to get a little crowded in there. Gary Turner, who was still behind the counter taking it all in, finally spoke. "If the fella you're after is as bad as you say, you might want to think about getting started after him. He took one of my best trucks, and he has enough gas in it to get halfway to Canada."

They all nodded in agreement and headed out the door. Charlie whispered in John's ear, "How did you make out in there?"

"Totally busted," was John's answer.

Demmy spoke next, "John, I seem to be missing some vital information here. Just who are we looking for, and what makes this guy so special?"

John turned to Demmy, and gave him a quick outline as to who Ivan was, and what happened to Ryan McWilliams.

Charlie introduced himself without mentioning he's CIA, and explained to Demmy Ivan's Soviet origin and training. "You know, that really gets my goat," Demmy said. What kind of a politician has people like that working for him?"

As they walked out to the truck Jay's phone rang. "Jay, this is Brian. I don't know how long it will last, but I hacked into a spy satellite and I'm scanning the area looking for Ivan now. Can you tell me real quick what he's driving?"

"What's the big deal? You've hacked into satellites before," answered Jay.

"That's true big brother, but this time I hacked into their control system and can steer the thing around. I'm now scanning the area."

"That's amazing Brian. Hold on and I will ask about the truck." Jay moved the phone away from his ear and said, "Brian hacked into a spy satellite over the area. I need a description of the truck Ivan has."

John looked at Charlie, who looked at Demmy. Demmy gave them a suspicious look before saying, "He's driving a light blue Ford pickup."

Jay gave the description to Brian. John waved to Jay to get his attention.

"Find out if Dave knows what he's doing," John said to Jay.

Jay asked Brian, and then relayed the answer to John, "Not yet."

John shook his head and said, "That's not good. Tell him to call Dave now, and be careful." Jay repeated John's message to Brian, and hung up.

"I think I need an explanation," Demmy said. "Just who are you guys anyway?"

Charlie gave a deep sigh, and pulled out his identification. He told Demmy because of Ivan's Soviet ties, the CIA was involved.

Demmy then looked at Jay and asked, "So, what's your story."

Jay looked at John for some guidance as to what to tell Demmy. John spoke instead of Jay. "Okay Demmy. You seem like a straight shooter and I'm going to trust you here. Jay is relatively new to the FBI. The person he's calling is his brother, who is one hell of a computer hacker we have working under cover. That's all I can tell you right now."

Jay's phone rang again. "Jay, this is Brian again. There is a truck off the road about twenty minutes east of you. It doesn't fit the description of Ivan's truck, but I think you should check it out. I need to warn you it's messy." Jay repeated the information to the group, as they all got into Charlie's truck. Out of courtesy John let Demmy have the front passenger's seat. One of the state troopers followed them as they drove up the road.

John sat quiet for only a couple of minutes before pulling out his phone. He hit the speed dial for Dave Gillian. "Dave, this is John. I'm just checking in. Right now we are on our way across the federal land covering the Cascade Mountains near Mount Hood."

"Yes, I know," Dave answered, "I just got off the phone with Brian."

"Did he tell you about his hacking into the satellite controls?"

"Yes he did. I think I got him protected for now. I was able to get two of my guys in the van parked outside his house. I admit I'm a little nervous about upsetting the military when they find out about their satellite."

John answered, "I just wanted to make sure you knew."

"Thanks John, I appreciate it. Now I want you to concentrate on getting Ivan. My bosses upstairs are now following your progress, so do what you have to, but stay safe."

John looked over at Jay, who was watching him. "Is everything okay?" Jay asked.

John nodded. "Yes, everything is fine, but there is something you'll need to watch out for. Dave sometimes will take risks that get him into trouble. I just wanted to make sure this time wasn't one of them, that's all."

Jay nodded and said, "I think I understand."

Ivan was feeling pretty good about the progress he was making. The dirt road was very smooth and he was going at a much faster pace than he originally thought possible. It was important to him to get across to Dalles as soon as possible. Since he had not seen any other drivers for a while, Ivan stopped slowing down for blinds curves.

He was approaching a sharp left when suddenly a logging truck coming the other way surprised him. Ivan swerved to the right and went off the road into a gully. He swerved again to the left after passing the truck and heard a large bang as he bounced back onto the road. He hit his head on the roof and was momentarily stunned.

The driver of the logging truck slowed down and looked in his rearview mirror. He saw Ivan's truck back on the road, so he decided to keep going. He couldn't afford to get off schedule.

Ivan sat there in the middle of the road for a couple of minutes rubbing his head. He looked down the road and watched the logging truck until it was out of sight. His truck was still running, so he stepped on the gas to keep going. When nothing happened, Ivan shifted to park and took his foot off the brake. The truck started to roll backwards, so Ivan used the emergency brake before getting out.

Climbing out of the truck, Ivan could smell transmission fluid. He looked under the truck, and saw a puddle of transmission fluid and the front half of the rear driveshaft hanging in the dirt. Ivan walked over to the side of the road and looked in the gully. There were several large rocks in the gully, and one of them had a large scratch mark. Ivan guessed the rock must have broken the drive shaft under his truck.

Ivan got back into the truck, released the emergency brake and rolled the truck into the gully. He couldn't roll it far enough to get it out of sight, but at least it wouldn't block the road, which would attract even more attention. He sat in the truck and studied the map. He had about a two days walk from where he was, and that was if he went in a straight line. He was very concerned and rightly so. It wasn't that Ivan would have any trouble surviving; he had plenty of training for that. He needed to get out of the country as soon as possible.

Ivan folded up the map, and climbed out of the truck. He still had several more hours before dark. He had a tough choice to make. If he stayed on the road there was a small chance someone might come by giving Ivan a chance to take their vehicle. His other option was to hike in a straight line to Dalles through the woods.

Jay was still on the phone with Brian as they approached the place where the truck rolled down the embankment. "Stop," Brian said to Jay. "Stop right there and cross the road."

Charlie pulled over to the side of the road and all four of them got out. They all walked across the road and looked down the hill.

Demmy was the first to start down the hill followed closely by John and Charlie. Jay was a couple of steps behind them, but the closer they got, the slower Jay went. This was slowly widening the gap between them. The state trooper went back to his car to call for an ambulance.

"What a mess," Demmy said as he looked over the area.

The driver had gone through the windshield and left a long blood streak across the hood of the truck. When Demmy, John and Charlie walked around to the front of the truck Demmy said, "That's too bad. You can't even recognize this fella."

By this time Jay had caught up to them. He looked at the body and quickly turned away. His could feel his stomach start to churn. John touched him on the back and said, "Don't feel bad. You're not the only one about to throw up."

Demmy went back to the truck to look around. He noticed shell casings scattered all over the truck and the empty box. He picked one of the casings up and smelled it. "This round was fired sometime today."

Charlie picked up another empty shell and asked, "How can you tell?"

"For one thing," Demmy answered, "It still smells fresh. Also, if you look inside the casing you can see that the powder is still very black." He then stuck his pinky in the case and rubbed it with his thumb. "The burnt powder is still very dry. That won't last long in this humid climate."

John looked around in the truck before turning to the group and saying, "If Ivan was here, it now means he has a rifle."

"Maybe so," Demmy said, "but at least it's a caliber that's hard to get ammo for. This is a .50-70, which is a discontinued round."

Jay picked up another empty cartridge and examined it. "It looks like a huge bullet goes in here."

"It was a round used for buffalo during the old west," Demmy said.

The four men climbed back up the hill. Demmy handed his empty cartridge to the state trooper. "We're only guessing, but the guy we're looking for might now have a rifle."

The trooper looked at the cartridge and shook his head. "That's a lot of lead to throw. I have some bullet proof vests in the trunk. It's still going to hurt, but they might work with this old round."

Demmy nodded his head and said, "Thanks, I think we're going to take you up on that. I feel somewhat responsible for bringing these city fellas back in one piece." The trooper nodded as he turned to open his trunk.

Demmy called the other three over to the trooper's car trunk. Jay's phone rang again as they were walking over. "Jay, this is Brian. I think I may have found the truck. You guys are a little less than an hour away. The only part I can't figure out is why it's not moving. I'm trying to scan the area around it but if he's hiking through the woods the trees are too thick for me to see him."

Jay told the others what Brian just told him. They each grabbed a vest from the trooper and headed for the truck. Demmy also grabbed a backpack and put it over one shoulder. "Can I carry that for you?" Charlie asked.

"I got it," Demmy answered, "but you could open the back hatch for me." The trooper agreed to stay behind and wait for the ambulance. He stood there watching as they sped off.

Ivan decided to hike along the road for a while and see if anybody drove by. The going was much easier, and as of yet there was no sign of anybody following him. He double-checked his rifle. There was a new scratch on the scope from the accident but it still looked okay. He unloaded it and looked down the barrel. It looked clean so he closed up the action without loading it and dry fired it. Everything seemed to be in working order so he loaded in a round, and kept the other two in his pocket.

"Your turn off is coming up," Brian said to Jay, who quickly repeated it to Charlie.

Suddenly Brian said, "Uh-oh," and Jay could hear his computer beeping in the background. He then heard the phone drop and what he thought was the frantic pushing of computer keys in the background.

After a minute or two Brian picked the phone back up and said, "Jay, are you still there?"

"Yea I'm still here. What happened to you?" Jay asked.

"I'm afraid I lost my satellite connection. They tried to trace back the line but I think I shut down before they could get to me. I'm sorry about that but you're on your own now."

"We appreciate what you've done so far Brian."

John looked at Jay and asked, "What happened?"

Jay answered, "Brian lost the satellite connection, but thinks he shut down before they could trace the line."

Just then Demmy turned around and said, "Don't hang up yet. Let me talk to him."

"Brian hold on a second," Jay said before handing the phone to Demmy.

"Hello Brian, this is Hank Deminkoski, but please call me Demmy. We are going to need a little more information to locate the truck. I'm pretty familiar with the roads up here, but they do go all over the place. Were there any land marks near the truck?"

Brian answered, "I'm going back now to open up one of the pictures I copied when I was looking through the satellite. Okay, there it is. All

300

I see is woods. Mount Hood is on the left, about at a ten o'clock position. There is a long straight and then sharp bend to the left at the spot where the truck is sitting."

Demmy thought for a moment before asking, "You said that Mount Hood is on the left at about a ten o'clock position?"

"Yes," Brian answered, "The truck is parked on the side of the road right at the beginning of that turn."

"Okay, thanks Brian. I think I know the spot."

John and Jay sat quietly in the back as Demmy gave directions to Charlie. Demmy seemed to know the roads without a map. Finally Demmy pointed up the road, and everyone could see the truck parked in the gully. Charlie slid to a stop next to the truck. John and Charlie quickly jumped out and ran over to the truck. With their guns out John opened up the door. The truck was empty, so John climbed inside and looked around.

Demmy walked out into the middle of the road and examined the oil stain. Jay decided to follow Demmy. Demmy then retraced the tire and oil tracks back and saw where Ivan had driven the truck into the gully. Demmy pointed at the rock with the gash mark and said to Jay, "Look there. That's why he left the truck."

By this time Charlie and John were walking up to meet them as Demmy headed over to Ivan's truck. He looked underneath and viewed the damage. The other three stood and watched as Demmy walked around the front of the truck. He pointed at the side of the road and said, "It looks like he decided to walk along the road. Charlie, get the truck and let's drive down the road for a while. This may be our chance to catch up to him."

Charlie ran back to get the truck as the other three continued to walk along the road. It didn't take long for Charlie to catch up to them. Charlie rolled down the window and said, "We won't be making any progress if you guys don't get in."

John and Jay immediately turned to get in the truck. Demmy said, "Just a minute. I want to make sure he didn't double back and head in another direction." Demmy continued to walk along the road for another five minutes before getting into the truck.

Charlie hit the gas but Demmy immediately said, "Slow down. I need to make sure I can see his tracks. If he turns to start hiking in the woods it does us no good to drive right by."

They continued this way for several miles. Charlie was beginning to think Demmy was putting them on because he couldn't see any footprints in the dirt.

Ivan heard a car coming slowly up the road and quickly ran into the woods. He had to jump across a drainage ditch and left several deep footprints in the mud. He continued to run until he was about fifty yards into the woods. He ducked down and watched a white SUV slowly drive by. Ivan continued to watch as the SUV drove about twenty more yards before stopping. A man Ivan didn't recognize got out of the passenger's side front seat. Ivan raised his rifle and considered taking a shot, but he changed his mind when he saw two more men get out of the back.

"Charlie, hold up a minute. I don't see any more footprints," Demmy said.

Charlie hit the brakes and Demmy jumped out even before the SUV came to a complete stop. Jay and John jumped out and followed behind Demmy as he worked his way back up the road.

"There," Demmy said as he pointed to some footprints in the mud.

"How fresh are they?" John asked.

Demmy answered, "I'd say less than ten minutes."

"How can you tell?" Jay asked.

Demmy squatted down and pointed to one of the footprints. Jay immediately squatted down with him. "Do you see the water slowly filling up the heel print?"

Jay nodded his head yes. Demmy stuck a finger in the water to gauge its depth. "The cavity made by the print looks about half full, and I'd say judging by the rate the water is soaking through the ground it would take about another five to ten minutes to finish filling up."

"That means he's right out there," John said.

"He might even be listening to us," Demmy added.

You bet I am, Ivan thought as he slowly and quietly started to head deeper into the woods.

Charlie pulled off the road and got out of the truck. He headed to the back and opened up the hatch. All of the men put on a bulletproof vest under their jackets. Demmy grabbed his backpack and put it over his shoulder. John offered to carry it for him but Demmy gave him an insulted look without saying anything. Demmy then turned toward the woods following the footprints. "Remember boys, just because you got dressed up for a hike doesn't mean you're ready for one," Demmy said.

John and Charlie looked annoyed and said, "Don't you worry about us. We'll keep up."

Jay quietly followed. He knew he was in better than average shape and shouldn't have any problems.

The woods on the mountain were very dense and seemed to hold in the moisture. They were hiking for about an hour, and it seemed like they were going up the whole time. John and Charlie were showing signs of tiring, and Demmy was keeping an eye on them. When he could see they needed a break he would stop for a moment and pretend to lose Ivan's trail. This would give them a chance to catch their breath. Demmy would also make a pile of rocks or sticks to be used as a marker to find their way back. Demmy was also pleased to see Jay keep up. At the last stop he even gave Jay the backpack to carry.

Ivan looked down the mountain using the zoom of the riflescope to see. He was surprised to see the four men following him. He thought they would have quickly lost his trail. Obviously at least one of them is an experienced tracker, but Ivan didn't know which one he was so he couldn't just shoot him. It was time to try another way to lose them. Ivan looked up and headed to a narrow trail farther up the mountain.

Along the way Demmy was working with Jay, showing him some of the signs to look for to track Ivan. He was pleased to see how eager Jay was to learn. They came up to a narrow path with a cliff rising on the right, and a drop off on the left. The trail itself was dirt and stone, and well weathered. Charlie was in lead, with John behind him, then Jay, and finally Demmy taking up the rear.

John was commenting to Charlie how he preferred the rocky trail to the thick woods they just left when suddenly one of the rocks Charlie stepped on moved, sending his foot out from under him at an un-natural angle. Charlie went down and grabbed his ankle. He rolled to his side holding his ankle, in obvious pain. John was first at his side, grabbing Charlie so he didn't roll off the edge of the cliff. Demmy ran up and while carefully cradling Charlie's ankle took off his boot. "I can't believe I twisted my ankle," Charlie said.

Demmy said nothing as he examined Charlie's ankle. "Do you think it's broken?" John asked.

"No," answered Demmy, "but it is badly sprained."

"So what do we do now?" Jay asked.

Demmy put Charlie's boot back on and laced it up tight to hold back some of the swelling. He then looked at Charlie and said, "Do you think you can make it back to the truck?"

"I think so," Charlie said.

"Maybe I should go with him," John said.

Charlie shook his head no and said, "You need to keep going. I'll make it back. We all have cell phones, and I can call you if I get into trouble."

Demmy doubled back to a spot where some small trees were growing. He cut down a tree with two forked branches at the top, which made a crude crutch. Bringing it back, Demmy held it next to Charlie and trimmed it to its final length. Charlie tried it out and seemed to manage okay. John walked over to him and said, "Are you sure you'll be okay?"

Charlie said, "Just go do what you have to do. I'll be fine."

Jay was watching Demmy closely as he knelt down where Charlie had slipped. "Look at this. Do any of you see anything unusual here?" Demmy asked.

John and Charlie looked, but were silent. Jay asked, "How do you think that pile of green leaves got under that rock?"

Demmy looked up at Jay. "That's right Jay. This is an old trick."

Demmy got up and walked up another five feet and knelt down again. The others, except Charlie, quickly followed him. Demmy turned over another rock and said, "Here's another. We'll need to be careful from here on in."

Above them, Ivan stood and watched as they patched Charlie up. Well that's one down, Ivan thought. He debated about trying to take a shot at one of them but decided he was too far. This old rifle, he thought, will hit hard at close range, but Ivan wasn't sure how much the big round would drop at longer ranges. Having only three rounds to work with wasn't helping either. Besides, he had other ideas to slow them down.

Ivan turned to continue. Looking over the landscape he saw a shallow plateau on the mountain that seemed to collect a lot of water. It was a swampy area with thick ferns growing throughout. It was so thick he couldn't see below his knees as he walked. Ivan continued on for about thirty yards and looked back. He was halfway across, and noticed that he left a visible path across the ferns.

John, Demmy, and Jay stood and watched as Charlie headed back down the mountain. With the crutch Demmy made he seemed to be limping along well enough. Charlie turned to them and yelled, "What are you waiting for? Get going before he gets away."

John turned to the others and said, "I feel bad about leaving him."

Demmy said, "Look at it this way. In about an hour and a half he'll be sitting in the truck with the radio on taking a nap!" Everyone laughed as they turned to press on.

Chapter 22

Ivan finished crossing the swamp and traveled up the next hill for about forty more yards. He spent a lot of time in the swamp, but felt that it was worth it. He estimated they were only about five minutes behind him. Just ahead of Ivan was a rock formation consisting of two large boulders with several smaller rocks piled between them. He walked around the back of the rocks and stretched out between the two boulders to wait.

John was glad to see the end of the rocky trail. Although they found only a couple more booby-trapped rocks, he was getting tired and the added stress of watching every step was wearing on him. Demmy stopped and studied the path through the ferns. He took two steps and said, "Don't put your foot down until you can see where you're stepping."

"How are we supposed to do that?" John asked.

"Like this," Demmy said as he demonstrated, "brush the ferns away with your foot and look before putting your foot down."

"What are we looking for?" Jay asked. "It's hard to say for sure," Demmy answered.

As they started to walk across John and Jay noticed Demmy was not using the same path across that Ivan made. He was off to the right about two feet. John and Jay followed several yards behind Demmy. They continued to walk across taking their time as Demmy instructed.

They reached the halfway point when suddenly a shot rang out, and a clump of mud exploded to their left. John and Jay started to run back to the safety of the rocks behind them.

Ivan quickly loaded the next round and looked at the scratch mark on top of the scope. He guessed the scope must have been knocked out of alignment during the accident after all. He estimated it to be off about two feet at the distance they were at, and would have to compensate for the next round.

Demmy decided to run forward after the first shot. He got about two steps before yelling out in pain and falling to the ground. When John heard him yell he stopped running and turned around. As he did so the second shot rang out, hitting him in the chest, about four inches to his right. The force of the bullet knocked him over.

Jay dove behind the rocks and took out his gun. He looked around and could see Demmy rolling around in pain but did not see John. Jay scanned the area and caught a reflection off of Ivan's gun. Jay aimed carefully and fired two rounds.

Ivan heard the bullets Jay fired ricochet on the rocks around him. He loaded the last round and took aim. Jay fired again, and Ivan fired back. The bullet from Ivan's gun hit the mud in front of Jay and sprayed him with dirt. Jay jumped back behind the rocks. He sat there for several seconds. He thought about his situation, and became enraged. He rolled back out from the rocks to look across where he saw Ivan. He looked carefully but didn't see anything.

Ivan rolled down from his perch. He looked at the rifle and tossed it into the brush. After taking about two steps he stopped. He turned around, grabbed the rifle, and climbed back up the rock pile. Ivan carefully set up the rifle pointing toward his pursuers. As Ivan slid down the hill he chuckled to himself. Assuming there is any fight left in them when they see the rifle it should slow them down for a while as they carefully approach it.

Jay waited another moment before starting to crawl out toward the others. John started to groan, and slowly stood up. "Get down!" Jay yelled.

John didn't hear him and continued to walk toward him. He looked stunned and was moving slowly. He was also holding his right side, and having some trouble breathing.

Jay stood up and ran toward him. John was in a lot of pain and Jay helped him sit back down. Jay opened up his jacket, and looked at the bulletproof jacket underneath. The bullet was gone, but the vest stopped it. Jay next looked under the vest and John's shirt. He could see a large bruise on his chest. It was red, black, and blue and half of John's chest was starting to swell. John looked at Jay and gave him a weak smile. "Demmy said the vest would stop the bullet, but I didn't think it would hurt that much."

Jay shook his head and said, "I thought you were a goner."

Jay got back to his feet and headed toward Demmy. When he got close Demmy yelled, "stop!" as he held out his hand.

Jay froze where he was as Demmy continued, "Watch where you're stepping."

"What am I looking for?" Jay asked.

Demmy reached over and pulled a stick out of the ground. He tossed it to Jay and said, "This is what you're looking for. I don't know how many are here, but if you step on one it will go right through your shoe."

Jay examined the stick closely. It was about six inches long and had a sharp point on one end. The other end was obviously stuck in the mud, leaving about three inches pointing up from the ground. Jay slowly walked over to Demmy checking every step before putting his foot down. Along the way he pulled up three more pointed sticks.

When Jay finally got to Demmy his boot was already off. Jay could see some blood and asked, "How bad is it?"

Demmy looked up and said, "It's not good. It looks like your friend got me. Can I have my backpack? I have some bandages in there."

Jay slid the backpack off his back, opened it up and handed it to Demmy. While Jay was doing that Demmy asked, "How's John doing?"

"John got hit, but the vest stopped the bullet. He's still pretty bruised up though."

Demmy nodded and said, "Well, it could have been a lot worse."

Jay helped him bandage his foot, and together they put his boot back on. Demmy also pulled out some duct tape, which he used to cover the hole in his boot. "Help me to my feet, will ya?" Demmy asked.

Jay reached over and helped him up without saying anything. As Demmy stood up Jay noticed his pants were also torn on the upper right thigh. There was a little blood stained around the tear. "What happened to your leg?" Jay asked.

"I rolled onto another stick when I went down. Fortunately I was only scratched a little," Demmy answered.

Jay thought it looked like more than a little scratch but didn't say anything else.

When Jay and Demmy got to John they helped him to his feet. Jay helped both of them as best he could back through the swamp to dry ground. When they reached the entrance to the swamp they all sat down on some rocks.

"Now what?" Jay asked.

John answered, "Welcome to the real world. Sometimes the bad guy wins. I'd say Ivan got us good here."

Jay looked over at Demmy, who continued to look straight ahead. "I'm not hit," Jay quickly snapped back, "and I'm going to get him."

Demmy looked at Jay and said, "Take no offence my friend, but you don't stand a chance. It will be dark in about two more hours and you will get lost for sure." Jay was angry but the truth was he would get lost, so he said nothing more.

Jay's phone began to ring. He looked at the display before answering. It was an unknown number. Jay answered, "Hello?"

"Jay, this is Brian. A lot has happened here since we talked last. Dave picked me up and I'm now on a secure line in the FBI building. I also got control of the satellite again and want to know why you three are sitting there goofing off!"

Jay stood up so fast he almost jumped a foot in the air. "Can you see Ivan?" Jay asked.

Brian answered, "He's ahead of you and moving pretty fast. The path he's on makes a wide loop around a rock formation. It looks like there is a way straight through it and if you hurry I could show you how to get to the other side first." Jay put down the phone and shared the information with the others.

Demmy and John looked at each other. Demmy shook his head no, and said, "It's not worth it. Somebody can pick him up on the other side or in Washington State. Besides, it will be dark in a couple of hours."

John turned to Jay and said, "He's right. We are in bad shape."

Jay thought for a moment, and then put the phone back to his ear. "Brian, can you track Ivan or us in the dark?"

Brian's answer was "No," but Jay didn't share that information with the others.

John looked up at Jay and said, "Forget it Jay. You're not going."

311

Jay didn't answer John, and the last thing he said to Brian was, "I'll call you back in a few minutes."

John looked at Demmy. They both already knew if Ivan kept walking after dark he could not be tracked by satellite and would be lost. They both also knew that's exactly what he will do. John was hoping not, but apparently Jay figured it out too.

John quietly slipped his hand in his pocket and grabbed his handcuffs. As Jay stood up John lunged toward him to try and grab his arm and handcuff him. Jay hopped out of the way and started back across the swamp. He didn't see the handcuffs. John moaned in pain.

"You probably cracked a rib," Demmy said.

Jay looked over at John and said, "I'll be careful, but I have to go."

John reached for his pistol, but by the time he got it out Jay was halfway across the swamp. "If the handcuffs didn't work I was going to threaten to shoot him in the foot," John said to Demmy.

"Maybe he'll step on another one of Ivan's pointed sticks," Demmy said. The two of them watched in pain as Jay crossed the swamp. Jay was doing it right and checking each step before putting his foot down.

When Jay got to the other side he pulled out his phone. He hit the redial to Brian. "Brian, where is Ivan now?"

"He's about halfway around that rock formation. You need to hurry."

Jay looked to his right and saw the rifle sticking through the rocks. He quickly ducked behind a tree. "Brian, can you look at the rock pile to my right? Somebody's there with a rifle."

"Hold on a minute," Brian said.

Jay waited behind the tree for a couple of minutes before Brian called him back. "There's nobody there," Brian said.

"Are you sure?" Jay asked.

"I can't zoom close enough tell a rifle from a stick, but there are no people there."

"Okay," Jay said as he walked toward the rocks.

Jay climbed up the front of the rock pile where Ivan had sat when he ambushed them and picked up the rifle. He opened up the action and pulled out the empty cartridge. He closed the action back up and tossed the rifle to the side. He called Brian back and said, "Tell me which way to go."

"Start heading east toward the next hill and I will call you back and tell you where to start climbing."

Jay followed the trail east as instructed. When he got to the rock formation his phone rang.

"Brian, so which way do I go?" Jay asked without even saying hello.

"Start climbing, but stay to the left of the peak," Brian answered.

"Are you sure about this? It looks like tough going," Jay asked.

"Yes I'm sure," Brian answered. "Go up about a hundred feet or so and you will see a path. The going will be easier as soon as you get over the first part."

Jay reluctantly started to climb. As soon as he got to the path Brian spoke of he called him back. "Brian, I think I found the path. How am I doing with catching up to him?"

"Jay you are a little behind Ivan so you will have to hurry. Is your phone okay? You're starting to fade out a little."

Jay looked at the display on his phone. "My batteries are getting a little weak. I'm on the path, so I'm going to hang up now. Call me back if I start to get off track."

"Okay big brother. I'll be here." Jay took another look at the display before hanging up. He really needed to shut the phone off but couldn't. To make matters worse, he switched his phone to vibrate instead of ring because he was concerned about how far the sound could carry.

Jay picked up the pace as best he could. It has been a long day, he thought, but he couldn't let Ivan win.

As Ivan made his way around the rock formation he did his best to look all around him. What a waste of time to go around this, he thought. When he got to the other side he turned to start descending down the mountain. A couple of crows screeched in the trees on the hill behind him before flying away. I'm a little too far away for them to be crowing at me, he thought. Ivan stood behind a tree and stared up the hill for a minute. He spotted someone just past the peak and heading down toward him. He waited another minute to see how many there were. When he was satisfied there was only one, he turned and continued down the hill being careful to keep out of sight. Some people just don't know when to quit, he thought.

When Jay reached the path around the rock formation his phone vibrated in his pocket. Jay knew it was Brian and answered, "Hi Brian, which way do I go now?"

"It looks like he's heading down the hill."

"Brian you are fading out some, so you will need to speak up. How far away am I?"

Brian answered, "Let me put it this way: I may need to speak up but you need to keep your voice down. I also have to tell you the woods you are in will get thicker as you descend down the mountain and I will have more trouble seeing through the trees."

"Okay Brian, I will be careful." Jay hung up his phone and put it back in his pocket. He stopped for a moment to look down the mountain.

As Ivan descended down the mountain he was considering all his options. Should he try and out run this person following him, or should he wait and ambush him. Looking down the mountain he spotted several large trees growing together about forty yards in front of him. This is perfect, he thought.

As Ivan descended down he moved over to his left where his follower should be able to see him. He continued along out in the open being careful not to turn around until he got past the trees. He stepped behind them and pulled out his knife. He looked through two of the trees watching as Jay continued toward him. He saw Jay carrying his gun and thought it will be good to get it.

"There he is!" Jay mumbled to himself. Jay pulled out his gun and picked up his pace down the hill. He lost sight of Ivan when he went around those trees and all he could think about was not losing him. His adrenaline was flowing, and his highest priority was catching Ivan. He was also starting to sweat, and considered taking off the bulletproof vest, since he felt Ivan was probably not armed anymore.

Jay stepped up to the trees and as he past them he caught a shadow suddenly move toward him. He tried to point his gun in the direction of the shadow but was not fast enough. He watched as Ivan's knife headed straight for the center of his chest. At the same time Ivan knocked the gun out of Jay's hand.

Ivan made a fast stab with the knife and quickly pulled it back to make another. Jay's training took over as he grabbed the forearm of Ivan's knife hand and at the same time turned his body in to elbow him in the solar plexus. Jay then snapped his fist back to give Ivan a back fist to the face. Jay continued to turn around until he stood right in front of Ivan with his back to him and flipped Ivan over his back. Ivan hit the ground with a thud but was instantly on his feet again. At least the impact sent the knife flying out of Ivan's hand.

Jay felt his chest looking for a knife wound. His jacket was torn but the bulletproof vest had saved him. Jay quickly looked around for the knife or his gun but couldn't see either. He then turned all his attention to Ivan as the two men stood there sizing each other up.

Ivan made the first move going for a roundhouse kick to Jay's head with his right leg. Jay stepped toward him blocking the kick with the pointed bone of his elbow to Ivan's thigh muscle. Before Ivan could put his leg down Jay also went to punch Ivan in the face. This was blocked, and Ivan returned a punch, which caught Jay in the left cheek. Although Ivan was slightly off balance, which resulted in a punch without much power behind it, the ring on his finger cut Jay's cheek.

Ivan could feel the muscle in his right thigh start to spasm as he applied weight to it. Jay could feel the blood start to ooze from his cheek.

"You will find I'm not as easy as the Chinese," Ivan said to Jay.

Jay just stood there ready to fight. His adrenaline rush was in high gear and was not influenced by what Ivan had to say. Ivan wasn't sure what to make of Jay's silence, but he found it a little unsettling.

Ivan faked a right and connected with a left, this time hitting Jay in the eye over the cut. This sent Jay back about two steps. Ivan followed up with sweeping kick that knocked Jay off of his feet. Ivan moved in to kick Jay again while he was down but Jay spun around on his hip and kicked Ivan in the kneecap. Jay could hear Ivan's knee pop. Ivan staggered back about three steps before falling into a brush pile.

Jay quickly sprang to his feet and rushed over to finish Ivan off. Ivan was lying on his stomach but rolled over on his back before Jay could get there. Jay heard a shot and felt pain in his chest. The impact knocked him over and stunned him.

The next thing he knew Ivan was standing over him, and his one leg was twisted slightly. He had Jay's gun and was pointing it at him. Jay figured that he must have found it when he fell in that brush pile. As Jay laid there flat on his back a rage went through him. He refused to give up and desperately searched for way to strike back. He felt around for a rock or something to use as a weapon.

"It looks like the American loses. That bulletproof vest will not stop a head shot," Ivan said with a smile.

As Ivan carefully pointed the gun at Jay's head blood suddenly sprouted from his chest followed a second later by the sound of a gunshot some distance behind them. Ivan fell backwards and did not move. Jay rolled to his feet and pulled the gun from Ivan's hand. Ivan lay there motionless, his eyes staring straight up.

Jay looked up the hill and saw John wave as he headed toward him. Jay breathed a sigh of relief before heading up to greet his friend.

As Jay got closer, he noticed John's right arm was in a sling, with his gun still in his right hand. "I didn't think you broke your arm," Jay said.

"I didn't," answered John, "but my right side is all bruised up and I think I may have cracked a rib. It hurts less when the arm is in the sling."

Jay grabbed John's left arm and helped him the rest of the way down to where Ivan's body was. The two men stood there in silence for a few moments. "I'm sure glad you showed up when you did," Jay said finally breaking the silence.

John didn't look up when he answered. "I had to come. I promised Dave I wouldn't let anything happen to you."

After a moment of silence Jay said, "John, I'm not so sure I'm cut out for this FBI thing."

John looked up and studied Jay's face. His eye was starting to swell shut, and he had a stream of drying blood on his cheek. "Why do you say that?" John asked while struggling to keep a straight face.

"I was almost killed today. If you hadn't shown up and made that incredible shot I would be dead."

"Jay, your only mistake was taking on Ivan without backup. I tried to stop you. Besides, you weren't the only one almost killed today. Four of us went up against the best the old Soviet Union had to offer. Overall, I think you did excellent, and let me tell you something else. I would take you for a partner any day." Jay smiled, but said nothing more.

Jay sat down on a rock and looked down the mountain. John sat next to him. "What do we do now?" Jay asked. "It's starting to get dark, and I don't think we can find our way out of here in the daytime."

John answered, "I'm not sure. It's also starting to get a little cold. Do you know how to build a fire?"

"Do you have a match?" Jay asked. The two of them looked at each other and started to laugh.

"What's so funny?" someone yelled behind them.

John quickly turned around and Jay stood up. In the fading light they saw Demmy leaning against a crude looking crutch made from a tree similar to the one Charlie used. "You traveled all this way using that crutch?" John asked.

"I had to make sure you city boys didn't freeze to death tonight."

"Did you bring a match?" John asked while looking over at Jay. They both started to laugh again.

John said, "We have to stop this. It's too painful."

Demmy smiled, but didn't say anything.

Demmy took off his backpack and started to clear a spot. Jay bent over to help and asked, "What are you doing?"

Demmy answered, "I'm clearing a spot for a fire. Since you can obviously still walk, why don't you collect some firewood? I have a couple of cans of beans we can heat up. No sense in going hungry tonight. Tomorrow morning we can hike out of here."

John walked over to Ivan's body and searched it. He found his phone first and turned it on. "Hey check this out. Ivan has a couple of numbers saved in his speed dial." The others nodded but said nothing.

John pulled out his phone to call Dave. "Dave, this is John. We got Ivan."

"Is he still alive?" Dave asked.

"No, he fought us to the end. The reason I called is I have his cell phone. I want to read off a couple of phone numbers he saved in his speed dial directory."

John read them off as Dave copied them down. Brian was next to Dave in his office on his computer. He entered the phone numbers in his computer. "I will see if I can trace them. How are you guys doing? Is anybody hurt?" Dave asked next.

John answered, "We all have our bruises. I think I might have broken a rib, Demmy has a hole in his foot, and Charlie has a twisted ankle."

"How's Jay?" Dave asked. John said, "He looks the worst but is doing the best. He will have a black eye for a couple of weeks, and might need a stitch or two in his cheek, but he's okay."

"John is that your campfire starting up?" Dave asked.

John turned around to look at it before answering. "Yes, that's us."

"Give me about two hours and I will have a rescue team up there to bring you guys back. Brian tells me he has your coordinates."

"Thanks Dave, we appreciate it," John said.

"Is there anything else I can do?" Dave asked.

"Yes, one more thing," answered John. "Can you let Jay's brother Brian book our flight reservations home?"

"What's that supposed to mean?" Dave asked. John just started to laugh as he hung up the phone.

Chapter 23

When Jim Gallagor's phone rang the first thing he did was look at the clock. It was 2:30 in the morning and Jim had only been in bed a couple of hours. "Hello?" Jim said.

The other voice said, "Don't speak, just listen. Your guy didn't make it. It was sudden so he didn't have time to empty his pockets. You need to dead end all trails." The other person hung up. Jim hung up and sat up in his bed.

He now knew that Ivan was killed, and he didn't get a chance to destroy his identification, and probably his cell phone. Jim picked up his cell phone on the table. He scrolled through the list of incoming calls that were saved. Ivan's number came up several times. He got up and walked down to the kitchen. With a bottle of degreaser and a few paper towels, he wiped the phone clean of all fingerprints and put it in a plastic bag. It was unfortunate, he thought, but circumstances like this are why he had taken the precaution of sending Allen out to run his errands. All of the phones used between him and his staff were in Allen's name.

Jim looked at the clock again. It was now a little after 3:00 in the morning, and he had to hurry. He went down to the basement, and moved some boxes that were stacked up in front of the wall. Behind the boxes the cinder block wall looked the same as everywhere else in the cellar. Jim pushed on a certain block and it slid back. He reached behind the wall and pulled out a plastic bag. Inside the bag was a box. Jim took out the box and opened it. Inside were several small gray boxes about half the size of a cigarette pack, with a metal clip on each and a switch on the side. Jim took out three boxes and what looked like a transmitter. He closed up the box, wrapped it back up in the bag and put it back behind the wall. He then replaced the cinder block and restacked the boxes before going back upstairs.

Jim quickly got dressed in a black sweat suit and black sneakers. He looked like he was going for a jog. The items from the cellar were on the kitchen counter. Jim picked the first gray box up and opened it up with a screwdriver. From a drawer in the kitchen he pulled out a bag from the local pharmacy. Inside it were several watch batteries the size of a dime. He pulled out each of the gray boxes and put in a fresh battery. The transmitter got four fresh AAA batteries.

Jim scooped up the items, his car keys and headed for the door. It was now approximately 3:45 AM and Jim had about another hour and a half of darkness left. He still has a thirty-five minute drive to Allen's house and was cutting it close. On his way out Jim suddenly stopped. He reached over and grabbed the phone he put in the plastic bag, thinking to himself how he almost forgot it.

Jim went down in the cellar again. He had a tunnel that led to a shed on the corner of his property. He climbed up into the shed, and quietly slipped out. There was a side access gate through the fence that circled his property. It was hidden behind some shrubs from the outside. Jim carefully unlocked it and squeezed through. Down the road was an older car Jim kept for this type of emergency. Although the car looked beat up from the outside, Jim had just about every moving part replaced or rebuilt so he could be confident it was reliable. With the press watching his every move so close to the election he was actually considering getting a second car to park next to this one to use as another back up.

Jim got to Allen's house in record time. He seemed to hit every light just right. Parking his car down the street from Allen's house, Jim was able to walk up to Allen's car unnoticed. Fortunately for Jim, Allen lived a rural area and the streets are dark at this time.

The first thing Jim did was crawl down to the passenger's side front wheel. He felt around in the dark for the brake line. As soon as he located it he reached in his pocket and pulled out one of the small gray boxes. He followed the line to where it met the frame of the car and clipped on one of the gray boxes. He then turned the three position slide switch to the A side. Jim did the same thing to the driver's side.

The third box required Jim to crawl under the car and locate the fuel line. He found it using a small pen sized flashlight he held in his mouth. This last box was mounted on the fuel line as close as he could get to the exhaust manifold. He switched this box to the B position.

Crawling back out of the car Jim hit his head. He cursed under his breath and thought about Ivan. This kind of thing is normally his job. Ivan will need to be replaced, and Jim wondered if Mike could be trusted to handle these types of operations.

The last thing Jim did was take out the key he secretly had made of Allen's car. He unlocked it and tossed the phone in the back being careful not to leave any fingerprints on it after taking it out of the bag. He relocked the car and went back to his. It was now time for him to get back in his car and wait for Allen to come out.

Brian rolled over in bed and looked at the clock. It was almost 5:00 AM and his alarm should go off soon. Yesterday was such an exciting day he had trouble sleeping. The van out front was gone, now replaced by two men in a parked car. This meant he was still guarded, but was now free to use his computer. The only thing still bothering him was calling work and telling them he was sick yesterday so he could help his brother. He also thought about the phone numbers John gave Dave last night from Ivan's phone. He hadn't bothered to look them up since there was nothing he could do with them anyway. Dave said he would handle it, and Jay's flight was not due back until this afternoon.

Jim thought about how he hated this part. He was sure if elected he would have access to people who can do these things for him. He looked at his watch again. It was approximately 5:45 AM. He decided to call Mike and tell him to stay home today.

Mike's cell phone was plugged in charging on the nightstand beside Mike when it began to ring. He was in a deep sleep and didn't move until his fiancée Sara, who was next to him, gave him a nudge.

"Hello?" Mike said in a sleepy voice.

"Mike, this is Jim. I have some things happening out of town today. Why don't you stay home and I'll call you tomorrow."

Mike sat up and thought for a moment. "Is something wrong?" Mike asked next.

"No, nothing is wrong. I've got to go. I'll call you later," Jim said.

Mike sat on the side of the bed and tried to think. "Is something wrong?" Sara asked.

"No," was Mike's short answer. As a habit Mike didn't tell her anything about his work. The truth was Mike was worried. The last time he saw Ivan he was acting strange. Now Jim was acting strange. He needed time to think about all of this.

Jim watched as Allen's garage door opened up. Allen walked out of the garage and got into his car. He started it up before closing the garage door from inside the car. Jim started his car but waited for Allen before pulling out. He was several car lengths from Allen as they pulled out onto the highway. They drove for about fifteen minutes before Allen signaled to turn off. The exit ramp made a gradual right, and then a sharp left. The gradual right seemed to draw people into the left too fast and if you were to stand off to the side near the sharp left you would hear tires squealing all day.

Jim turned on his transmitter and waited with his finger over the A button. When Allen was too far along the exit ramp to get back on the highway Jim pressed the button. Allen heard a small pop and looked in the rear view mirror to see if he ran over something. He saw nothing so he kept going as he approached the gradual right. He gently applied his brakes but nothing happened. He released them and pressed again. This time they went to the floor.

Allen's tires screeched around the right turn. He knew he was going too fast to make it around the sharper left so he tried to downshift.

The left turn came up too fast and he slid off the road. When the car finally shifted into second gear Allen was completely on the wet grass heading down an embankment. Allen tried to turn up the embankment and the car flipped over. Jim now hit the B button as the car turned over on its roof. The gas line burst open and the electric pump still running in the gas tank began spraying gas all over the hot engine. The car continued to roll down the embankment, which sent gas everywhere. Allen was knocked unconscious as the car went up in flames. When it reached the bottom of the embankment it ended up on its roof.

The flames roared from the car as several people stopped to try and help. One man got within five feet of the car before the flames drove him back. Jim slowed down to watch but did not stop. He couldn't afford to be seen just in case someone was taking pictures. Mission accomplished, Jim thought as he drove home.

The sun started to come up and Jim knew it would be harder for him to sneak back into his house now. He was hoping for a little luck as the night shift reporters who were anxious to go home by now may not be watching too closely. He parked the car, shut off the motor and looked around for a moment. Studying both of the other two cars parked within sight Jim determined they were empty. He got out, slipped back through the gate and into the shed.

Sara was in the shower getting ready for work. Mike had just made some coffee and decided to turn on the television. Since he had the day off he was curious what the weather would be like. Sitting down watching the local news, Mike was only half paying attention to it as he thought about his boss Jim. Something was wrong but he couldn't put his finger on it.

The local news station went to their chopper in the sky report. The chopper was zoomed in on a car fire that was still burning. Traffic was backing up quickly. The reporter in the studio was asking the chopper pilot the usual questions, which for the most part was not holding Mike's interest.

When the chopper pilot zoomed in on the car, he got a real close shot of the back. The rear bumper was not burned yet and Mike spotted a bumper sticker advocating Jim Gallagor for U.S. Senate. "That sure looks a lot like Allen Bismark's car," Mike mumbled out loud.

Sara, who was out of the shower, dressed in a robe getting a cup of coffee said, "What? Did you say something?"

"Nothing, never mind," was Mike's answer.

Sara shrugged her shoulders and went back to the bedroom to finish getting dressed.

Mike stood up and walked back to the bedroom to get his phone. He tried Allen's cell phone number but only got his voice mail. He hung up without leaving a message. Sara was in the bathroom doing her hair when Mike walked in.

"How is your mother doing?" Mike asked.

Sara looked at him through the mirror. She gave him a funny look because she knew Mike didn't really like her mother, and was too self absorbed to really care. "She's doing about the same, why do you ask?" Sara answered somewhat sarcastically.

"Do you still want to go see her?" Mike asked next.

Sara stood up and turned toward him. They just had an argument about this two days ago. Sara's mother had been ill and Sara was gone for about a month, two months ago. Mike complained about the length of time she was gone and when she mentioned she wanted to go back for another month the argument started.

"Sara, I need to check some things out this morning. If I give you a call at work and tell you to go I want you to go straight to the airport and visit your mother. Stay there until I call you."

Sara knew Mike's work was sometimes dangerous but he never really explained it too her. "Why, what's going on?" Sara asked.

Mike had a couple of long rehearsed excuses to give her, so he was ready for the question. "Jim said not to worry, but when an important election like this gets close to the end occasionally you get lunatics making threats. I'm doing what I think is best to keep you safe."

Sara studied Mike's face before answering. "I'll pack a bag before I leave and call on some flights when I get to work. What should I do? Should I wait to hear from you before booking a flight?"

Mike answered, "No, don't wait for me. Go ahead and book it." Sara took that to mean go if he calls or not.

Brian was a half hour late when he got to work. His boss Ed passed him in the hallway as he made his way to his office. "How are you feeling today?" Ed asked.

"I'm feeling better, but the traffic was terrible."

Ed answered, "I heard. There was a car fire on one of the exit ramps that has traffic backed up for miles."

"I saw the smoke," Brian said, "did anyone get hurt?"

Ed nodded his head and said, "Yes, unfortunately one guy was killed. That's why things are so backed up. The police are investigating."

Brian continued to his office without thinking too much more about it.

When Dave walked into his office the information on two phone numbers from Ivan's phone were on his desk. One was a number in Russia that could not be traced. The second number was to a phone registered to a Mr. Allen Bismark. Dave wanted to send some of his own guys but nobody was left. He had two more guys working for him, but they were both getting ready to retire soon and were not part of his inner circle.

Dave punched Allen Bismark into his computer, and reviewed his profile. He was never arrested, and owned his own house. He had a wife and two kids, who were both teenagers. There were two cars registered in his name. Dave looked at his watch, and decided to take a ride past Allen's house. He printed off several pages of information, including the descriptions of both Bismark cars to bring with him.

Brian started up his computer and was actually looking forward to a quiet day at work. He decided to wait about an hour and then call to see how his brother was doing. The last thing Brian did last night was book first class tickets for all three of them. He smiled when he thought about how Jay would react when he gets to the airport. Brian made sure they get the total V.I.P. treatment from the airlines per the orders of their board of directors. Brian never references a single name, so there's nobody to call and verify the information he types in. It's on-line booking taken to the next level.

Mike walked back out to the kitchen and looked at the coffee pot. He was nervous, and his mind was thinking of all the possible scenarios. He was not trained for this kind of thing; Ivan always knew what to do. He went back into the bedroom and put on an old pair of jeans and an old T-shirt. He quickly walked back out before Sara could see him.

Mike walked out the front door, and into the driveway. His car was parked behind Sara's. He got down on the ground on his back and crawled under his car. Although Mike was not really sure what to look for, he looked around all four tires. Mike examined all the brake and fuel lines. Satisfied everything was okay; he made the same checks to Sara's car.

When Mike was satisfied both cars were not tampered with, he walked back to his car and pulled it into the street. Sara would need it moved before she could go to work.

When Mike walked back into the house, Sara was eating breakfast. "Where did you go?" she asked.

"I just went to move my car," Mike answered.

Sara gave him a strange look and asked, "Why are your hands greasy, and why is your back all dirty?"

"I thought I saw some oil dripping somewhere from the motor, and I guess I got a little carried away looking for it," Mike answered. Mike knew she wasn't buying it, but she said nothing more.

Sara finished up her breakfast, put the bowl in the sink, and grabbed her stuff. Mike carried Sara's suitcase and walked her to the car. Mike said, "The election is less than one week away. This will all be over by then."

Sara reached over and kissed him on the cheek. "Just be careful," was all she said. Mike stood in the driveway and watched as she drove away.

Dave was halfway to Allen's house when he got a phone call from his secretary. "I'm sorry to bother you Mr. Gillian, but I have some additional information to add to the Allen Bismark file you asked me to start."

Dave's first thought was after two years he still can't get his secretary to call him by his first name. "What is it?" Dave asked.

"There was an accident this morning involving Mr. Bismark's car. He is believed to be dead, but the body is pretty badly burned so it will take a day or two for positive identification."

"Were there any other cars involved?" Dave asked.

He heard some tapping of computer keys before she said, "No."

"My God, it's starting already. Can you give me directions to where the accident is?" Dave asked.

As soon as Dave got the directions he made a U-turn across two lanes of traffic and then across the grassy center median to the other lane. Rush hour traffic was winding down but Dave still managed to get at least three drivers mad at him as they swerved out of his way.

When Mike got back into the house he sat back down in front of the television. The latest poll results showed Gallagor trailing behind Senator Stone by about two points. It was going to be a close election. Mike wasn't sure what to do next. He was wondering if Jim does get elected, would that make him a greater threat or not? Mike decided to shower, change and take a ride. There was a cabin up in the woods Sara's parents owned. Mike knew it would be empty and decided to hide out there until after the election. The cabin is several hours away and also in the next state. Mike would make sure to bring his hunting rifle and shotgun, as well as his handgun.

Jim Gallagor was back in his house watching the news. He had a rally to go to in the afternoon on his behalf. He was tired, and decided to go back to bed. It might be another long night tonight if he decides to get Mike out of the way too.

Dave pulled over when he got to the crash site. He waved his badge to the officer directing traffic, who then showed him where to park. Allen's car was no longer on fire, and the tow truck was moving into position to start the process of flipping the car over. They still had not removed the body yet. Dave guessed they were going to have to cut off the roof once the car was turned over.

Dave looked at the tracks in the grass and noted something wasn't quite right. Assuming Allen knew he was off the road there should be more torn up grass to show where his front tires were not turning, assuming his brakes were working. Instead all Dave saw was what looked like Allen's back tires only were trying to stop the car. This fact became very obvious when the car started to slide sideways before it flipped.

Dave followed the tracks back up to the road. There were very light tire marks about half a tire width on the road, but no actual skid marks. The marks Dave saw were most likely created from the front tires turning too sharply without the brakes applied.

There were two uniformed officers standing next to a patrol car. Dave walked over and showed them his badge. "Can you back up your car and block off the exit ramp for about ten minutes," Dave asked.

The two officers looked at each other first, before one of them said, "I'll do it. Just let me know when you're through." The officer then jumped in the car, turned on his lights and backed up the ramp.

When the officer was in place blocking the ramp, Dave walked up to the start of the tire marks. He stopped to get a better look at them before continuing to walk up the ramp. The other officer followed quietly behind. When Dave got near the top of the ramp he found a couple of fresh oil stains each about the size of a nickel. He turned to the officer following him and said, "Do you have any paper towels or anything?"

"All I have is my ticket book," answered the officer.

Dave held out his hand and said, "Hand it over."

The officer hesitated for a moment. He was studying Dave's face. Dave saw this hesitation and started to get annoyed. "Come on, hurry up," Dave said.

The officer reluctantly unclipped the ticket book from his belt and handed it to Dave.

When Dave got the ticket book he opened it up and tore out two plain pages, leaving the carbon paper between them. He then laid them across the oil stains letting the fluid soak in. He gently stepped on the paper to try to speed up the soaking in process. After a couple of minutes Dave picked up one of the sheets of paper and examined the oil stain on it. "What does that look like to you?" Dave asked the officer.

The officer took the paper and held it up in the sunlight before smelling it. "It doesn't seem like engine or transmission oil to me," he said.

"What about brake fluid?" Dave asked next.

The officer shrugged his shoulders and said, "Maybe, but I hate to say without knowing for sure."

Dave picked up the other piece of paper and said, "That's fair. Now do me a favor. Can you bring that piece of paper to whoever is investigating this accident? I'm going to take this other piece back with me. Oh, and tell the other officer he can open the ramp back up." The officer nodded and waved his partner back in.

Dave walked back to the crash site. The tow truck was in place, and the firemen were making sure it was safe to flip the car over. They didn't want the car to catch on fire again. Dave walked up to the front tires and front brake assembly. The rubber brake lines were burned away, so there was nothing to see. Dave tried to find the fuel line but most of that had melted away too. In fact, it was hard to make sense of what was left of the car it was so badly burned.

Dave turned to go back to his car. There was not much evidence against calling this an accident, except for the speculation someone might have wanted to silence Allen Bismark. Dave thought of the phone number trace to Bismark's cell phone. There are always leaks in an investigation, but Dave wondered if he could ever build a case against Gallagor if Gallagor can get information and react faster than Dave can.

Jim Gallagor slept for a couple of hours, and was now up watching the midday news. Although he was still a couple of points behind in the polls, the television news channels were using the margin of error

332

in the polls to call the race a dead heat. Jim had a lot of speeches planned before the election beginning with the one tonight, and still felt he had a chance.

Brian was in his office working through lunch. He took another bite of his sandwich when his cell phone rang. "Brian, this is Jay. How's it going?"

"I'm okay, just working through lunch. How are you, and where are you?"

"We are in sitting on the runway of our last flight about to take off. Should be landing in about 3 hours. John says thank you for the great seats, and so does his cracked rib."

Brian laughed and said, "Tell him I said you're welcome. Anything for saving my brother."

"Anything new going on?" Jay asked next.

Brian thought for a second. "Not really. I haven't talked to Dave all day, have you?"

Jay answered, "I haven't but John did. Apparently one of the phone numbers John got from Ivan's phone led to someone named Allen Bismark."

"Did they question him yet?" Brian interrupted.

"I'm afraid not. He died in a car accident this morning. Real convenient huh?"

Brian shook his head in disbelief. "So there's no way to tie it to Gallagor?"

"All I know is they are still working on it," Jay said.

As Jay was talking Brian got on the Internet to check the online news. "Jay, I'm looking at the latest poll results and it says Gallagor is only a point or two behind. Some people are using the margin of error to call it an even race. This guy would be unstoppable if he gets elected."

"We know that," Jay interrupted, "We hope Dave can come up with something."

Brian saw his boss Ed walk by and said, "Jay, I've got to go. I will see you when your plane gets in."

Brian sat back in his chair and thought for a moment. His computer chimed which signaled he got a new email message. He clicked on his computer and saw it was Dave Gillian. Brian opened the message and read it. Dave explained to Brian about the car crash this morning, and asked him to identify the picture he attached to the email. Brian clicked open the picture and studied the face.

Brian wrote back that he hadn't seen that person before. The person who hung out with Ivan was named Mike, but was not sure of his last name. Brian also included a brief description. Hopefully you can find him, Brian wrote back. He sent the message off to Dave and sat back in his chair to think. He wished there was something more he could do. After a couple of minutes, he leaned forward and started typing away on his computer.

Chapter 24

Charlie was the first one to come down the exit ramp from the plane into the terminal. He was on crutches. John was next, and he had his right arm in a sling walking slowly behind. Jay was in the rear, carrying three bags. He was moving well, and if it wasn't for the black eye and bandage under his eye Dave Gillian might have thought he wasn't injured at all. They were all dressed in jeans, flannel shirts and their hiking boots. None of them had shaven either.

"Aren't you three a comical sight," Dave Gillian said. "You look like a bunch of lumber jacks that fell out of a tree."

"Yea, yea, whatever," John said. "At least we all made it back, and in a couple of weeks will be as good as new."

Dave reached down to grab one of the bags Jay was carrying when a large baggage handler stepped up behind him and took all three bags. He piled the bags in the back of an electric cart and waited for them to get on. Dave looked at John and said, "How did you manage all this?"

John smiled, nodded his head over in Jay's direction and said, "Ask him. Somehow his brother had us traveling as special guests of the airline."

Dave looked over at Jay. Jay waved back but said nothing. Although this trip gave Jay a big boost in confidence with the group, he was still a little uncomfortable about making wise cracks to his new boss. Dave studied his face and said, "That's quite a shiner you got. How many stitches do you have under that bandage?"

"Only three," answered Jay.

"Have you thought up a good explanation for your wife yet?" Dave asked next.

Jay thought for a second and finally decided a question like that needed a smart remark. "I was thinking of telling her you hit me for going," Jay answered.

John and Charlie started to laugh, and Dave did his best to fight off a smile, but was unsuccessful. "We can talk about that later," Dave finally said.

The four of them crowded onto the electric cart and headed down toward the parking area. When they were halfway there Jay pointed toward Brian who was heading back to their terminal. "Hey Brian." Jay yelled. The driver stopped as Brian walked over.

There was no more room on the cart. They tried to squeeze over but Brian said, "How about I meet you by the baggage claim."

"All we had were carry on so how about we meet you in front of the parking area," Jay said.

Brian nodded and said, "Okay."

The driver of the cart pulled up to the door leading out to the parking area. He asked about a wheelchair for Charlie, but Charlie declined. "I'm going to get the car and pull up to the door for him," John said.

"Where are you parked?" Dave asked Jay.

"I was running late and had to park in the hourly lot."

The other three started to tease him about being too good for the daily lot when Brian walked up.

Brian stood there and took a good look at Charlie, John, and then finally his brother Jay. "What happened to you guys?" Brian finally asked.

Jay quickly spoke up and said, "It's a long story, and I will fill you in later."

Dave jumped in next and said, "Speaking of getting filled in, I need everyone to come back to my office. I need some information to finish my report, and I can give all of you the latest news."

John looked at his watch and said, "I will need to call my wife and tell her I'll be late for dinner."

Dave replied, "I'm sorry about this and I promise we won't be too late. I'll even order dinner. Does Chinese sound okay for everyone?"

Everyone nodded yes and before they split up Dave said, "Brian, I want you there too."

Mike drove for several hours, and had just crossed the state border. He pulled into a local grocery store, which was the last one he would pass on his way to the cabin. He would soon turn off the main road and follow a dirt road the rest of the way. He was confident that at least so far, he was not being followed.

Jim Gallagor had passed by Mike's house on the way to his rally. He was now on his way back and decided to again see if Mike was home. Jim had tried to call Mike's cell phone several times, but it didn't seem to be working, and he didn't want to call his house phone. Jim was concerned Mike's caller ID would show a record when he called.

Jim drove by the house, but there were no cars in the driveway. He pulled into the driveway and went to knock on the door. Nobody answered, so Jim looked into the garage. Mike had a small one-car garage, and when Jim saw all of the stuff stored inside he knew that no cars were kept in there. He got back in his car and drove off. If Mike didn't show up by morning Jim would have to assume he's a security risk too.

Brian and Jay were the first to arrive at the FBI parking lot. They waited about five minutes before John and Charlie drove up. John got out of the car and said, "Have you seen Dave yet?"

Jay answered, "No."

John nodded and said, "Let's wait for him in his office. He probably got delayed picking up the food for dinner."

The four men entered the building and followed John to Dave's office. It was late in the day and a security guard replaced the secretary who is normally in the front lobby. When they got to Dave's office everyone walked over to his table. Jay and Brian sat down but John didn't. Instead he said, "Can you guys excuse me for a couple of minutes? I want to go back to my desk and check my messages."

Jay and Brian shrugged their shoulders and said, "Okay."

Charlie followed John out and said, "I need to use the phone too. I'll only be a couple of minutes."

Jay looked over at Brian, who was looking at some files on the table. Brian slid one over to Jay and opened another as Jay said, "I don't think you should be doing that."

Brian whispered, "This one is on Gallagor. Look at all the old pictures of him. Here's one of Ivan and him taken a long time ago. I think this was taken in Moscow. Look at the buildings in the background."

Jay looked over at the picture. "I can't believe the FBI can have pictures like this and not be able to do anything about him," Jay whispered. "Now, hurry up and put it back before someone comes."

Brian started to put the picture back, but then noticed there were two copies of the photo with Ivan. When they heard Dave's voice Jay looked toward the door giving Brian the chance to slip one of the pictures in his pocket.

Dave entered the room and Jay got up to help him with the bags of food. They put the food on the table, and Dave began stacking up all of the files on the table. He moved the files to his desk and asked Jay to start setting up the food. John and Charlie walked in and they all sat down at the table.

As they were eating, Dave picked up one of the folders on his desk, and pulled out a picture. Dave began, "I'm not sure if everybody heard yet, but one of the phone numbers on Ivan's phone was traced to Allen Bismark. Unfortunately he was killed in a car accident this morning."

Dave handed the picture to Brian. "This is not the guy I saw with Ivan. His name was Mike," Brian said.

"Is there a police report yet?" John asked.

"They are listing it as an accident," Dave answered. "I went out to the crash site this morning. The car was badly burned, so there wasn't much left. I'm guessing his brakes failed, but the fire destroyed any definite proof of that. I did find a couple of drops of brake fluid on the road though."

Dave pulled out the paper with the brake fluid stain and passed it around. "It's just not enough to go on," Dave said.

"Isn't there a link between Gallagor and Ivan we can prove?" Brian asked.

"We have plenty of thirty year old history on Ivan and Gallagor, but nothing recent enough to use by itself, especially before the election," Dave answered.

Jay looked over at Brian, who caught his glance. Dave could see Brian getting frustrated, so he reached over to grab the Gallagor file. "The issue Brian," Dave continued, "is the FBI must stay neutral during an election. We have information that could hurt most politicians from both sides. If we announced an investigation now, we would be accused of using his past to make him lose."

"And if he gets elected we can't touch him either," Brian interrupted sarcastically.

Charlie looked over at Brian and said, "Hey, get used to it. We do the best we can, and sometimes it takes a while to get them."

Dave walked over and closed the door to his office. As he was walking back he said, "This is why we got together, remember? I have bosses to answer to, and most of them are career politicians themselves. We stopped Senator Stone from getting killed, and were able to stop Ivan before he escaped. We have a few victories here. The rest is going to take more time."

"What about Mike, the guy who hung around with Ivan?" Jay asked.

Dave answered, "We did find someone named Mike Buelle on Gallagor's campaign staff, but when we sent someone over to ask him a few questions he wasn't home. So unless we can quietly find him, I'm afraid we are at a dead end."

"I hope he's not dead too," John said.

Jay looked over at Brian again, who silently stared at the floor. Jay knew his brother, and for him to give up this easy meant that he had another idea. Unfortunately, Jay thought, he was probably the only one to understand that.

Dave continued, "For now I think it's important for you guys to get healthy. Jay you take a couple of days off too, and we can start again next week. Remember Tuesday's the election, so let's hope Gallagor loses. It will make our life easier."

"The last thing I have is information on Ryan McWilliams funeral." Dave handed everyone a piece of paper as he continued. "The address and time is on the front, and a map on the back. I'll see all of you there at ten o'clock."

When it was time, everyone quietly got up to leave the office except Dave. He stayed seated and opened up another file. When they got outside Jay walked with Brian to his car. "I don't know what you have in mind, but don't do it," Jay said.

Brian turned to him and said, "I don't know what you mean."

Jay rolled his eyes, turned toward his car, and said, "Just stay out of trouble and I will see you tomorrow."

Mike pulled up to the cabin, and parked the car under some trees. The cabin was up on a small hill, and Mike hid the car the best he could. He was thankful to get there before dark. Mike got out of the car and went straight to the trunk. He loaded the shotgun and walked around the cabin. Satisfied there were no signs of any human visitors for a long time, he went into the cabin.

Pushing the key into the padlock, Mike was actually happy to be struggling with the lock. He took it to mean the lock had not been opened for at least a few months. When the door finally opened, he cautiously walked in.

It was a two-room cabin. The main room was set up as a living area and had the kitchen to one side. In the back was a smaller bedroom. The bathroom was an outhouse around back. Mike searched both rooms, but could see from his footprints on the dusty floor he was the first person there in a long time. He went back outside to get his groceries.

Mike got to work unpacking, sweeping, and setting up a bed. It took him almost an hour to get the pump working in the kitchen, but when he finally did the cold fresh water coming out was worth the effort. It was dark now, and Mike lit one small lantern on the floor in the center of the room. It had been a warm day, but with nightfall it was cooling off fast. Mike didn't want to block the windows before the cabin cooled off but didn't want to be seen either. He considered one lantern a tradeoff.

Dinner was a cold TV dinner and a warm beer. Tomorrow Mike would chop some wood and get the fireplace going. He bought several novels, and there was fishing equipment packed in the attic. Mike planned to go fishing in a stream over the next hill, which had plenty of trout. If it wasn't for the fact he was in hiding, Mike would consider this a decent vacation.

Jim Gallagor slept in on Friday morning. Mike had been missing for two days now, and Jim was concerned. Did he go to the police, and are they building a case, Jim wondered. Although Jim had a large staff of volunteers to help him, Jim didn't have anybody left from his inner circle. His secretary helped with his appointments, but Jim knew he would soon need to replace both Ivan and Allen. Jim hoped Mike would help him. The greatest risk is finding the first person to trust. After that, there is always at least a one person buffer between him and the next new person.

Jim went down stairs and turned on the television. He wanted to check out the latest polls. The news had been getting better for Jim all week, and although it would be close, he really felt he had a chance.

Ed Bell walked past Brian's office. Except for the funeral yesterday morning Brian had been working non-stop. The only problem, Ed thought, was that he had no idea exactly what Brian was working on.

As Ed walked into Brian's office he said, "How's it going?"

Brian hit a button on his computer to switch screens before speaking. "Hi Ed, Dok Rhee gave me some things to work on until we get the first security program to decipher. I want to continue to make a good impression and one of the best ways to do that is to respond to his requests as quickly as possible. Do you want to come around and see what I'm doing?"

Ed looked at his watch. "I've given up a long time ago trying to follow your programming. Besides I have a meeting to go to."

Brian looked up and nodded, but didn't say anything more. Ed shook his head. "Just stay sharp. You know how much is riding on this."

"I know," Brian said. "We'll be fine."

Ed turned to leave, and Brian felt a twinge of guilt. Although he had been busy these past two days, Brian was really working on what he liked to think of as his undercover job.

Since Jim Gallagor next speaking engagement wasn't until this evening, he decided to catch up on some paperwork. Yesterday he was given a file on what happened to Ivan, compliments of a connection he had made through his political party. Jim hated to admit it, but he was feeling a little down about Ivan. The two of them went back more than thirty years. The least he could do if he became a Senator was make the people who killed Ivan suffer a little.

He opened up the folder for the first time and carefully read through the report. He was pleased to see that Ivan went down fighting. Each of the three FBI agents and one CIA agent were injured. Jim read through the names of the agents. Chestburg seemed to be familiar name, and it was bothering Jim that he couldn't place it.

Jim got up and opened a file cabinet in the corner of his office. He pulled out another file and carried it back to his desk. This second file was on Brian Chestburg. Jim looked again at the first file. That name was Jay Chestburg. "There're brothers!" Jim said out loud.

It was early Saturday evening, and Brian and Julie were over at Jay's house for another barbeque. Jay couldn't help but notice that something was up with Brian. He must have looked at his watch at least one hundred times, and Jay was curious why. Even Rebecca noticed something was up.

Finally, when it was a little after 9:00 PM, Brian stood up and he had to go. Julie made a face but stood up anyway. Jay was guessing Brian talked to Julie beforehand. Jay asked, "What's your hurry Brian? It's still early."

Brian answered, "It's been a long week, and I'm tired. I will give you a call tomorrow morning."

On the way home, Brian said to Julie, "I have something to take care of which will take me a couple of hours. If you want to come over, you can watch television or something until I'm done."

Julie knew Brian well enough to know he didn't mean it the way it came out. She answered, "Okay."

After Brian and Julie left, Rebecca turned to Jay. "What do you think that was all about?" she asked.

Jay shrugged his shoulders and said, "I'm not sure, but something's up. Maybe I should wait about half an hour and drive over for an unexpected visit."

Rebecca asked, "Can I go? I can keep Julie company. I'm guessing she will be on the couch watching television."

"It's up to you," Jay answered.

Brian pulled into the driveway and shut off the motor. He was used to waiting in the car until the FBI agents following him had a chance to park out front. It was a suggestion from Dave Gillian. Brian got out of his car and walked over to the agent's car.

As Brian walked up to the car one of the agents rolled down the car window. "Can I get you guys anything?" Brian asked.

"We've been through this before Brian. You're supposed to pretend we're not here, remember?"

"I know it guys, but it seems so boring out here. I'm going to put on a pot of coffee, any takers?"

The two agents looked at each other. "Okay, we give in. Some coffee would be great."

Brian and Julie walked into the house, and Brian went straight upstairs to turn on his computer. Julie went into the kitchen to make some coffee. She knew Brian was up to something, but when he tried to explain his plan he deliberately focused on the technical parts first and lost her. It was enough for her to know he needed a couple of hours upstairs before he could be with her.

Jay pulled into the driveway and parked behind Brian's car. Rebecca and Jay got out of the car at the same time, and Jay walked over to the agent's car parked in front. On the way over he pulled out his badge and held it up as he approached the car. One of the agents recognized him and waved. Jay waved back and headed back to the house.

When Jay walked in Rebecca was already in the kitchen with Julie. He decided to tip toe upstairs and see what his brother was doing. Jay walked into the open doorway of Brian's computer room and stopped to watch. Brian was typing away at his computer. Jay looked over Brian's shoulder at the monitor and saw what looked like a newspaper on the screen.

Jay stood there for several minutes as Brian rearranged what looked like the front page of the local newspaper. Finally Brian heard something and turned around. "Jay! What are you doing here?"

"I wanted to see what was so important tonight," Jay answered.

Brian turned back around to face his computer and said, "Then, come on over. I might as well show you what I have planned."

Jay pulled up a chair and sat down. Brian said, "This is what I'm doing. First, I tapped into the AP wire and posted a story about Ivan Spelluchuvik and his attempt to kill Senator Stone. I then go into his Soviet Union background, and how he met Gallagor. I also included the picture of them together in Moscow, and finish with the need for an investigation."

Brian took a breath and continued, "Now comes the hard part. I tapped into fifteen separate newspapers around the state, and I'm in the process of rearranging their front pages for the Sunday morning paper.

"Why bother with the AP wire?" Jay asked. Brian zoomed in on his article. He pointed under the title and said, "I referenced the AP wire for the source, which gives it credibility. And just in case an editor does some last second checking before publishing, the story is there."

Jay leaned back and shook his head. "You know, this is going to get back to us. Dave Gillian could get into trouble."

"Jay, I've got that covered too. If you read the article, my imaginary AP reporter quoted unnamed sources in Portland Oregon after Ivan's death."

Jay took another moment to think some more. Finally he said, "It looks like you have everything covered, but how are you going to get through to that many papers tonight?"

Brian said, "Now that you're here, why don't you help?"

"How do I do that?" Jay asked.

Brian got up and walked across the room. He pulled his laptop computer out of its case, along with some wires. Brian brought it over to the table, and plugged it into the back of his main computer. As he was turning it on, Brian said, "I will show you what to do. It's really pretty easy once you get started."

Brian looked at his watch before continuing. "My plan is to get all of the papers ready to go, and right before the deadline make the changes all at once."

"How much time do we have?" "Only about two hours max, so let's get started."

About a half hour later Rebecca came upstairs to check on Jay and Brian. Jay turned when he saw her. She asked, "How's it going up here. You two are awfully quiet."

"I know," answered Jay. "We will be about another hour. I can explain everything to you then."

"I'm hearing that a lot lately," Rebecca she said before turning around to leave. Rebecca was still getting used to Jay's career change and figured she would deal with this later.

About another hour passed before Jay leaned back in his chair and said, "I think I'm finished. How are you doing?"

Brian looked at his watch again before answering. "I think I'm finished too. Now all I have to do is send them. I wrote a program to automatically send them all at once. I was concerned sending them one at a time would take too long."

Both brothers stared at the computer screen as the program worked. When the task-completed message came up, Brian gave his brother the high five. "I sure hope this works as planned," Jay said.

Brian gave him an annoyed look. "Of course it'll work," Brian insisted.

Chapter 25

It was early Sunday morning, and Dave was still in his pajamas as he walked barefoot down his driveway to get his Sunday paper. It was a beautiful morning, and the sun was already taking the chill out of the air. The paper was wrapped in a plastic bag, which was wet from the evening dew.

Dave carried the paper in and unwrapped it in the garage. He brushed his feet off before walking inside. On his way to the kitchen table he happened to glance at the headline on the front page. Suddenly he stopped, and reread the headline several times.

Dave continued to stand in front of the kitchen table carefully reading the front-page article. He studied the picture of Ivan and Jim Gallagor. He knew the picture came from the file in his office. His wife Jamie, who was making coffee, noticed Dave's unusual behavior. Finally she asked, "Is something wrong?"

"It can't be possible," Dave said.

Jamie gave him a strange look and asked, "What can't be possible?"

Dave handed her the paper and said, "I can't believe he could have pulled something like this off!"

Jamie took the paper and quietly read the article. Dave walked over to the television and turned it on. It was still too early for any of the morning talk shows to react.

Jamie looked at Dave and said, "Wow, that's some article. Where do you think the reporter got the information?"

Dave answered, "I'm not sure, but I wouldn't be surprised if we never find out who wrote the article."

"Who do you think did this?" Jamie asked.

Dave looked at her and said, "I'll give you one guess. When my bosses read this I'm sure to get a phone call."

"Maybe so," Jamie answered, "but it says in the article the leak came from Portland. That's not your fault. Besides, from what you told me about Gallagor, it might still be worth it." Dave looked up at her and stared.

Jay's phone rang. He knew from his caller ID it was Brian. "Did you see the morning paper?" Brian asked.

"Not yet," answered Jay as he walked out of the house to get the paper lying in his driveway.

Brian continued, "There's an interesting article on the front page about Jim Gallagor." Brian was careful not to say anything incriminating on the phone.

"I see it now," Jay answered playing along. "Give me a chance to read it and I'll get back to you." They both laughed as they hung up the phone.

John was upstairs playing video games with his son when his wife Tara walked in. "Take a look at this," she said as she handed the Sunday paper to John.

As John read the article his jaw dropped farther and farther. "I can't believe it," he said as he sprang to his feet. John groaned when he stood up. He was so excited he forgot about his broken rib.

John walked out of the game room and into his bedroom. Tara stood there and looked at her son. "Is Dad coming back?" he asked. "We're in the middle of a game."

Tara looked toward the door and said, "I think your Dad needs a few minutes. He'll be back later."

John called Charlie, who was reading his paper as his phone rang. "What do you think?" John asked.

Charlie took a deep breath before answering. "I'm not sure. Is it possible our computer friend was able to do this?"

John answered, "That's what I was thinking, but I don't know for sure."

"Did you call your boss Dave yet?" Charlie asked.

John laughed before answering. "There's no way I'm going to call him first! I'm not sure how he's going to take it, and I'm especially not sure how well his boss is going to take it if he thinks one of us is involved somehow."

"The article does mention a source in Portland, so maybe that's your way out," Charlie explained.

"I hope so," John said.

Jim Gallagor sat down with his morning coffee and opened up the paper. He read the front-page headline and dropped his coffee, which spilled across the kitchen table. As he was reading the article, he could feel his stomach tighten up in knots. He grabbed his cell phone and made several phone calls. He called several of his campaign volunteers who lived throughout the state. Apparently every major paper in the state has run the same front-page story. "I'm through," Jim mumbled as he hung up the phone after his fifth call.

Jim walked over to turn on the television. He knew it was only a matter of time before the 24-hour news shows would start covering the article. Although he might be through for now politically, he doubted there was enough evidence for anyone to convict him. He would need to disappear for a couple of years, and maybe try again in another state.

A few days later Jim Gallagor was sitting quietly watching television when his phone rang. "Hello, Mr. Gallagor? I'm not sure if you will remember me, but my name is Kiev Ruskof. I'm calling long distance, and I hear you might need someone with my experience."

Jim thought for a moment. "Why yes Kiev I remember you, it's been a long time…"